Sunset in Silvana

Book 1 of

The Da'ark Nocturne

Sunset in Silvana

by

Paul Sims

&

Robert Warr

First Published in Great Britain
by Bellorum Publishing, 2015
(contact: laughinlabrador@aol.com)

ISBN 978-1-517-03870-0

Cover design by I.Designs –
www.indyscribabledesigns.com

This book is dedicated to Sue Sims, Paul's wife and one of the best friends you could ever hope to have. She also, with great patience, corrected some of the more interesting deviations from Standard English that we committed as well as copy editing the book.

We would also like to thank, in no particular order, Howard, Neil, Jonathan, Bob, Julian and Martin, who helped develop the story and the characters.

Chapter 1

Talia Milanova woke that morning with a smile on her face, as she had for as long as she could remember – though that, she had to admit, was only a few months. *I'm so lucky to live in Silvana Zelyna,* she thought sleepily, *especially as a Hero of the Republic.*

She stretched and yawned, luxuriating in the soft cotton sheets, a privilege provided by the state. *I really don't think I deserve such special treatment, whatever Major Valentine says. And I don't feel much like a 'role model'. Perhaps one day I'll wake up and it'll all have been a dream. I'd better make the most of it.*

She rose and walked over to the window, where she leaned on the windowsill to watch the city awaken. The sun was still below the horizon, but the ringlight gave plenty of gentle illumination. The view over the bay and along the chain of islands that reached out into the distance was beautiful. It was softened by a light sea-mist that partially obscured the detail, lending an air of fantasy to everything but the large concrete tenement blocks that marched down the hill with regimented precision.

Talia had seen pictures of the area before the liberation of Silvana, with its attractive but wasteful arrangement of small villas in landscaped parkland, all set about with glow-trees. Unfortunately, the need to house several thousand good Zelynan families, many of them refugees from Pregeor, took precedence over the comfortable existence of a few hundred privileged Silvanans. *Since I'm one of those who benefited, I shouldn't really be critical, but it* was *rather beautiful.*

As she watched the water lapping at the docks, a shuttle rose from the Skyport on a plume of flame, starting its journey to Restavic High Space Station. *I wonder if Johan's at the controls,* she mused. *It's a while since we've seen much of him – he practically lives at the 'Port nowadays*

The sun rose, and a melody played through her mind, as it did every dawn. *I wish I knew what this song is. I ought to sing along, but I've don't remember the words. I've forgotten where I first heard it, but it speaks to me of peace and freedom, and fills me with optimism for the day ahead.*

Once the sun was fully revealed, the music faded, and Talia breathed a happy sigh and began her daily exercise routine. *It wouldn't do for a Hero of the Republic to get flabby.* She usually found the exertion invigorating, but today she felt a tinge of sadness because of the absence of her friend and regular exercise partner, Anoushka.

They were the only females in their small group of Heroes. That, and being set apart from the normal citizens by their status, thrust them together a great deal – an arrangement both of them enjoyed. Anoushka wasn't Talia's equal physically or intellectually, but she had a light-heartedness and a gentle nature that Talia envied. Whenever Anoushka entered a room she brightened the atmosphere, which – besides making her company a real delight – also proved of great value at the Restavic Down Medical Centre, where they both worked, Anoushka as a Senior Nurse and Talia as a Nurse Manager.

As she stretched, Talia thought back to when they'd first met – as far as she knew – when they were recovering together from the incident at Pregeor in a small private ward in Restavic City General Hospital. They – and the other survivors of the disaster – had amnesia, their whole past erased by the trauma.

Since they had been kept in medically-induced comas as their bodies healed, the physical effects of the incident had largely been mitigated when they'd recovered consciousness, and their doctors soon began encouraging them to regain their full fitness through physiotherapy. Talia had found the recommended exercises rather basic and boring, and had soon graduated to her own set of dance-based katas. As with so much, she'd forgotten where and when she'd learnt these, but her muscles still remembered them well.

She remembered Anoushka watching her for a while, and then asking if she could join in. Indeed, once she'd started, tentatively, to copy Talia's movements, Talia remembered some sequences that were meant for two people, where the actions of each of them complemented those of the other. From then on, they'd exercised together whenever possible.

Despite her relative inexperience, Anoushka enjoyed every moment of their shared callisthenics: sometimes, when they moved in true harmony, her pleasure was almost palpable, and even when she lost her balance and ended up flat on the mat, she took it in good heart.

Talia smiled as she remembered when, three days previously, Anoushka had landed on her bottom during a particularly tricky manoeuvre. When Talia had leaned down and offered her a hand up, Anoushka had grabbed hold of it and jerked Talia off balance. That she had ended up spread-eagled on top of Anoushka was enough of an indignity, but Anoushka had the temerity to tickle her as well. Talia had retaliated, and they probably would have been late for their shift if Boris hadn't looked in and commented on the lack of decorum displayed by *some* Heroes of the Republic. It was later that very day that Anoushka had a flashback to Pregeor, and now she was back in the hospital, undergoing treatment in its psychiatric wing.

Talia's exercises seemed rather flat without her friend, so once she'd done enough to work out the kinks in her muscles and generate an internal glow, she showered, dressed, and went in search of breakfast.

"Morning, Talia." Boris Dechorsky was another of her tight-knit group. He was actually her closest friend, apart from Anoushka. He was a couple of inches taller than she was, and a few years older, but they rarely disagreed about anything, and often seemed to know what each other was thinking. On the other hand, though he knew no more than she did about their lives before Pregeor, she somehow felt that his history was a sad one – maybe it was the lines on his face, which seemed to indicate that he'd faced a lot of pain in his past.

"Good morning, Boris. Is there coffee brewing?" She knew there would be, and he nodded as he poured a steaming mug and handed it to her. "Thank you, Comrade. How are things at the Skyport?"

He grimaced. "A bit slow at the moment. The tension with Telphania means we get less traffic, which means less to fix. Ivan and I fill our time doing maintenance checks, but it's hardly entertaining. Speaking of Comrade Baranov, I wonder where he is? I don't want to be late."

The young man in question chose that point to appear. He was still half-asleep, and had not yet shaved. Ivan Baranov was another of their small band – the youngest, apart from the boy Josef, he found his new-found celebrity a great advantage when it came to his social life. His devil-may-care attitude sometimes grated, but he could be good company – when he didn't have a hangover. Boris glowered at him, but he just yawned noisily and scratched himself, poured himself some tea, slumped down in a chair, and rested his head in his hands. "Just gimme a couple o' minutes," he muttered.

"Have a fun evening, Comrade?" Talia asked brightly.

"More fun than this morning." Ivan gave her a slightly resentful glare. He knew she realised how much he drank on poker nights, and the delight she took in teasing him. As recompense, despite Boris's look of disapproval, she poured Ivan a small measure of vodka, which he downed gratefully.

"Thank you, Comrade Talia – you're a life saver."

"I hope so. Yours would be the third life I've saved this week – though the others were in more danger, and their conditions were hardly self-inflicted. Now go and shave before Comrade Boris here has apoplexy."

Boris raised an eyebrow as Ivan shuffled off. "Yes – you stopped Leon bleeding to death yesterday, didn't you?"

"I suppose so – but to lose half his arm like that... a turbine, wasn't it?"

"Yes. Didn't look where he was going, the young idiot – but at least half a future is better than none." They sat in silence until Ivan returned and he and Boris set out for the bus.

Talia wondered how less enlightened nations managed without such a fine public transport system. Boris and Ivan would be at work exactly on time. She was on the afternoon shift, so she had time to eat a good breakfast and study for a couple of hours before she caught the shuttle herself.

She felt fortunate to have been made a Nurse Manager at the Medical Centre. Though she couldn't remember it, she'd been told that she'd been a Senior Nurse at Pregeor General Hospital. Apparently, when the disaster occurred, she had succoured and treated the injured, and, like her fellow Heroes, had refused to leave before the last of the survivors had been rescued. The Comrade President had been so impressed by her bravery and dedication that he had personally appointed her to her current position.

She had made many friends at the Medical Centre. One of them, Dr Julia Romanova, had noticed how quickly she mastered new techniques, and had been sponsoring her medical studies. She had been given an exemption from pre-medical training and the first year of a part-time medical degree due to her training and experience as a nurse, and she was three months into her second year. That morning, she became so engrossed in her studies – she had just completed a course on 'The Effects of Gradual and Explosive Decompression', and was beginning to get to grips with 'The Physiological and Psychological Effects of Exotic Atmosphere Leaks' – that she nearly missed her bus.

Being a Hero of the Republic could have its downside: because of your celebrity, you had no privacy when in public, and always had to be ready for the curiosity of other citizens. She could cope with formal occasions, but found impromptu encounters difficult – it was like being continually on parade.

Normally, she travelled with Anoushka, and they could lessen interference by sharing a seat and talking to each other. People are less likely to interrupt a conversation than to address someone sitting on their own. But on this occasion she was by herself, and the bus being nearly full, had to share a seat. The elderly man she sat next to noticed the starburst on the collar of her uniform. He kept looking at her, then looking away, but in the end he plucked up the courage to address her.

"My apologies, Comrade Hero, but I notice that you were at Pregeor," he began. "Are you by any chance Comrade Hero Talia Milanova?"

She nodded and smiled, but her heart sank within her. Yet again she missed Anoushka, who always took these encounters in good heart, and shielded her from the worst of them.

One passenger, a girl of about eight, said proudly, "My name's Talia, too – and when I grow up I'm going to be a Hero, just like you."

"Good for you," Talia replied, forcing another smile. "But remember that every citizen who does their duty for the Republic is a true hero."

The girl nodded vigorously. "What was it like at Pregeor, Comrade Hero?"

"Hush, Talia," said a middle-aged woman who sat next to the girl, who Talia judged to be her mother. "Don't bother the Comrade Hero. I'm sure she doesn't like to be reminded of that horrible day."

Talia gave the woman a look of gratitude. "Thank you – you're right. I'm sorry, young Talia, but I don't even like to try to remember it. When I do, it makes me shiver and shake, and all that I can remember is the fire, and someone's face melting." Even as she tried to talk dispassionately about Pregeor, Talia could feel her heart beginning to race and the sweat building, but luckily she was just about to reach her destination, and could wrench her thoughts back to her duties. She made her exit to a chorus of sympathetic farewells.

The day passed uneventfully. Since, apart from providing emergency treatment for workers at the Skyport, the Centre primarily catered for tourists, they had few patients for the same reason that Boris and Ivan's workshop was lightly loaded – the tension with Telphania meant few traders and even fewer passenger liners were currently visiting Ruine.

There had been border troubles for many years, especially since the citizens of Silvana chose the joys of freedom as part of the Republic over slavery to the repressive government of Telphania, but recently tensions had escalated. When the investigations of Zelyna's security forces had laid the responsibility for the devastation at Pregeor squarely on the shoulders of Telphania and its allies, the citizens of Silvana had become incensed, and had volunteered in droves for the armed forces. Reports of Telphanian soldiers massing on the border meant it was likely to be only a matter of time before violence erupted.

The journey back that evening was quieter, and mostly spent in pleasant anticipation, as Talia was to have dinner with Major Valentine. She knew it was part of his job as Security Liaison Officer to talk to them all regularly, but somehow these evenings had become more to her than just duty. She spent especial care preparing, and chose her best dress - something Ivan noticed only too well.

"Oh, Comrade Talia, you *do* look seductive tonight," he said.

She felt her face redden. "It's only a security briefing, Comrade," she replied tersely.

"I bet you wish it was more than that."

She dug her nails into her palms, and would have slapped Ivan had she been near enough. She knew he was only teasing and meant no harm, but it was near enough to the truth to hurt. The Major *was* attractive, as well as being considerate and charming company, and she sometimes found herself imagining what a deeper relationship with him would be like. However, as Ivan well knew, the Major seemed to harbour no reciprocal desires – indeed, although he seemed friendly most of the time, there were some days when he treated her with an icy, almost inhuman, detachment.

Boris sprang gallantly to her defence. "Leave her alone, Ivan. Remember, she lost more than you at Pregeor. You weren't married."

"It'd take someone special to catch *me*," Ivan boasted. "Until that happens, I'll play the field. There are untold benefits to being a Hero of the Republic." He gave a sly smirk, and Talia was about to retort when the intercom buzzed. Her lift had arrived.

The limousine drew up outside the best restaurant in Restavic City, and she was escorted to the usual booth, where Major Valentine was waiting. He smiled, got to his feet, and took her hand.

"Comrade Talia, thank you for joining me."

"My pleasure, Comrade Major. I always enjoy your company – and the food here is exquisite."

"Please, sit – I've taken the liberty of ordering you an aperitif."

"Thank you."

Only inconsequential matters could be discussed while the waiters fussed around them, but once their main course was delivered, the Major broached more serious concerns.

"How is your memory?" he asked. "Is it becoming any easier to recollect your past?"

Talia shook her head sadly. "Not really – someone asked about it on the bus today, and... well, let's just say I still don't want to try."

"I'm sorry." He seemed frustrated at her lack of progress, but also, for an instant, she felt he was oddly relieved. "What about your comrades? Have they remembered anything?"

"I think Boris is a little nervous about what he'd find if he dug too deeply. Ivan couldn't care less – he's too busy revelling in being a Hero – and you know what happened to Anoushka. It's only the amnesia that's keeping her sane at the moment." He nodded understandingly. "I haven't seen much of Johan recently. With the current international tension, he tends to spend more time at the Skyport than in his apartment, and our shifts don't often coincide anyway. As for Goran, you know how he and I don't really get along. He spends most of his time at the *Comet*, and keeps young Josef with him. He treats the poor boy as a kitchen slave — it's easy to see how much Josef resents it. Still, it's not my place to criticise."

"It's important for the young to do their duty."

Talia grimaced. "I know, but it seems a bit harsh on an orphan who went through such hell to make him the ward of such a man."

"That man led the resistance at Pregeor."

"That's true, but that doesn't necessarily make him a good father-figure. Anyway, enough about him – is there any news of Anoushka?"

"She's doing well, and should be back with you in a few days."

"Oh, that's good." Talia smiled, but shook her head in exasperation. "I blame myself."

"For what?"

"Her breakdown."

"Surely not."

Talia sighed. "If only I'd been quicker… I know all about her sensitivity, and everyone on the permanent staff knows not to involve her with burn victims, but that paramedic wasn't one of the regulars. It's true it was an emergency, but there was no call for him to manhandle her like that. When he forced her to look at that poor girl's flash-burnt face and she collapsed, I just had to go to her. I deserve a reprimand: I should have left her where she was and helped with the emergency."

"It was an understandable reaction."

"Yes, but not very professional. Nobody said anything, but I could feel their disapproval."

"You're imagining things. From what I've been told, you couldn't have done anything more than your comrades did to save the burns victim, and nobody I've talked to has any complaints about your behaviour."

"But it is the duty of a Hero of the Republic to act in an exemplary fashion at all times."

"Psh! Don't put too much of a burden on yourself – or your comrades. You're human, all of you, and your very humanity shows the rest of our citizens that they, too, can aspire to be Heroes. Anyway, what about Comrade Ulanova? Fainting like that was hardly exemplary."

Talia bridled. "That's different."

Major Valentine looked her in the eyes. "No, it's not. I've noticed the pressure of duty you put yourself under, and if you don't cut yourself some slack, it could be you in the psychiatric ward – and not because of Pregeor either. Heroes of the Republic should not have nervous breakdowns, so from now on, please regard it as your duty to relax as much as possible."

Talia's shoulders sagged. "If you put it that way…"

"I do – and I'll do my best to enforce *that* duty," he said with mock severity, but after a second or two, his face softened. "And on the subject of relaxation, have you any plans for the weekend?"

"Well…"

"Well what?"

"We were hoping that, since it is the weekend of the President's Birthday, and we have four days off instead of three, we could go to that dacha up the coast that you sometimes let us use. It's so beautifully peaceful, and the weather's not yet too cold for swimming."

"I thought you might ask for that, so I've already ordered it prepared."

"That's marvellous. You take such good care of us."

"Nonsense. I'm simply doing my duty."

Talia wondered whether she was imagining things, but she felt the look in his eyes belied his words. "I wish there was some way I – we – could thank you."

"There is."

"Oh? And what is your wish, O master?" Talia bowed her head in mock obeisance.

He laughed. "*My* masters would be grateful if you would visit a couple of our schools the day before the holiday – and perhaps you could persuade Boris and Ivan to do the same?"

"That shouldn't be a problem – the lure of a long weekend at the dacha will easily entice them, and things are pretty slow at the Skyport at the moment."

"That may well change."

"Really?" She gave him a speculative look, but he seemed unwilling to divulge anything more, so, after a short pause, she continued. "Anyway, they won't mind – and you know I'm always ready to spend time inspiring future Heroes. You'll have to provide cover for me at the Medical Centre, though."

"Everything's already arranged."

"You know, you seem to almost know what I want before I do."

"As I said, it's part of my job. There'll be a helicopter waiting for you at six that evening. Take some clothes for Comrade Anoushka."

Talia's heart leapt. "Of course."

As they were finishing their coffees, the Major said, "Comrade Talia, I don't want you to be alarmed, but because of the increased international tension, you may notice a little more security around than you've been used to."

"Are we in danger?" She bit her lip and he laid his hand reassuringly on her bare arm.

Despite her nervousness, a shiver of pleasure ran through her, and she almost missed what he said next. "You're in no more danger than any other public figure, Comrade, it's only a precaution. Unfortunately, the Telphanians and their allies, the Silvanan Free Army, have been becoming more active recently."

"I wish I understood why the Telphanians hate us so much," she said. "It's probably the result of the trauma of Pregeor, but I can't remember anything about how we got into this situation. Peace between neighbours – especially neighbouring countries – is what we need. We don't want another incident like that."

"No indeed, but that's not just up to us. Since Silvana chose to secede from Telphania and join our Republic, the Telphanians have used all the means at their disposal to destabilise our government in the hope of recovering their lost province. Pregeor is only the worst of it – they sponsor the SFA, and their agents infiltrate everywhere. We must be on our guard at all times."

Sunset in Silvana

"Surely they wouldn't actually invade Silvana? They wouldn't stand a chance with their soft, undisciplined troops against our elite forces."

"They have help – mercenaries and advanced weapons provided by their off-world allies. But we have friends too – the Dainworlds Federation have proved staunch comrades-in-arms."

"But what do these off-worlders hope to gain in return for their aid? Our small planet seems pretty unimportant in the cosmic scale."

"This planet was once vital to older galactic powers. You probably don't remember much of our history, but most of Ruine was ravaged some thousands of years ago by the Forerunners and the Ancients."

"Forerunners? Ancients?"

"The light and dark forces of legend. They fought over this planet, and in its skies, which is why so much of the surface is barren and dead, and why we're surrounded by a ring of debris where there used to be several moons. From what I've been told, having devastated much of the galaxy, both races simply disappeared. Nobody today knows much about them, but they did leave several strange constructs on Ruine, on the only continent left relatively untouched – our own. From what I can tell, the major galactic forces of today are curious about these artefacts, and want to access them – which is why they're so interested in us."

"But where are these 'artefacts'? I can't remember hearing about them before now."

"That's because they're mostly in Telphania – apart from the strange spiral of monoliths in Duplif-al-Starel. Now, I mustn't take up any more of your valuable time. Thank you for your company, which has been as delightful as always."

"The pleasure is all mine. I do so look forward to these occasions."

He took her hand and led her back to the limousine for the return trip, which passed in a happy reverie. The threat of Telphania seemed unreal, and anyway, she had Major Valentine to protect her. She changed into her sleepwear and lay down on her bed thinking happily how good life was.

Chapter 2

Boris Dechorsky woke the next morning bleary-eyed and depressed. His head told him that he should be grateful for his privileged life as a Hero of the Republic, but his heart told him otherwise – somehow, almost everything about his life felt empty and hollow. He yawned, stretched and tumbled reluctantly out of bed. He stood under the shower, hoping that the cold water would wake him up and lighten his mood. It managed the former, but signally failed at the latter. He sighed and began to dress.

He dragged himself to the washbasin and began to shave. He sometimes felt that he'd look better with a beard, but Senior Mechanics at the Restavic Down Skyport did not wear facial hair. Anyway, even if he had wanted to stop shaving, the official policy for all the Heroes of Pregeor was that they should look as similar as possible to their clean-cut images on the patriotic posters, as reproduced on the new set of stamps celebrating their actions during the disaster. The special framed cover on the wall looked down on him with an air of superiority; how could anyone hope to live up to those heroic archetypes?

A noise from outside the window caught his attention, and he looked out to see a van from one of the local co-operatives draw up outside the block. The concierge, Olga, came out to speak to the driver. They haggled for a few moments, and Boris could see that he was a rather surly lout. Boris judged from his manner that he wouldn't help Olga with her purchases, but would leave her to struggle with them on her own. He turned from the window and ran to the hallway and down the stairs, pulling on his coat as he did so. He emerged into the cool air just as the van drove away leaving the old lady to cope with the boxes and a large, heavy-looking sack.

"Let me help you, Mother Olga," he said as she strained to lift the sack. "After all, you bought some of this for me and my comrades."

She glanced up, surprised, but when she realised who it was, she gave him a broad smile. "Thank you, Comrade Boris," she said with a sigh. "You're up early. I was wondering how I'd manage to carry it all in. I've purchased a good selection of vegetables, *and* I managed to persuade the driver to sell me a small crate of freshly-caught flickerals.' She gestured at the uppermost box, which was full of the slender finger-length fish.

Boris lifted this and the carton of bread beneath it and put them into Olga's arms before slinging the sack over his shoulder. "Lead on, little mother – let's put this stuff away before it loses its freshness."

He followed her into her ground floor apartment and helped her to separate the provisions that she'd bought for him and his comrades from those that were for her own use. "Would you like a coffee as a reward for helping a poor, frail old lady?" she asked, as she started to put things away.

"Yes, please," he replied. "But you can't fool me – I've seen just how hard that 'poor, frail old lady' works keeping this block clean for us."

She laughed. "A lifetime of toil builds the muscles, but I *am* getting less flexible – and I'm truly grateful for all your help this morning."

As he sat down and accepted a mug of strong coffee, one of Olga's cats, a grizzled black-and-white tom that she called Vanya, landed heavily in his lap. "Comrade Olga," he said as he scratched the intruder behind his ear, "I'd be interested in buying some of your flickerals – or, if you are going to use them to make some of your delicious chowder, perhaps you could spare a pot of that?"

The old lady nodded her agreement. "I'm sure we can come to an arrangement," she said with a smile.

"For a pot of your chowder, whatever you wish to ask."

She laughed. It was a good system: she would supplement her wages by dealing with the co-operatives – and occasionally cooking her tenants some food – while freeing them from the need to go out to the vans early in the morning.

A thought seemed to strike her and her face took on a troubled cast. "Comrade Boris," she said half hesitantly, "there's something I feel I should tell you."

"Yes, little mother?" he replied, expecting some routine matter.

"Major Drovsorsky's assistant came to see me yesterday – and something about her manner chilled me."

"More than normal?" Boris chuckled. "Captain Reynard is the original Ice Queen."

The old lady didn't smile. He reached across and reassuringly patted her shaking hands, but she just shook her head. "Comrade Boris," she said, "there is never anything remotely funny about that woman, but this time she was so intense that it frightened me – it was as if she was a predator and I was her prey."

He started to speak but she waved him to silence and, having taken a sip of coffee, she continued.

"The Captain was very interested in how you and the other Heroes were behaving. She reminded me of the time that you and your friends spent in hospital last month. She said that you had been suffering from paranoia brought on by a drugs imbalance and that she wanted to ensure that none of you were suffering any sort of relapse. She actually seemed rather disappointed when I told her that you were all quite well."

"Surely she's just doing her job," he interjected. "Isn't it just an indication of the Republic's solicitous care for us?"

"Perhaps – but she insisted that I should report any odd behaviour directly to her, rather than to Major

Drovsorsky, and there was something about the way that she said it that made my blood run cold. What's more, the Major had actually spoken to me about the same matter himself just last week." She paused. "I thought I should tell you, that's all."

"Thank you for your concern, Comrade Olga. I know you find Captain Reynard unsettling, but perhaps it's just the weight of her responsibilities that make her so intense?"

"I don't think so – the Major has greater responsibilities than she does, but *he* never seems threatening. When he comes to see me, we just chat over coffee and he always pets any of my cats who are around, and sometimes he even brings them a tin of pluny – but when Captain Reynard visits, the cats all hide, and I feel like joining them." She paused and sipped her coffee. "No, I never look forward to interviews with her, but there was something different about her this time – a focussed cruelty that I didn't like – I didn't like it at all."

They finished their coffee in silence and, having thanked her for her hospitality, Boris lifted a protesting Vanya from his knees and dumped him on the sofa. He paid Olga for his group's share of the food, and carried it upstairs.

As was customary when Talia was not on early shift, Boris had been the first to rise, and had both coffee and tea brewed by the time she joined him.

"Good morning, Talia."

"Morning, Boris." She yawned decorously, covering her mouth with the back of her hand.

"How was your evening with Major Valentine?"

"As pleasant as always – he's very good company."

"Anything I should know?"

Her brow furrowed. "Anoushka's doing well, and should be back with us any day now... Oh, and

I've arranged for us to have the dacha at Plune over the weekend…"

"Good. It will be nice to get away for a while."

"But in return, the Major wants us to do some school visits the day before."

"Of course – it'll be better than another day of tedious maintenance."

"He said that might change…"

"Oh?"

"That's all he said. I couldn't get him to elucidate any further. Now, I'm sure there was something else… Oh, yes – there's going to be a bit more security about because of the situation with Telphania."

For some reason that made Boris uneasy, but he simply shrugged. "Coffee?"

"Please." She took the steaming mug, sipped and gave a deep sigh. "Oh, that's better… Standard shift today?"

"More of the usual, I reckon. I hope this trouble blows over soon, or I'll go mad from the tedium. At least you have your studies to keep you interested."

She looked at him sympathetically. "Up to a point – but you'd be surprised how often I read something which should be new to me and find that somehow it's already familiar." She gave a little puzzled frown. "Anyway, if things come to a head, we'll all be busy enough – me with casualties, and you and Ivan repairing battle damage."

Pat upon his cue, Ivan arrived. He looked as dishevelled as always, but at least he'd already shaved, and he didn't have a hangover this morning. "Battle damage?" he said quizzically as he poured himself a cup of tea. "Have I missed something, Comrades?"

"No, Ivan. Comrade Talia was simply talking about how busy we'd be if a war breaks out."

Ivan frowned pensively. "D'you think they'd send us to the front?"

Talia shook her head. "We're too valuable. They might send us to a base camp or two to raise morale, but they won't risk us getting killed."

"You're right," Boris said. "People seem to have taken us to their heart. Now, Comrade Ivan, drink up – we've got a bus to catch."

"But Comrade Talia hasn't told me the sordid details of last night's encounter with Major Valentine yet."

Talia stuck out her tongue and retorted, "The only thing in here that's sordid is your mind."

Ivan laughed.

"Come on, you dirty old man." Boris took Ivan by the arm. "I'll give you the news on the way."

"Not so much of the 'old' – I'm a good few years younger than you." He shook Boris off, but downed his drink, got to his feet and headed for the door.

Being on early shift had its compensations: it meant they shared the bus almost exclusively with their workmates each day, and with them, they had long since lost the status of celebrities. The journey passed in companionable silence, but as they approached the 'port, it was obvious that something unusual was happening outside it: not only were there more mechanics around than normal, but there was also a heavy security presence.

"What's going on?" Boris asked a guard as he and Ivan were escorted into the machine shop.

"We had a special delivery of agricultural machinery from our allies in the Dainworlds Federation." A familiar voice came from behind them, and they turned; to their surprise, the speaker was Major Valentine.

"What brings you here, Comrade Major?" Ivan asked.

"Has Comrade Talia told you about the increase in security because of the threat from Telphania?"

"Yes."

"Well, I'm simply here as part of that extra security." He turned and made his way back toward the gate.

Boris looked at Ivan, but he just shrugged his shoulders and said, "It makes sense, I guess – at least now we've got something useful to do." He turned and made his way to their workshop, and as Boris followed him, he realised that Ivan was right – this was more like it: transit damage to repair, the odd replacement part to fit or manufacture – real work.

It was about mid-morning that Boris got an inkling of something odd: he realised that the part that he was straightening was a firing pin from a 45mm cannon. How he recognised it, he had no idea – he could only assume he'd come upon something like it in the past. He had a sudden flash of memory: he was standing beside such a cannon, dressed in armour and carrying an advanced combat rifle. He tried to hold on to the vision, but it shredded to tatters as his heart began to race. *Better not to think on the past,* he decided.

As the day wore on, he found himself recognising more and more military components among those he was servicing. He kept his suspicions to himself, however, until Ivan came over with a puzzled expression and said, "This panel I'm flattening out is too heavy for a tractor – it's some kind of armour. I wonder what's going on."

"I don't know," Boris replied, "but some of these parts are definitely not for agricultural equipment – unless they're building cultivators with mounts for surface-to-air missiles nowadays."

"Should we talk to Major Valentine?"

"Oh, he must know – and he must realise we'll work out that these parts are military. The foreman told me that he wants to address us all at the end of the shift. Let's wait and see what he has to say."

Ivan nodded his agreement.

"Anyway, at least we'll have something interesting to tell the others this evening."

"Too right." Ivan returned to his task.

It should have been Anoushka's turn to cook that night, but since she was still indisposed, the duty fell to Boris. Ivan wasn't around – the usual situation when there were chores to be done – so Talia volunteered to help him prepare the vegetables.

"How was your day?" she asked as she peeled a potato.

"Different," he replied, and she looked up at him, one eye-brow raised. "We spent it doing transit repairs on some new agricultural machinery."

"Really?"

"Yes – sent by our allies in the Dainworlds."

"We could do with it – just look at this." She held up a scrawny excuse for a carrot. "What sort of equipment? Tractors? Combine harvesters?"

Boris thought for a moment. "That's funny – do you know, I can't remember precisely what it was – just general farming equipment, I suppose." He shrugged. "Anyway, how was your day?"

"A bit tedious – I'm looking forward to the weekend."

"So am I."

The stew was bubbling nicely when Ivan turned up. "Anything I can do to help?" he asked with wide-eyed innocence.

Talia raised a cynical eyebrow, and he had the grace to blush. "Well, you could help us eat..." she said.

"Hah! I'm always ready to do my duty for the Republic – however onerous." He grinned.

Talia shook her head slowly and sighed. "Pour yourself a drink and sit down. Boris tells me you had an interesting day."

"It was certainly a change," he said as he sank down into a chair. "A shipment of agricultural machinery – and your lover-boy was there, too."

Talia's cheeks coloured slightly. "Oh?" she said with careful nonchalance.

Boris could see that Ivan wanted to tease her further, so he gave him a warning look. "Isn't today check-up day?"

"I guess so." Ivan sighed. "I'm getting fed up with being pushed and prodded every week. How much longer is this is going to go on?"

"As long as necessary," Talia told him as she served the stew. "And don't think I haven't noticed the way you ogle some of the nurses."

Ivan gave a wicked laugh and tucked into his meal.

The medics turned up at ten o'clock precisely. They always arrived just as everyone was preparing to go to bed, as their patients needed to be sedated in order to perform the more intrusive tests. These were, Boris and his comrades had been assured, simply intended to ascertain how well their bodies were recovering from the effects of Pregeor.

Boris lay on his bed as the nurse assigned to him expertly located a vein in his left arm and he felt his mind dissolve in warmth.

Chapter 3

Talia woke on the eve of the weekend in an even happier frame of mind than usual; of all her responsibilities as a Hero of the Republic, visiting schools was the least onerous. Addressing young, enthusiastic students on the glories of the Republic, and the necessity to work hard and be vigilant in its service, could actually be enjoyable. She showered, dressed and exercised, in keen anticipation of the pleasures of the day, and of the four days of holiday that would follow it.

The visits all went well: the children welcomed her with true revolutionary fervour, and listened intently. She autographed so many of their books that her wrist was beginning to go numb. She had a slightly guilty feeling of relief when she was introduced to her last group, a set of eleven-year-olds at the President's High School for Girls.

Their teacher, Miss Sikorski, introduced her: "Class, as you will all be well aware, this is Comrade Hero Talia Milanova, one of the Heroes of Pregeor. Karla Karensky, please remind the class of what happened at Pregeor."

One of the girls rose to her feet and began the familiar description:

"A year ago, foreign agents incited a treacherous group of deviant, recidivist, counter-revolutionary malcontents to plot against the Comrade President and to attempt to seize the Pregeor region for their sponsors. These criminals were well armed with off-world weapons and overcame our peace-loving police force. But in the moment of their victory they lost everything when the loyal people of Pregeor, realising what had occurred, rose up against them.

"Armed with chair legs and spades they fought against gauss rifles and plasma guns. Fought and won, although hundreds had been slain by the time Goran Ardy, an unassuming worker from the Pregeor Tractor Works, was able to lead a group of patriots into the rebels' strong point. Knowing all had been lost, the rebel leader, whose name has been expunged from history, decided that he would destroy the city he could not steal. To this end he triggered an atomic demolition charge he had placed at the city's chemical plant. It exploded, releasing a devastating, burning cloud of corrosive and radioactive gas.

"A small band of heroes worked in this cloud of death to save their fellow citizens and restore power to the monorail system. They saved over twenty thousand people from dreadful injury and agonising death, but only a few of them survived, all badly injured. Physically and mentally scarred, they spent months being treated at the Restavic City Hospital.

"The Comrade President declared all those brave men and women to be Heroes of the Republic, and decreed that on recovery they would take up new and important positions in the capital city, where they would be a living example to us all."

After a brief pause, the teacher said, "Thank you, Karla. Now, everyone, the Comrade Hero will address us. Please be as quiet and attentive as you can."

Talia delivered her standard speech of encouragement to the eager youngsters. There was a moment's silence as she finished, then a spontaneous cheer that warmed her heart. She smiled and, aware that she had a few minutes to spare for the first time that day, asked if anyone had any questions. A forest of hands shot up and the teacher indicated a bespectacled girl in plaits.

"Olga Korsova."

Olga blushed and got to her feet. "Comrade Hero, what's it *like* being a hero?" One or two of her classmates giggled at her presumption, but most looked at Talia intently.

She paused and considered. "I... I'm not sure, Olga... I don't *feel* very heroic most of the time... I just try to do my best for the Republic – and the Republic is very generous in its appreciation."

"Tatiana Golova."

"Were you scared at Pregeor, Comrade Talia?"

Talia shook her head. "I wish I knew, Tatiana – I expect I was terrified, but I still can't remember it at all. One final question."

"Jana Klevik."

"Are you still ill, Comrade Talia?"

"Well, I – like all my fellow Heroes of Pregeor – still have to carry two small auto-injectors that dispense drugs into my system every day, to prevent any cancers that might be caused by lingering effects of the fallout and to promote the continuing regeneration of my body." Talia indicated the bulge at her waist, and with that her duties for the day were over, apart from the last batch of handshakes and autographs.

She'd arranged to meet up with Boris and Ivan afterwards at their favourite café, and they brought along Josef, who had been freed from servitude at the Tangled Comet to visit an Old Comrades' Home. They ordered drinks, and the youngster cupped his hands around his mug of hot chocolate and gave a deep sigh of contentment.

"You seem happy," Talia commented.

"Why shouldn't I be? I've no tables to wait on, no washing-up to do – and no-one looking over my shoulder all the time, making sure I'm always busy."

"Well, the weekend should be fun."

"Old Grumpy will find things for me to do – and I bet he's arranged more boring lessons, even over the holiday."

She looked at him sympathetically. "Doesn't Comrade Goran ever let you have any fun?"

"Not that I noticed. I wish I was *your* ward – or Comrade Anoushka's – or even Comrade Boris's." He took a pensive sip. "Comrade Talia, did you and your husband have any children?"

"No…" He hit a sore point: Talia had been told she had been married at Pregeor, but somehow that didn't seem right. She couldn't be certain whether or not she'd ever been married, but, as a nurse, she could tell that her body had never borne a child.

"What about the others?" Josef persisted.

Talia shook off her confusion. "Comrade Anoushka has never been married, and as for Comrade Boris, –" (she looked over towards the latter and pondered the haunted look in his eyes) "well, I don't know, but I think he'd make a good father." She paused and looked back at Josef sympathetically. "Look, I know you're not happy where you are, and I've told Major Drovsorsky so, but I'm afraid you're stuck for now."

He gave a grimace, then shrugged. "That's a strange-looking couple." He inclined his head towards the door.

One glance told Talia what they were. "Tourists. Off-worlders – just ignore them, and they'll go away." Indeed, their garish clothes and crude manners labelled them indelibly. The Heroes all tried to follow Talia's advice, but the female tourist's tone grated and they couldn't avoid hearing words such as 'quaint' and 'adorable', so they soon drank up and left.

As they passed the visitors, Josef stumbled slightly and knocked into the male tourist. "I'm sorry, sir – please excuse my young friend," Talia said, noting that Josef did not intend to apologise. She glared at the boy, but he simply shrugged.

"No problem," the man replied, but as they went through the door she heard him comment to his wife about "backworld manners", and for once she had to agree.

They walked back to their block to pack for the dacha. Though public transport was copious – and free to Heroes of the Republic – it was an idyllic autumn day, and the stroll along the banks of the river was truly delightful. The air was clear and sharp, with none of the pollution that Telphanians had to put up with, and each lungful made Talia glad to be alive. The leaves on the trees were just beginning to turn golden, and a few seasonal pioneers crunched beneath their feet. A skein of geese flew over, their melancholy cries echoing off the buildings lit by the afternoon sun.

While the rest of them prepared for their holiday, Josef sat and watched a programme on the television about the history of Silvana, and its fight for freedom from Telphanian tyranny. From the glimpses Talia caught of it, it was very inspiring, and featured many interviews with happy citizens of the liberated province. They had finished packing and were waiting for their lift to the helipad when the youngster looked up and asked, "Comrade Talia, what's a swan?"

"A big white bird with a long neck."

"I've never heard of them before. Have you ever seen one?"

A flash of memory: a lake, a flock of swans, a man – Jimmy? – by her side; then it was gone. "I have... but I can't remember where or when... Why do you ask?"

He flourished a piece of paper. "One of those tourists dropped it." Talia looked at him speculatively. "Well, I'm sure he would have if I hadn't liberated it from his pocket."

"Josef!" She acted shocked, but wasn't really. He always was an inquisitive child.

It was a news sheet from something call the *Lyric Swan*, which, from the context, had to be the space-liner that the tourists hailed from; hence his question. They all knew they shouldn't soil their minds with enemy propaganda, but even Heroes of the Republic can be curious, so they gathered around him to read it. It was primarily concerned with information for visiting tourists about their planet, including a warning about wearing nose filters to counteract the sulphur in the atmosphere.

One item annoyed Talia intensely, so much so that she burst out with, "What do they mean, branding our Republic a 'totalitarian dictatorship'? Who do they think they are? Don't they realise that under the benign rule of the Comrade President we enjoy a standard of living undreamed of by those who live elsewhere?"

"Calm down, Comrade Talia." Ivan gave her a pitying look. "They clearly don't know what they're talking about. Look – they say here that our government has purchased some grav tanks and is preparing for war. That's poppycock. If they had, Boris and I would have heard something about it." Boris looked a little perplexed, but nodded his head in agreement. "Anyway," Ivan added, "we have a right to protect ourselves from those Telphanian warmongers."

There was one further surprise in store: what did the sheet mean by calling what happened at Pregeor an accident? Talia was about to draw this to the others' attention when the intercom buzzed; the car had arrived to take them to catch their helicopter. She screwed up the contentious document and threw it in the rubbish bin, dismissing its uninformed drivel from her thoughts.

It was a brief but pleasant flight to the dacha, which was some miles up the coast from *The Tangled Comet*. The sun was low in the sky, and the rose-pink sky boded well for the morrow. Even Josef seemed happy, though his separation from his guardian obviously had an influence on his mood. The fact that Anoushka was due to join them during the weekend also lightened Talia's heart.

The shadows were beginning to lengthen when they arrived. They dispersed to their rooms and unpacked and, having put away the things she'd brought and stowed her suitcases under the bed, Talia changed into her swimsuit. Since men have much less luggage than women, Boris had finished well before she did, and he had already made up some punch. He, Ivan and Josef had changed into casual clothes and were sitting on the veranda, drinking and taking in the view.

"Anyone else fancy a swim?" she asked.

"It's not really my idea of fun," Ivan said with a grimace.

"Perhaps tomorrow," Boris added, more kindly. "Let's have a walk along the shore, Ivan."

"Why not, Comrade?"

"And I want to make a sand-hovercart," Josef said as he jumped down.

After the bustle of Restavic City, the peace and calm were delightful. There was a broad sandy beach which ran back towards the woods behind the dacha. Since it was early autumn, there was a sprinkling of reds and golds among the many shades of green.

Talia lay out on the beach for a short while, breathing the clean, resin-scented air and soaking up the setting sun. As its last rays bathed the sands in a warm glow, she decided to have her swim. Boris and Ivan had returned from their stroll, and had sat down a little way up the beach. The water was deliciously cool and invigorating, and she lingered for some time; eventually, however, she decided that she needed a drink and made for the shore. As she was leaving the water, she was surprised to see a young woman approaching her along the strand, wearing a rather attractive flower-print dress and carrying a shoulder-bag.

"Hello." Talia smiled at her. "We don't usually have visitors here – this place is pretty remote. Come and have a drink."

The girl glared back at Talia. "Murderer!" she snarled.

Talia's jaw dropped. The girl seized the opportunity to pull some sort of contraption from her bag and point it at Talia. The analytical part of Talia's mind screamed that she ought to react, but the rest of her was too dumb-founded to move. Luckily, the girl was no expert, and the contraption jumped in her hand as she pulled its trigger. A metal ball flew at Talia's eye, but at the last second she moved just enough so it buzzed past her left cheek. She staggered backwards.

The girl muttered a curse, took another ball from her bag and started to reload her weapon. Talia came back to her senses. Instinct was telling her to run, but she realised that if she did, she wouldn't get very far. She glanced at Boris and Ivan, who had started in her direction, but could see that they wouldn't reach her in time.

As the girl pointed the weapon at her again, Talia swallowed her fear and launched herself at her attacker. She caught hold of the girl's wrist in both hands and twisted it sideways before she could fire again. The girl grabbed Talia's hair with her free hand and snapping her head back. In her pain and shock, Talia loosened her grasp, and the barrel of the gun swung inexorably toward her face. She covered her eyes with her forearm, and her world exploded in agony.

Chapter 4

Boris and Ivan sat in relaxed silence, gazing at the setting sun. They were a little way up the beach from where Talia was bathing, and were alone, apart from the birds and a slender spotted feral cat that wandered the dunes. As they watched, the interloper waded out some yards, stood in rapt attention, waggled its rear, and pounced. There was a splash or two and the sodden feline returned to the shore with a fish in its jaws.

Boris idly picked up a small stone and hefted it into the water. The ripples spread out, catching the golden rays of the sun. As they died away, he picked up another pebble, intending to send it after its fellow, but Ivan interrupted him.

"It's a bit cold for a swim, I'd say." He indicated where Talia was cleaving the clear water, sending up splashy diamonds that caught the low beams of light and split them into rainbow colours. "Still, she doesn't look bad in a swimsuit."

"Getting ideas?" Boris gave Ivan a sardonic grin.

The younger man grimaced. "What? Me and Talia? Nah – she's not my type: too serious. I'd have thought you might be attracted to her, though."

"I might – it's just that she's not – oh, I don't remember who she's not, but she definitely isn't…"

Ivan laughed. "You're getting senile, old man. Anyway, Anoushka's more my style."

Boris was suddenly serious. "Just be careful. You hurt Anoushka, and Talia will happily gut you with one of her scalpels – and if she didn't, I would."

"Only joking, honest. Anyway, what about the bit in the news sheet about grav tanks? I just don't know where these people get their information."

"I don't know – there's been something odd going on at work the last few days: all that security, just for a few tractors – and have you actually seen any agricultural equipment?"

"Sure I have."

"What sort?"

Ivan's brow furrowed. "Well... Nah – you're imagining things." There was a long pause, and Boris was about to push the point when Ivan shrugged and said. "Look, there's a girl coming our way. Now she looks more my type." He scrambled to his feet.

He was right: the sun's last rays picked up the outline of a slim young woman in a light summer dress. She looked exceptionally pretty, with long, shapely legs and long blonde hair. Talia had just reached the shore herself, and seemed to be greeting the newcomer when the latter shouted something. They couldn't hear what it was, but it certainly wasn't friendly. There was a cracking sound, and the two women grappled with each other.

By this time, Boris was up and running towards the scuffle, some yards behind Ivan, who had a head start. There was another crack and a scream, and Talia collapsed in a heap at the other woman's feet. She stood over Talia, muttering to herself and struggling with something metallic.

Boris's instincts took over and he did the only thing he could: he threw the stone in his hand at Talia's assailant. It missed her by a whisker but she was so engrossed in her task that she didn't appear to notice. By this time she was aiming the mechanism in her hand straight at Talia's head. It looked as if they would arrive too late, so Boris stooped as he ran, gathered up another rock and flung it at the girl in a single, instinctive, fluid motion. The missile hit her temple with surprising precision and she dropped as if pole-axed next to her intended victim.

"I didn't know – you could do that." Ivan gave Boris a surprised glance as they continued sprinting towards the two prone figures.

"Neither – did I." Boris shook his head in mystification as they reached the women. Of the two, only Talia was conscious, and she only barely. She was curled in a ball holding her right wrist and whimpering. Boris could see from the unexpected angle of her hand that the joint was badly damaged, but his priority was to ensure that the newcomer could do no more harm.

The girl began to regain consciousness, and moaned quietly to herself. Ivan retrieved her home-made gun and levelled it at her. "Before we hand you over to the authorities, you bitch, would you like to tell me why you tried to kill my friend?"

"You're another of those bastards – traitors and murderers, all of you." She spat at Ivan.

Ivan was taken aback. "What do you mean?"

"Whatever the propagandists say, we know now our own government triggered the explosion at the chemical plant, destroying Pregeor and killing thousands of Zelynans, including my family. We lived outside the blast radius, but the toxic chemicals killed everyone but me – and I'll soon be joining them – look!"

She pulled down her dress, showing that her body was covered with scars and burns, and in the dying light Ivan and Boris could see that her face, too, was scarred, and heavily made up to disguise the damage.

"I knew I'd never be able to get to the President or his lackeys, but you so-called 'Heroes of Pregeor' must have been involved somehow..." She sneered. "Anyway, *I* may have failed, but sooner or later, now people know the truth, *someone* will succeed, and you'll die – painfully, I hope. You deserve to share our agony." She spat at Ivan again and he recoiled from her venom.

Boris had opened his mouth to protest when an unexpected voice from behind him made him jump. "I'll take over now, Comrade Boris."

Boris looked round in surprise. "What are you doing here, Comrade Major?" he asked. "Your turning up unexpectedly is getting to be a habit – but if you'd come to protect us, you arrived a bit too late."

"A coincidence, Comrade Boris. I was just bringing a friend of yours to join your party." He indicated a helicopter a little way down the beach, from which Anoushka was disembarking. "Now let me take this creature away while you tend to Comrade Talia."

Anoushka could see something was wrong and hurried in their direction. As soon as she saw Talia's huddled form, she gave a wordless cry, ran to her and knelt at her side. "Oh, my poor Talia – what has that bitch done to you?" She glared at the interloper.

"I think her wrist is broken," Boris said miserably.

Anoushka rounded on Ivan. "Why haven't you done something for her?"

"We had to secure the prisoner," he mumbled resentfully.

Anoushka rolled her eyes. "Men! You're all useless! Go and get Talia's medkit. Move!" She turned to Boris. "And you – you go and get a mattress, so we can carry her inside."

Boris ran towards the dacha, but partway there he almost fell on his face as something shot between his legs; it was the cat they'd seen fishing in the surf. "Get out of my way," Boris hissed, but the creature just gave him a disdainful look and walked away, her tail held high.

By the time he had dragged Talia's mattress back to the scene of the battle, Anoushka had administered some morphine, and Talia was regaining a degree of hazy consciousness.

"'Noush – 'noushka?" she muttered.

"Yes, Talia: it's me. Now be a good girl and rest."

"But – but my wrist – it's shattered."

"That's what I thought the first time I looked at it, but it's actually not that bad. I removed this vile object," (she held up a large ball-bearing streaked with blood) "and when I went to immobilise the joint I found that the bones were whole and the major blood vessels intact. There's a nasty gash, but no long term damage." Anoushka bound Talia's wound and immobilised her patient's damaged wrist by strapping it to her chest.

"Thank God." Talia's tears began to flow as they helped her on to the mattress. The three of them, plus Major Valentine, who had returned from dealing with Talia's attacker, carried her inside, one at each corner.

They settled her in the living room, and sat around in a confused daze. Ivan broke out the vodka, poured them all liberal glassfuls and kept the bottle for himself. "Major," he said, "that woman claimed *we'd* attacked Pregeor…"

"Don't believe anything she said. I've checked – " (Boris felt a small surge from one of his auto-injectors) "and she's delusional. She escaped from a party of mental patients that are using a dacha just up the coast. Her carers will be severely reprimanded."

"But her wounds…"

"Self-inflicted, I assure you."

Boris nodded in agreement, but, for some reason, he found himself mentally reciting the alphabet, over and over. He felt his mind clearing, and realised that the others seemed to be hanging on the Major's every word.

"Now I must leave you." The Major got to his feet and turned to Ivan. "I'd better take that weapon and dispose of it, Comrade – it's a nasty contraption." Ivan handed it over and the Major looked over at Anoushka. "And its ammunition…" She gave him the ball bearing. "I suggest you all get a good night's sleep." With that, he departed.

Once he had gone, Ivan went straight to bed, taking the vodka bottle with him, but Anoushka sat on

Talia's mattress with her back against the sofa, cradling her injured friend's head and stroking her hair.

"I still don't see how those wounds could be self-inflicted," Boris said quietly, so as not to disturb the patient.

Anoushka was concentrating on Talia, and absent-mindedly said, "I know – I only caught a glance as they led her away, but her condition was shocking. She'll die unless they get her into an Autodoc."

"What's an Autodoc?"

"Hmm? Sorry?"

"I said, 'What's an Autodoc?'"

Her nose wrinkled in thought. "I don't remember hearing that term before."

"But you just used it."

She shook her head emphatically, "All I said was that poor girl was going to die. Now get to bed. I'll look after our casualty."

As Boris lay down, he crimped the tubes on his auto-injectors to disable them. If his suspicions were unfounded, they were due to be checked in a few days anyway, and he could explain it away as accidental damage caused during the scuffle with Talia's assailant. And if not…

He awoke in the early morning, his bladder distended. Oddly, as he regained consciousness, he seemed to hear someone talking quietly, but as he moved, the voice stopped. Now he was awake, he listened in puzzlement. There seemed to be a gentle susurration, as of a number of people whispering at once. It seemed to be coming from several places, including the living room.

After a few seconds, he raised his head to try to make out what was being said, but as soon as he did so, the noise stopped. He struggled to his feet, went to the bathroom and relieved himself and, as he made his way back, he looked in on the others to see if anyone was awake. They were all deeply asleep. To be honest, he wasn't surprised, as the voice he'd thought he'd heard didn't sound like any of his companions, but he was disconcerted.

Anoushka had fallen asleep where she sat with Talia. Boris gently raised her head and slid a pillow behind it. He ran the murmur he'd heard while half-asleep through his mind. He could have sworn he'd caught the phrases 'nothing else happened' and 'slipped and caught it on a bolt...' He shook his head in bewilderment and returned to bed.

Chapter 5

Talia awoke in pain and confusion; her wrist hurt, and it was strapped to her chest. She opened her eyes and looked up into Anoushka's face. Her friend smiled and said, "Good morning. How does your arm feel?"

"Really sore," Talia said. "I can't believe that a simple bolt could do so much damage."

"Let's have a look at it." Anoushka undid the strapping and removed the blood-sodden bandage. The wound had mostly closed, but there was still some minor bleeding, so she anointed it with antibiotic cream and rebound it, but more lightly. "I'm not going to strap it down again, but there's to be no heavy exercise for you today – we don't want it to reopen, do we?"

Talia pouted. "You don't have to talk to me if I'm seven years old, 'Noushka."

"If only I could be sure you wouldn't *act* like a seven year old…"

"I'll be a good girl, Nursie – honest." They laughed, and Talia's cares melted. "Oh, it's so good to have you back." She gave Anoushka an impromptu one-armed hug.

"Breakfast," Ivan called from the kitchen. Indeed, he needn't have bothered – the smell of frying bacon was beginning to draw everyone like moths to a flame. As Talia wolfed down the artery-hardening, cholesterol-rich, but totally delicious fried meal, she looked over at Boris, who was pushing his own food distractedly around his plate.

"What's the matter, Comrade? Toothache?"

He shook his head. "I need a walk to burn up some of these calories. Care to join me?" They all agreed, and once Anoushka had washed up (she refused to let Talia get her wound damp), they set off on a gentle stroll up the shoreline.

Once they'd walked a hundred yards or so, Boris turned to Talia and said, "Talia, do you remember what happened yesterday evening."

"Yes, of course I do – we arrived and unpacked. You sat on the beach while I went swimming. On the way back, I damaged my wrist when I slipped and caught it on a bolt protruding from the veranda rail. Nothing else happened."

"Don't you remember being attacked?"

Talia stopped in her tracks, looking confused, and shook her head. "Being attacked?"

"It happened just as Anoushka arrived," he added.

"What do you mean?" Anoushka said pensively. Her eyes widened and she gasped. "It's all coming back to me now. You were injured when a girl attacked you. That's why you were on your mattress in the living room this morning – we'd had to sedate you and carry you back from the beach. The girl accused you – and us – of causing the disaster at Pregeor."

A pulse in Talia's temple started to throb and all her muscles seemed to tighten. "Boris – 'Noushka – it's very strange, but now I've got two sets of memories of last night. I – I know you're right: I can see the girl's face now – it was all creased up. She was screaming at me. But I still remember catching my wrist on that bolt as well – horrible, ugly thing sticking out of the veranda. They can't both be true."

"Which of them seems the most real?" Boris put his hands on Talia's shoulders and his eyes bored into hers.

"I – I don't know…" She turned her head away, unwilling to meet his eyes. "I really don't want to think about it."

"Please, concentrate – it's important,"

Talia closed her eyes and took a deep breath. What could she be certain of? She remembered their arrival, changing, and that exhilarating swim. Then, as she left the water… Suddenly the incident with the bolt fled before her internal gaze. "I was attacked," she said firmly, turning her gaze back to Boris.

"Good girl!"

At this point Ivan, who had been lagging behind, caught up with them and asked, "What's going on?"

"We were discussing last night's attack," Boris replied.

"Attack? What attack?"

"Don't you remember? The one where that woman shot Talia in the arm."

"Begging your pardon, Comrade Anoushka, but there was no attack – she merely slipped and caught her wrist on a bolt protruding from the veranda rail. Nothing else happened."

"Same phrases, same fiction," Boris said, half to himself. "I swear I heard those same words when I got up to relieve myself last night. I believe we're being brain-washed."

"The only thing that your brains have been washed in is too much vodka." For some reason, Ivan was getting agitated.

"Calm down, my friend – it's just that I think that someone's been messing with our minds – and our memories."

Ivan snarled. "You're delusional, Boris. My mind's fine – and my memory."

"What about Pregeor?"

"What about it?"

"What really happened there?"

"What do you mean? We *know* what happened."

"Do we? Are you positive? We only know what we've been *told*. Maybe our memories need jogging."

"I'll jog *your* memory!" Ivan swung at Boris and hit him full in the face, and the older man crumpled to the sand.

"What did you do that for?" Anoushka knelt down beside Boris, and reached into her bag for a tissue to stem the bleeding from his nose.

Ivan seemed confused. "He – he insulted me! Implied I was crazy." He turned on his heel and stamped off back in the direction of the dacha.

Talia joined Anoushka at Boris' side and examined him. The flow of blood soon lessened, and they were able to help him sit up. He was still very muzzy, but despite the anger in Ivan's blow, there seemed to be no major harm done. Boris followed Talia's finger with his eyes, and his pupils seemed fine, so there was no sign of concussion.

When the stream of blood had become a trickle, Talia checked the inside of his nose. It didn't seem badly injured, but while she was examining it she caught a glimpse of something odd. There was a strange plastic device deep in the nasal passage. She wanted to take a closer look, but felt she couldn't reach it without reopening the wound, or at least causing Boris severe pain, given the bruising surrounding it, so left it where it was.

"He should be fine," she told Anoushka. "Let's get him back to the dacha – a couple of painkillers should have him feeling better." Anoushka nodded, and helped Talia get Boris to his feet. As they slowly made their way along the beach, Talia looked over at her friend. "Anoushka, back in the city, before we came here, Josef 'liberated' an off-world newssheet from a tourist."

"Did he, indeed?" She chuckled. "Young delinquent. What did you do to him?"

"Nothing – we were too curious about what it said. It made some scurrilous claims about our Republic, but there was one thing it mentioned that's just come to mind..."

"Oh? What's that?"

"It recommended that visitors to Ruine should wear nasal filters."

"I vaguely remember hearing something like that before – something about our atmosphere being rich in sulphur."

"And I know we've got air filtration units in several of the rooms at the Medical Centre set aside for off-worlders. I've never had call to use them myself..."

"... but they're there for those who can't tolerate our atmosphere," she finished. "Interesting, but I don't see what you're getting at."

"Well, while I was treating Boris's nose, I noticed that there's something that looks suspiciously like a filter deep inside it." They had reached the veranda, and sat their still-dazed charge down. "Could you look after him for a minute while I get something?"

"I'd be happy to."

Talia returned seconds later with the pencil torch from her medkit. A few minutes investigation confirmed her suspicions: Boris and Anoushka had similar devices in both nostrils. "Look here." she showed Anoushka the contraption in Boris's left nostril. "Would you check my nose?"

She put her head back so that Anoushka could shine the torch up her nose and peer inside. "You're right," Anoushka said after some seconds, "You've got them, too."

Talia sat up and thought for a few seconds and said, "Look, 'Noushka, I want to do an experiment – I'd like to see the effect if one of those devices is removed. I'd try to take out one of mine, but I'd have to use a mirror, which always makes manipulation difficult – and after what Ivan did, I don't want to disturb Boris's for fear of doing more damage..."

"... so you'd like to remove one of mine."

"It might hurt a bit... *You* could always extract one of *mine* – under my supervision."

Anoushka shook her head. "Oh, no – you're far defter than I am, and you'd do it faster, and do less damage in the process. Don't worry – you remove one of mine. I know you'll do your best to keep the discomfort to the minimum. Anyway, here comes Ivan – do you think we should tell him?"

"He still looks agitated. We should keep this from him for now."

"Look at this," Ivan said as he approached. "Now who's imagining things?" He directed the others attention at the veranda rail, and indeed one of the bolts securing it had some dried blood on it. There seemed no point in arguing with him, so Talia simply nodded.

"How do you feel?" Anoushka asked Boris, who was slowly regaining his faculties.

"Bloody," he replied, and smiled tentatively. He looked up at Ivan, who, seeing Boris's discomfort, was clearly beginning to feel rather embarrassed. "Why'd you hit me, Ivan? I was only trying to get at the truth."

"We all *know* the truth – look, here's the bolt Comrade Talia hurt her wrist on." He paused. "Look, I'm sorry I lost control. I shouldn't have lashed out like that, but I thought you were implying I was going loopy."

"But –" began Boris.

Talia interrupted him. "It all seems clear now, Comrade – we must have been wrong. It must have been some sort of a bad dream." Ivan looked relieved. "Why don't you go and get some drinks while we tend to Boris?"

"That's a good idea."

Once he had gone, Talia turned to the others and murmured, "Look, if something odd is going on here, if we're being manipulated in some way, we don't want to raise anyone's suspicions."

"True," Boris responded. "And if Ivan is under an external influence, he might give us away, either accidentally or intentionally."

"Yes," Talia mused, "lashing out unexpectedly like that implies an inner conflict, though – maybe if we just give him some time…"

"I agree. Now, just in case the drugs they're feeding us are part of the conditioning, I've crimped the tubes on my dispensers. Let's do the same to yours."

Talia shook her head. "Too suspicious – it'd be better to drain their contents. If I store them in some of the sample jars in my medkit, I might be able to get the drugs analysed."

Anoushka frowned. "But won't that put our health at risk?"

"I don't think so," Talia replied pensively. "If Boris is right, it won't do any harm. If he's wrong, the dispensers are due to be refilled next week anyway."

"But if they're empty, won't that look odd?"

Talia shook her head indulgently. "Don't worry, 'Noushka – I'm not that stupid. I'll change the drugs for something innocuous for now and replace them before our next check-up."

Anoushka wrinkled her nose and stuck out her tongue. Talia laughed, and at this point, Ivan returned with a tray of drinks and a dishevelled Josef, who had just got out of bed, so they postponed future discussion until they were alone again.

Chapter 6

The pills Talia had given Boris worked as efficiently as all her remedies, and the pain subsided to something more or less bearable. Boris thought sardonically that Ivan's vodka had probably been just as helpful: if only it could restore memories as well. That, however, was going to be up to him.

He stood up. "I need to clear my head. I'm going for another walk."

Anoushka looked concerned. "Are you positive you feel up to it?" she asked.

"Yes. Why don't you *all* come with me, just in case?"

Boris guided their stroll to the part of the shore where the attack had occurred, but when they reached the area, all traces of the struggle seemed to have been swept away, naturally or otherwise. He caught sight of something glinting amongst a patch of scrubby grass.

He pretended to stagger. "I feel a bit woozy again," he said. "Can we sit down here for a while?"

Talia looked at him quizzically, sensing his artifice but unaware of his purpose. She shrugged her shoulders, helped him to seat himself on the sand, and reclined beside him. The others joined her and they were soon relaxing in the warmth of the sun.

Boris had positioned himself carefully between the object he'd seen and Ivan – if possible, he wanted the younger man to be the one who discovered it. He could sense that nobody wanted to discuss anything personal, so he raised the subject of the advantages – or otherwise – of hovercraft over conventional vehicles.

Talia and Anoushka looked at each other; the latter rolled her eyes and sighed while the former shook her head pityingly. They both lay back in the sand and pointedly ignored the men.

Boris kept hoping that Ivan would notice what he'd seen, but the latter was initially oblivious to it. Boris had almost given up, and was about to 'discover' it himself when, to his relief, Ivan frowned and said, "What's that?"

"What's what?"

"There – in the grass – something metallic."

"Where?" Boris feigned confusion, so Ivan got to his feet, walked over and picked the object up.

"That's strange," he said

"What is it?"

"This is a ball-bearing from a heavy ball race. What an odd thing to find in a place like this."

It was the first missile that the girl had fired at Talia the previous evening. Boris could see that Talia and Anoushka recognised it as well, and they all waited in anticipation for Ivan to remember the incident. There seemed to be no immediate effect, though he did seem distracted by his incongruous find, which he inspected for a few seconds before thrusting it into his pocket.

Boris had done what he could, so he lay back down on the sand and relaxed for a few minutes, before sitting up and saying, "I fancy a mug of tea – I'm positive that would complete my convalescence. Let's go back, and I'll make us all a drink." The others murmured agreement, and they got to their feet and strolled back to the bungalow.

He was fulfilling his promise when Josef poked his head around the kitchen door and said, "There's a 'copter coming, Comrade Boris."

He joined the others just as the Shiskin landed and Major Drovsorsky jumped out. He seemed concerned. "Comrade Talia," he began, "I've come to see how you are this morning, and to apologise for the incident which occurred last night. The young woman who attacked you has been returned to the asylum."

Talia gave him a vacuous look that almost made Boris laugh aloud. "Attacked me, Major? Nobody

47

attacked me. We had a quiet evening. Nothing happened of any consequence, apart from the fact that I slipped and caught my wrist on a bolt protruding from the veranda rail." She held up her bandaged forearm.

The Major looked extremely puzzled. "Really? Please excuse me for a moment," he said, and returned to the 'copter where he consulted someone via its radio. It seemed a fairly animated discussion, and Boris guessed that he hadn't been told about the modification to their memories. On reflection, perhaps this was part of some sort of power-play by Captain Reynard. He knew the Captain coveted the Major's job.

The Major returned, looking rather embarrassed. "I am so sorry I disturbed you, my friends. It appears that the message I got was garbled, and the incident I was informed about took place at the next dacha up the coast. I apologise for interrupting your holiday."

"Not a problem," Boris replied. "Was anyone hurt?"

"I don't believe so." He turned back to Talia. "I am, however, sorry about your injury, Comrade Talia."

"Don't worry - honestly." She laid her good hand on the Major's arm. "It's only a scratch, really."

"Well... I hope it'll heal quickly. Anyway, I won't trouble you any further, and I hope you enjoy the rest of your stay." With that, he bowed politely, turned, and strode back to the 'copter. It rose into the air and hovered for a moment, before flying away in the direction of Restavic City.

Ivan, who had been strangely quiet through the visitation, was fingering the ball bearing he'd found with a puzzled frown. To the others' chagrin, he shrugged and put it back in his pocket.

Once Boris had finished preparing drinks and served them to the others, he dismissed his concern for the moment and lay down on the beach in contentment, revelling in the warmth, and the gentle breeze, and the sound of the lapping waves. He had closed his eyes and was half asleep when a hand touched his arm. He looked up into Talia's face and opened his mouth to enquire what she wanted, but she put her finger to her lips and pointed at Ivan, who was snoring loudly. He got to his feet and followed her back to the dacha, where Anoushka was waiting.

"I've already changed the contents of Anoushka and my dispensers, and I managed to do the same to Ivan's while he slept. Let's deal with yours." She drained both containers into separate sample jars and replaced the contents with a clear liquid.

"Nothing dangerous, I hope."

"No – just some blood plasma from my medkit. Hmm…" She frowned. "Odd – you and I had two different-looking drugs, but Anoushka's and Ivan's seem the same… Ah well, I'll have to wait till I can run them through the analyser at the Medical Centre."

"Is that everything you wanted?" he asked.

"Not quite. While I was treating your nose this morning, I noticed that you had something artificial buried deep in your nasal passage. I examined Anoushka and she checked me, and we found that we both had similar devices. I'm going to have a go at removing one of Anoushka's to see what they're there for. Could you keep a lookout for us?"

Boris checked that Ivan was still asleep, and that Josef was busy: the boy was building yet another model hovercart in the sand, which was taking all his attention. Since the coast was clear, Anoushka lay down on her bed, and Talia began a gentle investigation of her left nostril. The device was so deeply imbedded that it took some time to remove, and caused the patient a fair amount of discomfort, but after some moments it lay in Talia's palm.

"Now take a small breath," she told Anoushka.

The latter did as she was told and wrinkled her nose in disgust. "Ech!" she said. "What a horrible smell. It's a good thing *I* eat sensibly, or you'd be clearing up my vomit."

"It's just as I thought," Talia said as she worked to replace the device. "Remember the news-sheet that suggested filters for visitors to Ruine?" Boris nodded. "Well, I think that's just what we are – visitors, and this is all some sort of elaborate charade. They probably change them during our weekly check-ups."

"Why doesn't our food taste sulphurous?" Boris asked.

"Maybe it does, but we're just used to it," Talia replied. Her patient gave a yelp. "Oh, sorry, 'Noushka – it's damnably tricky to re-seat this thing without the right tool."

"Hey, what's going on?" Ivan's voice, edged with suspicion, came from the doorway, and Boris jumped. He had been so engrossed by the procedure that he'd forgotten to keep a lookout.

"Anoushka's got a nose-bleed," Talia said smoothly, and indeed a slender trickle of red was obligingly proceeding from Anoushka's nostril.

"Humph!" He stomped off.

"Sorry about that," Boris said, shamefacedly. "I'm – we're all going to have to be more careful." The others nodded agreement.

He re-joined Ivan on the beach. They sat together for some time in uncomfortable silence until Ivan sighed and said, "I'm sorry about hitting you earlier, Boris. I don't know what came over me. I shouldn't have reacted like that."

"Apology accepted, Comrade," Boris said. "Let's forget it and enjoy the view." He indicated the girls, who were wading into the sea. Ivan laughed and the tension vanished.

Boris was about to lie down and close his eyes when he caught sight of a motor launch anchored fifty yards or so off shore, with a man fishing from its stern.

"That's an odd place to fish," he said to Ivan, inclining his head towards the boat.

Ivan raised his head. "Seems all right to me."

"But he won't catch much moored there," Boris persisted. "I've been out fishing here with Goran, and he always anchors further out – and so do all the other fishermen I've seen."

"Perhaps he just wants some peace and quiet – or perhaps he's a novice and could benefit from your sage advice." Ivan raised his voice and called out in the direction of the boat, "Comrade! You don't seem to be having much luck. Why don't you come and share some vodka with us? Then Boris here can advise you on the best places to fish."

The fisherman looked startled. He poked his head into the boat's cabin and seemed to be talking to someone inside. "Sorry, Comrade," he called after some seconds, "I'd love to join you, but unfortunately there's something wrong with my engine."

"We're mechanics," Boris called, "we'll come and give you a hand," and in a great show of solidarity, he and Ivan scrambled to their feet, stripped down to their shorts, waded out into the water and started to swim towards the boat.

The fisherman sat where he was, looking rather nonplussed, and before the swimmers were halfway to the launch, its engine surged into life. It shot away from the beach, and the putative angler fell forwards and let go of his rod. Trying to regain his balance, he grabbed at a towel draped over a protrusion on the boat's roof. As the yacht dwindled into the distance, Boris noted that the item this revealed was a parabolic microphone.

Chapter 7

Once Boris had followed Ivan back to the beach, Talia checked the filter she replaced in Anoushka's nose, before turning her attention to her own injury.

"Don't fiddle with your dressing, Talia," Anoushka said with mock severity as she sat up.

"But it itches, Nursie."

She sighed. "All right, let me have a look at it." She carefully removed the bandage and gave a sudden intake of breath. "That's not right," she said, a puzzled frown across her forehead. Apart from an area of scarring and mild bruising, Talia's wrist was now fine. "Nothing heals that quickly."

"I know what you mean," Talia said. "It should have taken ages for it to mend that much." She began examining the unnaturally-healed wound, but was distracted by a strange vibration against her leg. Looking down, she saw a small cat rubbing against her calf and purring.

Anoushka followed her glance. "What a beautiful creature," she said, and reached down to stroke the newcomer. As she did so, the young feline sprang onto her right shoulder, wound round the back of her neck and rubbed its forehead against her left cheek. Anoushka grinned. "I saw her roaming around last night. She seems to be feral."

"She seems friendly enough." Talia looked into the cat's eyes, which were like liquid gold. There was something strangely familiar about that gaze. She scratched between the interloper's ears and the cat closed her eyes, purring ecstatically. "Perhaps she's hungry." She stood up and walked into the kitchen and her question was answered, as the cat leapt decorously down from Anoushka's shoulders and did figures-of-eight around Talia's ankles as she opened a tin of pluny.

She emptied the fish into a bowl and lowered it to the floor. The animal was clearly hungry, but had the good manners to give a courteous "Mrowp" of thanks before she began to eat, delicately but efficiently.

Talia turned back to Anoushka. "Well, I don't know how my arm healed so quickly, but at least I know I can go for a paddle now, can't I?"

"As long as I go with you to keep you safe," Anoushka replied. "But *no* swimming – we can't be sure that the tendons are fully healed."

They left the cat to her meal, changed into their swimming costumes and returned to the beach. As they walked down into the cool, refreshing water together, Talia's mind was distracted by their recent discoveries. She turned to say something to Anoushka, but her pensive mood was shattered as she received a face-full of spray.

"You – you – you –" she spluttered, but Anoushka just giggled and waded away from her as fast as she could. Talia was determined to have her revenge, however, and dived under and through the water in her friend's direction. She tackled Anoushka around the knees and pulled her over, ducking her under the surface in the process.

Anoushka came up coughing and spluttering but still managed to splash Talia again as she did so. "I thought I said no swimming," she cried when she'd got her breath back.

"You made me do it," Talia retorted. "But at least it proved that my wrist is just fine." She emphasised the fact by using the newly-healed arm to send a wave of water towards her friend.

Anoushka was preparing for round two when suddenly she stopped. "What are those two miscreants doing?" she asked, looking behind Talia. Talia was suspicious that this was a ploy to distract her, but the sudden sound of an engine in that direction backed up Anoushka's story. She turned just in time to see an

Arkan VII hydrofoil take off like a bat out of hell. In between it and the two girls, Talia could just make out the heads of Boris and Ivan facing the departing boat. As she watched, they turned and set out for the shore.

"I wonder what that was about," she said as she turned back into another cascade of water. She dived for Anoushka's knees again, but her friend managed to dodge her and hold her head down under the surface. She thrashed about until she managed to free herself, and as she surfaced, spluttering imprecations, Anoushka waded away. Talia chased her this way and that through the shallows, and though she was faster, Anoushka somehow kept managing to evade her grasp. At last, with a triumphant cry, Talia caught her friend around the waist and was about to exact her revenge when someone pinned her arms to her side from behind, forcing her to let go.

From behind her left ear, Boris's voice said, "OK, ladies, we need to talk, but we've got to be careful not to make Ivan suspicious. For the moment, let's just keep up the horseplay." This seemed to be his justification for lifting Talia up bodily and dunking her under the surface head first, but the smirk he gave after she regained her footing showed a little too much relish. Talia took her revenge by diving for his legs and toppling him backwards into the surf.

She glanced over to the beach, where Ivan had lain down again and was dozing in the sun. "I think we can talk n-" she began, but her sentence went unfinished. She heard Anoushka laugh behind her as a beach-ball hit her in the middle of her back and she fell face-forward with an almighty splash.

Talia was about to retaliate when Boris said, "You're right – let's just throw the ball around while we talk." She grunted her reluctant agreement as Anoushka smirked and stuck out her tongue. "That fishing boat was eavesdropping on us."

"How do you know?" Anoushka asked, and he told them about his and Ivan's adventure, and the parabolic microphone that he'd seen on the roof of the launch. "Anyway," he added, "I retrieved the rod dropped by the 'fisherman', and I don't see how he expected to catch anything without bait – or a hook."

"It didn't look like a fishing boat to me," Talia mused. "I've seen something like it before, but with some sort of insignia on the side."

"What sort of insignia?"

"A capital M with a capital I superimposed on it. I should know what that means, but I just can't bring it to mind." She sighed in frustration.

"Doesn't mean anything to me." Anoushka wrinkled her nose in thought.

"Or me. But I think we've got to be careful." Boris was visibly concerned. "This looked too well-organised to have anything to do with last night's amateur assault – and, given our nose filters, I think we're not who we've been told that we are. I'd reckon that we're under observation to ensure we don't find out – or remember – the truth." He paused, before adding. "We can't trust the others not to give us away, for the moment at least, so we've got to keep this to ourselves."

"I agree," Talia said, and Anoushka nodded her assent. "Now let's take a break. We're due at the *Comet* for lunch in an hour or so." They emerged from the sea and lay for a while in the sun before returning to the dacha to shower and change.

As a reward for his heroism in leading the resistance at Pregeor, Goran Ardy had been made the owner/manager of *The Tangled Comet*, a high-class restaurant and wine bar by the waterside on the eastern edge of Restavic City. Talia didn't get on with Goran, and he disliked her intensely, but their mutual status as Heroes of the Republic required that they spend *some* time in each other's company; and anyway the food at the *Comet* was good. What's more, Goran was a consummate yachtsman, and the whole group planned to take a leisurely cruise on his catamaran back along the coast to their dacha.

They dressed appropriately, and were ready when the helicopter arrived to transport them to the restaurant. Unexpectedly, before they could board it, it disgorged a party of security troops. "Good morning, Lieutenant." Talia smiled her most winning smile at their leader, a fresh-faced young man in his twenties. "To what do we owe the pleasure of this visit?"

He smiled back. "I'm afraid it's not for pleasure, Comrade Hero, delightful as that would be. I'm taking these new recruits on a training hike, and simply thought that we'd catch a lift with your transport – to kill two birds with one stone, as it were."

"What a pity. Perhaps you could come by yourself sometime. Our status means that we have few visitors, and I – we – would make you very welcome." Talia laid her hand on his arm and squeezed it gently.

He blushed. "I – I would like to – if and when time permits." To cover his confusion, he turned to his squad. "Sergeant, move the men out." Turning back, he said, "I'm sorry – I must go."

"Of course – but remember my invitation."

"I – I will."

Boris's expression was disapproving as they made their way to the helicopter. "I wish you wouldn't do that sort of thing," he said.

"Why not?" Talia countered. "It kept him off-balance, and allayed any suspicions he might have had, didn't it? And I've been given these 'gifts'" (she waggled her hips) "so I might as well use them to my – and our – advantage. Anyway, did you notice his men? They didn't look like raw recruits to me."

"No – and they were pretty heavily armed for a hike in the woods. I wonder what's up."

Talia looked back, and saw Ivan standing by the veranda, fingering the ball bearing. "Aren't you coming?" she called to him.

"I don't think so," he said pensively. "I'm feeling a bit odd. I think I'll lie down and rest for a while."

Chapter 8

The helicopter landed on the beach by the *Comet*, and Talia, Anoushka and Boris disembarked. The latter looked back at Josef. "Not joining us, Comrade?"

"I've got to visit my tutor for some classes. Anyway, ol' sourpuss would only have me washing up – that's worse than lessons. Peter will be there with me, and maybe we can get the old duffer to talk about hovercart design. It used to be his hobby, you know." He grinned at the prospect as the others entered the restaurant.

Goran himself met them and led them to a table by the small stage where a folk band often played. "Welcome, Comrades," he said expansively. "Comrade Anoushka, it's so good to see you back with us." He gave her a broad smile as he pulled out her chair and helped her to be seated, then stepped up onto the stage. "Comrades," he announced loudly, "Today, in honour of our glorious Comrade President's Birthday, we have a special treat in store. May I introduce Political Commissar Tatiana Cheslenko, who will address us concerning 'Our Children – Our Future'."

A young and personable blonde woman in a uniform took his place and began to speak. Until recently, she would have had Boris's full, if slightly reluctant, attention, but somehow the rhetoric seemed even more empty than usual to him that day, and he had other things on his mind. He was so wrapped up in his own thoughts that he jumped as Goran led the applause at the end of the oration. "Bravo, Comrade Commissar," their host cried as he got to his feet and escorted the young lady from the podium. "Now come and join us for lunch."

"I'd be honoured, Comrade Hero, to be part of such an august company – if only for a few moments."

Sunset in Silvana

He helped her into a spare seat that he'd reserved for her. "Nonsense, my dear – we are the ones who would be honoured. Did you hear what she said about the duty of children to be obedient, Comrades? I only wish Josef hadn't missed such an interesting and informative talk. I'm all in favour of education, but this was far more relevant than some dry, dusty history lesson. Comrade Commissar, perhaps we could invite you to visit us at our dacha tomorrow? You could repeat your sage advice for Josef's benefit – and maybe we could get to know each other a bit better. What do you say?"

"It would be a pleasure. I'm positive I can rearrange my schedule for such a worthy cause. And please, call me Tatiana, all of you."

Goran beckoned the Head Waiter over and said, "Well – Tatiana – what would you like to eat?"

The Commissar perused the menu and pursed her lips. "I'll have the Flickeral Salad," she said, then gave a slightly embarrassed smile, adding, "followed by the Butterscotch Pudding. It's a bit decadent – but it's irresistible."

"Don't worry," Anoushka said, laying her hand lightly on the visitor's. "You're among friends – we won't tell. Anyway, I feel the same way – I'll have the same."

"And me," Talia added. "It sounds like a delicious combination."

"What about you, Comrade Boris?" Goran asked.

"I've always enjoyed your Pork in Red Wine, Comrade – with potatoes and vegetables, please – and I'll follow that with Chocolate Cake and Cream."

"I'll just have a portion of the stew," Goran told the Head Waiter. "When I've been supervising – and tasting - the cooking all morning, I find I haven't much of an appetite, Comrades," he added by way of explanation.

Boris had expected the Commissar to act like her public persona, but was pleasantly surprised: she deliberately eschewed politics, changing the subject if the conversation turned in that direction, happily chatting about music, video programming and sport, and discussing clothes and make-up with Talia and Anoushka.

"Ah, well," she said as they finished their coffee, "Now, I must bid you farewell and return to my duties. Until tomorrow –"

"Until tomorrow," the others replied as she waved goodbye.

They made their way to the *Comet*'s private quay and boarded Goran's Meteor catamaran, the *Grim Reaper's Darling*, its name reflecting his rather macabre sense of humour. He began setting the sail as Boris cast off and pushed the boat out from the shore. He took the tiller, and Talia and Anoushka lay out on the cabin roof together, basking in the afternoon sun. Boris joined him at the stern as they began their cruise along the coast.

"Comrade Goran…" he began.

"Please don't call me Comrade when we're alone," Goran said. "It doesn't sound right, for some reason."

"That's one of the things I'd like to talk with you about," Boris continued. "It's hard to explain, but…the girls and I have a strange feeling that we're not what we're meant to be…that we're being – manipulated somehow."

"Manipulated? That's interesting. Go on."

Boris outlined the recent events: the attack on Talia, the implanted memories, the fishing-boat with the microphone and the discovery of the nose-filters.

As he talked, Goran's eyes widened, but he looked more relieved than surprised. "This would explain a lot, including some of the strange dreams I've been having."

"Dreams?"

"Yes – mostly they fade when I awake, but sometimes a bit lingers. They normally involve you and the others, but we seem to be in some sort of military detail."

"Talia thinks that the drugs in our injectors might be keeping away our true memories and making us suggestible," Boris said. Goran raised a slightly contemptuous eyebrow. "Look, I know you don't like her, but she *is* a nurse, and she knows what she's doing – she found our nose filters, for goodness sake. I think she's right, and she's drained our dispensers and replaced the drugs with blood plasma to see what will happen. I suggest you let her do the same to yours as soon as possible."

Goran shrugged, and Boris made his way forward, where he was soon sitting at the front between the hulls, dangling his feet in the spray and fishing. The sun was warm and the fish were biting, and soon a couple of good-sized pluny lay beside him on the deck. He had just re-baited his hook and was about to cast it again when the peaceful afternoon was rudely shattered. There was a strange whistling sound, followed by a splash off the port bow, a muffled explosion and a fountain of water.

"Mortar!" he yelled instinctively.

Goran immediately heeled the boat over to starboard, while the others dived for cover. There was another splash, a muted 'whump' and another cascade.

By this time, Talia and Anoushka had rolled off the roof. The former landed behind Boris on all fours like a cat, and he could sense she was ready to respond to the danger. There was a tense silence for some seconds before she called, "What do we do?"

"We've got to keep going and get out of range as soon as possible," Goran shouted back. "The shore is too shallow here to beach the boat and make it to cover safely. Anyway, whoever's doing this may have friends waiting for us if we try. But there are some dangerous shoals if we go out too far. Here comes another shell – brace yourselves." He threw the tiller over and the yacht yawed to port instants before the muffled report as another mortar bomb was fired.

"I think I can see where they're coming from," said Boris, pointing into the woods just ahead of them. It was perhaps surprising that Goran had known the shell was coming before it had been fired, but he was too concerned with keeping hold of the boat to worry about that. The shell hit the water and exploded to starboard, but closer this time.

"I wish there was some way we could fight back," Talia shouted. "Is there nothing we can do?"

"Oh, sure," muttered Boris. "We can install a top-of-the-range interceptor system – just check in your handbag, Talia, love." Aloud, he called back, "We can just pray that we won't be hit, and that they haven't any snipers with them. We're sitting ducks out here, and a wooden boat is scant cover from a high-powered rifle bullet."

"Can't you go any faster?" Anoushka asked Goran in a tremulous voice, clearly trying to fight off hysteria: she gave a yelp as he heeled the boat over to avoid the next missile.

"We're at the mercy of the wind," he replied. "It's driving us onshore. While we run ahead of it, we've got enough speed that I can just about avoid being hit, but I have to tack out to sea sometime soon or we'll run aground. Once I do that, we'll lose momentum and become an easier target."

"Leave it as late as you dare," Boris advised him, as the boat swung again and a shell exploded disturbingly close, "We're past their launch point now, and when we change course we'll be heading away from it. Hopefully we'll soon be out of range."

Goran threw the tiller over again: there was another explosion to starboard, but further away this time. Anoushka gave a shrill giggle with no humour in it, and Talia exclaimed, "Missed again!" The next shell fell thirty yards astern, its noise now muffled by the spray thrown up as the catamaran swerved and zigzagged further out to sea.

"It's OK, 'Noushka," said Talia, putting a reassuring arm around Anoushka's shoulders, "it's stopping. They can't reach us now."

When there had been no bombs for several minutes, Goran changed course once more. "We can't go much further out," he said. "There's an underwater reef that would rip us to pieces. Let's shadow the coast till we reach the dacha."

"Are you certain it's safe?" Anoushka asked.

"We're well out of range," Goran assured her. He started to smile, but then his jaw dropped. "Me and my big mouth – get down!" he shouted as he once more turned the boat sharply towards the beach. There was an explosion just off the starboard hull and everyone was drenched by the spray of an all-too-near impact.

"Where'd that one come from?" Boris yelled.

"Up ahead," Goran called back as he swung the yacht out to sea once more. So began the second instalment of their dance with destruction.

"Do you think it's the same mortar?" Talia called.

"Does it matter?" Boris replied, looking back at her.

"I suppose not." She shrugged hopelessly.

Goran chose that very moment to react to the next shell. Unfortunately, this time Anoushka's grasp slipped and she slid across the superstructure. Goran instinctively let go of the tiller to catch her and the catamaran slid back on course. The shell exploded just under the starboard bulkhead. The boat was thrust sideways and there was an ominous cracking noise. The tiller jerked in Goran's hand, and he had to let go of Anoushka to control it. She gave a cry of despair as she slipped into the water.

Before Boris could react, Talia dived after her. He knew that Talia was a far stronger swimmer than he was, so he waited, his nerves taut, for a chance to retrieve the two of them. He tried to keep an eye on how they were doing, but the waves and the frequent course changes made it difficult: at one point he saw that Talia had got hold of Anoushka, and they were only a few yards to starboard, but a few seconds later they were much further away. *At least those bastards are firing at the boat rather than Talia and Anoushka,* he thought. *It'll give them a fighting chance.*

After one particularly violent turn, he lost sight of the two girls. Several minutes passed as the boat continued its evasive course and Boris scanned the surface of the water in vain. "I think we've lost them," he called to Goran, his heart sinking.

The sombre mood was broken when a voice from below gasped, "Don't – give up – on us yet." Astonished, Boris looked over the front of the superstructure. Underneath, between the hulls and clinging by her right hand to the hindmost inner strut of the starboard one, was Talia, her other arm round the chest of a bedraggled and stunned-looking Anoushka.

"The girls are hanging on to the boat between the hulls," he called to Goran as he made his way towards the back. "Try and keep her steady while I pull them aboard."

"I'll do what I can," Goran shouted back as Boris roped himself to the back rail, but the latter had just reached down and grasped Anoushka round the waist when Goran yelled, "I've got to turn to port – now!"

Talia gave a surprised yelp as Boris yanked Anoushka from her grasp, and her body swung away from the hull as the boat heeled over. He lowered his burden as gently as he could down into the cockpit.

He was worried that they lost Talia during the last manoeuvre, but she still clung on, though her knuckles were bloodless. He took her now-free left arm and managed to haul her up onto deck and lowered her down beside Anoushka. She slumped down on the one end of the bench, gasping for air and kneading her hand, while Boris checked Anoushka over at the other end. Both girls seemed to be exhausted but otherwise uninjured.

By now, they had once again reached the limit of the mortar's range, so there was a short period of blessed peace, but after some moments, it opened up again from further down the coast.

"How's she handling?" Boris called to Goran.

"Listing a little to starboard. I think she's shipping water. We may have to swim for it."

Boris looked over at Talia, who shook her head. "I don't think the girls are in any shape for that," he said. "We may have to take our chances with the shoals out to sea."

"Wait," Goran called out. "What's that?" He pointed back towards the city. Boris squinted in that direction and saw a small dot in the air. Soon, to his relief, it resolved into a helicopter. Once it got close enough, he could see its security markings, but his celebrations were tempered when he saw that it wasn't a gunship – only an unarmed transport.

"I don't think he's come to rescue us," Talia said breathlessly.

Indeed, presumably noticing their predicament for the first time, the pilot veered his craft sharply away as another mortar bomb exploded just in front of the boat. He hovered uncertainly for a few seconds, then seemed to make up his mind to help. He swooped down and a security officer leaned out to the side and tried to engage their hidden assailant with a rifle. In riposte, after half a minute or so, a Surface-to-Air Missile came screaming from the same direction as the mortar. The pilot banked left and dropped, but the missile seemed to be a heat-seeker, and followed its target. It hit the 'copter's engine and the aircraft disintegrated into a fireball.

The officer with the rifle was thrown clear of the explosion and fell into the sea where he ended up floating face down about twenty yards in front of the boat, just off the port bow. There was a short lull in proceedings, presumably while their enemies exulted over their kill. Goran used the time to manoeuvre the boat close enough to the floating man that Boris could snag him with a boat-hook and pluck him from the water. He laid the unconscious officer out on the superstructure, and Talia checked him over as Goran tacked the yacht away from the next bomb.

"He's very badly concussed, and has a couple of cracked ribs, but I think he'll survive," she said, "– at least, as long as we do."

"Look." Anoushka pointed back towards the city, where another dot had appeared. "The helicopter must have called for help."

This newcomer approached far more rapidly than before, and turned out to be a jet scrambled from the Restavic Down Skyport. It swung out from the shore, banked sharply and headed landwards.

Another Surface-to-Air Missile was launched from the woods behind the beach. It flew straight towards the jet. This time, however, its target had more speed and mobility, and the aircraft's pilot was able to release a flare and pull its nose up just in time. The missile skimmed the plane's fuselage and homed in on the decoy, exploding harmlessly over the sea.

The pilot fired two of his own rockets into the woods before soaring steeply upwards. There was a massive explosion as a small copse of trees was demolished. The aircraft circled over the area to confirm its kill, before slowing on its hover jets. It hung in the air, at a distance where the wash from its jets would not endanger the boat. Its pilot seemed to satisfy himself that they were OK, before making an odd three fingered gesture.

Talia and Anoushka waved their thanks, and Goran and Boris raised their arms in salute.

After a few seconds, the pilot fired his main jets, gained altitude, turned and flew back the way he came.

"That was close." Talia sighed. "I wonder what that gesture meant."

"It was vaguely familiar," Boris said, "but I can't place it."

Once the plane had disappeared into the distance, Anoushka asked, "What do we do now?"

"I'm continuing on to the dacha," Goran said. "We can make a landfall there quicker than at the *Comet*, and there's no suitable landing place between here and there. What's more, it's where Major Drovsorsky will expect us to go."

"Good idea," Talia agreed. "Anyway, this man needs proper medical attention. Anoushka, could you give me a hand?"

Boris was about to volunteer in Anoushka's place, but when he opened his mouth to do so, Talia gave him a frown and a slight shake of the head. He understood, and closed it again: Anoushka was clearly badly rattled, and activity was the best medicine Talia could offer her. The poor girl took a deep breath and acceded to Talia's request.

Talia looked back at Boris. "This soldier has lost his rifle, but he's got a pistol in his holster…" she said.

"He could easily have lost it in the water," he replied, picking up on her unspoken suggestion.

"Yes," she agreed, "the strap could have come undone when he hit the surface. Goran, is there anywhere on this boat that you could hide a gun?" she asked.

Goran gave her a wicked grin. "Oh, I can think of a few places… Anyway, I ought to go below and assess the damage. Hold the tiller for a minute or two, would you, Boris?" Talia removed the pistol and handed it to him as Boris took his place and he slid down through the hatch.

He was gone for some minutes, and when he returned, he looked concerned. "It's just as I thought," he told the others, "there's a crack in the starboard hull and we're shipping water. It's not too bad – we'll easily make it to the dacha – but she's going to need quite a bit of work before I can take her out again. My poor *Darling* – you nearly lived up to your name today."

As they neared the dacha, a helicopter with security markings flew over them and landed on the strand. Soon, they could see Major Valentine and Ivan waiting for them on the jetty.

"Comrade Heroes," the Major called as soon as they were in earshot, "are you all right?"

"We're fine," Boris shouted back, "thanks to Goran's skill and a fair slice of luck – and we rescued one of your men from the helicopter that was shot down. Talia has stabilised him, but he needs proper treatment."

"Thank God you weren't hurt," the Major continued as he and Ivan helped them moor the catamaran. "I've brought a medical team to treat any of you that had been injured – they can look after the wounded man. Now would you all please come with me – I need to talk to you."

Ivan helped the girls ashore, then stuck out his hand to Boris. His grasp as Boris took it conveyed more than just an aid. "I'm sorry about my bad manners earlier," he said, sotto voce. "After what the Major told me about your yachting adventure, it's obvious that *something* odd is going on. I'm still not sure what it is, but I don't want to lose your friendship over it, and I somehow think we need to be able to depend on each other."

The Major waited impatiently while Anoushka and Talia changed out of their wet clothes, assembled the party in the dacha's sitting room, poured them all large glasses of vodka, and addressed them.

"My friends, I must apologise for deceiving you," he began. "We've known for some time that members of the Telphanian-hyybacked rebellion have been plotting to kill you, but we've taken the attitude that you were suffering from enough stress as it was, and it would be better to keep the knowledge from you. But now the cat is well and truly out of the bag."

"But why do they want to – to k-kill us?" Anoushka asked with a shiver. She hugged her shoulders and bit her lip as Talia put her arm around her protectively.

"We don't know for sure, Comrade Anoushka – we think it's an attempt to deal a propaganda blow to the Republic – but I want you to be assured that your lives are under our full protection, and your security is our paramount concern. From now on you will be safeguarded by as many resources as we can spare, given the current situation with Telphania. In addition, I want you to take these and carry them with you all times." He handed everyone a small personal communicator. "They provide direct access to Security Central. Use them whenever you need to. Just press the red button and you should be answered immediately. Now, if you'll excuse me, I have to get back to co-ordinate the search for the rebels who attacked you."

The injured security guard had already been loaded onto the helicopter and, as soon as the Major was on board, it flew off in the direction of Restavic City.

Once it was out of sight, Boris turned to the others and said, "Why don't we barbecue the fish I caught, and have a supper party here on the beach?"

"Do you think it's safe?" Anoushka looked worried.

"Safe as anywhere. Remember those security men that came earlier for a 'hike in the woods'?" he reminded her.

"Yes…"

"I'll bet they're out there watching over us."

She gave him a wan smile. "I hope so."

The party was a welcome release from the stress of the day, and the barbecued fish and sausage were consumed in large amounts accompanied by slabs of bread and large glasses of vodka.

Their feral feline neighbour took the opportunity to scrounge up a meal, not that anyone begrudged her a tit-bit or two except Goran. When that curmudgeon lifted a stone and went to hurl it at their guest, Talia slapped his arm aside, her eyes flashing. They looked at each other unblinking for some moments, until Goran dropped his gaze, shrugged and pointedly turned to talk to Ivan. For the rest of the evening, Talia kept protectively close to the cat.

As things were winding down, Boris remembered what he'd overheard the previous night, and determined to make it as difficult as possible for them to be re-conditioned.

"Let's sleep out under the stars," he suggested.

Talia caught his drift immediately and said, "What a good idea – yes, let's. It may be the last chance before it gets too cold. I'll get some blankets." The others chorused their agreement – all except Ivan, who grumbled about the discomfort, and insisted on dragging his mattress out from the dacha.

As they lay down and looked up at the stars, Ivan drew Boris's attention to Talia and Goran going off in the bushes together. "Wonders will never cease," he said, his eyebrows raised in amusement.

Chapter 9

Between the columns of greasy grey smoke, the sky was of a deep shade of blue, without the yellowish tinge Talia had grown used to on Ruine.

Bullets and laser bolts flew over her head as she crawled through the mud toward a wounded soldier. He was clutching his arm, blood streaming between his fingers. A badge on his shoulder showed the same capital 'I' superimposed on a capital 'M' that she remembered in connection with the fishing boat. The same badge showed on the left breast of her uniform, accompanied by a red cross on a white background and the nametag 'Miller'.

As she bound the wound, she looked up and saw a face she knew – the face she'd seen in her vision of the park with the swans. She realised that this was her future fiancé, Jimmy; then, as she woke, it all changed, and she was looking at someone else. "Bartes?" she said.

The man she'd known as Boris smiled. He bent his mouth near to her and whispered, "So, you've recalled my real name, have you, Tanya?"

"I – "

He touched a finger to her lips. "Careful – don't give us away."

"Yes, I remember who you really are – and my name, too. And I'm positive there's lots more that will come to me as I think things through. What have you remembered?"

"Quite a bit, but I think it's better if you work everything out for yourself. I'm glad that our minds are starting to clear, but we're going to have to keep an eye on the others, to ensure they don't give us away as their memories return. And keep playing your part as Talia, too. We may know our real names now, but we'll need to use those we've been given unless we're certain we can't be overheard."

The newly-rechristened Tanya lay back and started to examine her real memories. She was interrupted by the loud chug of a helicopter landing some yards along the beach. Disgorging Major Valentine, it took off again.

"What are you doing here, Major?" Ivan asked as Major Valentine approached them.

"I've come to see how everyone is," came the reply, "and to share one of Comrade Goran's magnificent breakfasts."

"Coming right up," Goran replied, and he disappeared into the kitchen while the others gathered on the veranda around the Major.

"Are you going to stay here and protect us?" Anoushka asked him.

"Comrade Anoushka," he replied, slowly shaking his head, "I know that you must be shaken by yesterday's attack, but I do have other duties." She looked crestfallen. "I have, however, arranged for more security to be flown in. They'll be arriving soon, but I must fly back as soon as they do."

The food and coffee that Goran served was most welcome, and they all fell on it as though they were starving. Towards the end of the meal, Tanya had an idea.

"Comrade Major…"

"Yes, Comrade Talia."

"I feel a bit guilty."

He looked puzzled. "And why is that?"

"Well, Dr Julia expected me to do some reading over the weekend about the effects of exotic atmospheres on the human body, but in the excitement of the holiday, I completely forgot, and left the relevant books back at the Medical Centre."

"I could have them brought here."

Tanya managed to force a blush, and continued, shamefacedly, "I don't even remember where I left them. I really need to go and locate them myself. And anyway, I feel that four and a half days is perhaps too long to leave my post unattended, and I would like to check that everything is running smoothly."

"Very conscientious, Comrade Talia – I commend you for your devotion to duty. As it happens, I have arranged for a helicopter to bring Political Commissar Cheslenko here this afternoon, for the visit Comrade Goran arranged. I'll arrange that it picks you up and takes you to the Medical Centre first."

"Thank you, Major."

"I'll come too, if it's all right with you, Major," Bartes said. "Comrade Talia should have an escort in these perilous times."

"Very gallant, Comrade," the Major replied, "but quite unnecessary – my men will keep Comrade Talia safe. But if you fancy a scenic flight over the mountains, I'm positive we can find you a seat."

After another quarter of an hour or so, a large troop helicopter arrived and disgorged a number of soldiers plus Josef and his friend Peter. Most of the soldiers disappeared into the trees, but a few started digging foxholes either side of the dacha. The Major consulted briefly with the Lieutenant in charge, made his farewells and left in the 'copter.

"That was exciting," Josef said. "One of the soldiers even let me hold his gun."

"Where have you been?" asked Goran, scowling.

Josef gave him a sullen look. "After we'd finished our lessons, we started talking about hovercart design with our tutor. Did you know that he raced them when he was young?" Goran shook his head disapprovingly. "We got so involved in our discussion that we didn't keep track of the time, so when we *did* notice, we realised we couldn't make it back here, so he let us sleep in his spare room."

"Well, now you're here, you can wash up the breakfast things."

"But…"

"No buts. You and Peter can talk about hovercarts while you work."

Josef ground his teeth and stamped away with Peter in train. Halfway to the dacha, he turned and looked back. "Comrade Boris," he said, "when you have some time, could you come and talk with us? We're thinking of entering for an amateur race in a couple of months, and we'd very much appreciate your advice – and, if possible, your help – in building a cart."

Bartes followed them inside while Tanya sat and tried to recover her memories. It was like picking a scab – a tiny section falling away, then another piece lifting, and revealing –

– not new skin but old knowledge. True knowledge. The logo in her vision: M – I – Mercy Incorporated! She worked for the aid organisation, Mercy Incorporated. Now, why was she here, and not on Regni, where she'd been assigned as medic to Governor Anderson's bodyguard? And what about the rest of her team?

Oh, whoever had done the brainwashing had been very clever. Her teams' names had been changed, but mostly not so much: Tanya Miller – Talia Milanova; Bartes diCherval – Boris Dechorsky; Iain Browne – Ivan Baranov; John D'Arcy had been rechristened Johan Davidov; though why would their Team Leader, Richard Delmanes, known to all as RD, have been called 'Goran'? Perhaps they thought a Team Leader should have a special name. Oh, but they had a sense of humour. The full name they'd given him was 'Goran *Ardy*'.

But there were others, too. She could see why Anna Lawrence, as the Governor's Private Secretary, might be a target for abduction, but she had no idea why they would want Joseph Chaplet – after all, he was only the son of one of the Governor's aides. Joseph's father was a Baron, but – given their situation – it seemed unlikely that he'd been kidnapped for ransom. She didn't remember Peter at all from before Ruine, but perhaps they wanted to add a local boy to the group to provide Joseph with a friend – and to spy on the team.

But who their enemies were, why they were on Ruine, and why their group should have been targets – she could only speculate. And the possibilities that occurred to her all filled her with foreboding.

Chapter 10

Bartes wandered into the kitchen of the dacha and joined the youngsters, who were starting to wash the dishes. He even gave them a hand – after all, RD was definitely being unfair.

"That's moronic. Everyone knows the Atrix Swift exhaust system's about twenty years out of date…" Peter was saying.

"OK, I'm not saying the Swift's the best, but you must admit it's half of the price of the Cinta Airbrave. If you can afford that many zellars, fair enough, but… What do you think, Comrade Boris?"

"Hmm?" For a second or two, Bartes had forgotten his current name. "Oh. Oh, yes. Well, as far as I know, you're both right. It depends how much money you have to spend. How much do you have?"

Both boys looked embarrassed.

"Not a lot," Peter admitted.

"That's one of the things we wanted to talk to you about," Joseph added.

"I see," Bartes said. "You want to 'borrow' some from me. Doesn't Goran give you pocket money?"

"Only a pittance," Joseph told him. "I have to slave for him all day, and he acts as if I should be grateful for every cent."

"I'm sure it's not quite that bad," Bartes said uncertainly. "Anyway, I'll give it some thought. Now let's get this chore done."

As they finished the dishes, Joseph gave Bartes a pleading look. "Would you do me a favour, Comrade Boris?" he asked.

"And what would that be?"

"It's a long weekend, and they're having a hovercart grand prix and lots of other races on Lake Kuraken. Could you possibly ask the Major whether we could make it up there to see some of them? Don't mention it to ol' sourpuss, though – he's bound to veto it on the principle that I thought of it, and if the Major says it's OK, he won't be able to."

Bartes paused. *I'll bet it would be easier to escape from Lake Kuraken than from here,* he thought. "I'll see what I can do," he said aloud. "Now let's make some drinks and join the others."

As he sat on the veranda, sipping his coffee and pondering the situation, he reached out with his mind. :*Tanya,*: he sent.

Tanya jumped and almost spilled her coffee.

"Is everything all right, Comrade?" Ivan – Iain – looked slightly concerned.

Tanya smiled somewhat nervously. "It's nothing, really – just a chill running down my spine. I was thinking about yesterday, and I suddenly realised just how close we came to being killed."

:*Tanya, it's me – Bartes.*:

:*I'd forgotten we could do this.*:

:*So had I – until I just did it instinctively. How's your memory coming?*:

:*Patchy. I'm beginning to remember who we are, and I've recalled what we should be doing, back on Regni or wherever the Governor is, but why we're here and not there, and how we got here, is still a mystery. And I didn't realise I'd got any of my psionics back – or even remember that I had any – until you surprised me.*:

:*Sorry about that. Nicely covered by the way.*:

:*Thanks.*: Throughout their discussion, she managed to keep up her conversation with the others, and gave no hint of their telepathic dialogue. Bartes hoped that he'd concealed his half of their mental exchange equally as successfully.

When they'd finished their drinks, RD made a suggestion. "I fancy some exercise. I'm going for a walk in the woods."

"Sounds a good idea," Iain agreed.

"I'll come too," said Joseph immediately, before RD could assign him more chores. Peter also nodded his assent.

Anna, though, was still a bit rattled. "Are you sure it's safe?" she asked.

"Positive." RD gave her a reassuring smile. "Coming?"

"N-no." She shivered again. "Be careful."

"What about you, Boris?" RD asked.

"Why not," Bartes replied. "We might as well check out exactly how secure we really are. Talia?"

Tanya thought a moment. "No, I think I'd better stay here with Anoushka." Anna gave her a grateful look. "But before you go, I can see there's something wrong with your drug dispensers, Josef. Come with me." She took the young man into the kitchen.

As they entered the woods, Bartes skimmed his leader's mind to see what mental state he was in. RD turned towards him instantly, his eyes flashing dangerously. "I'll thank you not to mess with my head," he hissed.

Bartes was taken aback by his vehemence, but then he remembered RD's aversion and sensitivity to psionics. Their leader barely tolerated him, as the squad's licensed telepath, and it had been a source of antagonism between RD and Tanya from the day she joined the team. "Sorry," Bartes whispered, "I was only checking to see if you remembered who you are."

"You could have asked."

"I was trying to be discreet."

"Just don't do it again. If I catch you or that witch inside my head, I swear I'll kill you. And yes, as you can probably tell, I remember who I am – and who you really are."

"OK." Bartes paused. "Have *you* any idea why we're here on this planet?"

RD shook his head, frustration writ large on his face. Suddenly, his expression changed. "Look up ahead," he said in an undertone, "a couple of yards to the right of this track."

Bartes looked in the direction RD had indicated, and could just make out a camouflaged foxhole. He stopped, breathed deeply and looked around as if just out for a stroll. "There's another one further on, on the other side. Do you think they've spotted us?"

"Let's find out." RD indicated to the others to move as quietly as possible as they approached the cordon.

It was only when they were within a couple of strides of the nearest dugout that there was a guilty start, and a fresh-faced private lifted his head, pointed a rifle at them and called "Who goes there?" rather too loudly.

"The people you're *supposed* to be protecting, out for a walk. Were you asleep or something?"

"N-no, Comrade Heroes," the boy replied, his dishevelled state indicating otherwise, "merely keeping a low profile."

RD grunted. "Well, you can go back to keeping a low profile – but try not to snore so loudly."

The young man blushed and muttered, "No – that is, yes, Comrade Hero. Thank you, Comrade Hero."

As they walked on, Bartes said, "I didn't hear any snoring."

"Neither did I," RD replied, "but I know that sort of soldier – I was one once." He gave a wolf-like grin. "I'll bet he needs a change of underwear now."

They walked on for a few hundred yards, then it was their turn to be surprised when another soldier stepped out in front of them from behind a tree, his gun raised. "You'll have to turn back, Comrades – this is the limit of our protection," he said.

"Of course, Comrade Sergeant. It's good to see that *you* know what you're doing at least - the troops manning the inner cordon seemed to be handpicked for idiocy."

"Did you spot that sergeant?" Bartes asked RD as they headed back to the dacha.

"No," RD replied. "It seems that some, at least, of our guardians – or, perhaps, our jailers – know what they're doing."

Chapter 11

As the others walked off into the woods, Tanya sat down next to Anna and put her arm round the girl's shaking shoulders.

"Oh, my poor Anna," she said.

"Who?" Anoushka/Anna's momentarily puzzled expression gave way as her eyes widened. After some moments she swallowed. "Yes, that is my name, isn't it? I'm Anna Lawrence – and your name's Tanya Miller. It's all coming back to me now."

Tanya let her think for a while. "It's all rather a shock, isn't it."

"Y-yes." Anna looked up into Tanya's face and sighed. "You and the others can cope with this – they're military, and although you're a doctor, you're with Mercy, but I'm just a s-secretary, and I don't know how to deal with being brainwashed, and with - with people trying to kill us. How do you manage to be so calm about it all?"

A shiver ran down Tanya's spine and she sadly shook her head. "I'm not – not on the inside, anyway – I've just learnt to act as though I am. If I ever grew indifferent to the danger, the pain and the suffering, I'd be no better than a robot – or, more likely, I'd be dead. Whatever happens, whether I want to scream, or cry, or roll up into a ball and hide, I have to keep my emotions under control and do what I can to deal with the situation."

"But what *are* we going to do?" Anna asked, her despair showing in her voice.

Tanya held her and stroked her hair gently. "We're going to go home, Anna. Somehow, I swear, I'll get you back to Regni. And we're going to deal with the bastards who did this to us – to you. For the rest of us such things go with the territory, but not for you – or young Joseph. I don't know who caught you up in this, but I promise you I'll find out – and they'll pay, whoever they are. Now dry your eyes, and let's prepare some lunch."

Anna set to concocting a salad as Tanya poured her another coffee – and added a tot of vodka. "Drink this – it'll make you feel better."

Anna sipped the hot drink and gave a tentative smile. "Thank you, Tanya. You always know just how to lift my spirits."

Tanya laughed. "You just drink *that* spirit. Anyway, I feel the same way about you – and I'm not sure *your* good opinion of *me* is really justified. I don't remember much of my life before all this, but I have a feeling I'm not as nice a person as you seem to think. And call me Talia for the moment – we can't be certain when we're being overheard, and we don't want to be reprogrammed."

"So that's why you turned on the tap when we came in: to cover up our conversation."

"It's an old trick, but it works. We can only talk freely if we know no-one can hear what we're saying." Tanya scanned the kitchen. "The only microphone I can see is in the far corner, behind the bread-bin. Don't look at it!"

"Why not?"

"There's a mini-cam in the opposite corner, above the wall-cupboard. If someone's watching, we don't want to give away that we know we're being spied on – or let them read our lips."

"You *are* paranoid."

"Paranoia keeps you alive." There was a short pause as they laid out the meat, cheese and bread, and carried the platter, the salad and the relishes out to the picnic table. "Anna, I'm going to try something which might help."

"Okay." She sat on the bench. "But call me Anoushka – I rather like it, and I plan to keep it – it sounds much nicer than Anna, and it's the same name really.

:*Can you hear me, Anoushka?*: Tanya sent psionically.

"Yes," the unrechristened Anoushka said with a puzzled look. "But you didn't move your lips. Was that telepathy?"

:*Yes. I know that you're not a telepath, but you don't have to be to 'talk' to me. I can do all the work. Now try thinking of something or someone I wouldn't expect, but would recognise.*: Anoushka's brow furrowed, and a picture of John D'Arcy came into Tanya's mind. She was so surprised that she blurted out, "John? I didn't realise you found him attractive."

Anoushka blushed. "I didn't think *that*'d come over."

"Emotions are easier to read than ideas. Don't worry – I'll keep your secret."

Anoushka frowned. "I hope he's all right."

Tanya patted her hand. "Don't you worry about him. The security at the Skyport is very tight."

Anoushka paused and her brows wrinkled. "Who else knows who they really are?"

"I know Bartes does, and it shouldn't be long before the others remember the truth, now they're no longer being drugged, but we'll have to keep play-acting for now." Tanya heard a noise and looked up. "Anyway, hush – here they come."

As they ate their lunch, Tanya informed Bartes of her conversation with Anoushka. :*I've made a mental link with her,*: she told him. :*Hopefully, I can strengthen it till we can communicate at will.*:

:*Don't try it with RD,*: he replied.

:*I wouldn't dream of it. I remember how much he hates telepathy. I wish I knew why he detests psionics – and me – so much.*:

It was in the middle of the afternoon when the helicopter arrived for their trip to the Medical Centre. It was a large troop-carrier, and as well as the pilot and his co-pilot, it was carrying two heavily-armed marines to act as a bodyguard. The latter conducted Tanya & Bartes to their seats and sat either side of them. The flight passed quietly, as their guards seemed unwilling to engage in idle conversation. To their relief, given their recent experiences, it was also without incident.

Tanya felt odd entering the double doors of the Centre – strangely nostalgic. She realised that she'd been happy there: her job had been easy, her colleagues agreeable and the stress levels relatively low – apart from the odd emergency. She'd usually been able to take the bus home after each shift with the warm feeling of a job well done. Now everything had changed, and not for the better. She shook herself. That life was a sham, she told herself, and couldn't have continued forever.

They'd asked their guards to wait outside for them, as they didn't want to alarm the Centre's staff. The security guard on detail glanced at their identity cards, but he wasn't really interested, as there were no high security patients in residence. He waved Tanya and Bartes through and returned to watching football on a portable video screen.

Tanya found the duty nurse, Olga Poliakova, and asked her to keep Bartes company while she checked on the patients in the few beds that were occupied. That task complete, she made her way to her office. She noted that she was the only senior staff member present – even those who should have been in attendance had been allowed to be with their families for the holiday, though they were on call if needed. She was sorry to miss Dr Julia in particular. They'd become quite close, and she owed the doctor a lot. She would have liked to have made a proper farewell, even if she daren't have revealed that's what it was.

She ran the drugs that she removed from the group's dispensers through the spectral analyser and compared them with the pharmacopoeia. It was about what she had suspected: for RD, Anoushka and Joseph, both dispensers contained Hyperon 9, a banned hypnotic, though this *was* mixed with a basic radiation palliative for some reason, but for Bartes and herself, one contained Psigon, a psionic inhibitor.

She picked up Iain's sample to load into the analyser and paused.

Why is it a deeper amber than the others? she wondered. *Methaqualude? That would explain a lot...*

Methaqualude it was. *And that,* thought Tanya, *accounts for 'Ivan' being so different from the team-mate I've always trusted to have my back in tricky situations.* She knew that this particular drug was only used – normally to treat depression – in extreme cases, as it tended to have an effect on the personality of the patient. *Hopefully, now he's no longer under its influence, he'll soon be back to normal.*

She erased the results from the analyser's data bank, retrieved her personal medical kit and added to it a selection of drug components; she had her own ideas about ways to aid their escape. She also located a couple of instruments that could be used to facilitate the extraction and replacement of the nasal filters, picked up the books she ostensibly came for, then went to have a coffee with Bartes and Nurse Olga.

"I'll have to drag Boris away now," Tanya said after a while. "We've got to pick someone up for a visit to our dacha."

"Must you?" Olga wrinkled her nose. "It's so slow around here today, and I'm bored."

"You should be reading improving text-books or medical journals." Tanya frowned theatrically and waggled her finger in false admonition, but couldn't keep a straight face.

Olga laughed. "You get yourself off to your beach," she said, "and don't think of us poor workers.

Wait until the revolution, when we throw off the shackles of you bloated aristocrats!"

They parted in good humour, but for Tanya there was a tinge of sadness: if things went as she hoped they would, this would be the last time she and Olga would see each other. And if they ever did meet again, their relationship could never be the same. Unless Tanya had been re-programmed, and that thought made her shudder.

The helicopter flew to Restavic City's main helipad, where Political Commissar Tatiana was waiting. She looked quite different out of her uniform and with her hair free. She exchanged greetings and the standard pleasantries with Tanya, but was sensitive to the latter's pensive mood, and left her to her brown study while she chatted to Bartes.

Tanya sat, chin in hand, looking out of the window as dusk began to fall, the oncoming darkness echoing her mood. They were flying over the mountains, which were sprinkled with early snow, when she was momentarily distracted by a flash of flame from the forest. She disregarded it, unwisely as it turned out. A moment later there was a cry of "Incoming!" from the co-pilot and the helicopter lurched sideways as the pilot took evasive action. Seconds later, there was an explosion at the rear of the helicopter, and it began to spin out of control.

The view through the windows was disorientating, but with every rotation, the waiting trees were closer. Instinct told Tanya that she might be able to do something about their predicament with her mind: she reached out and tried to stop, or at least slow, their spin, but there was nothing to push against. Just before impact, she found she could thrust mentally against the ground a little, though the strain was excruciating.

Whether her efforts made any difference, she couldn't tell. From the feeling of dizziness and nausea after they hit, she knew that she had at least survived – and almost wished that she hadn't.

Chapter 12

They were not too high when the missile hit, and somehow their pilot managed to avoid the dense forest and crash into a clearing. They hit the ground nose first and the snow was quite deep, so although the impact was serious, it wasn't fatal to those in the rear, though Bartes' glance at the flight crew showed they hadn't been so lucky.

He looked over at Tanya, who was bleeding from the nose. "Are you all right?" he asked

She wiped the blood with the back of her hand. "I've got a splitting headache," she said, "but I'm fine otherwise."

"I seem to have survived as well", the Commissar added, "apart from a few bruises. At least the seat-belts proved adequate."

The door on the right side of the helicopter had been wrenched off during the crash, and as Bartes undid his belt, he saw their guards make their way out of the jagged hole it had left. There were two almost simultaneous bursts of gunfire followed by a thump as something large and heavy fell against the side of the helicopter.

He and Tanya looked at each other in consternation. :*What's happening?*: she asked him telepathically.

:*I don't know,*: he replied. :*Nothing good. I can sense a group of people out there. I doubt they're friendly, since they just shot our escort.*:

:*Are they dead?*:

:*One is – the other is dying. I think we're in deep trouble.*:

Two figures dressed in paramilitary gear looked in through the serrated tear in the fuselage. They were armed with advanced combat rifles, and the way they carried their weapons looked less than friendly.

Sunset in Silvana

The Commissar rose and drew a pistol from her handbag. She opened her mouth to challenge the intruders, but the nearer figure raised its rifle and fired a short burst before she could do so. She blinked twice and looked in surprise down at the red stains spreading over her white blouse. She gave a couple of gasping breaths and a bubbling cough, then subsided, her eyes glazing over and blood trickling from the side of her still-open mouth. Tanya and Bartes immediately raised their hands.

"Please don't kill us," Tanya begged.

"And why shouldn't we?" a female voice sneered.

"We're not who you think we are."

"We know *just* who you are," the woman replied slowly and grimly. "You're 'Heroes of Pregeor'. Our allies tell us that you massacred your own people for your cursed government. To be honest, we don't really care about that – the deaths of Zelynans is all to the good, but *your* deaths, now – they could deal a blow to your pestilential regime, and help free Silvana from its rule."

"We aren't! We didn't! We're not Heroes – or villains – we're just scapegoats."

There was a tense pause and the figures disappeared. There was the sound of animated discussion from outside, but Bartes and Tanya couldn't make out the words and, by common consent, daren't risk telepathy in case the intruders were sensitive to it and took exception. The strain was almost unbearable by the time the voice said, loudly, "All right, come out of there and explain yourselves – but no funny business or we shoot."

As he and Tanya emerged, Bartes stumbled over the body of one of the bodyguards, and saw that the other lay off to one side. They were both covered in blood and very dead. Six people stood in a semi-circle, all with rifles pointed in their direction. One of them, the stocky woman who seemed to be their leader, took a couple of paces toward them.

"Now what do you mean by scapegoats?" she asked.

"Look, we've only just found out who we really are. We'd been brainwashed into thinking we're Heroes of Pregeor. We weren't actually there – we're not even from this planet," Bartes said. "We're off-worlders who were kidnapped by the Zelynan Government, and we have no more love for them than you have. We're their prisoners and we want to escape. Please – help us, and we'll do our best to help you."

Most of their captors seemed incredulous, and one or two roared with laughter. Their leader shook her head in disbelief and snorted. "I knew you'd say anything to avoid being killed," she said, "but that's ridiculous. Say goodbye to each other." She signalled, and her team raised their weapons.

"No! Stop! Look, we can prove it," Tanya pleaded.

They paused. The leader's gun was pointing between Bartes' eyes, and everything was frozen in agonising detail. He swore later that he could see the rifling in the barrel, and even the nose of the bullet deep within. Part of his mind noted that one of their captors hadn't aimed at them, and was deliberately looking away, but also observed dryly that five executioners would prove quite adequate. After a few heartbeats that seemed to last forever, the leader grunted and lowered the muzzle of her gun a few inches.

"How?" she demanded tersely.

With a gasp Tanya released the breath she hadn't realised she'd been holding. "We have filters in our noses to help us cope with the sulphur in your atmosphere."

The leader signalled to the girl who'd been unwilling to kill them. "Maria! You check her story. We'll cover you."

90

The youngster, who looked about seventeen, walked tentatively forward. She took a torch from her pack, peered up Bartes' nose with it, and extracted one of his filters. She took more care than he'd have expected, and even apologised for the discomfort. The unfiltered atmosphere was unpleasant, and he nearly vomited. She examined the tiny plastic apparatus with a puzzled expression, looked up Tanya nose to check that she had similar devices, and took it over to the leader.

"Hah – this could be anything," the stout woman said. "And anyway, even if it is a filter, what does that prove? You could still be willing collaborators – or even Dainworlders."

"But we aren't!" Tanya almost screamed. "And we could help you."

"And just how could you do that?"

"If we escape – and we intend to – it would be a major distraction for your – our – enemies."

The woman thought for a moment, before shaking her head. "How can we know if you're telling the truth?"

Tanya bit her lip in consternation, but then she had an idea. "Test our blood," she said. "It will show you that we're from the Terran Union – which is no friend to the Zelynan government."

"And if you're lying?"

"I'm sure you can find us again and finish the job – or perhaps you don't think that's possible."

Good tactic, Bartes thought. *She won't want to seem weak in front of her team.*

The woman bridled. "Of course it's possible. If we wanted to kill you – anywhere, any time – nothing – and no-one – could stop us. Dieter, take blood samples from them while we discuss this. Maria, you keep them covered."

A young man came over to them, took a medical kit from his backpack, removed a couple of small jars and emptied the pills from them into his pockets. "Put out your hand," he said. When Tanya did so, he sliced her palm with his knife and collected some of her blood in one of the jars, before repeating the savage process with Bartes and the other container. Before he returned to his companions, he shoved Bartes' filter into Tanya's other hand. "You – put this back," he said.

As Tanya replaced the apparatus as delicately as she could, the rebels discussed their fate. Bartes had little hope for their survival – and indeed, after a few minutes, it seemed that the tide was turning against them. He overheard the phrase, "a beached pluny is worth a river-full of fish," and decided to take one last gamble. He reached out with his mind to the youngest of their captors.

:*Maria,*: he sent quietly. The girl jumped and looked around wildly, but the others' discussion had become animated, and they didn't notice. :*Maria, it's me.*: She looked over in his direction and he nodded imperceptibly. She opened her mouth to say something, but he forestalled her. :*Please – don't give me away. Just think: I can read your mind.*:

You're telepathic, she thought.

:*Yes. You know they're going to kill us, don't you.*:

They might decide to let you go.

:*I can see you don't really believe that – and I know you don't want us to die.*:

There's already been so much death: my father, my brother, so many of my friends... but I can't let my team-mates down.

:*We've got team-mates depending on us, too. We're going to have to make a run for it. It's not far to the trees, and you're the only one between us and the forest. If you don't shoot, we might just make it.*:

He could sense her indecision, and saw her take a steadying breath. *All right, but you'll have to hit me as you go past, or Martje, at least, will suspect something. Wait till I look over at the others. I'll claim I was* distracted by their discussion. *Good luck – and look out, there are other teams in the woods – we were just the nearest to the crash site, and got here first.*

:*Get ready to run as soon as Maria looks away,*: Bartes told Tanya. :*I've persuaded her to let us escape.*:

Their muscles tensed as they watched Maria.

The girl took another deep breath, set her lips and deliberately looked away.

Tanya and Bartes took off towards the woods without a glance back. As they passed Maria, Bartes clipped her across the chin, hard enough to knock her down but without causing any real damage.

They had almost reached the tree-line before their erstwhile captors recovered from their surprise and opened fire. Bullets flew past them on both sides. They dived headlong over a fallen tree-trunk, and hit the ground.

Bartes had just raised himself on his hands and knees, ready to crawl away, when Tanya yelped. "What's wrong," he asked.

"M-my back," she said through gritted teeth. "I've been hit."

Bartes glanced down. "It's a splinter of wood. It must have been knocked off a tree by one of the bullets. Come on." He got to his feet, and reached down to help Tanya up.

She took his hand, but when she tried to rise, she gave a cry of pain. "There's no way I can move," she said, shaking her head. "Leave me."

"Don't be stupid. We have to find somewhere to hide."

"Where? ...Oh!" Tania's voice surged with a sudden hope. "Lie down next to me," she said urgently.

"We don't have time for that sort of thing."

"Idiot," she said, and chuckled briefly at his gallows humour. "Just do it!"

Her peremptory tone shocked him into obedience, and he threw himself down, twigs snapping beneath the weight of his body. They heard their pursuers fall still, listening. After a couple of seconds, the rustling of a clump of ferns nearby told them that the chase was nearly upon them.

:*God, Tanya, they can't miss us,*: he sent. :*That guy – Dieter – he's coming our way. He'll be on us any moment.*:

:*Keep still. He* won't *see us – not unless you panic,*: Tanya sent, her 'voice' sounding strained. :*And keep the heavy breathing for later – when we're alone.*:

It was all Bartes could do not to laugh aloud. :*Now who's being an idiot,*: he sent. :*Why can't he see us?*:

:*It's one of my talents,*: Tanya replied. :*Just be quiet and think like a log. I've got to concentrate.*:

Dieter scanned the area where they lay. Bartes felt it was only a matter of time before they were located. The young man look straight at him, and Bartes braced himself for a struggle, but just as the tension was becoming unbearable, Dieter turned away and called, "They're not over here. I could have sworn they went this way. I'll look deeper in." He walked past the fugitives, his boot landing within inches of Bartes' head.

More rebels arrived to join in the hunt, and Bartes and Tanya heard them calling to each other as they systematically searched the area. Bartes heard a heavy tread coming their way.

"They must be somewhere round here," a familiar voice said.

"But, Martje, I checked this area – it's completely clear," Dieter replied as they came into sight.

"I want to check for myself."

Bartes glanced at Tanya. Her face glistened with sweat; her eyes were closed in concentration. He knew better than to disturb her, and watched as the rebels came closer. Ten metres – eight metres –

My God, he thought, *they're going to fall over us.* :*Tanya – your leg - get it out of the way – quick!*::

Martje froze in mid-stride.

"What is it?" Dieter asked.

"I heard something move," Martje said. "Quiet!"

"Can you see anything?"

Bartes held his breath.

"No," she replied after a couple of seconds. "It must have been a squirrel or something." She gave an exasperated sigh. "Dammit," she added. "They must be a long way away by now – we'll never catch them. Maybe they'll get lost in the forest and die of exposure – we can only hope. Anyway, we'd better get out of here before any rescuers arrive. Let's round up the others."

Tanya and Bartes lay prone and silent as they moved away. Their voices receded, and after what seemed like an eternity, all was quiet. :*Do you think they've gone?*: Tanya sent after some moments.

Bartes reached out with his mind. No human thoughts within range... "I think so," he whispered. "How did you manage to keep them from seeing us?"

"I'm not really sure." She sounded mystified. "I just realised I could make them see what I wanted them to. It's a good thing none of them were psionic, or they might not have been fooled. Doing it for so long took a lot out of me, though. I feel exhausted. Can we call for help?"

Bartes pressed the activation button on his communicator, but got only static. "We appear to be out of radio range."

"Those things weren't meant to be used out here in the wilds. The helicopter crew must have got off a mayday, but even if they didn't, we'll soon be missed. Major Valentine's people are bound to come looking for us, and that wreck should be pretty visible."

"I hope they find us soon. It's getting dark."

"And cold." Tanya shivered, then gave a sharp cry of pain. "I think this splinter is pressing on a nerve. Every time I move, I get a jolt down my left leg."

Bartes looked over at her, and could see the bloodstain on the back of her dress, surrounding the piece of wood that protruded from it. "Is there anything I can do? Could I remove the splinter?"

"No! No offence, Bartes, but it seems to be touching a major nerve, and you could do more harm than good – and anyway, you might leave some shards behind. But the external wound does need to be cleaned and dressed – and so do our hands. Do you think you could get my medical kit from the helicopter?"

"I'll do my best."

He made his way cautiously back to the wrecked vehicle, mindful that their assailants might yet be around, but the area was deserted. He confirmed his suspicion that he and Tanya were the only ones left alive, and located her medkit. Luckily it had been strapped down, and seemed little worse for the impact of the crash. He carried it back to where she lay, along with some emergency gear and supplies he found in the helicopter's lockers.

Once he'd returned, he took an energy bar from one of the ration packs he'd found, half stripped it and put it into Tanya's uninjured hand. Mumbling her thanks, she devoured the bar and gave a sigh. "Is there any more?" she asked, and he passed her another. As she consumed it in a more leisurely fashion, she said, "Look, I'm getting pain if I move, and it'd be dangerous to try and treat myself blind like this, anyway. You'll have to do it for me."

"What should I do?"

"Cut away the cloth for a few inches all the way around the splinter." She sighed. "It's a pity – I rather like this dress."

"It's not really suitable for the snow."

"It's better than n-nothing."

"Try not to shiver while I'm working on your back – it makes it hard to avoid disturbing the splinter."

"I'm d-doing my best."

Once he had cut away the cloth, he inspected the wound. The splinter was about an inch across at its widest, and an eighth of an inch at its thickest and protruded a couple of inches from her back.

"Ouch," he said. "It's like a dagger blade. It's not far from your spine."

"That's what I was afraid of."

"Do you want me to break off the protruding part?"

"No!" She inadvertently shook her head and gave another cry as the sudden movement tweaked the nerve. She gave a couple of shuddering breaths and continued. "Now, open the bottle of surgical disinfectant and clean the area around the wound with a pad of cotton wool... Ow! Gently! That's better – the cold of the alcohol is beginning to dull the pain. Now give me a shot of local anaesthetic. Use one of the small vials in the top left compartment, and inject half of it in each side of the thickest part of the splinter, about half an inch from the wound... Good." She sighed as the pain-killer began to take effect. "Now unwrap a number 3 dressing, cut a hole for the splinter and cover the area with it – don't worry about antiseptic, the dressing is already impregnated with it."

When Bartes had finished, he cut a slit in a blanket and covered her exposed back with it, carefully threading the splinter through the hole. He folded another blanket and put it under her head. "What about our hands?" he asked.

"The cuts look bad, but they're pretty superficial, really. They'll have to be cleaned up, though, to avoid infection."

"It's not that – won't it look a bit suspicious if we have identical wounds?"

"I hadn't thought of that." Tanya pondered a moment. "Look, clean your hand and anoint it with antiseptic, and cover it with a length of surgical tape. You'll have to try to keep it out of sight as much as possible – with any luck it won't be noticed. Once you've done that, we'll deal with my hand."

"What do you mean?" Bartes asked as he followed her instructions. "Can't we do the same for you?"

"Because I'm injured, they'll check me all over, and there's no way this looks accidental, so we'll have to disguise it somehow."

"How?"

"Well, could you clean it up first, and apply some local anaesthetic?" She reached around her with her other hand and found a piece of flint.

"What're you going to do with that?"

"Watch."

Bartes winced as she deliberately drove the jagged edge of the stone into the wound and tore the edges of the previously straight cut. He could see from the tears in the corners of her eyes that it hurt despite the anaesthetic.

"N-now, c-could you get a f-fire going?" she asked, as she cleaned the now-jagged wound again and put a dressing over it. "I can f-feel that I'm g-going into shock."

He quickly gathered some fallen branches and ignited them with a fire-lighter from the emergency kit. "How do we explain our escape without mentioning what we told the rebels?" he asked Tanya.

She held out her hand towards the growing blaze. "Ooh, that's better… We'll have to pretend we fled before they arrived."

"But the Commissar's body is in the wreckage. They'll know we didn't have time to get out before the rebels turned up."

"You'll have to get her corpse out into the open and pose it as if she was shot outside."

"What about the bloodstains inside the helicopter?"

"Clean up whatever you can. Let's just hope they don't look at the wreck too closely. We can always claim they were caused in the crash, when I gashed my hand."

Once the fire had taken hold and Tanya had stopped shivering, Bartes took some more branches back to the clearing where they'd crashed and lit a beacon, and laid the Commissar's corpse out as Tanya had suggested.

He returned to Tanya's side and they waited, huddled close to the fire. Gradually, a little warmth crept into their bones, and they relaxed. Tanya's eyes were beginning to close and Bartes was starting to doze in sympathy when she gave a little gasp.

"What is it?" he asked with concern.

"Talk to me."

"What do you mean?"

"Talk to me. I was beginning to drift off into unconsciousness. That's not a good thing to do when you're in shock, particularly in this cold."

"Uh... What should I talk about?" His mind went momentarily blank, but soon the obvious hit him. "We've got to get away from here," he began.

"I know. I hope they find us – and soon."

"So do I, but I don't mean here here – I mean this planet here. We've got to get back to Regni before something awful happens."

"What d'you think is going to happen?"

"Whoever kidnapped us probably has substitutes masquerading as us. I don't think we're important enough for anyone to spend so much effort just to capture and reprogram us – no offence intended."

"None taken – but if my people, at least, knew I was missing, they'd be looking for me – and they're quite resourceful." Tanya frowned. "We're such a close-knit group that replacing all of us would make discovery less likely than only swapping part of the team – though it must have been quite a complex operation. I think you must be right, but what d'you think our impersonators are planning to do?"

"I don't know," Bartes exclaimed in frustration. "If I did, I wouldn't feel so exasperated."

"But how *can* we escape? They're watching our every move, and eavesdropping on our conversations."

Bartes put his tentative thoughts into words. "Joseph suggested this morning that we take a trip to Lake Kuraken, because they have hovercart races there this weekend. I'm not certain where this lake is, but I remember someone at work telling me about it. He'd been there on a skiing holiday, so it must be up in the mountains, and from his description, it's pretty large, and surrounded by some very wild country. We stand a much better chance of getting away from our guards in a place like that."

"That's all very well, but it won't take us off-planet. We have to get home before your unknown disaster strikes – if it hasn't already."

"True – but at least it's a start. Have you any better ideas?"

Tanya was silent for a while, long enough that Bartes looked down at her to check that she wasn't losing consciousness. "Not really," she said eventually. "Do you know how far it is from this lake to the Skyport?"

"I'm afraid I don't – but it's up in the mountains, so it must be quite a distance. Are you thinking of stealing a spaceship?"

"If we could reach the Skyport, perhaps we could locate John and undo his conditioning. He might be able to 'borrow' a shuttle, and arrange for us to be smuggled aboard an outgoing vessel. At the very least,

I might be able to persuade someone to contact Mercy for me."

"That's all very well, but how do we get to the Skyport?"

Tanya's forehead wrinkled. "Look, if we can get to this lake, and can somehow get hold of a map, we might be able steal a boat, sail to somewhere remote and make our way to the Skyport on foot. It would all take time, but it's all I can think of at the moment, and it's better than just waiting and hoping the security forces don't find out we've broken their programming."

Bartes had a flash of inspiration. "We've *got* a boat – or at least RD has."

"But that one's at Plune."

"I think my workmate mentioned that they had yacht racing on the lake. If we could only persuade Major Valentine to transport RD's boat to the lake to take part..."

"Seems a pretty long shot. And that's if he'll even let us go."

Bartes shrugged. "It's worth a try…"

As the sun was finally setting, they heard noises from the direction of the wrecked helicopter. Tanya dared not move, so Bartes staggered to his feet and called out. Neither of them cared by this point who their rescuers were, as long as they had more blankets and some hot drinks.

The newcomers were a security team that had been searching for them, and Major Valentine was with them, along with a couple of paramedics. They had landed by the crashed helicopter, and were beginning to check through the wreckage when Bartes emerged from the edge of the forest and called for help.

When he saw Bartes, Major Valentine cried out and ran towards him. "Comrade Boris, thank God you're alive." The Major looked genuinely relieved, but his expression changed to one of concern. "But where's Comrade Talia?" He shone his torch to either side.

"She's been injured. She's lying behind a fallen tree-trunk a few yards into the trees."

"What happened?"

"The rebels who downed our helicopter were trying to kill us. We got out before they arrived, and reached the trees before they started shooting, but Talia was struck by a splinter from a tree that was hit by one of the bullets. Please, it's lodged near her spine and she needs proper medical attention."

"I'll see to it at once." The Major sent one of the paramedics with a couple of his men to attend to Tanya, and escorted Bartes to his helicopter, where he was handed a mug of blessedly hot coffee. The Major gave him a few minutes to recover before asking, "Now, can you tell me what happened?"

"I'm still a bit confused," Bartes prevaricated. "I gather from what the co-pilot shouted that someone fired a missile at us."

"We saw that on our radar scopes."

"Well, the pilot managed to keep a degree of control even after we were hit, and we survived, even though he and his co-pilot didn't make it. We got out of the wreck as soon as we could, and saw a number of armed people coming out of the trees. They were dressed for combat and had rifles, but weren't soldiers or security troopers. They raised their guns so we ran for our lives."

"We found your bodyguards and Political Commissar Cheslenko with the wreckage. They'd been shot."

"I know. After we were certain the coast was clear, I went back and found them. I did what I could for them, but they were already dead. You call *us* heroes, but they were the *true* heroes, especially Commissar Tatiana. As we fled, I called to her to follow, but she insisted on staying to cover our retreat."

"You and Comrade Talia were lucky to escape, Comrade. Commissar Cheslenko was right to do what she did, but she paid for it with her life. I will see that she is suitably honoured."

Tanya had been stabilised and retrieved and now lay face down on a stretcher, sipping her own steaming mug of coffee. She sent to Bartes, :*Not totally convincing, but it'll have to do.*: "The crew and our escort, too," she said, "after all, they all gave their lives to save ours."

"Truly commendable," the Major replied.

"And if there's anything we can do for their families –" she continued, "– to show our solidarity with them in their grief, we must do whatever we can."

"I agree," the Major replied, "but why didn't the rebels come after you?"

"They did. We could hear them searching for us, but we kept quiet, and luck must have been with us." Tanya's look of wide-eyed innocence almost convinced Bartes!

"It seems odd to have gone to so much trouble, but not to make sure of finishing the job…"

It seemed like the Major would pursue his suspicions further, but at that point a medical transport helicopter arrived and the paramedics had Tanya and Bartes transferred across to it, releasing the Major to join his team scouring the forest for the long-departed rebels.

Chapter 13

"What seems to be the problem, Comrade Hero?"

The voice broke into the reverie Tanya had slipped into when Bartes left to greet their rescuers. "Hmm?" she replied drowsily.

"How can I help?"

"Oh... oh, yes - I've got what feels like half a tree trunk lodged in my back. Actually, it doesn't, because Bar – Boris injected it with local anaesthetic, but you know what I mean." Tanya hoped her obvious confusion would cover her blunder.

The medic shone his torch on her back. "I see... Can you move?"

"Yes, but I think the splinter is pressing on a nerve, because if I *do* move, I get a jolt of pain down my leg."

"Tricky – I think I'd better immobilise you until the full medical team arrive."

"Good idea."

"First let's get you off this frozen ground and onto the stretcher. You –" (he pointed to one of the soldiers who had accompanied him) "lift her legs, with one arm supporting her calves and one under her thighs. You –" (he pointed to the other) "use one arm to lift her shoulders and the other under the blanket supporting her head. I'll lift her torso and we'll move her gently onto the stretcher face down. One – two – three – lift!"

It was smoothly and easily done, and Tanya felt nothing untoward. "Thank you," she said as they began strapping her body down.

"No problem." The medic held Tanya's hand to reassure her as she was lifted and transported to the rescue 'copter. Coffee had been brewed, and Tanya was handed a mug. She clutched it in her frozen hands and almost dropped it at the painful return of sensation. She splashed a little, but retained hold and forced a trickle of fiery liquid down her throat.

Bartes was trying to explain why they were still alive, and Tanya was grateful that she was not the one being grilled. She breathed a figurative sigh of relief when they were transferred to the newly-arrived medical 'copter.

Once they had taken off, a nurse removed Tanya's shoes and Bartes' boots and checked their feet. "You're lucky, Comrade Heroes," she said. "Neither of you have any signs of frostbite."

"I don't think we were out there long enough – though it seemed like ages, especially when the rebels were searching for us."

She looked at Tanya's hands, removed the bloody dressing from the gash, and gave a sharp intake of breath. "That's nasty," she said, "but it seems to have been cleaned up pretty well." As she redressed it, she glanced over to where Bartes was now relaxing. "Did you suffer any injuries, Comrade Hero?"

"None at all – I was very lucky," he answered. He kept his injured hand in his pocket throughout the journey to maintain the fiction.

Once the nurse had done the basics, she called the team's doctor over to deal with the splinter in Tanya's back. The doctor removed the blanket and the dressing and inspected the damage. "Hmmm – your splinter's not as big as all that," she said.

"It's not *my* splinter," Tanya retorted.

"You seem pretty attached to it," the doctor replied dryly.

"I'd as soon see the *back* of it."

"You make puns like that, I'm almost tempted to leave it there. Actually, it's pretty deeply embedded, and you're fortunate that it just missed your spine. Drink this – it'll help deal with the pain as I remove it."

She poured some vodka into a plastic cup and handed it to Tanya. As her patient swallowed it, she cleaned the area around the wound yet again and administered some more local anaesthetic. She had a steady pair of hands, and cut the splinter out smoothly and cleanly, before cleaning the wound and sewing it up.

"I wouldn't to lie on it for a while," she advised Tanya, "even padded, it'll hurt once the anaesthetic wears off."

"Thanks." Tanya smiled and made to sit up.

"Oh no, no you don't. You stay where you are."

"But –"

Suddenly, the doctor's eyes widened in recognition. "I know you." Tanya sighed and waited for the expected request for her autograph, but she'd mistaken the doctor's meaning. "You're a Nurse Manager at the Restavic Down Medical Centre – Talia Something-or-other. I've seen you there a couple of times when I've brought in patients." She shook her head and gave a wry grin. "No wonder you're so difficult: nurses make the worst patients – apart from us doctors, that is."

Tanya laughed. "Hoist by my own petard," she admitted. "You're dead right. Okay – I'll be good."

Tanya spent the rest of the journey back to the dacha helping to regenerate the damaged tissue psionically. By the time they had reached their destination and were landing she was able to struggle to her feet.

"What did I tell you? Lie down again immediately," the doctor told her.

"I can't," the patient insisted. "If I'm carried in lying on my belly, I'll never hear the end of it. Anyway, you did such a good job – it feels a thousand times better."

The doctor rolled her eyes and sighed. "Nurses! At least let me check the stitches before you go."

As she was doing so, they touched down and Tanya soon heard a familiar voice. "Talia! Oh, Talia, what happened to you?"

"It was only a splinter, Anoushka. I'm going to be fine."

"But what *happened*? We heard that your helicopter had been shot down. I was so worried."

"Once we've got Talia into the dacha, we'll give you the full story," Bartes said.

"Of course. I'm sorry, Talia." With Anoushka and Bartes supporting her, Tanya carefully made her way from the helicopter into the dacha's lounge and lowered herself gingerly into a padded chair. The others were desperate to know what had happened, but Bartes forestalled them until they were sat comfortably with large glasses of vodka in their hands.

"We were flying back from the Medical Centre," Bartes told them, "when we were shot down."

"Did you pick up Political Commissar Cheslenko?" RD said with a frown.

Tanya sighed. "She was with us when we went down. She didn't survive."

Anoushka gasped. "How – how did it happen?" she asked.

"It wasn't the crash," Bartes said. "The pilot and co-pilot were killed when we hit the ground, but those of us in the passenger compartment were left shaken up, but alive – until the rebels arrived, at least. Our bodyguards and Commissar Tatiana gave their lives so that we could escape."

Anoushka and RD needed to know the truth of the matter, but with Iain, Joseph and Peter there, Tanya and Bartes realised that they had to be careful. As Bartes was answering the others' questions, Tanya reached out mentally to Anoushka. :*It wasn't quite like that,*: she sent.

Anoushka's gave a shiver, then she recovered her composure, glanced in Tanya's direction and nodded imperceptibly. Tanya could 'hear' her consciously forming words in her mind. *Sorry, Tanya, I'm not yet used to this.*

:*We were captured by the rebels,*: Tanya 'told' Anoushka. :*We tried to tell them they were making a mistake, that we weren't who they thought we were. They may even have believed us, but it looked like they were going to execute us anyway. Somehow Bartes managed to persuade our guard, a young girl called Maria who didn't want to kill us, to let us escape.*:

Once the initial inquisition was over, Bartes invited RD into the kitchen, ostensibly to discuss dinner, but really to update him on his & Tanya's adventures verbally.

Tanya had lapsed into that strange feeling of post-traumatic euphoria when Major Valentine arrived. He seemed distracted.

"Comrade Heroes, I beg your indulgence," he began.

"What can we do for you, Comrade Major?" Anoushka asked.

He looked faintly embarrassed. "I apologise in advance, particularly to you, Comrade Talia, and to you, Comrade Boris. When your helicopter went down, the rebels broadcast a bulletin on their pirate radio station claiming that you had been killed in the crash, and they had 'executed' you as 'traitors'."

A cold feeling ran down Tanya's spine. They'd been oh-so-nearly correct. "But that's not true. Surely you could issue a rebuttal?" she said.

"We did, but lies like that spread quickly, and my superiors have suggested that you and Comrade Boris make a public appearance this evening to prove the rumour-mongers wrong. Tonight is the premiere of a new production of *Comrade Jones* at the State Opera House in honour of the President's Birthday, and we have invitations for you all."

Tanya sighed. "To be honest, Major, I'm very unwilling to sit for hours in a theatre seat, given the state of my back."

"I know, Comrade Talia, and I can only apologise again. Alas, when my superiors 'suggest' something like this, it is unwise for me to ignore their suggestion – or you their 'invitations'." His voice had an ominous tone that would have made Tanya shiver, had she been able to do so without pain. "You will have your own box, and I will ensure that plenty of cushions are provided. At least there will be a sumptuous reception for the President and his guests as part of his Birthday Celebrations."

Bartes exchanged glances with Tanya. "Very well, Major, but there's a favour we'd like in return," he said.

"And what's that, Comrade Boris?"

Bartes took a deep breath. "It's becoming clear that our enemies will stop at nothing to kill us, and we are making it easy for them by doing the expected. I feel that we should move from this dacha to somewhere less predictable."

"That's a very good idea, Comrade. You surprise me. I should have thought of that – I am, after all, supposed to be the expert in matters of security."

Bartes shrugged, but sent Tanya the succinct message :*Oops.*:

"And where would you suggest we take you?" the Major added.

"What about Lake Kuraken? Josef suggested we take a trip there to see the hovercart racing." The young man in question nodded enthusiastically. "If nothing else, it might throw our enemies off-balance – and they would have to change any plans they have for other assassination attempts."

"That's a good idea, Boris," RD interjected. "Perhaps you could arrange for my catamaran to be transported there, too, Comrade Major? It's boat-racing season, and I'd like to try my luck."

Major Valentine pursed his lips and said, "Very well, I'll see what I can arrange."

"In that case," RD continued, "I'll stay behind and prepare the *Darling* for transport – and repair the damage done by that damned mortar. Unless your superiors require my presence?"

"No, Comrade – only Comrades Talia and Boris were named by the rebels. Feel free to stay behind and do what you need to."

"Thank you, Comrade Major." RD gave Tanya an infuriatingly smug look. "Enjoy your evening, Comrades."

As Tanya glared back at RD, the Major turned to Bartes. "Now let's go, Comrade – the opera awaits."

Tanya yelped. "Major, you can't possibly expect me to attend such a prestigious occasion looking like this? And with a hole in the back of my dress?"

"Very well, Comrade Talia. How long will you need to get ready?"

"At least an hour."

He consulted his watch. "You have five minutes."

"Men! It's all right for you."

He gave a deep sigh and shook his head. "Ten, then."

As it was, the girls managed to drag out their preparation time to a quarter of an hour before the Major took each of them by the arm and ushered them physically – but reasonably gently – to the transport helicopter. Even so, they had to finish their make-up in transit, which was a nightmare – trying to apply mascara in such a situation is not to be recommended.

As they flew to Restavic City, Tanya realised how regaining her memory had changed her perspective. She was now unpleasantly aware of the poor quality of the rather utilitarian clothing and accessories they had been provided with, even for an occasion such as this. A vision intruded on her mind: a grand state banquet. Oddly, instead of being there on duty, she was one of the important guests. She was wearing a formal dress of midnight blue silk, with long drooping sleeves and a skirt that trailed a little behind and swished as she walked, and she was quite young. She tried to remember more, but as usual, the picture fled before her gaze. Where it had come from, she had no idea, but it didn't tally with anything else she remembered. Yet another puzzle.

The centre of the square outside the Opera House had been cordoned off by a platoon of soldiers, and the transport landed in the middle of it. Once the troopers who had been escorting them disembarked and formed a line either side of the red carpet that had, no doubt, originally been laid for the President, Bartes, Tanya and the others were permitted to alight. Their presence had unquestionably been trumpeted, as demonstrated by the crowds, who broke into apparently spontaneous cheers. :*If only they knew who we really are,*: Bartes sent to Tanya as they waved and made their way along the red carpet.

As well as the soldiers guarding them, there was a strong and noticeable security presence, and, as they made their way toward the Opera House, Tanya saw that there was a pair of uniformed officers on its broad steps, one at each side. They were scanning the crowd suspiciously and she could detect an undercurrent of mental activity. Tanya guessed that they were there to detect anything psionically significant, and was instantly concerned they might have noticed Bartes' telepathic message. She leaned over to him, inclined her head slightly in their direction, and whispered, "Sniffers – we'd better keep our thoughts to ourselves."

Bartes nodded his understanding as they mounted the steps.

Sunset in Silvana

Just before Tanya followed the Major and Bartes into the foyer, she turned to give a final wave to the crowd. As she did so, she caught sight of one of the sniffers as he suddenly turned his head and stared firmly towards the far right edge of the crowd. He had been gazing in that direction for some seconds when he suddenly clutched his chest and grimaced. She could feel his agony psionically as he sank to his knees before collapsing forwards onto his face. As his consciousness faded, his still-beating heart appeared where he'd been standing, sprayed its contents liberally around, and fell onto the marble between his twitching feet.

There was a second or so of stunned silence, followed by screams and pandemonium everywhere. With a wordless cry, the dead officer's partner ran to his side from the other end of the steps. Several bodyguards surrounded the corpse, while the others clustered protectively around Tanya, though what they could hope to do against such a form of assassination baffled her.

Having ascertained that her partner was definitely and irrevocably dead, the other sniffer scanned the crowd with a snarl of fury and tears in her eyes. *Those two may have been partners in more ways than one,* Tanya thought. The surviving sniffer, too, soon focussed her gaze on the far right edge of the crowd. Somehow, Tanya knew what was about to happen, and watched in horrified fascination as the girl gave an uncannily accurate repeat performance of her partner's act of Grand Guignol. *Whether or not they were lovers in life,* thought Tanya ironically, *their hearts are now together in death.*

Tanya looked over in the direction that both victims had been staring when they'd been killed. Just at the edge of the crowd, she could see a slender young woman who was moving quietly away from the commotion.

:*Nicely done,*: she sent without thinking. :*A bit showy, but effective.*:

The girl turned her head momentarily towards Tanya, but without changing her pace. :*You're very kind. It's nice to get a compliment from such an accomplished Aelumi psionic,*: she sent. She seemed to know Tanya, but although something about her was familiar, Tanya couldn't remember when – or if they'd met before.

The confusion continued for a few seconds, until Major Valentine came back out onto the steps. He called for silence, and the crowd complied with his command preternaturally quickly. "Nothing untoward has happened," he announced in a stentorian voice. "There has merely been an accidental spillage of red paint. Would those of you whose clothes have been splashed please join me here. The rest of you should go about your business. I hope you all enjoy the opera."

To Tanya's astonishment, as soon as he'd made that announcement, the whole crowd began to behave as if nothing odd *had* occurred. They ignored the bodies, and those cleaning up the mess, and one or two who had collapsed regained their feet, brushed themselves down, and acted completely unconcerned. Even those spattered with blood seemed unbothered; they assembled as requested and were escorted away, presumably to be cleaned up.

Tanya, however, *was* concerned, and she turned and entered the Opera House in a quandary: she had only just found out who she thought she really was, but she wasn't an Aelumin, was she? She'd heard of those psi-witches, and the idea of being one of *them* made her uncomfortable. Her regained memory told her that she'd been born and raised in a middle-class suburb on Ataraxia, but how did that tally with the stranger's odd salutation? And what about that odd vision on the helicopter?

Then it struck her: where had the thoughts she'd directed to this young woman come from? They'd been totally instinctive, and she hadn't really considered what she'd sent at the time, but now they came back to her, and the recollection made her feel cold all over. She was a doctor, wasn't she, dedicated to the preservation of life? And yet somehow she was now aware that she'd taken more than one life, and in stealthy, underhand ways. What she'd said to Anoushka was all too true: she wasn't really a very nice person.

She had a glass of champagne thrust in her hand, and had to cover her inner turmoil when she was personally greeted by the Comrade President. "Comrade Talia, how very nice to meet you again. You are well, I hope?" he said loudly.

"Very well, thank you, Comrade President." She bent her knee slightly as he kissed the back of her unbandaged hand. "Congratulations on your birthday."

"Thank you. And you, Comrade Boris, you are also as fit and healthy as a Hero of the Republic should be?"

"Very much so, Comrade President, thank you for asking. And may I add my good wishes on your birthday to Talia's."

"You are too kind." They exchanged a few more pleasantries. All the media were in attendance, and the President made a particular point of being photographed several times with Bartes and Tanya, both singly and together.

Eventually, though, he moved on, and Tanya looked round for the others. She noticed with some concern that Iain, who'd already had several glasses of vodka before he came, seemed to be imbibing rather heavily, as did the two youngsters. She was about to have words with Joseph when a bell rang and one of the ushers announced, "Distinguished Comrades, would you please take your seats?"

They had been assigned their own personal escort, who led them up to the box on the right of the President's own. Most of them followed her, but Iain decided to be awkward.

"I wish to sit with my comrades, the workers," he announced imperiously, as he made his inebriated way through the tunnel that led to the stalls.

Bartes and Tanya looked at each other in chagrin. After what they'd seen outside, they were both chary about communicating their fears telepathically, but they didn't really need to. It would be ironic if one of them who *hadn't* broken his programming drew enough attention that they were rumbled.

Iain perched on a step and turned to a young woman who was sitting on the aisle seat next to him. "D'you know this opera?" he asked her.

"N-no, Comrade Hero," she replied, leaning away from him.

"I hope it's funny," he continued. "I don't mind a good tragedy, something with lots of blood." He belched loudly. "Oops, par' me. What I really like is a good laugh."

Major Valentine bustled over. "Let me conduct you to your proper seat, Comrade Ivan," he said.

"If you don't mind, Major," Iain said imperiously, "this lady and I were having an interesting conversation."

It was obvious that the girl's opinion differed, and she gave the Major a pleading look. Several of the Major's men hovered around them uncertainly, and one of them whispered in his ear. He shook his head and said, "No – hopefully, it won't come to that. Just keep him out of trouble," then, to the girl's obvious horror, walked away.

The lights dimmed and there was an expectant hush as the overture began. The music itself was strangely familiar, though the rest of the opera was not. And the former was as good as the latter was dire: the story was dull, the staging heavy-handed, and the lead tenor, though politically correct, should have been more so musically. The lead soprano had a pleasing, if unremarkable, voice.

> "Work for your commune,
> Give it all you've got.
> Work night and day,
> Work night and day..."

The chorus had just begun this interesting, if vaguely familiar, refrain when Tanya became aware of an extra voice from the stalls. Iain had recognised the song as having been plagiarised from a different opera, and when he joined in, using what he considered were the *correct* words, she recognised it too, as a corruption of the Toreadors' Chorus from the ancient opera *Carmen*. There was a mutter in the audience, which rose in volume as Iain stood up, clambered up onto the stage and joined the cast, still singing loudly.

When some of the actors and the stagehands moved to restrain him, he staggered towards them with his arms extended in greeting. Though he seemed to be enjoying himself, they were clearly irate. One of them took a swing at him and a scuffle began. Iain's escort of security officers had initially been surprised by his sudden move, but now they jumped on to the stage, appearing uncertain as whether they should remove him or protect him. Some of the crowd began to cheer: perhaps they thought this was part of the opera, but perhaps they just found the slapstick violence a refreshing break from the tedious dogma.

Iain continued struggling with a couple of actors until a piece of wood wielded by a stagehand caught him under the right ear and he sagged to the ground, senseless. The security officers surrounded him, and Tanya realised with alarm that the Major might have him dragged off for treatment. It could be disastrous if he did so: her subterfuge with the dispensers might be discovered, and all would be up. She turned around to ask Bartes what he thought they should do, but he wasn't in his seat.

As she looked around for him, she became aware of another voice singing the Toreadors' Chorus. In a box on the other side of the auditorium, a security general had picked up the baton that Iain had dropped. After a couple of minutes of confusion, several security men appeared in the back of his box, at which point he stopped singing and looked around himself with a puzzled expression. Meanwhile, a well-dressed middle-aged woman on the opposite side of the stalls took up the refrain, until she in turn was surrounded. The chorus was continued by unsuspecting patron after unsuspecting patron as the security team tried vainly to regain control.

Major Valentine got up onto the stage and started scanning the audience. After a few seconds, he focussed on the back right of the circle. Tanya looked in that direction and saw a slender, familiar, female silhouette with a blue glow at its throat. The woman, whoever she was, was standing by an Exit sign. The Major drew his gun and fired at her, but she nonchalantly dodged the bullet and disappeared through the door. He pointed out where she'd gone to his men and left the stage to join in pursuit, but Tanya felt certain she wouldn't be apprehended.

As the disturbance subsided, the stage curtains closed, the safety curtain lowered, and a projector started somewhere at the back of the auditorium. On the safety curtain appeared a rather grainy but recognisable representation of some large military-looking vehicles being unloaded by soldiers from a space shuttle with the insignia of the Dainworlds Federation. A narrative began, and a clear contralto voice said:

"This is the 'agricultural equipment' imported at your Skyport over the last week. These are actually grav tanks, over a hundred of them sent from the

Dainworlds, with a cost much greater than your country can afford. I have a message for the Comrade President: if you start a war, you yourself will not survive it."

Above the pictures bold, blood red letters, appeared:

WAR = DEATH
YOUR DEATH!

Tanya had been vaguely aware of the frantic search for the source of this intrusion, which clearly met with success when the projection suddenly cut out.

After a short but restless pause, Major Valentine again mounted the stage. "Ladies and gentlemen," he began, "nothing untoward has happened. You have just taken your seats after the interval. Please be quiet, as the opera is about to continue." By now Tanya was used to the way the audience complied with every instruction they were given, but she continued to wonder how the Major was able to dominate people so easily.

In all the confusion, Bartes had been able to retrieve Iain, and helped him up to their box. "Are you all right, Ivan?" Tanya asked the impromptu baritone *sotto voce* as he sat collecting his addled wits.

"My head aches – and call me Iain," he muttered. "I'm sorry for how I've been behaving."

She blew out her cheeks. "That's a relief. It was getting hard to keep things from you," she whispered.

"How did they manage to keep us so deeply programmed?" he asked in mystification. "We're trained to resist this sort of thing."

"They used drugs in our dispensers, but I exchanged them for something harmless as soon as Bartes told me of his suspicions."

"Who else knows who they really are?"

"Bartes, Anna – who has adopted her new name, Anoushka – and RD."

"What about the others?"

Bartes interrupted. "Young Joseph hasn't yet regained his memory," he whispered, "and I'm worried about John. There's not a lot we can do till we see him. If the worst comes to the worst, we'll have to escape without him."

"Escape without him?" Anoushka interjected in alarm, a little too loud.

"Shh!" Tanya put her finger to her lips. "Yes, Anoushka, we may have to." She put her arm around her friend. "What else can we do?" she whispered. "We have get back to Regni – who knows what's happened – or is going to happen while we're away. If John is at Lake Kuraken, we'll try to take him with us, but it's vital we get home as soon as we can. Look, we'll talk later, but for now, we've an opera to endure."

Comrade Jones had restarted, and plodded through its rather predictable ending without further interruption. Somehow they managed to stay awake, and even to simulate enjoyment.

As they had been promised, a luxurious buffet had been laid on after the performance for the President's special guests. Tanya assumed that he was supposed to be present, but he wasn't. She put this non-appearance down to caution. After the impromptu extra 'entertainment' they'd witnessed, she'd have thought twice about making herself vulnerable, had she been in his shoes.

The use of psionics is physically draining and leaves one hungry, so it was interesting to note the number of security personnel who attacked the buffet with gusto; the catering staff were having to work hard to keep it replenished. Although Tanya had not been very psionically active, the amount of 'fallout' flying around had left her quite peckish, so she, too, made a beeline for the food.

She loved savouries, and the seafood canapés looked particularly delicious, but the need for quick energy led her to the fruit meringues. She took three, and was liberally anointing them with cream, when the security general who had unwittingly followed Iain's lyrical example earlier approached her. "Comrade Hero Milanova, may I introduce a friend of mine who is eager to meet you?"

"Why, of course," she replied with a smile, which broadened as she realised the friend was, in fact, the young woman she'd seen twice earlier. She noticed that, unsurprisingly, the girl's plate was piled high.

"My name is Sophie," the newcomer said, "Sophie Mikova."

"As I'm sure you know," the general continued, "Sophie is one of our most talented ballerinas. She is currently staying with me at my dacha."

"I am so glad to meet you, Comrade Mikova."

"Call me Sophie," the girl gushed. "Grigori, darling, would you please get me another glass of champagne?"

"Coming right up, my dear." The general disappeared in the direction of the bar.

Sophie winked at Tanya. "I would so like your autograph, Comrade Hero."

"You must call me Talia." Tanya dared not use telepathy in such close proximity to all the security officers, some of whom were probably trained 'sniffers', and she knew Sophie would feel the same, so they bent over the piece of paper Sophie brought out from her handbag and conferred *sotto voce* as Tanya slowly wrote her 'name'.

"You know who I am?" Tanya whispered.

"Yes – don't you remember *me*?"

"I'm afraid not. I – and my team – have been brainwashed, and we're only just breaking the conditioning. Are you here to rescue us?"

"I didn't even know you were here until recently. I have my own mission."

"I saw – look out, here comes your tame general"

"And what are you young ladies talking so seriously about?" the general asked.

Sophie gave a vacuous laugh. "Just girlish things, Grigori darling. You men don't know the importance of just the right shade of lipstick."

The general laughed indulgently and said, "Sophie, I'd like you to meet some more of my comrades. If you'll excuse us, Comrade Hero?"

"If I must," Tanya said. "It has been such a pleasure to talk to you, Comrade Sophie. I hope we meet again soon."

"As do I," the faux ballerina replied as the general whisked her away.

Chapter 14

Once the purgatory that was *Comrade Jones* was over, Bartes and Anoushka escorted the still slightly bewildered Iain to the reception – Bartes reckoned that he needed to be chaperoned until he came to terms with his new/old self. As they led the young man to a sofa, a harassed-looking Major Valentine button-holed them.

"Could I have a word with you, Comrade Boris?" he asked.

"If you wish, Major. Would you look after Ivan for a while, Anoushka?" When she smiled her assent, Bartes followed the Major to a quiet corner.

"How is Comrade Ivan?" the Major began. "He was behaving rather strangely."

"He has a lump on the side of his head," Bartes replied, "but he seems all right otherwise. He's had a bit too much to drink. He does that from time to time, as you well know. I do apologise on his behalf."

"Please try to keep him under control, at least in public."

"I'll do my best."

"Thank you." He gave Bartes a weary look. "Enjoy the rest of the reception," he added as he made his way toward the buffet.

Bartes surveyed the throng. Iain and Anoushka were chatting quietly together, Tanya was talking with a slender young woman and a security general, neither of whom he recognised, and Joseph and his friend Peter were eating pastries and drinking wine.

He was a little concerned at the increasing inebriation of young Joseph. *If he recovers any of his memories while he's drunk,* he thought, *he could easily give us all away. I think I'd better do something about this.* He had started toward the boys when one of the serving staff, a rather attractive young blonde, bent down and whispered in Peter's ear. The boy looked round at her nervously. His eyes widened in apparent recognition, he swallowed and nodded almost imperceptibly. She moved away and Bartes saw her go through the door to the fire stairs. After a couple of minutes, Peter slipped away from Joseph and cautiously moved toward the same exit.

Bartes looked around for Tanya, and saw that she was just leaving the powder room. He caught her eye, inclined his head in Peter's direction, and set off after him. He tried to catch up with the boy, but before he could reach him, the lad started down the stairs. Bartes followed, but before he'd gone more than a few steps, he heard voices: Peter's and a young woman's. They seemed to be arguing in whispers about something. Tanya had, by now, caught him up, and they slowly and carefully descended together. There was a brief moment of panic when Bartes' foot slipped on a discarded waitress's uniform. The noise was slight, but the voices instantly stopped.

They froze and held their breath. It seemed an age before the whispering restarted and they could continue their descent. They'd just reached the top of the last flight of stairs when a brief breeze indicated that the external door just below them had been opened. They were just in time to see the waitress, now dressed from head to toe in black, hold the door open for Peter and slide through after him.

Bartes was about to follow when Tanya laid a restraining hand on his arm. She had seen a woman in security uniform lurking in the shadows at the bottom of the staircase. When the woman emerged from the darkness, they saw it was Captain Reynard. Fortunately, she was so intent on her prey that she didn't look up. If she had, she could hardly have failed to notice them. She too, went out of the fire door, and she seemed to be whispering into a comms link as she did so.

"What are we going to do now?" Tanya whispered.

"The sensible thing would be to go back to the reception. Peter's not one of us, after all, so it's not really any of our business."

"And if we're caught, it could mean reprogramming – but I'm curious..."

Bartes sighed. "So'm I – let's go after them." They carefully descended the last few steps, and Bartes opened the door just wide enough so they could see out. There was a large waste hopper several metres to the right, behind which the Captain was crouching, cradling her pistol. She was oblivious to them, her concentration on the yard in front of her. Motioning Tanya to follow, Bartes slipped out, and they crouched behind a pile of crates on the other side of the door.

In the yard was an unmarked black van, and two sable-clad figures were helping Peter into the back of it. Neither they nor the absconder had seen Captain Reynard. Suddenly, there was the sound of running feet from the side of the Opera House and a security detail came boiling around the corner. This was clearly what the Captain had been waiting for. She rose to her full height, stepped out into the light, raised her gun and yelled, "Stop right where you are!"

One of the figures, the ex-waitress, spun on her heel and yelled "Get Peter to safety" to her colleague, and launched herself at the Captain, a wicked looking knife in her hand. The Captain's gun barked once – twice – a third time – and the girl fell in an untidy, twitching heap.

"Bastards!" her companion shouted. He had closed the van's back door and, as it began to drive away, he heaved something in the direction of the oncoming security detail before he, too, was cut down. The grenade exploded not far from Tanya and Bartes, and there was the sound of shrapnel and other, more organic, fragments hitting the far side of the crates they were hiding behind. Several of the troops had moved to cut off the van, but it knocked them aside, and drove away followed by a hail of gunfire.

The fallen girl lay in the shadows, a couple of yards from Bartes and Tanya. Her dead eyes seemed to look straight at them and a wisp of blonde hair that had escaped her woollen headpiece blew in the night air. Strapped across her back was a compact laser carbine.

"I want that gun," Bartes told Tanya. "I'm going to get it while they chase the van." He began crawling toward the corpse.

"Don't be an idiot," Tanya hissed, "You'll be caught."

She was in no position to stop him without drawing attention, though, and Bartes was soon struggling to free the weapon. He couldn't get it over the cadaver's shoulder, so he began to undo the sling. It was sticky with the girl's life-blood, and proved difficult to release – so much so that he hadn't finished when some of the van's pursuers started to return.

Tanya swore a most unladylike oath. "If this works, you'll owe me big time," she muttered as she got to her feet and walked out into the light as far from Bartes as she could. "What's going on?" she called in a tremulous soprano. She looked around in feigned horror, screamed and collapsed.

As the returning troops rushed to her side, Bartes completed his task and melted back behind the crates. While he was disassembling the firearm and hiding its components in his clothing, he heard a familiar voice.

"Comrade Talia! Wake up, Comrade." It was Major Valentine.

"Wha – where am I?" Tanya's voice had an artful tremble that deserved an Academy Award.

"You're in the courtyard of the Opera House. There's been an incident."

"O – Of course." She swallowed. "It's – it's just – all the blood – and there was somebody's arm, just lying there and – and still twitching." She paused and shuddered, her eyes closing as if to erase the sight.

"Come along, Comrade, you've seen worse: you're a Nurse Manager, for goodness sake."

"You don't understand: at the Centre, you expect it, and can divorce yourself from the misery. Here it's different – oh, so different." She seemed to gather herself, and took a deep breath. "All right. What can I do to help?"

"Go back to the reception."

"What? But…"

"No buts – we have our own medical team available, and I'd hate to spoil your dress." He paused. "What were you doing down here, anyway?"

"It was rather stuffy and hot up there, with so many people wanting to talk to me, so I came down for a break, and a breath of fresh air. Boris was going to follow me, but he got caught up in a conversation just as I left."

Pat upon his cue, Bartes emerged from the shadows. "What the devil's happened here?" he asked, putting as much concern in his voice as he could. "Talia, are you all right?"

"I'm fine." She smiled wanly.

"Not another assassination attempt, surely." Bartes frowned at Major Valentine.

"No, Comrade Boris – young Josef's friend Peter has been kidnapped, and Comrade Talia simply came upon the aftermath. Would you please escort her back to the reception?"

"As you wish. I hope you recover the lad quickly. Josef will be desolate without his friend."

"Not to worry. Captain Reynard is in pursuit of the perpetrators, and I doubt they'll escape her clutches." His voice held barely-concealed contempt for his subordinate.

As they mounted the stairs, Tanya rounded on Bartes. "That – that was – was so far beyond stupid that there isn't a word for it," she said in a low growl.

"I'm sorry," Bartes said defensively, "but, given the circumstances, we could do with a weapon, and it seemed too good an opportunity to miss."

"You're lucky no-one saw the blood on your hands. You'd better wash it off before we re-join the party."

"Right away."

Bartes performed the necessary ablutions, and as they approached Iain and Anoushka, Tanya whispered, "Where did you put that bloody gun, anyway?"

"I disassembled it and hid the parts under my clothes – so if I walk a little stiffly, it has nothing to do with your obvious charms – this time, at least."

She snorted, giggled, then laughed aloud, and Bartes joined her.

"What *has* got into you two?" Anoushka asked.

"I'll tell –" Tanya got out between fits of giggles, "tell you – later."

She and Bartes tried to regain a semblance of composure, but when Iain muttered about "too much vodka", the floodgates opened again.

About a quarter of an hour later, Major Valentine re-joined the reception and approached them. "Comrades," he said, "you've had a very busy day, so I've arranged for transportation back to your dacha."

"Thank you, Comrade Major," Tanya said with a sigh. "I am so very tired, and my back is still painful."

"Once again, I apologise for putting you through this evening. Now, if you'll finish you drinks and follow me..." He paused and looked around. "Where's young Josef?"

Bartes had a sudden palpitation that something had happened to the boy while he and Tanya had been distracted with Peter's abduction, but Anoushka spotted him. "Over there – under the table," she cried.

127

Indeed, Joseph lay in a drunken stupor, a vacuous smile on his face, and Bartes had to hoist him over his shoulder and carry him. The Major led them down the fire stairs they'd used earlier, and out into the courtyard. The bodies and other detritus had been removed, and the pools of gore sprinkled with sawdust. Indeed, the clean-up operation had been so efficient that Iain and Anoushka didn't notice anything until Bartes pointed things out as their helicopter rose into the air.

The same vehicle that brought them to the opera was used to take them back to the dacha. It was a heavily armoured gunship, and they were accompanied by several troops in full battledress. When Bartes gave a look of envy at their advanced combat rifles, Tanya scowled at him, sighed theatrically, and muttered, "Boys and their toys…"

They landed on the beach by the dacha. Major Valentine alighted with them and they were met by RD, who took one look at Joseph and figuratively exploded. "What's happened to him?" he asked, his eyes flashing.

"Too much vodka," Anoushka replied.

"I'll give him 'too much vodka' in the morning," RD growled ominously.

"I'll put him to bed," Iain volunteered, rather uncharacteristically, and he took the boy and carried him to his room.

The rest of them assembled in the lounge. "Have you eaten, Goran?" Anoushka asked.

"Been too busy…" RD seemed a bit tongue-tied.

"Then it's a good thing I brought you a doggy-bag, isn't it?" She produced a large paper sack full of goodies, got a couple of plates from the galley, and laid out the food. "Now eat. We don't want you collapsing in the middle of a yacht race."

He grinned. "Thank you, Anoushka," he said, and began eating with obvious hunger.

Bartes looked at Anoushka. *She lifts the spirits of everyone around her,* he thought. *Perhaps she has a wild talent for psionic empathy. I'll have to ask Tanya to investigate when she has time. She certainly has an effect on RD that I wouldn't have predicted.*

"Comrades –" Major Valentine had waited until Iain had returned before addressing them. "I have made enquiries, and in tune with Comrade Boris's clever suggestion, you are to be ferried to a dacha at Lake Kuraken tomorrow evening. I'm sorry we can't move you earlier, but we need to make the appropriate preparations."

Bartes smiled wryly. He had a feeling that the preparations in question were more to keep them imprisoned than to keep them protected. He'd hoped that the unexpectedness of the change of location would catch the security forces on the hop, but there seemed little chance of that. *Ah, well,* he thought, *it was worth a try.*

"I'm afraid, however, that my superiors have made another 'suggestion': that you have lunch tomorrow at *The Tangled Comet* as if there is nothing wrong."

"Won't that be dangerous?" Anoushka asked.

"We'll have things wrapped up tightly. Nobody will be there but security personnel, the accredited media and a few selected citizens whose loyalty is without question. We will also evacuate the whole area – and all to show that it's 'Business As Usual'." He paused. "On the other hand, I have called in a few favours, and a heavy freight helicopter will pick you up, along with Comrade Goran's catamaran, in late afternoon. You will be flown directly to Lake Kuraken."

Bartes raised a sardonic eyebrow at Tanya and sent, :*Well?*:

She wrinkled her nose: :*Smugness doesn't become you. I still can't see why the Major is doing this.*:

Bartes shrugged. :*Perhaps he has his own agenda.*:

"Comrade Davidov will be joining you there," the Major added. "Now, I suggest you all get a good night's sleep."

Tanya's heart leapt. If John was to be there, they'd have a chance to break his conditioning and all escape together. "Shall we sleep out under the stars again?" she suggested.

"I wouldn't recommend it," the Major responded. "With all that's been going on, I think it'd be safer to stay inside." And with that he departed, but as they waved him off, Bartes noticed that the troops that had escorted them had been left to augment their bodyguard.

RD made everyone a nightcap, and as they sat around drinking it, with the radio as audio camouflage, Tanya told them about her new acquaintance.

"Who d'you thank she works for," RD asked.

"She recognised me, so she's probably a Mercy agent," Tanya replied. "She's an extremely powerful psionic – and she has that particular brand of self-confidence that normally characterises an Eranian Commander."

"At least it means we're no longer entirely on our own." Anoushka verbalised the relief they all felt. "What do we do about sleeping tonight, though? I know it's not likely to affect us now, but the idea of someone whispering lies in my ear gives me the creeps."

"Hmm…" Tanya said. "I've had an idea." She disappeared into the kitchen and was gone for some time. When she returned, she handed each of them two pads of cotton wool that felt slightly moist. She pushed two in her ears and the rest of them followed suit. Once they'd been inserted, all anyone could hear was their own breathing and heartbeat.

:*Clever,*: Bartes sent to her.

Sunset in Silvana

:I *rather thought so,*: was the slightly self-satisfied reply.

Chapter 15

Tanya woke in silence with someone shaking her. She opened her eyes and saw it was Anoushka, who seemed rather agitated. She was talking, but Tanya couldn't hear what she was saying.

"'Noushka? What – what is it?" Her voice sounded strange, and it took her a couple of seconds to remember that she was wearing earplugs and remove them.

"– it's Joseph. He's fighting with RD – Goran. Please – we need your help."

"All right – I'm coming." Tanya rose and hurried to the kitchen, blinking the sleep from her eyes as she did so, but the sight that greeted them almost made her doubt them. Bartes stood to one side of the kitchen holding Joseph from behind. He had the boy's arms pinned to his sides and had lifted his feet clear of the ground. Joseph's eyes were flashing and he was mouthing obscenities. He was flailing with both feet and hands, and in one of the latter he was holding a blood-stained kitchen knife. RD stood on the other side of the room, holding his left arm. His right hand was covered in gore and more was streaming down his forearm. As she watched, Joseph gave Bartes a vicious kick on his left shin with his heel.

"Turn on the taps, then help RD," she told Anoushka before turning to Joseph. "Right," she said to him quietly, calmly and deliberately. "The sensation you are beginning to feel is called apnoea. I am psionically closing your windpipe. You have two choices: drop the knife and cease struggling, or wait until you lose consciousness and it happens automatically." He gave one last heave before reluctantly complying with her instructions. "Good choice," she said as she released his trachea. "Now keep your voice down and tell me what all this is about."

"That bastard!" the boy said through gritted teeth. "When I think of the way he's treated me."

She was slightly taken aback. "I know he hasn't been the best of guardians, but you've never attacked him before."

"That's because I didn't know who I was. He made me a slave, when *he* should have been *my* servant, if anything."

The penny dropped. "You know?"

"Yes. I woke up this morning in silence and my mind was clear. So I went looking for revenge."

Tanya sighed. "And just what was that going to accomplish?"

The boy looked sullenly at her for some seconds. "Satisfaction…"

"And if your satisfaction results in us all being reprogrammed?"

"I didn't think of that…"

She snorted. "Of course you didn't. Look, do you want to go home or not?"

He looked at her incredulously. "What do you think, you idiot!"

"Do you want me to close your windpipe again? Permanently, perhaps?" Tanya clenched her teeth.

"No…" He resumed his previous sour demeanour.

"Then keep a civil tongue in your head. Now, let's examine the possibilities – question one: do we want to escape? Quiet, that was a rhetorical question – of course we do. Question two: how do we keep our captors from reprogramming us? Answer: we give them no reason to suspect we've broken their conditioning. Now, if – and I repeat if – you haven't completely screwed up our chances with this ridiculous display, we'll have to continue our charade."

"Does that mean I have to slave for *him*?" There was an audible sneer in the boy's tone.

"At least enough to allay any suspicions the security men might have." She turned to RD. While she and Joseph had been talking, Anoushka had started dressing the gash on his arm and bandaging it. "And as for you, Comrade, you'd better be careful. I know this one's a brat, but his father is one of the Governor's top aides."

"I'll take any reprimand his dear daddy orders," RD replied with a scowl, "when we're safely home."

Tanya returned her gaze to the boy. "Let him down, Bartes. Listen, *child*, unless we can be certain we won't be overheard, we use the names our captors gave us *at all times*. Why did you think I asked Anoushka to turn on the taps? It covers up conversation. Now, since RD, Bartes, Iain and I are all experts in this sort of thing, you'll obey any instructions we give you instantly and without questioning – understand?"

"I suppose. Even Anna? She's just a secretary."

Tanya gritted her teeth again, and somehow stopped herself from hitting the boy. "She's worth a dozen of *you*, boy. True, this is all new to her, but so far she's coping remarkably well. If you want to survive to get home, I'd remember that we're your only ticket back. If you aggravate us too much, we could dispose of you and simply blame it on our captors if – when – we get home."

As Joseph stamped off to his room, his fists balled, RD's gaze fell to the floor and his brow furrowed. Catching Tanya's eye, he pointed silently to where a bottle of cooking oil had fallen and spilt during the fracas.

If he's expecting me to clear it up, he's got another think coming, she thought, but then she realised what he was trying to show her. There was an area of tiles about a metre square that the oil hadn't covered: it was apparently seeping down cracks on all four sides.

She raised an eyebrow at RD and nodded. The floor here wasn't solid. This could be an access hatch.

After breakfast, which was quiet and rather strained, Tanya decided to check the drug components she'd brought from the Medical Centre. Although one or two vials had been damaged in the previous day's crash, most had survived intact. It was her turn to wash up, and as she did so, she checked the kitchen thoroughly for surveillance devices, but found nothing more than the microphone and mini-cam she'd already noticed. She set up her equipment out of sight of the camera and started making up a number of doses of a basic combat drug.

She was part way through the synthesising process when there was a shout from outside. A group of locals had driven up in a lorry with some fresh vegetables for sale. She emerged, only to stop dead in her tracks: one of the "locals" was Maria, and some of the others looked familiar. As she passed Tanya a basket of cabbages, the latter asked her quietly, "How's your chin?"

The girl smiled ruefully. "A bit sore," she whispered, "But your friend's blow did no real harm."

"Good." Tanya grinned back. "Why are you here?"

"Well, we checked your blood, and you're right: you're not from this planet, or from the Dainworlds. Your colleague is from the Terran Union, but as for you, your blood is – different."

"What do you mean?" Tanya asked.

"They wouldn't tell me," she continued. "Anyway, Martje and the others were still suspicious, and they decided to take no risk and finish the job – they planned to do it this morning, despite your guards." Tanya looked around in sudden panic, but saw nothing untoward. "Don't worry. Something must have happened overnight – I don't know what – and this morning our leader told us we had to help you rather than kill you. So we've sent word to our people to halt all assassination attempts, and we've brought you a few weapons to help you escape. You'll find them in the bottom of the baskets."

Tanya breathed a sigh of relief. "Thank you. You're taking a bit of a risk." With a slight nod of the head she indicated the security guards, who were looking on suspiciously with their fingers on their triggers.

Maria shrugged. "Our friends are covering us from the trees – and anyway, something about what you said yesterday made me think you're in a lot more trouble than we are."

"Is there anything you can do to help us get away?"

"No – we have our own problems, and limited resources – and although we know you're not the traitors we thought, we still don't know who you really are."

"We're…"

"And we really don't want to know. So I'm afraid you're on your own. Good luck." Tanya thanked her as she paid her a suitable amount for the vegetables. With that, the girl and her companions drove away with a cheery wave and Tanya returned to the kitchen.

Once she completed her task, Tanya concealed the drug in her medical kit and found RD, who was tinkering with his boat. "Those villagers that came with vegetables this morning were members of one of the rebel groups," she told him, "the ones that nearly killed us up in the mountains. We've been able to persuade them that we aren't their enemies, and they've provided us with some weapons to aid our escape."

"That's very altruistic of them," he said suspiciously.

"Not really – any attempt we make to flee will draw attention away from their activities."

"I suppose that makes sense…"

"Anyway, the weapons are hidden in the baskets of vegetables we bought, but I'm not sure how we're going to transport them to Lake Kuraken. There's also Bartes' precious laser carbine. We might be able to hide some things among our baggage, but it would be better if we could cache everything on your boat, so they'll be there already if we try to escape across the lake."

"Hmm," he said. "Leave it to me. I'll need your help, Josef."

"Why?" The boy glared at him.

"There are some places we could hide the weapons which are unlikely to be searched. I can't reach them, but someone smaller, like you, can."

There was a short pause before Joseph replied. "All right," he muttered.

"You and the others pack your bags, and we'll stash them on the boat for the trip," RD told Tanya. "That'll help conceal the contraband."

They had just finished loading the boat when a helicopter gunship arrived to take them to the *Tangled Comet* for lunch. The flight was quiet and tense. Anoushka was looking worried, so Tanya swapped seats with Bartes so she could sit next to her. "Relax," She said in an undertone as she put her arm about her friend. "It'll be all right – you'll see."

"What if we're attacked again?"

"I don't think it's likely, but if we are, we'll manage somehow. Look, Anoushka, I stood up for you in front of young Joseph this morning. I said you were worth a dozen of him, and I meant it – please don't let me down."

Anoushka took a deep breath and squared her shoulders. "You're right," she said, "I can't afford to go to pieces. I know I'm not as prepared for situations like this as the rest of you, but at the very least I can't – I mustn't – be a liability." She gave Tanya a wan smile.

"Good girl." Tanya squeezed her friend's arm. "Just leave things to the professionals, and we should be all right. And if anything *does* happen, take cover until it's been dealt with."

When they landed at the *Comet*, their guards disembarked first and established a protective perimeter. Major Valentine had been as good as his word, and the place was crawling with security personnel. He greeted them at the door. "I've prepared a special table for you, my friends. Please follow me."

"Sorry, Major – I'll be needed in the kitchen. It *is* my restaurant, after all. Come along, Josef."

Joseph opened his mouth to complain, but Tanya's glare silenced him; he balled his fists and followed RD.

To Tanya's surprise and delight, Sophie and her tame general were sat at the next table. She was wearing a pure white cotton dress, simple and elegant, and looked radiant. "Comrade General, Comrade Mikova," Tanya greeted them, "Do you know Major Drovsorsky, our security liaison?"

"I do," the General said, "Good afternoon, Comrade Major."

"Sir." The Major saluted.

"No need for too much formality, Valentine, we're all friends here. Have you met Sophie Mikova, the ballerina?"

"I don't believe so…" Valentine's brow furrowed, then cleared as he took and kissed the lady's hand. She gave him a strange look in return, and smiled back.

"Sophie is staying with me at my dacha for the holiday."

"And these are my companions, Boris, Ivan and Anoushka," Tanya interjected.

"I'm so pleased to meet you, Comrades." Sophie's smile was dazzling.

Sunset in Silvana

They sat and made small talk as their orders were taken, and they ate their entrées and their main courses. After Tanya had finished her pluny en croute, she had an idea. "I'm just going to freshen up," she said, and raised an eyebrow in Sophie's direction.

"I'll join you," Sophie said, taking her hint.

Once they had their voices covered by the sound of running water, they began to confer. "How are things going?" Sophie asked.

"Well," Tanya began, but at that point one of the other diners, a reporter for *The Silvanan Times*, entered the rest room and interrupted them.

"Comrade Milanova, may I have a moment of your time?" she asked.

Tanya frowned. "Not now," she replied. "Can't you see I'm talking to a friend?"

"Very well, I'll try again later." The reporter didn't leave, however, but began a leisurely survey of her make-up, clearly hoping, as all of her profession do, to overhear something interesting.

:*Let's communicate psionically while we chat about innocuous things.*: Sophie sent.

Tanya looked round nervously. :*Aren't you frightened we'll be caught with all the 'sniffers' round?*:

:*Not really.*: Sophie seemed supremely confident. :*They can detect the use of psionics, but none of them are good enough to eavesdrop. I've finished with this persona, anyway – and I can handle anything* they *can do.*:

:*I guess. Well, if you're so positive…*:

:*I am.*:

:*We've all broken our conditioning to a large degree – although I now have a confusingly large number of different sets of memories vying for my attention – and we need to get off this planet. We believe that we are being impersonated back on Regni, and that whoever is doing it intends to cause some sort of catastrophe.*:

:*You could be right: I'm in regular contact with Regni, and I didn't even know you were here until I arrived a few days ago and if they thought you were missing, I'd have heard* something.:

:*And nothing's happened to the Governor?*:

:*Not that I'm aware of.*:

:*Then it may not be too late if we can escape. Can you do anything to help us?*:

:*I'd like to, but I've got my own mission here…*:

:*…to stop the war. I'm aware of that, but surely there's* something *you can do?*:

:*Let me think a minute.*:

:*While you're thinking, have you any idea why everybody is suddenly trying to kill us?*:

:*Yes. Have you ever seen a copy of* The Free Silvanan?:

:*That scurrilous rag? Once or twice.*:

:*Well, let me show you the front page of the latest issue.*: A picture formed in Tanya's mind: under a banner headline of **HEROES – OR VILLAINS?** there was a cartoon that displayed a perversion of the first day cover recently issued to commemorate Pregeor. It showed a group of dead and dying women and children under a mushroom cloud, and overlooking the carnage were unflattering distortions of the stamps representing Tanya and her fellow Heroes. These vile caricatures seemed to indicate their pleasure in the carnage illustrated below. Tanya's image, with its devil horns, vampiric teeth and salacious grin, was particularly horrible.

:*Why now, after all this time? I don't think we were even* there.:

:*You weren't – but the government has associated your names with the tragedy. Something happened at Pregeor – something pretty horrendous that I won't burden you with at the moment. The government gave orders that the city be destroyed in order to prevent it spreading further. They blamed Telphania, and the resistance believed them, and broke off relations with their allies across the border. Last week, though, someone leaked evidence of what really happened to the Telphanians, and they wasted no time in presenting this to the resistance in hope of re-establishing their alliance. That put you at the top of everyone's hit list – and the newspaper article gives anyone who lost friends or family at Pregeor a reason to hate – and perhaps try to kill – you.*:

:We have to get away before one of those assassination attempts succeeds. Have you thought of anything to help us escape?:

:If you could get to Telphania...:

:But the Telphanians think that we're Heroes of Pregeor. We'd end up being arrested, and put on trial. Even if we could persuade them that we're not who they think we are, I can't see them just letting us go...:

:I'm here with blessing of the Telphanian government, and I've already sent their people a message to inform them of your real identities, via my contacts in the Silvanan Free Army.:

:So you're the reason Maria and her friends didn't follow up on their threat to kill us. I thought it might be your doing.:

:Guilty as charged. They're useful allies. If you can get to Brogovel Shuttle Port, there may be a way off planet. Find a contact of mine called Dick Haraldson, who works for Merrywine Intoxicants and say, 'For Mercy's sake, I need a crate of Regnian Ale'. He should be able to help you.:

:Can you at least tell me who I really am? I'm feeling very disoriented.:

There was a pause. *:No – I think not. Your life is confusing enough as it is, and I think you're going to have to act quickly and decisively very soon. I don't want to make things harder for you. Just concentrate on being Tanya Miller for now. It'll come back to you in its own time. Trust your mind – it knows what's best* *for you. Now let's get back to your companions. Don't worry – I'll keep in contact...*:

:*But how?*:

Sophie gave a knowing smile. :*Never mind. If you* do *manage to escape, head east and I'll do what I can to help. If not, I'll come for you when my mission is completed. Oh, by the way, be wary of Valentine.*:

:*Why?*:

:*I've met him before, elsewhere. He's not what he seems.*:

:*I can tell he's psionic.*:

:*Yes, and he's no more a native of this planet than you and I are.*:

:*Is he the one that kidnapped us?*:

:*Possibly, but I don't think it was his idea.*:

Tanya frowned. :*I get the feeling he wants us to escape.*:

:*If he does, I doubt it's for your sake. No, he has some sort of agenda of his own – opposed to that of his mistress.*:

:*His mistress?*:

:*The one pulling his strings. She's the one responsible for your abduction. But I don't think she quite realises the determination of her puppet to have his own way.*:

:*So he might be on our side.*:

:*Possibly – for the moment – but I wouldn't trust him: things can change in an instant, and he wouldn't hesitate to sacrifice all of you, either for his own purposes, or because his mistress commands it. He might regret it, but he'll do it – just like you or I would.*:

:*Am I really like that?*:

Sophie gave a sad smile. :*'Fraid so – circumstances sometimes force people like us to make uncomfortable decisions. Now let's get back to your friends.*:

Sophie and Tanya made their way back to their seats, and as they began to eat their desserts, there was a commotion outside. A cocky-looking security lieutenant, accompanied by six subordinates, pushed his way into the room and announced in a loud voice: "I'm sorry to disturb your meal, Comrades, but we're searching for a dangerous off-world fugitive." His team spread around the room and started looking around intently, and Tanya felt a significant increase in background psionic energy. She guessed they'd detected Sophie and her 'conversation', and that things were about to get ugly.

Suddenly, the Lieutenant looked at Sophie and froze. He gasped, clutched his chest and fell as she 'signed her signature' on proceedings. His squad, all of whom had drawn their weapons, turned towards her and fired, but the bullets passed through the empty air where she no longer was. After a moment of stunned silence, everyone panicked at once.

More security troops arrived, both through the door and from the veranda. Tanya looked around for Sophie in the confusion, and caught sight of her across the room just as several poppies seemed to bloom on the white cotton of her dress. The red stains grew and merged as her eyes widened and her jaw dropped. She'd been knocked back against a partition and slumped slowly to the floor leaving a broad smear of blood behind her.

Chapter 16

When the security detail entered the restaurant, Bartes was on his way back from the lavatory. *Oh my God*, he thought, *we're really in the shit now. What can I do?*

It was clear, though, that there was nothing he needed to do: Sophie was giving an encore of her previous performance. Tanya had described her abilities, but the reality was more impressive still. *She's literally a heart-breaker*, thought Bartes, smiling sardonically at his own wit – *and... dear God, she used psionic blur to avoid those bullets. Where the hell has she gone? Did she manage to escape?* He looked around and noted that the security detachment had sealed the room.

Another volley rang out. A figure in a dress no longer white lurched against a partition and collapsed in a bloody heap.

Bartes' reflexes took over. He broke into a run, but before he could reach Sophie's body, a security guard dived in front of him. She was shorter than Bartes, and over her head, he could see the crumpled corpse. Sophie's corpse... *No. Something's not right*, he thought. *It looks like Sophie all right – but it doesn't feel like her.*

He cleared his mind and looked again. Now he saw the body of a woman in a security uniform – a woman who looked strangely like the one that was now standing in front of him. The latter winked at him, whispered, "Thank Tanya for teaching me that trick, would you?" and walked past him and out on to the veranda.

He returned to the table, where Tanya was comforting a near-hysterical Anoushka, and relayed the message to her in an undertone.

"Comrades, would you *please* remain in your seats while I ascertain what happened," Major Valentine said as he sat down next to Sophie's general, who was looking completely bewildered. "Just where did you meet that young lady, General?" he asked.

"At the ballet – just last week," the General told him.

"Did you see her perform?"

"N-no..."

"Then how did you know who she was?"

"She told me. A-and you could tell she was a ballerina, just by looking at her."

"And she's been staying with you? And meeting all your friends?"

"Yes..."

"Hmm... I think you'd better get yourself home now. I'll visit you later to discuss what she may have learned."

As the General got unsteadily to his feet and staggered off toward the cloakroom, the Major turned back to the others. "Comrades," he said, "it appears that the young lady who was accompanying the General was a spy."

Tanya gasped and put her fingertips to her lips. "Was she here after us?" she asked.

"I don't think so. I think she was gathering information from the General and his acquaintances for the Telphanians. She was a very talented psionic, so the General shouldn't be blamed – although no doubt he will be. I wish we could have captured her quietly for interrogation, but my over-zealous colleagues chose to shoot her instead. They will be severely reprimanded, not just for the loss of a valuable prisoner, but also for alarming you, our guests. In the meantime, let me assure you that you were in no danger, as she was unarmed. Now, please excuse me while I check on my other guests."

As soon as he was out of earshot, Tanya muttered, "Who needs weapons with psionics like that?" She looked pointedly in Bartes' direction.

"Well-armed is well prepared," he replied.

She shook her head. "You shouldn't rely on artificial aids. You ought to practise with your mind more – let your brain take the strain."

Bartes laughed briefly, but no one else seemed to see the joke; their faces showed a mixture of puzzlement and distress. None of them could face much more to eat, but they drank a fair bit to steady their nerves.

Major Valentine circled the room, talking with the guests at all the other tables, giving everyone his personal reassurances, and no doubt subtly rearranging their memories. He came and sat with Bartes and his friends. "A terrible business," he began. "I know we're all under a great deal of stress, but Lieutenant Kaspertin should not have acted like that." He shook his head and sighed. "For once, though, my friends, it appears you were not the targets. That fake ballerina was obviously after the general. May I ask what you and she talked about in the Ladies' Room, Comrade Talia?"

Tanya's brow furrowed. "Nothing untoward, Major. Clothes, make-up – and one or two more personal feminine matters that I'd be happy to reveal to one of your female officers." She blushed artistically.

"I don't think that'll be necessary," the Major replied, his own face reddening slightly. "Now, when you've finished your meal, I suggest that I escort you back to the dacha."

"I don't think any of us wants anything more to eat," Bartes replied.

The Major looked around at the half-eaten desserts, and at everyone's ashen faces, and nodded. "I understand. Just wait here while I check on your transport."

As they boarded the helicopter for the flight back to the dacha, RD and Joseph joined them.

"What happened?" RD asked, looking with concern at Anoushka's tear-stained face. "We heard a commotion and some shots, but the Major's guards blocked the door and wouldn't let us out.

"There was another incident, Comrade," the Major explained as they took off, "but none of your friends were hurt. For once they appear to be innocent bystanders, to an attempt to capture a Telphanian spy who had infiltrated our gathering. Unfortunately, there was a brief fire-fight, and the spy was killed. Now, I suggest you put today's events out of your minds and look forward to the trip to Lake Kuraken. By the way, my superiors think that it is time you took an extended vacation."

"Now?" Bartes asked.

"Yes – at least until we're sure it's safe for you to go back to work. The incompetence of some of my men has put you in danger even when they're trying to keep you safe – how you'd fare unprotected I dread to think."

"But –" Tanya interjected.

"The Medical Centre can function without you for a week or two, Comrade Talia, and I know Boris and Ivan were bored with their work at the moment. And as for Comrades Goran and Josef, we'll put in a Temporary Manager at *The Tangled Comet*, and I'll arrange for the boy's tutor to come to him rather than the other way round."

"That reminds me: how badly damaged was the *Comet*?" RD asked.

"Don't worry," the Major replied. "My men will clean up and make repairs. Everything will be as it was before when you return from your 'vacation'. Oh, and I've ensured that the occurrence will go unreported so that your business won't suffer."

"Oh, I wouldn't be too concerned about that." RD's offhand manner surprised them. "Something like that would actually be good for business. It attracts the ghouls – and their money is as good as anyone else's."

Some minutes later, they landed by the dacha and waved goodbye to the Major. As soon as he departed, RD looked at Anoushka and his eyes softened. He took her by the hand, and led her inside and over to the sofa.

"Can I get you anything?" he asked.

"A-a drink?" she murmured dazedly.

"Coffee?"

Her eyes focussed and she shook her head emphatically. "No – vodka – lots of it. Enough so I can forget the look on that poor girl's face. If I ever c-can." She buried her head in her hands and her shoulders heaved as she sobbed uncontrollably. Tanya sat down next to her and held her close.

Iain and Bartes accompanied RD to the kitchen and the latter filled large glasses of vodka for them all. "What really happened?" he asked them.

"Tanya's friend from last night, Sophie the Psionic Ballerina, turned up with her tame security general in tow. Something alerted the security forces and they tried to arrest her," Iain said.

"They were no match for her," Bartes added. "She pulled the heart out of one of them and outran a hail of bullets. She swapped appearances with another officer – who was shot down by her own colleagues – and made her escape psionically disguised. I encountered her on her way out, and she even claimed that our Tanya had taught her the trick."

RD grunted. "I knew that woman was a witch."

Bartes gritted his teeth. "Whoever or whatever she is, she's one of us. It's all of us or none. We'll have to work together to have a ghost of a chance. You'll have to get over your prejudice."

RD's eyes flashed, but he swallowed his reply. He paused. "And what did *that woman* learn from her fellow sorceress?"

"She and Tanya went to the Ladies' Room together, but I haven't yet had a chance to talk to her about it."

"Well, let's go and ask her."

When they re-entered the living room with the tray of drinks, Iain switched on the radio and found a channel playing a patriotic march. "Was your friend Sophie any help?" Bartes asked Tanya quietly.

"Well, from what she told me, we've been set up: we were never at Pregeor, for a start. And the Zelynan government was actually responsible for what happened, so – as their figureheads – we're shouldering the blame."

"That makes sense," Bartes said. "Can she do anything to help us escape?"

Tanya shook her head. "Not really. She's a Mercy operative with her own mission: to avert war between Zelyna and Telphania – and as such, she's got her work cut out, without much time or effort to spare in our cause. She did say she'd got word to the Telphanians that we're not their enemies, and she gave me the name of someone at the Shuttle Port in Brogovel, the Telphanian capital, who might be able to get us off this dirt-ball."

"Then, by all means, let's get to Brogovel as quickly as possible," RD said.

Tanya nodded. "There's only one other way off this planet that I'm aware of – the Skyport. If we escape, our captors will assume we'll head there because we daren't go to Telphania."

"But what about John?" Anoushka asked.

"The Major told us that John would be joining us at the Lake. If we can break his conditioning there, we'll take him with us, but if not – well, the mission comes first. Sophie said to head east, and that she'd help as much as she could."

"Right, Telphania it is," RD said. "But, if I remember correctly, it's a long way from the Lake to the Telphanian border. We'll never make it on foot."

"We'll need transportation," Bartes mused. "If we can cross the lake in the *Reaper's Darling*, perhaps we can steal something. But I think we're getting ahead of ourselves. We've still got to get free from our 'bodyguards'."

"But at least we've got a plan now," Tanya said. "We can't do much more till we arrive at the Lake and see how the land lies."

"Did you pick up anything more from Sophie?" Bartes asked Tanya.

She looked pensive. "I don't *think* so – there was a horrible cartoon of us in *The Free Silvanan…*"

Iain shrugged. "So what else is new?"

Tanya's brows knit in thought. "There *was* one other thing: she said that, as far as she was aware, nobody back on Regni knew we were missing – but she thought nothing untoward had yet happened."

"That's a relief, but our doppelgängers must be intending some sort of mischief," Iain pointed out.

"But I still don't understand why whoever kidnapped us is keeping us alive," Bartes said.

"Probably so that we can shoulder the blame for whatever they're planning," RD said. "It's just one more reason why it's vital that we escape as soon as we can."

Anoushka had been drinking the vodka that RD had provided and her misery gradually subsided. Soon she was only producing the occasional sniffle, and she laid her drowsy head on Tanya's lap. After a while, she seemed to have fallen asleep and Tanya beckoned RD over. "I assume that you've finished your own preparations for the trip?" she asked *sotto voce*.

"Both the boat and I are ready to go," he replied quietly. "I've stored the weapons safely."

"Good." She lifted Anoushka's head and shoulders gently and slid from under them. "Sit here – I've got to go and pack for the two of us."

"But –" He seemed nonplussed.

"Don't worry – she shouldn't wake. Just stroke her hair every so often."

He sat and did what he'd been asked to do. He seemed rather tentative, and the confused look on his face told Tanya that, though he didn't really feel comfortable about what he was doing, in an odd way he was really enjoying it.

"I didn't realise the old man had a soft spot for Blondie," Iain muttered as Tanya passed him on the way to the bedrooms.

"Neither did I – but I wouldn't tease him about it – at least not until we've escaped. He's a bit touchy, and I wouldn't want to have to transport your unconscious body."

He guffawed. "Don't worry, I'll keep it to myself – for now."

Chapter 17

When their transport arrived, they were surprised to find that Peter was on board. "What happened to you?" Joseph asked him, as he sat down beside him.

"I don't know," the boy replied. "I can't remember anything between eating and drinking with you at the Opera House and waking up with a terrible headache at Security Headquarters."

"Nothing at all?"

"Nothing. They told me that I'd been found this morning, wandering the streets in a daze."

The Major confirmed the boy's story. "He must have escaped his kidnappers somehow," he said, "or they may have got the wrong person – perhaps they were after Josef and freed Peter when they realised their mistake." Given what Bartes and Tanya had seen, neither explanation held water – the boy had gone willingly. What mystified them now was why he was playing along with the Major's tale.

They arrived at the lakeside as dusk was beginning to fall. The helicopter lowered the boat into the water and landed beside it. Leaving RD to supervise as his precious catamaran was unchained and tied up to the jetty, the rest of them went inside their new dacha which, apart from extra heating and insulation against the cold, appeared to follow the same pattern as the one at Plune.

Tanya drew Joseph aside as they entered. "Could you keep Peter occupied as much as possible?" she asked him quietly. "We'll need to make plans, and I don't trust him."

"But I want to help!"

"Shh! You'll help most by keeping him out of our hair. Don't worry, you'll get plenty of excitement when we escape."

"Okay... but just 'cause *you* asked me," he muttered.

"Look, you'll have to get over your resentment soon," Tanya said. "The only way we'll get out of this predicament is to put aside our differences and work together - *all* of us." He shrugged resentfully and went off to distract Peter.

When they'd unpacked, they gathered in the lounge – apart from the two youngsters, who were playing chess in their room. They'd hoped the Major might have left them by now, but he seemed to want to help them settle in, so they sat and made small-talk. It was typical of Iain that he was the first to think of his stomach. "Whose turn is it to cook?" he asked, looking pointedly at Tanya.

There was a brief silence before Tanya said, "Well, *I* don't feel like making anything tonight."

"There's a superb restaurant by the lakeside," the Major told them. "I could get us reservations."

"Would it be safe?" Anoushka asked.

"I can't think that our enemies will be prepared to cause us any trouble up here yet," he replied. "Anyway, I'll make sure there's a heavy security presence. I'll go and make arrangements now."

Iain turned on the radio once he'd left. "Do you reckon that this would be an opportunity to escape?" he asked.

"I doubt it," RD replied. "We'd better keep our eyes open in case there's a chance, but we're woefully unprepared as yet. I think we need to know a lot more about the lay of the land before we make our move."

The Major returned. "Our tables will be ready in an hour," he told them.

"Let's have a coffee before we go," RD suggested. "I'll make it, if Comrade Talia will give me a hand," he added, and disappeared in the direction of the kitchen, with Tanya following. When they got there, he filled the kettle and, as he was transferring it to the cooker, he unaccountably dropped it. He cursed, and gave Tanya an exasperated look. "Well, don't just stand there," he snapped. "Help me mop up."

Tanya found some cloths and they started drying the floor. When they'd cleared up most of the water, RD gave her a knowing smile. With a slight inclination of his head, he indicated a similar drainage pattern in the floor to the one they'd seen at Plune, which showed that there was a trapdoor in exactly the same location as before – the two dachas *were* practically identical.

They sat making further small talk until the transport arrived – in the form of an Armoured Personnel Carrier. "This vehicle is not exactly subtle," Iain observed as they skirted the lake.

"But it *is* pretty safe," the Major replied.

"Perhaps – but doesn't it paint a big target on us?" Tanya said.

The Major shrugged. "It should deter most people, and we have patrols out searching for rebels and Telphanian infiltrators – and anyway, once we're at the restaurant, there will be some of my men in and around the building."

"For what they've been worth," Iain muttered.

"That's rather unfair, Comrade," the Major said, a degree of resentment in his voice. "The situation with Telphania has stretched my people very thin, and you're not the only ones under threat, you know."

Iain grunted dismissively but took his criticisms no further, as their vehicle had drawn up at the restaurant. They were greeted by the maître d', and shown to their table. The Major had ensured that they were in a corner far from the windows. Once he'd circulated around the room and shared subtle but significant glances with several of the other diners, he went outside, no doubt to check on the perimeter guards.

The menu was extensive – and expensive, though as the Republic would be paying, they didn't stint themselves. Among the items that made Tanya salivate was calamari – one of her favourite dishes – in an oyster sauce. Significantly, they all ordered non-alcoholic drinks – apart from Iain, who wanted vodka, and Joseph, whose request for beer was vetoed by his 'guardian'.

As the evening wore on, they gradually relaxed. Iain was availing himself of copious amounts of vodka, and Bartes became a bit concerned by his increasing inebriation. "Haven't you had enough, Comrade?" he asked the younger man.

He looked at Bartes and blinked. "You can never, *never* have enough vodka, Bar – Boris," he said owlishly. "Well *I* can't. Or pretty women for that matter." And he openly ogled the rather attractive girl at the next table, who was sitting on her own.

"Really, Ivan –" Bartes began, when his attention was distracted by an elderly man sitting nearby, who rose rather awkwardly to his feet, hobbled to the small dais at the end of the room opposite the bar, and rapped his walking stick hard on the floor. "Comrades," he began. "I would like to propose a toast to the Comrade President, whose birthday, I need hardly remind you, is tomorrow. I am old enough to remember the dark times before the revolution. When I was a mere lad..."

"Several hundred years ago," muttered Iain *sotto voce*.

"...my father worked long hours for a pittance. We had barely enough to live on, and we went to bed hungry every night..." He went on to elaborate – at length – on conditions long gone. "But then," he continued, "we rose against our oppressors, Comrades. None of you here were old enough to fight as I did. I was at the forefront when we stormed the parliament building."

"Must have been where he got his brain addled," Iain said a little less quietly.

"But I am unimportant."

"True." Iain giggled.

The elderly man gave him a glare before continuing: "The Comrade President was there that day, despite his youth, and fought beside his father, who became his predecessor in that onerous post." He began to outline the career of the Great Man in excruciating detail, from the period when he'd taken over from his ailing predecessor. He extolled their leader's magnanimity as he led the Republic in the liberation of Silvana from Telphanian oppression, and his decisive and humanitarian reaction to the tragedy at Pregeor perpetrated by those envious of his benevolent touch.

Most of the Heroes bore this stoically, but Iain yawned ostentatiously before leaning over towards the girl at the next table. "If I said you have a beautiful body, would you hold it against me?" he asked her with a leer. She moved her chair further away from him, but he didn't take the hint. "That's a gorgeous dress," he continued, "tight in all the right places…"

The elderly man had moved on to the benefits of the enlightened rule of the Comrade President. "Unlike the poor people of Telphania, we have full employment…"

"If you like being told what to do," Iain said to the girl.

"…good food…"

Iain grimaced. "If you don't taste it."

"…cheap and plentiful public transport…"

"But nothing worth visiting." Iain tried unsuccessfully to raise an eyebrow.

Tanya and Bartes looked at each other in exasperation. "Can't you stop him somehow?" Bartes whispered.

Tanya nodded. She concentrated for a second or two and their inebriated companion slowly slumped in his chair.

"What's wrong with Ivan?" Anoushka asked.

"Too much vodka," Tanya replied as she made the unconscious man comfortable, folding his arms under his head. He gave a loud snore and muttered something unintelligible under his breath. From the look that Tanya gave Bartes, he guessed that she had given nature a hand.

The elderly comrade's face had cleared when Iain lost consciousness, and he continued his toast. He seemed to take ages to wind up, but it could only have been a few minutes. He drew to a close with, "Comrades, I give you – the Comrade President."

Those still conscious raised their glasses and dutifully intoned, "The Comrade President," and drank.

The girl at the next table got up and walked off toward the telephone. Bartes felt that Iain had said rather too much to her, so he left his seat and intercepted her. "Please ignore my drunken friend," he said. "He tends to say stupid things when he's had too much vodka. Here, let me buy you a drink."

She ignored his overtures and walked past him, so he put his hand on her arm. "Let me go," she said, "or I'll charge you with interfering with me in pursuit of my duty. I am a security sergeant, and I have a report to make to my superior."

"Isn't Major Drovsorsky your superior?"

"I'm a personal aide to Captain Reynard, and she sent me here to keep an eye on you Heroes – and on the Major."

Bartes had half-expected something like this, so he drew in his mental strength and tried to calm her telepathically. His facility with his newly rediscovered psionics was not as good as Tanya's, however, and his target's shielding was very effective. She turned to him, her eyes flashing, and he'd braced himself for a painful riposte when he heard Major Valentine's voice behind him. "What seems to be the matter, Sergeant?" he asked.

"I have a report to make, Major," she asserted, though there was a slight tremor in her voice.

"Surely nothing happened of any importance."

She hesitated, before saying, with some reluctance, "No, nothing happened of any importance." Her face went blank for a couple of seconds, and then she smiled at Bartes. "I'm sorry, Comrade Hero," she said, "What were we talking about?"

"I was about to offer to buy you a drink as a way of apologising for the boorish behaviour of my drunken friend."

"I'd like that, Comrade," she said with a smile. He guided her to the bar and bought her a large vodka.

Chapter 18

Having used her psionics to slow the blood flow to Iain's brain just enough to induce unconsciousness, Tanya was still hungry, despite the substantial meal she had just eaten. She beckoned the waiter over.

"Could I have another portion of brandy pudding, please?" she asked him.

"Think of your figure, Comrade Talia," Major Valentine said archly. "We can't have Heroes of the Republic becoming overweight."

"Oh dear," she said in mock concern. "Do you think I look obese?" She smoothed her dress down over her waist and wiggled her hips.

"Well, no –"

"And I *am* still a little empty. I'll just do a bit more exercise tomorrow, that's all."

"Well, I'd like something more to eat as well," he said. "And I'll have some brandy pudding too, please, waiter."

"Very well, sir."

"But if we're going to gorge ourselves, Comrade, we ought to do some light exercise now to offset the effect of the food. Do you feel up to a little gentle dancing?" A small band had replaced the elderly comrade who had proposed the toast, and had begun playing dance tunes.

"I'd like that very much." She stood up and took his hand.

For such a big man, the Major was light on his feet, and moved with precision and elegance. When the music stopped, as he led Tanya back towards their table, she said, "You dance exquisitely."

"Thank you," he replied. "And so do you." She shook her head deprecatingly. "But now, before we rejoin the others, I have a request for you."

"Oh?"

"For Mercy's sake, please try to keep control of your companions. I don't want to live through this another time. And keeping people from noticing all your *faux pas* is giving me a headache."

He knows, Tanya thought, and in her confusion, nearly tripped over her own feet as the Major helped her to her chair. Leaving her to her perplexity, he addressed RD: "So, Comrade, I gather that you intend to race your catamaran while you're here?"

"Hopefully – if it's safe," RD replied.

"I'll do my best to make sure it is."

"Peter and I want to watch the hovercart races," Joseph added.

"I'll try to find you a secure vantage point," the Major said.

"If it's that secure, we won't be able to see much."

"Don't worry – I'll get you some binoculars if necessary." Bartes and Tanya exchanged speculative glances – that could prove useful.

She pondered the Major's words: did they mean that he was on their side? Or were they a trap, intended to get her to give herself away? She wasn't in the mood to take any more risks, though, so she kept off the topic as the evening ended and they set of for their new residence.

"That's odd," Bartes said as they approached the dacha along the lakeside road.

"What is?" RD asked.

Tanya saw what he meant. "There are lights on in the dacha, and I can hear music. I'm positive we switched everything off. Could it be your men, Major?"

"No, they've explicit instructions not to invade your privacy," he replied. "I think it's another guest." He was quite correct: when they entered the dacha, lounging on a sofa, right leg hooked over its arm and a large vodka in his hand, was John D'Arcy.

"John!" Anoushka cried and, unaware of her blunder, ran over to him.

He drew himself to his feet and put his arms around her in an affectionate embrace. "Hello, Anna, everyone – it's good to see you," he said as the others joined their enthusiastic greetings to Anoushka's – apart from Iain, that is – he nodded vaguely at John, slumped into a chair and promptly fell asleep.

"Welcome to Lake Kuraken, Comrade Davidov," the Major said. "I'm afraid you missed a superb meal. I'll leave your companions to bring you up to date. I have to get back to Restavic City to make my report, but rest assured I'll check that your guards are all in place and fully alert before I depart. I'll be back in the morning."

They bade him farewell, but once he'd left, Tanya turned to Joseph. "You and Peter had better go to bed, Josef," she said.

"But –" Joseph began rather resentfully.

She was in no mood for an argument. "Remember what I said earlier," she reminded him. "Anyway, you've had enough excitement for one day."

"Very well," he said grudgingly, and stamped away with Peter in his train.

She turned to the newcomer and said, "It *is* good to see you, Johan. We haven't seen you for ages."

"Don't you mean John?" he whispered in her ear. "After all, it's what Anna called me, didn't she?"

"So you know who you are."

"Yes," he said aloud. "It's about time you lot woke up – again. And anyway, you saw me a couple of days ago."

"What do you mean?" Tanya looked perplexed, but then her face cleared. "It was you in that jet, wasn't it – the one that saved us from the mortar attack."

"Guilty as charged – though RD seemed to be doing a good job of keeping you alive."

"It was only a matter of time… If you hadn't come along…" RD grasped John's forearm. "Thank you."

The two girls threw their arms around John and held him tight. "Whoa!" he said. "Don't smother me."

"I *knew* I'd seen that gesture before," Tanya said. "It was our team's 'All clear' signal, wasn't it?"

"Wait a minute," RD whispered. "We can't talk about this here – the room must be bugged."

"It is," John said, "but I moved the radio so it's on top of the microphone. Whoever's listening has heard nothing from this room but government-sponsored music and propaganda since I got here. And there's only one mini-cam in here, over in the top left corner as you enter the room, so as long as we're careful we can prevent anyone watching from reading our lips."

"Clever", Tanya said. "When did you regain your memory?"

"A long time back. Do you remember what happened the last time we tried to escape?"

"No," Bartes said. "I don't think any of us realised we *had*."

"I did," Tanya said, "or rather I've been told we had, indirectly."

"What do you mean?" Bartes asked.

"I didn't want to say anything while we could be overheard," she said, "but as the Major and I finished dancing together, back at the restaurant, he said something like, 'For Mercy's sake, please try to keep control of your friends. I don't want to live through this again.' He also said that keeping people from noticing our mistakes was giving him a headache."

"Do you think that his use of the word 'Mercy' was significant?" Bartes asked.

"From the way he said it, I'm positive. And intimating that we tried to escape before was a quite deliberate move on his part. I was just scared it was a trap."

Bartes shook his head slowly. "No. Given who he is, he could have had us all brainwashed on the slightest pretext. And now I think about it, it's probable that he's covered up our blunders on more than one occasion – such as Anoushka's little mistake when we met John tonight."

"What mistake?" Anoushka looked at him in surprise.

"You called him by his real name when we're supposed to think he's Johan Davidov,"

"Oh!" She put her fingers to her lips in dismay. "I'm so sorry."

"Don't worry. Just be a bit more careful in future – the Major may not be able to ignore it next time. You know, the more I think about it, the more I become convinced that he wants us to escape."

"I agree with you," John said. "They couldn't prove that I was part of our last escape attempt, but I'm pretty sure that the Major knew I was involved, and prevented them from re-programming me."

"What actually happened?" Bartes asked.

"Well, to cut a long story short, we'd planned for you to take the place of a family of tourists on a spaceliner that was about to leave the system. I was waiting in the Skyport to shuttle you up to the ship, but when the alarms went off, I realised that the game was up. Fortunately, I managed to persuade Major Valentine that my presence was a coincidence – though Captain Reynard was *very* suspicious.

"You were captured, interrogated and reprogrammed, though I was told a cover story: that you'd been on a visit to the 'port when there'd been an incident which had traumatised you all, bringing back your memories of Pregeor. They even arranged a suitable accident. The next time we met, you'd forgotten who you really are again."

"Why didn't they reprogram you, too?" RD asked.

"I was certain that they would, but you must have managed to keep my involvement secret. As it was, I was called in later for a 'check-up', and the doctors recommended some 'treatment', but Major Valentine vetoed it, saying that I was too vital to the operation of the Skyport to spare the time. Now you must bring me up to speed on all that's happened to you."

They brought John up to date with their own adventures, concluding with the incident at the restaurant. When they mentioned how the Major had dealt with Reynard's agent, John said, "That just backs up Tanya's conclusion that he wants us to escape."

"Well, from what he said about our 'protection', I don't think escape is an option yet," RD said. "Let's see if there's any information we can use in here." He picked up the folder provided by the Bureau of Tourism and shared out its contents.

"Dammit," Bartes said eventually. "There are no maps or guides to the area among all this bumf – nothing that looks at all helpful. I don't think we'll get any further tonight – we ought to get some sleep."

"I don't want to go to bed," Anoushka said. "I feel safer when we're all together."

"Couldn't we sleep in here?" Tanya said. "Iain's already well away, and we could make things reasonably comfortable."

"All right," RD said. "We'll do it for Anoushka's sake – the Major couldn't take exception to that. But I think it would be a good idea if some of us just kept watch – you never know what we might learn."

"You and Bartes are on the first watch," RD said quietly to Tanya as they were making themselves comfortable. "Wake John and me in a couple of hours."

Tanya settled down opposite Bartes and relaxed. It wasn't hard to pretend to be asleep – it was more difficult not doing it for real. In fact, Tanya might have already dozed off when she was roused by a scraping sound out from the direction of the kitchen. It was followed by a crash and a yelp, and a muffled voice that she didn't recognise said: "What the Hell is this ice doing on the ladder? I think I broke my ankle!"

She opened her eyes and looked at Bartes – he, too, was aware of the kerfuffle. She raised an eyebrow slightly. She didn't dare communicate telepathically in case one of their guards was a 'sniffer', but he understood her meaning, and shook his head slightly to indicate caution. They waited for what seemed to be an eternity while they listened to a distant discussion. They couldn't make out any words, but it seemed pretty agitated. It finished, and after a long silence they heard the muffled sound of an engine starting somewhere along the road to the north. It grew louder before passing outside the dacha and disappearing in the direction of the town.

It seemed that they might have an opportunity to check out "below stairs", so Tanya reached out carefully with her mind, ready to draw back if necessary. She detected the thoughts of only one person below, and his beta wave activity was at a low ebb, as if he were half asleep. She waited until he lost consciousness, before raising her eyebrow again to Bartes. She felt him reach out himself to check her findings, and they were clearly confirmed, for this time he nodded his head.

They got to their feet as silently as they could and made their way towards the kitchen. As quiet as they were, they woke Joseph as they passed his room. "Where are you going?" he muttered sleepily. Tanya put her finger to her lips and beckoned for him to follow.

When they convened in the kitchen, he'd shaken off his drowsiness and when they told him what had happened, he was keen to be involved. "I'll follow your orders to the letter, and I'll be as quiet as a silenced pistol," he assured them.

"All right, but first, go and rouse John – quietly! – and tell him what we're doing."

"Why?"

"So no-one will raise the alarm accidentally if they wake and find us missing. Anyway, Bartes and I are trained for this sort of situation, so we should go first and check what's down below. And try and keep out of sight of the camera in the living room as much as possible. It's in the top left corner as you enter."

He frowned, then shrugged. "OK – as long as I can join you down there afterwards."

"Very well – but be careful. From what we've heard, there's ice on the ladder, and we don't want you to slip and break something – or alert our jailers."

"Why let him get involved?" Bartes said after the boy departed.

"It's always better to keep loose cannons under supervision," Tanya said.

They raised the trapdoor and carefully climbed down the iron ladder. It was very cold below, and RD's earlier spillage had frozen on the rungs, making the descent really treacherous. They found themselves at one end of a short corridor illuminated by emergency lighting and lined with cables and rubber pipes. The pipes were attached to large gas cylinders at one end, and had valves to distribute the gas to each and every room in the dacha above. There were three cylinders: one green, one blue and one black with a skull and crossbones on it.

Slithering quietly through the door at the other end of the corridor, they found themselves in a small control room. There was a supply cupboard with coffee-making facilities to their left, and a table with four chairs and the remains of an interrupted three-handed card game in the middle of the room. On the right-hand wall was a small bank of monitors. In front of them, his feet up on the console and his cap over his eyes, was the slumbering form of a young security private.

A brief inspection told them that the monitors could show cameras in all the rooms upstairs, including – to Tanya's embarrassment – the inside of the shower. Others were trained on the area immediately outside the dacha, and confirmed that they were both well-protected and completely surrounded. One of the monitors showed John in the kitchen making coffee, and on another they could see Joseph waking the others in the living room, so Tanya switched them to other feeds to delay discovery if their watchdog woke.

There was another door in the opposite wall of the control room, and they made their way through it and along the rock tunnel on its other side. They reached an opening and found themselves in a rocky cave. From an old sign on the wall, this was normally a storage depot for the crews that looked after the roads and mountain trails of the area, and it contained two maintenance vehicles, several trailers and a variety of equipment. There was a set of recent tyre tracks that looked like those of a jeep, and the camouflage net intended to conceal the entrance had been pushed aside.

"Do you think they put in all this surveillance here – and at Plune – just for us?" Tanya asked Bartes.

He shook his head. "No. This is a paranoid society. They'll want to keep tabs on lots of people. I'm sure there are plenty of other places that are bugged – including our own apartment block."

Tanya shivered. "The thought of it makes my skin crawl... But wouldn't the maintenance crews that use this place know about the entrance to the dacha?"

"Perhaps," he replied. "But the entrance to the tunnel is very well concealed, and it would be kept locked. Even if they noticed something odd, they'd know better than to investigate."

She paused and looked around. "Could we escape in one of those?" she asked, indicating the vehicles.

"Hmm…" he considered, "that one's rather large and ponderous." Indeed, it was over forty foot long from the edge of the large front scoop to the cable roll at the back, and had a crane mounted on top. "The other one might do, though." They looked it over; it was a large green All-Terrain Vehicle built for off-road travel, with seating for six and a cargo space at the back. "Let's go back, talk to the others, and see what they think."

As they made their way back towards the guard-room, Tanya reached out with her mind to check that its occupant was still asleep.

Damn, she thought. *He's awake. OK, he hasn't noticed anything yet, but it's only a matter of time. :Bartes – it's not safe. He's conscious, and if he raises the alarm, we've had it.:*

:We'll have to kill him.:

She hesitated. *:Not unless we have to. Once we do that, there's no going back. Let me try something.:* She sat down with her back to the wall, let her mind relax and gradually synchronised her brainwaves with those of the young private. Once they were attuned, she began to impose her own rhythm on his, moving him from beta dominance to alpha, then after a pause to delta. It had taken a while, but it had worked. "He's asleep now, and he should stay that way."

"I can tell," Bartes replied. "He just snored. Where did you learn to do that?" She shrugged. "Well, you'll have to teach me how to do it someday."

They crossed the room and were met on the other side of the opposite door by a wild-eyed Joseph. "What happened to you?" Tanya whispered.

"I was on my way to join you, but as I opened this door, there was a bleep and the man in there woke up. I closed the door to a crack so I could just see and hear what was going on."

"What did you find out," Bartes asked.

"I overheard a conversation between the private in there and Captain Reynard. Apparently, she's worried that we're shaking off our conditioning, so she's sending a task force to take us into custody and recondition us."

"What about Major Valentine?" Tanya asked. "Surely he wouldn't let her do that."

"He's probably off duty," Bartes said, "so she's taken the opportunity to go over his head."

"Any idea when they'll be here?" Tanya asked the boy.

"Before morning. I think she wants to get it done before the Major can veto it."

"Damn!" Bartes interjected. "This was bound to happen, sooner or later, but at least now we might have a way out."

"What do you mean?" the boy asked.

"I'll tell you when we get upstairs."

"I'll stay here, just in case my 'patient' shows any signs of waking," Tanya said.

"Good idea," Bartes replied. "We'll be as quick as we can."

Chapter 19

Leaving Tanya to use her talent to keep the private asleep, Bartes and Joseph made their way upstairs. While they'd been investigating, John had made coffee for RD, Anoushka and Iain, and was forcing the latter's down his throat. He poured Bartes a cup while Bartes briefed the rest of them as to what he and Tanya had found below, and what Joseph had overheard.

"There's no way we can risk being reconditioned," RD said. "And I don't think we'll get a better opportunity to escape than this."

"I just wish there was some way we could retrieve our weapons from the boat," Bartes said wistfully. "I'd hate to leave that laser carbine behind – especially after going to such trouble to obtain it."

"I don't think so," RD said. "We'd alert the troops outside and the game would be up." He frowned. "Anyway, d'you think *you're* hard done by? When I think of all the time and effort I put into making that boat the best on the planet..." He sighed.

"One moment," Bartes interrupted him. "I've got an idea." :*Tanya?*: he sent.

:*Bartes?*: came the reply. :*D'you think this is safe?*:

:*I think it's worth the risk. I doubt there are any sniffers nearby, and I need your help.*:

:*Why didn't you just come and ask for it?*:

:*I've had an idea that requires the use of our telepathy, and we haven't a lot of time. We're going to make a run for it, but I think we need the guns that we stashed on the boat.*:

:*You and your weapons.*:

:*We're not all as talented as you are,*: he replied rather sharply. :*Without ordnance, we're sitting ducks. We wouldn't stand a ghost of a chance if we were cornered. Think of Anoushka, if no-one else – you* did *promise to get her home.*:

He detected a mental sigh. :*You're right – it just goes against the grain. What do you need me to do?*:

:*Can you use the monitors to guide me to the boat and back so I don't get spotted?*:

:*I'll do my best.*:

"I'm going out after the weapons," he told the others, "Tanya's going to keep a lookout for me using the monitors downstairs."

"Do you need any help?" John asked.

"No – it's a one-man job. I can manage all the weapons in one trip, and two people more than double the chance of being caught."

"I think you're taking an idiotic risk," RD said.

"How far d'you think we'll get without weapons?" Bartes asked. "Now, where on the boat are they hidden?"

RD followed Bartes to his bedroom, where Bartes began to change into black trousers and a dark grey sweater. "There's a panel near the front starboard corner of the main cabin," RD said. "It looks firm enough, but it isn't properly sealed. You should find it reasonably easy to remove. Use one of the screwdrivers in the toolbox under the bench on the port side. The panel gives you access to the starboard float. You may have some difficulty reaching the weapons, though – the boy climbed inside to put them there."

"I could come if you like." Joseph's eyes gleamed with excitement.

RD scoffed. "Not a chance," he said. "Bartes knows what he's doing and I think his chances of getting away with this are slim. If you tag along, we may as well surrender now."

"I'm sorry, Joseph," Bartes said, "he's right. I'll just have to use a boat hook." He donned a pair of dark gloves and made his way to the kitchen. "Anything in here I can use to black up?"

"The only things that might cover your face adequately smell strongly enough to give you away."

"Looks like I'll have to rely on good, old-fashioned dirt." Bartes eyes unfocussed again as he contacted Tanya. :*What's happening out there?*: he asked.

:*Not a lot at the moment,*: she replied. :*The APC's still at the back, and the troops that arrived with it have formed a perimeter arc around the dacha. As far as I can tell, they check in with each other, but not with this guardroom. They look like regulars, so they probably don't even know it's here. What's more, their perimeter doesn't enclose the underground exit.*:

:*Good.*:

:*At the front, there are a couple of guards dug in each side, but they're facing away from the dacha.*:

:*Even better.*:

:*The problem, as you may have noticed on the monitors when you were down here, is the Arkan VII tied up to the jetty.*:

:*Ah. I hadn't. Go on.*:

:*It's a standard military version with a couple of heavy machine guns, one each side, about a third of the way back. The crew seem to be alert, but not highly so. Its sensors look to be operating, but they shouldn't be able to detect you so close in. It's moored on the far side of the jetty, opposite the catamaran, but further out.*: She paused. :*As far as I can tell, everything's quiet. You're clear to move.*:

Bartes poured some cooking oil onto the hinges of the front door and opened it just wide enough to slither out.

"Good luck," Anoushka whispered.

He slid through and John closed the door behind him. He lay flat and still on the deck of the veranda and waited.

:*So far, so good,*: Tanya informed him. :*Crawl to the end of the veranda nearest the jetty and down the steps. Once you're at the bottom, the bushes should help conceal you – let's just hope that no-one looks too closely.*:

He followed her instructions, but as he put his weight on the last step, the wood creaked alarmingly. He froze and held his breath, and in the silence he heard a voice mutter, "What was that?"

"I didn't hear anything," someone replied.

"There was a noise."

"Well, if you heard a noise, you'd better go see what it was. I'm not moving. I just managed to make myself comfortable. I hate guard duty – and having to take orders from those black-shirted bastards."

"I wouldn't talk so loud, if I was you. You never know who's listening."

Bartes heard a movement from the direction of the voices and sank as quietly as he could onto the ground, trying to conceal himself under the edge of the veranda. It was scant cover and he was sure he'd be spotted. He rubbed some earth over his face in a futile attempt at camouflage. He dared not look up, but out of the corner of his eye he could see a pair of boots coming in towards him. He held his breath, cursed his luck and waited for the inevitable challenge.

Suddenly, something shot from behind Bartes, bounced on his backside and launched itself at the approaching guard with a hideous yowl. "Ow!" the guard cried. "It's a cat!" He stumbled backwards, flailing ineffectively with his free hand at the enraged animal that was clutching at the front of his fatigues.

The cat clung on for several seconds, hissing in the guard's face, before slashing his cheek with its right forepaw. It released its hold, dropped, and ran off into the bushes.

The soldier swore loudly and clutched at his cheek, then shouldered his rifle and fired blindly in the direction that the animal had gone. Bartes didn't think he'd hit anything. He breathed a quiet sigh of relief – at least the guard had been distracted from his search.

The disturbance brought the guard's fellow soldiers, but luckily their attention was on their injured comrade, who was bleeding profusely from three parallel gashes just under his left eye, and none of them noticed Bartes.

"Come on, you idiot, let's get you patched up."

"Serves you right for molesting the locals," said another with a guffaw.

"*It* molested *me*," grumbled the injured man.

"You must be used to being scratched by cats," one of his mates said. "Though in your case, they're mostly of a two-legged variety – and ugly as sin."

Their voices faded as they returned to their posts, but for some time Bartes could hear the wounded man muttering to himself as he was patched up.

:*Where did that cat came from?*: he sent to Tanya once all was quiet again.

:*I don't know – but I feel I ought to*...: she replied mysteriously. After a few tense minutes, she sent, :*Things seem to have calmed down now. I think it's OK for you to make for the boat.*:

Bartes crossed the gravel towards the jetty. There was a ticklish moment when it crunched slightly under him, but no-one seemed to notice this time. He slid smoothly into the water on the near side of the pier and waded slowly to the boat. Its shallow draft meant it could be moored close to the bank where the water wasn't too deep, and when he slipped between the twin hulls and reached its superstructure, he was able to stretch up and take hold of its rigging.

There was no way he could avoid making some noise, however carefully he pulled himself up onto the deck, so, after he did so, he lay prone for several minutes, his heart pounding, until Tanya again gave the all-clear.

Sunset in Silvana

It took some time to retrieve the weapons from where RD had hidden them. He had to move slowly and carefully so as to make as little noise as possible, but soon he was able to slide, fully laden, back down into the lake.

He made his way back onto the land with little difficulty, but as he crossed toward the dacha the treacherous gravel again rasped beneath him. He stopped dead in his tracks, fully exposed, fearful of making any further commotion, when he heard the voice of the injured guard.

"There's another noise," he muttered.

"It'll be that damned cat again," his mate replied. "Let it be – or do you want to turn the other cheek," he guffawed.

"Damn animal – I've half a mind to find it and wring its neck. Maybe I will when there's enough daylight."

"Leave it be – we've got a job to do. And remember what the Major said: anyone gets in – or out – tonight and we'll be shot."

Bartes slowly let out the breath he'd been holding and continued on his way. This time he managed to avoid the creaky step, and he reached the door without further incident. John let him in, and he collapsed on the floor of the living room and let the tension drain out of him while the others relieved him of his burdens.

"Well done," Iain said as he handed Bartes a mug of coffee. "We were watching from the front window. We thought they'd got you dead to rights until the moggy intervened. What a slice of luck."

"I'm not so sure," Bartes mused. "I think Tanya feels it was more than luck."

"Whatever it was, now we're loaded for bear." Iain rubbed his hands gleefully.

"You're sounding better – no hangover?"

"I'm feeling a bit delicate, but the prospect of escape sobers you up really quickly."

"By the way, the laser carbine's mine," Bartes told him. "I feel like I've earned it twice over."

"You've earned it," Iain said. "Now, there are four pistols, so that's one each for you, me, RD & Tanya – and there are enough combat knives for everyone."

"Can I have a weapon?" Joseph asked eagerly.

"You can have this," RD said, handing the boy the smallest knife they had. "Try not to cut yourself too badly. I'll have this beauty…" He held up a large knife with a serrated 8-inch blade. "… and the boot-knife. Now, let's get things together. Take the minimum necessary, and check everything – even what you're wearing – for bugs. And don't forget to leave your security communicators behind."

They dispersed to their rooms, changed into suitable clothes and collected together what they needed to take and ferried it to the maintenance bay in convoy. Anoushka had packed Tanya's stuff, and Bartes carried it with his own. As they passed through the guardroom, Tanya was looking strained, but still managed to smile her thanks.

:*You'll do anything to avoid hard work,*: Bartes sent to her. She didn't have the energy to reply. She just wrinkled her nose and stuck her tongue out at him.

They slung their bags into the back of the smaller vehicle. Iain and Joseph set about plundering the cave for useful equipment and extra fuel, while the others returned to the living quarters with several holdalls to scavenge what they could. They took all the food, filled all the empty bottles they could find with water, and acquired most of the kitchen equipment and everything else that might be of use that wasn't screwed down (and one or two things that were).

"What do we do about Peter?" Bartes asked RD as they checked around the kitchen for the final time.

"Leave him be. He must be a spy."

"I don't think it's that simple. If he's working for the Major, why was he abducted – willingly – from the Opera House?"

RD shrugged. "It's nothing to do with us. We have to escape, and we can't take the risk of taking him with us."

"What if he wakes up and raises the alarm when we've gone?"

"We'll tie him up."

"But what if he's as much a victim as we are?" It was Tanya, who had just climbed the ladder.

"What are you doing up here?" Bartes asked.

"I thought RD might try something like this," she said wearily. "We're taking the boy with us."

She and RD stared at each other for several seconds before the latter dropped his eyes. "Then he'll be your responsibility," he muttered.

Tanya sighed. "Very well. I'll try to keep him asleep until we're well away from here," she said, "but I won't be much good for anything by the morning. John, would you help me carry him down to the vehicle?"

"No," said John. "I'm not coming with you."

"What?" Anoushka asked, aghast. "Why ever not?"

"We daren't put all our eggs in one basket," he said. "If you're honest with yourselves, you'll see that you only have a slim chance of escaping this way. If I can persuade them that I'm still conditioned, I may get an opportunity to steal a flitter and get to Telphania. After all, I could have got away before, but I didn't want to do it without you. Now, from what you've told me, it's become urgent that one of us raises the alarm. I think that this is the best way to maximise the odds."

"What if they don't believe you're still under their thrall?" Bartes asked.

John shrugged. "They'll just re-indoctrinate me. Maybe you can rescue me later, if you get away. Now, you must tie me up and leave me here. I'll claim that

I'm loyal to the Republic, and you started spouting anti-revolutionary rubbish, and that you knocked me out when I threatened to inform on you – and if you do the job properly, they won't suspect me." Anoushka nodded dumbly. "I'll try to rendezvous with you in Telphania, if I can. All the attention of the security forces should be on you, so I should be able to 'borrow' a flitter."

Anoushka kissed him. "There'll be more of that waiting for you in Telphania," she promised. "Please, please be careful." Then Bartes hit him over the head.

As he slumped into unconsciousness, Tanya psionically checked inside his skull. "There's no permanent damage – though he'll be out for a while," she said with relief in her voice. "You've done that before."

"I must have done," Bartes replied, as they bound and gagged their unconscious companion and laid him as comfortably as possible on the sofa.

They made their way to the boys' room, where Peter lay comatose. "Can you keep him asleep – as well as the guard downstairs?" Bartes asked as he carefully lifted the boy. "I could bind and gag him."

Tanya shook her head. "That would most certainly wake him, but keeping him asleep will minimise the noise – and lessen the chance of alerting the guards outside. We can always tie him up once we're safely away."

Bartes passed the boy down through the hatch to Iain, and as they traversed the guardroom for the final time, Tanya's control over the mind of the security private slipped, and he half roused. He reached out and took hold of Bartes as he passed by. "Oh, Talia," he mumbled.

Tanya quickly slipped between them so that when the guard's eyes opened, all he could see was her face. To Bartes' surprise, she gave the young man a long, lingering kiss. :*For God's sake do something,*: she sent to Bartes. :*This is revolting!*:

Bartes looked around desperately, and noticed a bottle of water on the card-table. He picked it up by the neck and sent, :*OK, you can stop now,*: and, as Tanya disengaged herself, Bartes clubbed the guard with the bottle. The latter promptly collapsed.

Tanya grabbed the bottle, swilled her mouth out and spat the contents over the unconscious youth and slapped his face – hard.

"Why'd you do that?" Bartes asked, as he bound and gagged the young man.

"He was dreaming about... No, I'm not going to tell you what he was dreaming about." Tanya blushed. "Bleargh! My mouth tastes horrible. And I'm going to have to gargle with antiseptic. Come on, let's go."

"It's still some hours before dawn," RD said as they folded the camouflage net from the mouth of the cave. "We should to be long gone by the time the re-programming team arrives."

"I'm checking everything for bugs," Tanya said.

"And I've disabled the truck's tracking device," Iain added.

Bartes looked dissatisfied. "What about our auto-injectors? Couldn't they have locators inside them? We shouldn't be wearing them now, anyway."

Tanya's brow wrinkled. "There's nothing I can do at the moment. I'm a bit busy. Anoushka, you'll have to remove them. But keep the blood plasma that's in them – it might prove useful."

Anoushka swiftly removed their devices, starting with her own, drained their contents into containers from Tanya's medkit and discarded them.

Iain was the last to climb into the vehicle, but as he was about to clamber aboard, he suddenly stopped, turned, and ran back along the tunnel. Bartes jumped down and followed him back to the monitor room, where he was busy unloading the videotape machines.

"We don't want them to know what happened," he explained as Bartes joined in the task. "And if they saw these, they'd find out about John's plans."

When they carried the tapes back to the ATV, Tanya gave a look of chagrin. "Well done, Iain," she said. "I should have thought of that."

The path from the maintenance bay sloped gently down towards the road. RD released the brake and they coasted down onto the highway like a ghost. He engaged the gears and the vehicle's diesel engine shuddered into life.

They held their collective breath in anticipation of shouts and a hail of bullets from the dacha, but nothing broke the silence of the night apart from the sound of their own progress.

"Would it be a good idea to get off the road?" Bartes asked. "This is an all-terrain vehicle after all."

"We don't want to leave tracks yet," RD said. "Not this close to the dacha – it'd make it too easy to follow us."

"Shouldn't we have our lights on?" Anoushka asked.

"No. There's a chance we could give ourselves away. I doubt there'll be much traffic up here tonight, anyway – it's pretty remote. My night sight is good enough to see the edge of the tarmac, and if we see the lights of another vehicle, I'll pull in and park, and hope that whoever it is ignores us."

"Hold on – look what I've found." Bartes waved a map roughly in RD's direction and fumbled for a torch. "I've got a compass, too – they were in that pocket by the door. We need to go...west – no, north-west. That'll take us round the side of the lake."

The road away from the dacha led roughly north-west for several miles before veering gently northwards. At that point, however, RD continued straight on, taking the vehicle off the asphalt and through a gap in the trees.

"The ground's soft enough here to take tyre tracks," he said, and they followed a roughly northerly course. "This should help fool those who come looking for us, and hopefully trick them into wasting time searching in the wrong direction. It's a good thing that this vehicle was built for rough ground."

Although there was no longer any risk of something coming in the other direction, their new path brought different perils: hillocks, rocks and trees. Bartes tried to feel ahead with his psionics in the hope of warning RD of potential obstacles, but he had very limited success, and Tanya couldn't help him, as she was keeping Peter asleep with what little energy she had left. It was a relief to discover that, as well as good night sight, RD seemed to have some sort of innate danger sense, and – though they careened off one or two trees and the odd large outcropping – they soon managed to reach deep enough into the pine forest to risk lights safely.

It was now that Tanya's will finally gave out. "Tie the boy up, would you, Iain?" she mumbled, "I'm going to –" She was asleep in her seat before she could finish the sentence. Iain did as he was asked while Bartes reached over to make Tanya as comfortable as he could.

"Leave her to me," Anoushka said, as she guided Tanya's drooping head into her lap.

They continued to travel north until an exposed rocky plateau ran across their path. RD drove onto it and, once they were no longer leaving tracks, he turned the vehicle south-west. Just before dawn, the ground fell away in front of them as they found themselves on the bank of a broad, fast flowing river, which they were forced to follow to the south.

Some miles further, RD stopped the vehicle and turned to Iain. "Something worries me about the path in front of us," he said. "Could you scout ahead for a couple of hundred yards?"

"Sure." Iain dismounted and walked forward in the pre-dawn light to spy out the ground. It wasn't long before he returned. "Good call," he told RD. "The bad news is that this plateau ends in a sheer drop about a hundred yards ahead, where this river forms a rather spectacular waterfall. The good news is that there seems to be a sloping path down the face of the cliff about half a mile to the east. I can't be certain, but I think it's wide enough for this beast."

RD turned their transport away from the onrushing flood and they soon breached the slope that Iain had identified. The route they needed to take led down the face of the cliff toward the waterfall. The incline was quite steep, and rather narrow in places, but by common consent looked to be their only option. Twice they scraped against the rocky wall, and once one of the back drive wheels spun over the precipice and it took all RD's strength to keep them on the path. About three-quarters of the way to the floor of the valley below, as they neared the cascading cataract, the ramp opened out onto a scree slope. RD was about to turn towards the valley floor when Iain put a hand on his arm.

"Look," he said, pointing at the curtain of spray. "I think that ledge might lead to a cave behind the waterfall, which might be large enough to hide in. Let me go check it out."

"Good idea," RD said. "I don't fancy being caught in the open in broad daylight, and the land down here looks a little too domesticated to hide in." Indeed, in the growing light they could see below them a cultivated valley, complete with a village.

Iain again dismounted, and soon returned. "There's plenty of room under there, but the entrance is a bit cramped."

"It's our best choice," RD said, "Batten down the hatches."

Sunset in Silvana

They made the vehicle as watertight as possible as he gunned the motor and moved slowly forward. Spray hammered on the roof as he managed to negotiate his way along the ledge and into the cavern successfully. He parked the vehicle as close as he could to the back wall.

Anoushka settled Tanya on their bench seat while RD and Bartes, with help from Iain and Joseph, spread the camouflage net over the entrance around the vehicle. They could only start a small fire, for fear of it or its smoke being visible from the valley floor, but it was enough to make some hot drinks. By common consent, RD, who had done all the driving, was assigned the other bench seat in the ATV, while the rest of them spread the mattresses they'd liberated from the dacha on the flattest part of the cave floor. Bartes was grateful when Iain volunteered to take the first watch, and fell asleep as soon as he lay down.

Chapter 20

Tanya woke with a demolition team working in her head and a black hole in her stomach. She sat up and groaned, and someone put a hot mug in her hand. "Thank you, Anoushka," she said without opening her eyes, as she recognised her friend's scent and felt her calming presence.

"You're welcome, Tanya," Anoushka said in her gentle contralto. "How are you feeling?"

"Pretty bloody – and starving." Tanya opened her eyes a little and was relieved to find herself in semi-darkness. "What time is it?" She raised herself on her elbows, slowly and gingerly swung herself into a sitting position, and sipped the blessed liquid fire.

"Late morning. You were exhausted, and I didn't want to wake you. Here." Anoushka sat down beside her and handed her a tin of warm soup and a spoon. "Sorry, but we're having to rough it for the moment. We could only light a small fire, not enough to cook properly on, for fear of being seen."

"Who by? And where are we?"

"We're concealed under a rocky overhang behind a waterfall, which Bartes says is pretty much south-west of the lake. There's a village in the valley below, and despite our camouflage net, RD says a large fire would be visible."

"He's right. How did we get here?"

"You'll have to ask Bartes – he tracked our route, and maps and I have only a nodding acquaintance." She grinned, and Tanya suddenly felt much better.

"So we're on our way home."

"Looks like you kept your promises, Tanya." Anoushka squeezed her friend's arm.

Tanya finished her meal and climbed down onto the floor of the cave. "There's still a long way to go, though. Is there anything I can wash with?" she asked. "I feel really grubby."

Anoushka held out a plastic bottle of water. "Don't use too much of it – we haven't got a vast supply." She poured a little into Tanya's hands and the latter rubbed it over her face and into her eyes.

As Tanya took the cloth that Anoushka proffered and dried herself off, she glanced up and became aware of a small cat looking back at her from just beyond the camouflage net. "Don't I know you?" she asked the animal. "Weren't you at the dacha at Plune?"

Anoushka followed her eyes and gasped. "You know, I do believe you're right," she said. "Her markings are very distinctive."

:*And I'll bet you were the one who saved Bartes last night,*: Tanya sent.

:*That's right. I'm Slimmest,*: the cat announced smugly. :*My mistress sent me to help you.*:

:*And your mistress would be Sophie. I'd guess that she's a Beastmistress, and you're one of her team.*:

:*Of course – her team prime, actually.*: Slimmest preened herself. :*You'd remember me if you didn't have amnesia. We've met before.*:

"It *is* the same cat," Tanya told Anoushka. "She belongs to Sophie, who sent her to help us."

"How can *she* help *us*?" Anoushka asked incredulously,

"Oh, she has a lot of hidden talents – you'll see. Let's give her some rations. She must have travelled hard and fast to keep up with us."

"Why not?" Anoushka replied. "Here, puss," she called as she selected a tin of fish from their food supply to feed the new arrival.

:*I'll catch my own,*: Slimmest informed Tanya, her tail lashing slightly. The cat pointedly turned her back on them and stalked away.

"What's wrong?" Anoushka asked.

:*Please come back,*: Tanya sent, and told Anoushka, "You shouldn't call her 'puss'. Cats like her have a very strong sense of dignity."

"Then what should I call her?" Anoushka asked, dismayed.

"Just call her 'Slimmest' – it is her name – and try not to patronise her – she's pretty sensitive."

:*I am* not,: the cat stated imperiously, but at least she was now walking back towards them – in her most stately manner, tail held high.

"Pour the food into a bowl," Tanya continued. "She's not in the mood to eat out of the tin."

"As you wish." Anoushka located a china dish and tipped the provisions onto it. "Would you like some fish, Slimmest?" she asked the approaching feline, who gave a 'mrowp' and condescended to bury her nose in the pile of pluny pieces. "It's a rather odd name."

Tanya shrugged. "It has to do with the way telepathy works. You've had a little acquaintance with it now; how would you describe it?"

Anoushka wrinkled her nose. "It's a bit odd. Some of it is like pictures in my mind, and some is like spoken words."

"Exactly. And it varies depending on the 'sender'. Some people think almost exclusively visually, some verbally, and most somewhere in between. What does seem common is the visual representations of people and places. When I saw John D'Arcy in your mind, I knew who it was because I know him, and though your perception of him differs somewhat from mine, there was enough commonality for me to recognise him. But think what it would have been like if I hadn't met him – how would I have tried to work out who he was?"

Light dawned in Anoushka's face. "From what he looked like. So 'Slimmest' isn't a name…"

"…it's a description. Yes. I don't know her true name – at least not at the moment, and I suspect that I wouldn't, even if I had all my memories back. Eranians are careful about names. By the way, we'd better keep her away from RD as much as possible. You know how he feels about cats – and about psionics – and I want to avoid a serious confrontation between him and Slimmest's mistress at all costs. I don't think we can afford to lose him – yet."

Anoushka laughed, and frowned when Tanya didn't reciprocate. "You're serious."

"Deathly."

Once the newcomer was satisfied, she permitted Tanya to pick her up and introduce her to the rest of the party. She purred and nuzzled most of them and accepted their attentions in return, but, as Tanya suspected, RD simply grimaced and avoided all contact. "That animal is your responsibility," he told her. "Just keep it out of my way." He stamped off, muttering under his breath.

Tanya set the cat down and walked to the mouth of the cave, where she peered through the camouflage net to view the valley beneath. She drew in her breath, shook her head slightly and went to look for RD, whom she found sitting by himself in the cab of the ATV.

"It's a pretty big village down there – it's almost a town."

"Yes," he said. "The top of the valley's pretty wild, so we're unlikely to have any visitors, but if we try to move on before nightfall, we'll be seen. We'll have to hole up here, and hope none of the villagers are insomniacs."

"One of us should make a scouting expedition."

"And who would you suggest?" His eyes glinted in the darkness.

"Me."

"You are the best qualified," he replied grudgingly, "but I don't think you ought to go on your own."

"Why not?" she asked. "I can move more quickly by myself, and it's easier for one person to conceal themselves than for two."

"No, I won't have you going by yourself – Iain will go with you."

She opened her mouth to protest, but realised it was no use arguing – RD was, at least for the moment, in charge – so she closed it again and went to find her designated partner.

"We'll need a cover story, in case we're spotted," Iain said. "I know – when I was rooting in the back of our stolen vehicle, I found several sets of overalls. If we wear those, we could claim that we belong to a logging team that's working up country, and we've been sent to the village for supplies."

It seemed as good a plan as any, so they changed into their costumes and set out. Tanya asked Slimmest to scout ahead of them and give her a preview 'picture' of the layout of the settlement. It was, in fact, half village, half way-station, centred around a large hall which obviously functioned as a meeting place and held the office of the local security officer. Apart from several houses, there was an inn and a general store, plus a trading post which clearly dealt with hunters, prospectors and loggers. The latter had a large tank in a yard at the back, which appeared to contain diesel fuel.

As they neared the village, Bartes contacted Tanya from the cave. :*Hide yourselves,*: he sent, :*We can hear vehicles coming.*:

: *From where?*:

:*The plateau. No more 'talking' – they might have 'sniffers' aboard.*:

Tanya informed Iain, and they found some heavy undergrowth, lay down flat within it and waited. Almost immediately, a couple of hoverbikes were outlined against the sky next to the waterfall. They halted and both riders began to frantically wave their arms as a large troop carrier shot between them and over the edge of the cliff. In a magnificent feat of control, the vehicle's driver managed to use its hover fans to keep it level. There was, however, a sickening crunch as it met the floor of the valley. It bounced several times like a stone skipping across a pond and shuddered to a halt about twenty yards from where Iain and Tanya were hiding.

The riders of the hoverbikes drove along the edge of the cliff until they reached the path the fugitives had taken down into the valley. They rode their vehicles down it and, to Tanya's chagrin, one of them turned off and continued along the ledge towards where the others were hiding. She held her breath as he approached the camouflage net, but relaxed as he dismounted and faced the cliff wall to relieve himself.

Meanwhile, amidst a lot of vehemence and the shouting of obscenities, the troops in the vehicle had vacated it and were jacking it up so that the damage could be inspected. While the transporter's mechanic checked it over, the lieutenant in charge addressed a soldier who must have been the navigator. "Were you asleep, Private? The cliff is clearly marked." He waved a large map under the navigator's nose.

"No, sir!" The navigator stood at attention, but was shaking visibly. "And it's Sergeant, sir."

"Not any more, Private. It was only the driving of Sergeant Karlovitch that saved our lives."

"Thank you, sir." Another trooper, who was – for the moment – still wearing corporal's stripes, saluted smartly.

"Now take care of this Private, Sergeant, and make sure he doesn't make any more mistakes." He thrust the map into the navigator's quivering hands.

"Yes, sir!" The newly-promoted Sergeant gave his ex-superior an evil smirk. Tanya could see that their relationship had a history, and had just taken a turn for the worse as far as the new Private was concerned.

The Lieutenant strode over to the vehicle and addressed the mechanic's legs. "What's the damage, Corporal?" he asked.

The mechanic looked out from under the craft's skirt. "Not too bad, considering, sir. She's a sturdy old lady, aren't you, girl?" He slapped the side of the vehicle in an affectionate manner. "I'll have to unship one of the fans and straighten several blades, and replace a couple of bearings, but we'll be under way in a couple of hours – three at the most."

"Good – be as quick as you can, please." He strode over to where another trooper was fiddling with a radio. "How are you doing, Sparks?"

"The radio's fine, sir. I've informed HQ of our situation, as you ordered."

"Warn them that we won't reach Kije in time to join the President's bodyguard, will you?" He blew out his cheeks. "I just hope nothing happens."

As Tanya lay in her place of concealment, she became aware of a vibration at her side. She slowly moved her head so that she could see the purring cat and raised an inquisitive eyebrow.

:*Lucky for them,*: the cat sent.

:*What do you mean?*: Tanya asked, but the animal just gave her a smug look which said plainly, 'Wait and see'. Tanya shrugged slightly and gently stroked the cat, which served to increase the reverberation.

"Right," the Lieutenant said. "All those not involved in fixing the vehicle form up and follow me – we've got a job to do."

He led his squad down into the village square. The accident had not gone unnoticed, and most of the village had turned out to greet them, including a rather overweight security sergeant, who was red-faced and flustered. The squad checked everyone's papers, including the sergeant's. They went from building to building, ordering any occupants out and checking their papers too. Tanya could guess what – or rather who –

they were after, and her suspicions were confirmed when each of the villagers was checked for the nose-filters that would have given any one of the fugitives away. As each person's identity was confirmed, they were directed into the village hall.

Once everyone had been checked, the Lieutenant and two of his men entered the hall while the rest of the detail searched the other buildings. From the time they took, the check must have been pretty thorough. They still hadn't finished by the time the Lieutenant and his team left the hall about an hour later.

All this had taken some time, and Tanya was beginning to cramp up, but as her left thigh began to spasm, she became aware that Slimmest had stretched out alongside it, purring intensely. Her muscles relaxed and a feeling of mild euphoria seeped over her.

When the search was complete, the troops reassembled and returned to their vehicle, where they sat around waiting until the mechanic deemed it was ready to depart. There was a slightly unhealthy whine from the hovercraft's engine when it was started, but it managed to raise itself uncertainly on its skirts and limp away down the valley, escorted by the hoverbikes.

"I think we should go back now," Tanya whispered to Iain, as soon as it was out of sight, but he shook his head.

"We need better intel," he told her. "You go back – I'll take it from here."

"Be careful – if you get caught, we'll all be for it."

"Trust me."

A thought struck her. "I do. You know, you seem different now you're yourself again. The rest of us have changed a little, but you seem to have a completely new personality. A bit more serious, but definitely an improvement."

"I feel different," he said pensively, "almost as if 'Ivan' wasn't the real me."

"It wasn't," she said. "That was one of the things I discovered back at the Medical Centre. You were given a different drug to the rest of us – Methaqualude. It affected your personality."

"Hmm... That makes sense. I remember this medical I had some years back – they warned me at the time that I was allergic to most hypnotic drugs. Perhaps the security guys felt they had no choice. Anyway, I feel like myself now – not that I didn't before... Now, give me any money you're carrying. I might need it."

Tanya raised an eyebrow, but he just gave her a crooked smile. She passed him all the cash she had on her, and turned to crawl back up the slope.

:*Keep an eye – and your nose – out for anything we can use to supplement our supplies,*: she sent to Slimmest as they made their way slowly and carefully back towards the cave.

They slithered up the slope, but had only found a few wild asterberries and a handful of sage-grass by the time they neared the path up the cliff. Tanya had resigned herself to finding nothing really useful when Slimmest sent :*There's something in here.*:

Tanya looked around and saw the cat sitting by a large thicket. :*More fruit? Or perhaps some edible roots?*: she asked.

:*No,*: the cat sent. :*Fresh meat – very tasty.*:

:*I'll go round to the other side so I'm hidden from the village,*: Tanya told her. :*You chase it out that way and I'll try to catch it.*: She crept around the thicket, trying not to disturb their prey, detecting the pungent scent of ammonia as she did so.

Expecting something the size of a squirrel, or at the most, a small goat, she knelt and drew her knife as she heard a rustling in the undergrowth. The bushes parted. She raised her knife – and was confronted by a massive, disgruntled boar with red eyes and long curved tusks.

For what seemed an age, they watched each other. *Dammit,* she thought, *I'm no match for that thing.* She moved her free hand slowly toward her holster.

The hog pawed the ground, and shook its snout.

Perhaps I can get it to leave me alone. Tanya sent out waves of calming thought, but the boar appeared no more gruntled than before. She sighed. *Someone has to pay for disturbing its ablutions – and I've been elected.*

The animal threw back its head, gave a loud squeal, and launched itself at Tanya.

Had she not been psionically talented, Tanya would have been badly gored and trampled. As it was, she did the only thing she could: she blurred. The boar seemed to slow almost to a standstill as she drew her pistol and fired three times in quick succession. The bullets flew lazily between those piggy little eyes and buried themselves in the animal's brain.

Wild boars, though, are easier to kill than to stop, and this one was too stupid to realise that it was already dead. On it came.

Tanya tried to dive out of its way, but, despite her inhuman speed, getting her body to move took just too long, and, as the carcase passed her, its right tusk opened a large gash in her thigh. Its final revenge complete, the boar collapsed in the dust and lay still.

As Tanya cursed under her breath and tried to stem the bleeding, Slimmest wandered up and looked at her with wide, innocent eyes. :*My mistress would have brain-blasted the brute...*: she began, with a degree of self-satisfaction.

"Your mistress isn't here," Tanya said aloud through gritted teeth.

The cat gave a pitying look, and Tanya became aware of a glow beneath her furry chin.

"Thank you, little sister," Tanya said as the agony abated, "but please, next time, warn me."

:*I shall have to make allowances,*: the cat sent as she sat down next to Tanya.

Something suddenly struck Tanya. :*You healed my wrist, didn't you?*:

:*In a way. I do have a talent for healing, but not as good as yours, so I added yours to mine.*:

:*You could do that? Despite the drug?*:

:*The drug doesn't remove your talents – it just stops you using them. And I could only do it because we've done that sort of thing together before.*:

:*We have? When?*:

:*You'll remember in time. Now, shall I go and get help?*:

:*Yes, please. I'll need aid with skinning this carcass, if nothing else. 'Talk' to Bartes, and ask him to bring my medical kit, and something to put the meat in, but tell him to be careful, and to wait until he's certain no-one's going to come and investigate. I did make rather a lot of noise.*:

:*As you wish.*: The cat got up and trotted back towards the hidden camp.

While Tanya waited in trepidation, hoping that her gunshots hadn't drawn anyone's attention, she cut away the ruined leg of her overalls and tore it into two strips. She folded one into a pad and bound it over her wound with the other. It seemed that the villagers were still too stirred up by their recent visitors to show any curiosity about the noise she'd made, and she remained undisturbed.

It was some time before Slimmest returned with Bartes in tow. "What *have* you been doing?" he asked as he set Tanya's medical kit down beside her.

"I thought we needed some fresh meat," she replied.

"It seems like this beast had the same idea," he said wryly, indicating the dead porker. "Do you need any help with your wound?"

Tanya shook her head. "The antibiotic I just injected should take care of any possible infections, and this stimulant will keep me going for now. Once I've put a clean pad over the gash, we can butcher this damned hog."

They hacked and slashed at the dead animal's body – Tanya with perhaps slightly more violence than was absolutely necessary – and soon filled the containers that Bartes had brought.

"What shall we do with the rest of it?" Bartes asked. "We've got all we can use."

"I'll take the tusks," Tanya said. "They should prove useful for barter. We'll have to bury the rest to conceal that we've been here."

"We could always just hide it into the thicket. I don't think the locals come up here that often – at least I don't see any signs of it – or of any scavengers that might give the game away. I doubt anyone will find the carcase before we're long gone."

"You're right," she conceded, and helped him push the remains deep into the scrub and erase the signs of their presence.

The wound was still painful, so Bartes put Tanya's arm around his shoulders and helped her limp back to their hiding place. Anoushka was waiting anxiously just inside the net, and helped Tanya to sit down against the cave wall. As she settled herself, she looked around: Bartes and Anoushka both seemed sympathetic, but Joseph's look was amused, and RD's smirk was frankly insulting. When the latter opened his mouth to comment, she froze him with a look. "Don't – say – a – word," she told him. "And, yes, it does bloody hurt."

Once the pain had subsided to a dull throb, Anoushka helped her change out of her ruined overalls. A brief check of her thigh revealed that – mainly thanks to Slimmest – the bleeding had largely stopped, so she re-dressed the wound yet again, put on fresh clothes and re-joined the rest of the party.

Chapter 21

Iain waited until the furore had died down before walking into the village as if he had business being there. He received a few curious looks as he made his way to the tavern, but with an affectation of nonchalance he pushed open the door and strode straight in. The atmosphere was agitated when he entered, but the animated chatter dwindled to silence as he walked up to the bar.

It was similar to so many working bars on so many planets: smoky, with grimy windows and indistinct pictures on the wall, including a map of Silvana. Iain noted with interest that the flag on the corner of the map was that of the Telphanian province.

"What's wrong, Comrades?" he asked. "Never seen a logger before?"

"Sorry, my friend," the barman said. "We've just had a surprise visit that's left us all a mite on edge." Indeed, at that point several of the patrons jumped slightly at a distant but distinctive sound.

Hell's teeth, Iain thought, *that was a pistol. I hope nothing's gone wrong.* His mind raced. *Whatever's happened, I need to distract everyone here from investigating.* "I saw them leave as I was hiking down the valley," he said loudly. "They looked loaded for bear."

There was a mutter of agreement. "We haven't seen so many of those thugs – sorry, protectors of the people – since the invasion – uh, liberation." The barman reinforced his words by spitting into the sawdust on the floor.

"What were they after?"

"Wouldn't tell us, would they, lads." Another mutter. "Anyway, what can I do for you, friend? I haven't seen you round here before, have I?" His look, while not precisely suspicious, was definitely wary.

"Well, it's this way: me and my team have been working just upriver, and we've had pretty good fortune this trip. We're looking at a pretty hefty bonus when we get back to Tureskow, but that's a mite far away, and we got a hankering for a little premature celebration. The boss sent me down here to get some liquor, and I persuaded him to give me a little extra so's you good people could toast our luck, so it's drinks all round, Comrades."

"That's real neighbourly of you," the barman said, and the atmosphere relaxed markedly. "Though I wouldn't use the term 'comrade' around here, friend. People might get the wrong idea about where your loyalties lie – if you know what I mean."

"Right – friend." Iain nodded slowly. "You can call me Jan."

"And I'm known as Frank."

As the denizens of the bar gathered round Iain and collected their drinks, an elderly man peered closely into his face. "Haven't I seen you somewhere before, friend Jan?" he asked, and Iain inwardly cursed those damned posters, stamps, magazines – all the things that plastered his likeness before the public – a day's stubble was hardly an effective disguise.

"I don't think you could have, my friend," Iain told him. "I've never been up this way before."

The old man shrugged, and took his ale back to his seat, muttering and shaking his head.

"I wouldn't worry about old Michael," said a voice on Iain's left, "his memory's not what it was. He's always seeing people from his past – some of whom have been dead for years." Iain turned and looked straight into the face of the portly security sergeant he'd last seen in the village square.

Somehow, he managed not to panic. His heart threatened to burst from his chest, but he managed a smile and, without a tremor, replied, "Faulty memory is a problem we all face at times, Comrade Sergeant.

Why, my boss frequently forgets to pay me – or would if I let him."

The sergeant laughed, and Iain joined him, though more in relief than in humour.

"Anyway," Iain added, "I have one of those faces that a lot of people seem to recognise. I've been mistaken for other people many a time. I've even been confused with one of those Heroes of Pregeor – as if a common logger like me were anything like one of those pampered prima donnas. I have to *work* for my living, let me tell you." There was a burst of sympathetic laughter, and one of the other drinkers slapped him on the back. "But it's a little surprising to see someone of your obvious importance here at this time of day, Comrade Sergeant," he continued.

The sergeant cocked an eye-brow and wagged his finger at Iain like a schoolmaster. "Now, what did Frank say about using that word?"

"But I thought…"

"Harry's one of us," the barman interjected.

"Yeah, well, anyway, I needed a drink after the visit of that lieutenant and his goons," the Sergeant added.

"I'm surprised that they weren't friendlier, at least to a fellow officer like yourself."

The sergeant snorted. "Huh. They were as friendly as wild boar, and about as vicious. City-bred bastards – I'm sure my words won't leave this bar?"

"I've no time for them either," Iain assured him, and others murmured their assent. "That's why I work out here. Security men like yourself are much easier to deal with – you understand how to maintain order with the minimum of officiousness."

The sergeant nodded his head. "That's what I told His Officership, but he hauled me over the coals because a couple of the villagers' papers were a little out of date. Now I'll get a letter of reprimand from headquarters, and that'll mean I can say goodbye to any prospect of a pay raise this year." He sighed heavily.

"You poor fellow," Iain commiserated. "Why don't you join *us*? Plenty of fresh air and healthy exercise – we make a reasonable living and answer to nobody but each other, most of the time. The boss is a bit of a grump, but all in all it's a pretty good life."

"Don't you go tempting Harry away from here," the barman said. "Like I told you, he's one of us."

"Yeah," one of the other drinkers added. "When the damned Zelynans took over they sent one of their own people to 'supervise' our little community. Unfortunately, he had a little 'accident'." There was a chorus of sniggers. "They tried to foist another foreigner on us, and by some strange coincidence, he didn't survive long either. We're too remote and unimportant to waste a third man on, so they got the point and appointed a local – Harry, here. We really don't want to go through all that again."

Iain laughed, and Harry smiled and shook his head and hefted his considerable belly. "I haven't got the figure for 'healthy exercise', and anyway, I've only a few more years to retirement."

"Well," Iain said, "at least have another drink on me. Do *you* know what that surprise visit was about?"

"They wouldn't tell me." The sergeant bristled indignantly. "They rousted us all out, checked our papers and for some reason, they stuck their fingers up our noses."

"They seemed to be searching all the buildings very thoroughly as well," Iain said.

"From the time they took, they must have. They can't have been looking for the usual sort of stuff, though, or a number of the people who live in this village would be in trouble." Glancing round, he caught the eyes of several of the drinkers, all of whom looked away in mild embarrassment. "As would I for turning a blind eye to their little – frailties, shall we say? Now all

I've got to do is traipse around the outlying farms with these new security papers." He waved a sheaf of documents.

"So I suppose my mates and I will need some of those," Iain said.

"I've got plenty of spares, enough for you – and them as well. Let me know where you'll be working next week, and I'll come out and process you all."

"We're a couple of miles up the river at the moment," Iain lied, "but we'll be heading back for Tureskow after we've partied a little, so I wouldn't bother yourself overmuch – we'll get our new papers when we get back. Mind you, it might help if one of us had them. Perhaps you could process me now?"

"Why not? Let me have your old papers and I'll copy over the details onto one of these new sets."

Iain feigned checking his pockets. "Damn! I must have left them back at the tractor. You don't often need them out in the woods, and I'm still not used to having to carry them. Oh well – never mind."

The sergeant shrugged. "Don't worry about that, friend Jan. We've shared a drink and a confidence or two, so I know I can trust you. We'll do it from scratch: now, what's your full name?"

Chapter 22

The tension grew as they waited for Iain to return. It seemed like an age, but it must have been less than an hour after Tanya got back when Bartes, who'd been watching out for him, turned and said, "He's coming."

Tanya breathed a sigh of relief, but as Iain pushed aside the camouflage net and entered their refuge carrying a couple of bottles of vodka, her fears for him turned into anger. "What the hell took you so long?" she asked.

"Whoa!" He raised his hands defensively. "Who rattled your cage?"

"I'm sorry," she said, her anger dissipating. "I was so worried about you. What were you doing down there?"

He grinned. "Oh, just having a friendly drink with the locals."

Anoushka gasped. "You took an awful risk," she said.

"Not really – there's no love lost between them and the Zelynans. They believed my story about being a logger, but I'm pretty sure that they wouldn't have given me away even if they'd known the truth. And I even persuaded their security sergeant to given me these." He flourished his newly-acquired identity papers.

"You must be quite an actor," Bartes said. "I wish I'd been there to see it."

"Opera – theatre – all forms of performance at your command." Iain gave a florid bow.

Still tired from his exertions the previous night, RD lay down for a nap while the rest of them settled down to wait out the day. Tanya had almost dozed off herself when something occurred to her: their captive. "We'd better deal with Peter," she said quietly to Bartes.

"OK," he replied. "I'll wake RD."

Tanya shook her head. "I'd rather we did it without his interference." They made their way to the back of their purloined vehicle, where the boy had been dumped. He was still bound and gagged, though he was now awake. "Help me sit him up," Tanya whispered to Bartes, "and then go get Anoushka, Iain and Joseph."

They sat the boy against the side of the vehicle and, when they'd all gathered, Tanya crouched down in front of him and took out her knife. She laid it down between them and said, "I'm going to remove your gag now. If you make a single sound without me telling you to, you'll never make another. Nod if you understand me." The boy inclined his head in assent, so she freed his mouth. "Now, who are you really?"

"My - my name really is Peter, but my surname's Ackermann. I am the son of David Ackermann, the leader of the Silvanan Free Army." The boy paused. "Are you going to kill me?"

"Why should we do that?"

"For spying on you," he said glumly. "I'm not sure I want to live, anyway." He looked down, and tears formed in the corner of his eyes.

"Why ever not?"

"They'll kill her now, or worse…"

"Who?"

"My sister, Karla. Those damned Zelynans are holding her against my good behaviour, and now we've escaped..." He paused.

"Look, tell me all about it, and we'll see if we can help."

He snorted. "Why would you even want to? You're aliens, and you've got no real interest in us or our affairs."

"We're none too happy with what the Comrade President and his people have done to us," Bartes interjected. "We might be inclined to help you – if only to get up their noses."

"Well..." The boy took a deep breath. "My father was the Chief Sanitation Engineer for Restavic City when the Zelynans marched in. We thought our government would fight, but they just collapsed. My father said they were spineless idiots. He took all the maps of the city sewers, and told us that we were a resistance movement.

"He called us the Silvanan Free Army, but we weren't much of an army to start with – just Father and some of his friends – and Karla and me. But people soon got to know about us, and some of them joined up with us. We used to come out of the sewers after dark, like rats, and attack those bastards. We could do it from almost anywhere, and they couldn't catch us.

"Food was the trickiest thing. You don't want to eat the sort of stuff that comes down into the sewers. There were plenty of people on the surface who didn't want to join us, but they hated the Zelynans and were happy to give us food. The problem was that we had to get it below without the security forces finding out.

"That's where me and Karla came in. The blackshirts didn't bother about kids, mostly – it was the grown-ups they kept their eyes on. I told Father we could do the job right under their noses. He didn't like it, of course – after Mother died, we were all he had left – but after we managed two or three missions without any real difficulty, he realised it made sense.

"But in the end our luck ran out. We were making one of our regular runs on the west side of the city, and a friend of Karla's recognised her. Bloody idiot rushed over to us shouting Karla's name. Karla tried to shut her up, but it was too late. There was a security officer on the other side of the street, and he recognised us. He drew his gun and shouted for us to stop. We ran, but he radioed for help and two guards cornered us in a dead-end alley. I didn't have the strength to raise the only manhole cover I could find, so they caught us.

"They took us to the Blockhouse – Security Headquarters – and separated us. They interrogated me... I don't want to think about it. We heard a fair amount about the techniques they used – Father's friends talked about it enough times... persuasion first, then drugs... and no sleep... and no food... and when those didn't get enough information out of people, the pain... needles under the nails – I don't want to remember it...

"Anyway, I didn't tell them much, but to be honest, that was because I didn't *know* very much. I wish I could say they got nothing out of me..." He looked down and shook his head slowly. "... but that Major Valentine came and just sat looking at me for a while. Somehow, he pulled information out of my head, like where our headquarters were, as well as the other bolt-holes I knew about.

"I kept asking about Karla. I thought perhaps they'd killed her. I wished they'd kill me. It would've been better...

"Soon Captain Reynard came to see me. I don't know how long I'd been in the Blockhouse – you sort of lose track of time, you know. She had my sister with her. Karla looked – thin. Empty. But she knew me. She tried to run to me, but there was a guard. He grabbed her and twisted her arm behind her back. I couldn't reach her – there were two guards holding onto me.

"The Captain asked if I'd do a job for her, and I said, 'No – not in a million years.' She nodded to Karla's guard. He wrenched her arm again. She screamed... I think I was yelling too. I don't know –

"The bloody swine... She ordered the guard to take Karla outside, and told my own guards to let go of me. 'You do realise that I can make your life more comfortable?' she said, 'and even let you share a room with Karla? It wouldn't be a problem. You'd only have to perform a small task for me – really easy. If you don't... Well, is Karla a virgin?'

"'She's only eight years old,' I told her. 'What do you think?'

"'Well, isn't that sweet,' she said. 'What a dear little girl. If you don't do what I tell you, I'll get my men to make sure Karla isn't a virgin, before they cut her throat.'

It was a minute or two before the boy could continue. "What could I do? I agreed – for Karla's sake. That bitch had us moved into a cell together. It had beds with real, soft mattresses, and a proper bathroom. And we had food – real food. Two days later, the Captain came and told me about my assignment. She promised me I wouldn't be asked to do anything that would harm my friends. She simply wanted me to spy on 'a group of aliens who think they're Heroes of the Republic'. She wanted me to get close to you all, and to Joseph in particular, and warn her about anything odd you said or did."

Tanya exchanged glances with Bartes. "That explains a lot. But what happened at the Opera House?"

"Well, my father knew that I'd been seen with you people, so he was looking for a way to rescue me. When he heard we were going to appear at the Opera House, he took his chance. My cousin Marta stole a maid's uniform and told me a van was waiting for me downstairs. With Karla still at the Blockhouse, I didn't really want to go, but I didn't have a choice. Then everything went wrong."

"Bartes and I saw," Tanya said sympathetically. "Captain Reynard must have got wind of the attempt – or been well-prepared."

"M-Marta was killed – and her boyfriend Carl. She used to babysit me and Karla, you know. She had a lovely voice. I can still remember the lullabies she used to sing us..." The boy bit his lip.

"Anyway, the rest of us got away, and I was taken to meet my father. He hugged me and asked where Karla was. I had to tell him what happened, and that I had to go back, for Karla's sake. He frowned, and told me to get some rest while he talked to 'a friend'.

When he came back, he seemed different. He told me you'd met up with some of our people in the mountains, and that you weren't our enemies. He told me to stick close to you while his friend did something about Karla."

Tanya sighed. "Now, what are we going to do with you?" she said.

The boy shrugged. "Put me out of my misery. I won't struggle. Just... I'd be grateful if you'd do it relatively painlessly."

"Don't be stupid. I can tell that you're telling the truth, and my people only kill when it's absolutely necessary – and perhaps..." Tanya had a thought and looked over at Slimmest, who had also been 'listening' to the boy's tale. :*Could your mistress help?*:

The cat's eyes unfocussed momentarily. :*She's a bit busy right at this moment, as you'll hopefully see later, but she tells me that she's already been working on freeing the girl. Who did you think the 'friend' the boy's father mentioned is?* :

Turning back to the boy, Tanya said, "Peter, your father's friend is also a friend of mine, and I know that she'll free your sister if anyone can. Now, if you'll give me your word of honour that you won't try to escape or raise an alarm, I'll untie you." She looked around for confirmation: Anoushka and Bartes nodded agreement, Iain shrugged, but Joseph pointedly turned and looked away from his once-friend.

Peter thought for a few seconds. "Very well – I promise on Karla's life not to betray you."

"Fair enough."

As Tanya cut his bonds, RD strode up, his eyes blazing. "What the hell do you think you're doing?"

"Freeing an ally."

"He's a spy."

"He *was* – very unwillingly. Now he wants to help us escape, don't you, Peter."

"Yes." The boy stretched his cramped limbs and groaned. "Ow! My arms and legs hurt."

"It's just the circulation being restored," Tanya told him. "Don't worry, they'll be OK in a minute." Turning to RD she said, "I trust him."

RD grunted. "Your gullibility will get us all killed someday."

Bartes looked at him levelly. "I'll be keeping an eye on the boy," he said.

"So will I," RD added, ominously fingering the knife in his belt.

Bartes frowned in thought. "Peter…" he began.

"Yes, sir?"

"First of all, call me Bartes." The boy nodded. "And second, do you know anything about how we could reach Telphania?"

"Yes…" It was the boy's turn to look thoughtful. "If you'll trust me that is…"

"We've little choice," Tanya said, "but for what it's worth, I'm willing to give it a try."

The boy gave a grateful smile. "You could travel south-east till the mountains end and turn north-east – but you'd have to cross nearly 200 miles of settled land to reach the border, which is pretty well-patrolled."

Bartes sighed. "I thought it wouldn't be that easy."

"But there's an alternative. It could take a bit longer, but your chances of escape would be better. You could make your way through the forest to the southern mountains and cross them by a pass I know of. Telphania is just the other side, and the border isn't well guarded, because getting a large force through the mountains is nigh impossible. I could guide you."

Sunset in Silvana

"We'll have a go," Bartes said. "We've nothing better to try."

Chapter 23

The rest of the day passed peaceably enough, though military jets flew over the area at a low level a couple of times. During the afternoon, Tanya and Bartes explored the cave, which extended some way back into the hillside, and found an alcove at the far end of it where they could safely light a larger fire and roast the boar meat. Some of it made a good meal for them that evening, and the rest they packed away as trail rations.

The sun finally crawled below the horizon. They desperately wanted to move on, but didn't dare start out while anyone was awake down in the village. The bar Iain had visited did a roaring trade, and it was after midnight by the time all the lights were out and the village was quiet enough that they felt they could start the next leg of their journey. Guided by Iain, RD carefully backed the ATV out of the cave, while the rest of them tried to hide all traces of their occupation. They boarded the vehicle and coasted as quietly as they could down into the village, coming to a halt by the yard containing the fuel tank. It seemed that this was a general parking area, as several vehicles, including the security sergeant's jeep, lined the sides.

"Right," RD said quietly, "Bartes – you and Dr Miller check for signs of life, and warn us if you detect any. Iain – you and I will replenish our fuel supplies."

Tanya and Bartes cautiously felt around psionically for signs of wakefulness, but found none, apart from the local wildlife. Slimmest found a friend, though: a large ginger tomcat, who was initially hostile to the newcomer, but was soon rubbing cheeks with her. Tanya stifled a laugh, and when Bartes raised an eyebrow, she murmured, "It's nothing much. Slimmest was just commenting on the ease with which males can be manipulated. 'Poor, sweet, simple creatures' was approximately the thought she sent."

Fully refuelled, they cruised further down the valley until they felt it safe to start the engine. On Peter's advice, they spent most of the rest the night travelling roughly south-west along the bank of the river.

"Aren't we going the wrong direction?" RD asked him suspiciously.

"We can move faster by following the river," the boy said, "and the deeper we get into the woods, the less likely we are to be discovered."

Shortly before dawn, the course of the torrent swung round to the west, but they continued away from it, heading into the forest, seeking somewhere to hide during the daylight hours. They found a place where they could conceal their vehicle at least partially among the trees. RD guided the ATV into it, and they spread the camouflage net over the top and settled down for another day of nervous waiting.

For the first time in several days, Tanya saw the sun rise and found herself humming the melody she'd come to think of as her morning hymn.

Anoushka looked up from the peg she'd just hammered into the ground. "What *is* that tune, Tanya?"

"I really don't know. It's deep in my psyche, though – from well before we were brainwashed. I hoped I'd have remembered by now, but I still don't know where I learned it. What I *do* know is that it lifts my soul and makes me want to dance. I know – once everything is set up, let's exercise together. We haven't done it for the last few days – too much has been happening – and I don't want to get out of the habit."

"You couldn't if you tried, my dear – those exercises are as much a part of you as your arms or legs. I may be a bit rusty – you'll have to go easy on me."

About midday, Anoushka shared out a cold lunch of cold roast boar, cheese & bread. Tanya noticed that

Peter had taken his away and was sat on his own. She walked over to him and asked, "Do you mind if I join you?"

"No," he said. "If you don't mind sitting next to a spy, that is."

"I've been with worse – damn it, I'm pretty sure I've *been* worse," she said. "Are these the crystal woods we've heard about? They're certainly unusual."

"Yes – they're what makes Silvana so rich – and why those blasted Zelynans annexed us. You used to be able to make a good living as a logger around these parts. My grandfather spent sixteen years on the tractors, starting as a gopher –"

"Gopher?" Tanya looked puzzled.

"You know – whenever one of the loggers wants something, you gopher it. Anyway, he became a logger himself, then a foreman, and had saved enough to buy his own tractor. And then he met my grandma, and sunk the money into a small farm. I've spent a couple of summers working out here myself – that's how I heard about the alternative route to Telphania. Since the invasion, though, all the tractors belong to the government." Peter spat vehemently. "And they tax every log you gather."

"Let's get this straight," Tanya said. "Earlier, you called the annexation of Silvana an invasion, and Iain's experiences yesterday back your story up. We haven't any memories of it ourselves, but the line we've been fed is that it was requested by the Silvanans."

The boy snorted. "Propaganda. Zelyna's a poor country that envied our assets, so their President claimed that we asked for their help dealing with internal struggles – struggles that they themselves had been fomenting. They walked in, and our so-called government just rolled over and played dead. And because Telphania is a federation of free states, there was nothing much the rest of the country could do about it without a full-scale war."

They lapsed into silence for a while. Tanya said, "Tell me about the crystal woods."

"They're unique to Silvana, but our scientists can't explain how they came to be. The best we can come up with is that they were genetically engineered by one of the elder races. Their sap, when it solidifies, forms translucent crystal structures which are both very strong and very beautiful. As you can see, the trees themselves grow straight and vertical, and their branches are also very straight, and very regular. What's more, the sulphur in our soil gives the wood a deep, golden glow."

It was at this point that Slimmest wandered up. *:Have you any news?:* Tanya asked.

The cat took up a classic pose – front legs together and tail wrapped round her – and closed her eyes in meditation. *:My mistress has located the boy's sister,:* she sent after a few seconds. *:She's still being treated well, and my mistress wants to leave her where she is until we're ready to abstract her. Littlest is hiding in her cell and has made friends with her. She'll warn us if there are any problems.:*

"Peter," Tanya said, "I've been informed that our friend has found your sister. She's still being treated well – for the moment. And we've managed to get one of our agents close to her, ready to help if anything goes wrong."

He snorted. "Look, please don't try this on me – you can't *possibly* know that out here. I can understand that you're trying to get me on your side, but I'm not as much of a child as I look – you grow up fast in the Resistance. Can't you just accept my promise not to betray you?"

"Don't be so quick to condemn us," Tanya told him as she communed with Slimmest, asking for details. "They've given her new clothes," she continued, "but she refuses to put them on. She insists on wearing an old red cotton dress that's torn quite badly at the hem."

Peter's eyes filled with tears. "She's always loved that dress. It's really too small for her now, but Mother gave it to her before..." He took a deep breath. "It was torn when we were captured. I don't know how you can have found that out, but it's enough – I believe you now." He paused and looked up at her. "Could you do something for me?" he asked. "Could you talk to Joseph and tell him that I'm sorry? He's ignored me since I told you who I really am, and I miss his company."

"I'll do my best," she said.

As he turned away, shuffling into a corner to be alone with his thoughts, Tanya moved over to where Joseph was sitting. "You know, Joseph," she said, "Peter's feeling very lonely and lost at the moment. He needs a friend, and he'd really appreciate it if you'd forgive him. You used to get on so well."

Joseph's lips tightened and he looked away. "That slime *pretended* to be my friend. Why should I be sympathetic towards him – he never really cared about me."

"I don't think that's true. Anyway, it's not his fault – you heard his story."

"And why should I believe it? It could be a pack of lies, with no more truth than he told us last time."

"He's telling the truth this time – Sophie's cat has confirmed it. And he's all alone now, caught up in things beyond his control," she added. "He really needs a companion – or at least someone to talk to."

"Then he can talk to you."

It's no good, thought Tanya. *I can't get through to him.* Turning away, she saw Anoushka dozing on her bedroll. "Anoushka?"

"Hmm..." Anoushka blinked sleepily. "Yes, Tanya?"

"I've been talking to Peter, and he's rather lost and alone at the moment. Joseph won't have anything to do with him, and I can only do so much. Could you spare some time to befriend him?"

"Why not? It's not as if I can do much to help with our escape. It'd be nice not to feel like a fifth wheel for a change."

Later that afternoon, Tanya and Bartes were dozing when Slimmest suddenly called them psionically. :*I think you might like to see this,*: she sent. They joined the cat, who was sitting in the cab of the vehicle. The video screen was on and she was watching the screen intently.

It was showing a live outside broadcast: the Comrade President was standing on a podium in front of a large cheering crowd. He was accompanied by two other official-looking types that the subtitles identified as the Interior Minister (who was responsible for the security forces) and the Minister of War. A caption also identified the location as the State Tractor Works at Kije, and indeed an array of gleaming new forestry vehicles behind the dais testified to its truth. At the edge of the arena were two of the grav tanks seen on film during the night at the opera, and four armoured personnel carriers

Gradually the rest of the team realised what they were doing and joined them out of curiosity. Everyone had gathered by the time the President began his speech.

"Comrades," he announced, "we are here to laud the collective might and will of the Silvanan people." There was a loud cheer, and it was a while before he could continue. "But before I begin my inspection of this magnificent testimony to the ability and dedication of our newest comrades, I have a surprise for you." A buzz of puzzled expectation came over the audio channel, as he paused for effect. "There have been scurrilous rumours spread by reactionary malcontents," he went on, "that Silvana Zelyna has neither the will nor ability to resist the warmongering Telphanians and their off-world supporters. I would like to demonstrate

215

today, for both you and the watching public, some new forms of protection provided by our allies that will aid us all in our struggle with the forces of our enemy. You can see the grav tanks we now have –" (he gestured dramatically) "– but on a more personal note –"

He gestured again, and there was a collective gasp as a dozen security guards armed with rifles lined up in front of the platform and took aim directly at him. He waved his hands in front of him and, accompanied by a quiet hum, some type of energy barrier formed around the party on the dais that was detectable only by the minor visual distortion it caused. The guards fired their weapons, but the bullets failed to penetrate the shield. They could be seen to lose their momentum and fall to the ground.

The cheers were deafening, but after some seconds, they began to fade as the crowd seemed to be gripped by some form of unease. A ripple of silence spread out from a point at the back. The view on the screen changed to show the assembled multitude before locating and centring on the source of the disquiet. The throng parted to show Sophie, no longer dressed in white, but in a serious-looking black uniform with the sigil of Mercy on its shoulder and left breast. The guards in front of the dais – and all the others surrounding the area – turned towards her.

"I'm not here to hurt anyone – unless I'm forced to," Sophie announced in a voice that cut through the silence. "I just want to talk to your President."

The view changed again to show the podium, where the President stood in a state of agitation. "Kill her!" he shouted. "What are you waiting for?"

:*Shouldn't you be there to help her?*: Tanya asked Slimmest.

:*They can cope without me,*: she replied, apparently unconcerned.

The camera swung with the soldiers' weapons onto their target, who sighed and shook her head sadly.

Sunset in Silvana

The tanks and APCs all began to train their heavy weapons on the lone, slender figure. Tanya held her breath, fearing the worst, but before any of them could fire, a piercing actinic blue beam stabbed out from a bluff overlooking the tractor works. In quick succession, the barrels of each heavy weapon glowed cherry-red and drooped under the influence of gravity. One of the tanks, its crew oblivious to the damage, tried to fire. Its turret exploded in a gout of flame.

Sophie addressed the remaining troopers. "Those of you who want to live, drop your weapons." Most of them presumably felt that the risk of court martial was preferable to certain death, and complied. She blurred, and those who didn't respond fell in quick succession from single accurate shots to the head. A few soldiers managed to fire shots of their own before they died, but all missed their fast-moving target, one or two bullets hitting members of the crowd.

Sophie's movements slowed, she holstered her pistol and strolled forward toward the podium. A squad of four security men stepped between her and her destination. They obviously disdained guns, and simply stood looking at her. The tension mounted until one of the men gasped. The camera focussed on him as blood started to pour from his nose and ears. He opened his mouth and a crimson flood joined the lesser streams. He sank to his knees and collapsed.

A ripple went through the crowd, and Tanya could sense the apprehension of the three surviving men as they redoubled their efforts. She was aware that they would have cut and run if they could, but they were firmly locked into their futile struggle. Some moments later, a second, then a third of them followed Sophie's first victim's example. The fourth screamed as his heart was wrenched from his chest. The camera focussed on Sophie as she shrugged her shoulders and continued forward, stepping delicately over the bodies of her dead opponents.

It was clear that that, despite her display of *sang froid*, the silent battle must have taken quite a lot out of Sophie, and Tanya was concerned when her eye was caught by one of the troopers behind the girl. Slowly, cautiously, he was bending to retrieve his rifle. Two fingers touched the stock, but before he could grasp hold of it, a streak of fur hit him in the chest. He collapsed, trying to fight off a cat that was raking at his throat. :*That's Fattest,*: Slimmest informed Tanya, as blood spread over the guard's neck and chest. :*It takes a lot to get him moving, but he can be* very *effective when he does.*: A couple of other soldiers who had begun reaching for their weapons suddenly thought better of it.

Sophie addressed the President directly. "I warned you, but you wouldn't listen. This is your last chance – start a war with Telphania and you – will – die. And just to show you how I feel about your pathetic shields…" She looked at the Minister of War, took something from her belt and tossed it into the air. It disappeared, and her target jerked and put her hands on her midriff. Her look of surprise turned to one of agony as the micro-grenade exploded inside her abdomen, spraying the President and the Interior Minister with its contents. "If you don't sue for peace," Sophie told the President, "next time it'll be you."

With this final doom-laden warning, she spun on her heels and disappeared in a blur of speed. The camera could only just catch a glimpse of her as she ran *over the surface* of the river and disappeared into the woods beyond it. The blue beam sprang out again, less bright this time, but sustained. It burnt the words WAR – YOU DIE into the sides of the new forestry tractors. As the camera panned over the ominous message, there was an explosion. It swung back to show a cloud of dust and flame from the location of the source of the deadly beam. The screen went blank, and Tanya became aware of a very smug feline preening herself on her lap.

"Those tractors look pretty high-tech," Bartes observed as they began to disperse.

"Silvanan design," said Peter with pride, "and Silvanan construction. Those Zelynan bastards could never build anything like them. They've stolen the technology, just like that of the Skyport, and the high-speed monorail."

They set off again as soon as it got dark. They crossed one railway line, and it was about an hour after midnight when they came upon another, this one a single narrow track. Tanya turned to Peter and said, "Look, you know this part of Silvana better than the rest of us. Where do you think this line is headed?"

The boy thought for a moment. "I think that this must be the forestry railway between Kije and Varlov," he said.

"What's a forestry railway?" Bartes asked.

"The logging tractors have two sets of wheels," the boy explained, "all-terrain ones for harvesting the wood, and a second set that can be lowered onto the forestry railway tracks so the wood can be carried quickly and safely to the processing plant."

"I think we should follow this line," Bartes told the others. "It's going roughly in the right direction, and the ground will be pretty level along its route."

"What if someone comes along and spots us?" Anoushka said, anxiously.

"Well..." RD considered for a moment or two. "I don't think any tractors will be moving along it at this time of night, but we can't be too careful. Let's drive parallel to the line, but at a distance far enough away that we can hide in the event of something coming."

They followed his advice, and indeed, the line seemed deserted, but after an hour or so, Joseph said, "I think the sky's getting lighter ahead of us."

"Yes," RD replied, "but it can't be dawn. It's too early – and anyway the light is to the south rather than the east."

"It should be Varlov," Peter said. "It's the only place around here that would generate that much light."

"Should we detour round it?" Iain asked.

"No need to as yet," Bartes replied. "It's still a fair way off. Let's continue on for the moment." The glow was indeed caused by the lights of Varlov, and as they reached its outskirts the line led them through a deserted marshalling yard.

"Everybody disperse and see what you can find," RD said, "particularly fuel." He looked at Tanya and Bartes. "You two, keep an eye on that boy," he said.

As Peter, Tanya and Bartes searched the south side of yard, they came upon several large shapes sheathed with tarpaulins. Lifting the edge of the covers, they discovered three forestry vehicles. Tanya found RD and told him what they'd found.

"Just what we need," he muttered as he approached. "Let's swap vehicles. Fair exchange, and all that..." They pulled the tarpaulin off the middle tractor and Bartes hot-wired its starter. He drove it forwards, and once it was clear, RD backed their stolen vehicle into its place. They transferred their gear into their new transport, covered the ATV, and tried to make it look as if nothing had been disturbed. They reckoned that the exchange would not be detected, at least by a cursory glance. They found logging coveralls in lockers in their new vehicle and changed into them.

When they had refuelled the tractor, RD gathered them together. "I think our best course is to follow this railway south for now."

"You're right," Peter said. "The other side of the city, there's a line that runs south-east – towards the southern mountains."

"D'you think it's safe to go *through* Varlov?" Iain asked

"I don't see why not," Bartes said. "They don't yet know that we've changed vehicles."

RD raised his hand. "Quiet a minute," he hissed. "Listen." In the near silence, they heard the sound of rotors. "Everyone hide."

They watched as two helicopters flew nearly overhead and landed not a quarter of a mile ahead of them, close to the track. The 'copters disgorged a number of security men, who formed a line and began a sweep of the area, but – to their relief – towards the city.

Once they felt it was safe to emerge, RD looked at the rest of them and said, "That settles it: we skirt around Varlov and join the railway on the other side of it. Iain, you drive – I need a rest." They scrambled aboard the tractor, Iain started the engine and they set off to the east, following a trail into the forest, intending to give the city a wide berth.

Chapter 24

Some hours later they became aware, in the pearlescent pre-dawn light, that they were approaching a small logging town. "Look," Anoushka cried. "Let's stop and have some real breakfast."

RD pondered for a few seconds. "All right – but I'm staying with the vehicle. Be careful – and keep an eye on that boy."

"Don't be so paranoid," Tanya replied. "He's on our side now."

"I still don't trust him – or you for that matter." They locked gazes until the tractor drew to a halt in the town square, outside the local tavern.

As they dismounted from the tractor and entered the inn, the scent of frying bacon made them salivate. They ordered breakfast, but it left them almost out of money.

As they finished their meal, Tanya got to her feet. "I won't be long," she said. "Don't leave without me."

She made her way to the town's trading post. Since it was early in the day, although the post was open, there were no customers. The place was empty – apart from the owner, a middle-aged man with greying hair and a weathered but still handsome face.

"Can I help you, ma'am?" he said.

"I hope so," she replied. "Would you be interested in buying these?" She drew the tusks she'd removed from the dead boar from her pack.

"And how did you come upon those?" he asked.

She laid them on the counter. "*They* came upon *me*. I was relieving myself in the bushes up country when this massive boar suddenly went for me. I must've been peeing on one of his favourite spots, 'cos *he* was pretty peed himself! I tried to scare the bastard off, but he was having none of it, and he kept coming at me, so I had to kill him, but not before he gored my thigh. That's my blood on one of the tusks, by the way – do you want to see the scar?" She raised an eyebrow.

"Nah." He smirked. "I haveta run the store on my own today. Some other time, perhaps?"

"Maybe," Tanya replied with a smile, "if we come through this way again. We're just pausing for breakfast today."

"Ah well... Pity. Anyway, as it happens, I may just have a customer for your little trinkets. One of my contacts down in Duplif has a line in ornamental dagger handles, and they might be just up his street. How does 200 zellars sound?"

"I'd expect at least ten times that," Tanya told him, "and I'd prefer terras to Zelynan toilet paper."

He laughed. "How about 80 terras?"

"Hmm..." she said. "That's more reasonable. How about 120?"

"A hundred – that's my best offer."

She pursed her lips and nodded agreement.

"I haven't got that much Terran scrip here, I'm afraid. You'll have to wait while I go to the bank when it opens – unless you'd care to take something in part exchange."

"Well... I'd rather not hold my team up." She gave a sardonic laugh. "I'm not convinced they'd wait for me anyway. Let's see what you've got." She looked around, but nothing caught her eye. Then she had an idea. She felt she knew where the trader's sympathy lay, so she took a deep breath and said. "What I could really do with is something like a rifle."

His eyes widened. "Don't be stupid," he said. "If the security forces found me dealing in weapons, they'd arrest me and throw away the key. It's been like that since they brought in the ban on ordinary citizens having guns."

"It is a real pity," She said with a sigh. "I used to enjoy hunting."

"We all did," he said, "especially hunting security officers – that's why they banned our weapons." He paused and thought for a minute. "Look," he said. "Be honest with me – are you part of the Resistance."

"In a way," Tanya said evasively. "We're out to cause problems for the invaders, and help free Silvana if we can."

"I sorta guessed that," the trader said. "Wait here a minute." He disappeared into the back room, and returned carrying a tapering oiled leather case about 4 feet long. "I was keeping Winona here in the hopes that one day I'd be able to use her again. Maybe *you* could find a use for her." He held out the case.

Tanya took it reverently and laid it carefully on the counter. Unzipping the end, she drew out a most beautiful rifle, old-fashioned but well maintained. "She's worth far more than those tusks," she said in a hushed voice.

"Not if I can't use her – and I'm always a bit nervy that one of these days she'll be found in some random security sweep and end up in the hands of some Zelynan bastard who'll mistreat her." He paused and gave Tanya a shrewd look. "Now, I don't know what you're involved in – and I don't really want to know, for both your safety and mine – but I somehow think I'd approve of what you'll use her for."

"I'll tell you what," Tanya said thoughtfully, "I'll take her – and if things go well, I'll get her back to you somehow, someday – and hopefully with permission to use her again."

He nodded slowly. "You know, I think I actually believe you. Here's some ammunition –" He put five boxes of bullets on the counter and opened his till. "– plus 18 terras – it's all I've got – and 150 zellars. And you'd better take the old canvas bag over there to carry Winona's case in. You don't want anyone to recognise it for what it really is. Good luck."

"Thank you," she said as she opened the door. "You're very generous. I hope I'll be able to pay you back properly, someday."

She re-joined the others, who were waiting impatiently in the tractor. They set off again, and as they left the village behind, Anoushka said, "Well, that's the last of our money, but at least I got food for a few days. Where did you get to?"

"I knew we'd need funds, so I sold my boar tusks. The trader I sold them to was sympathetic. I got these – " She showed them the cash. "And he loaned me this." She revealed her treasure.

Bartes whistled, and took the rifle from her. "I thought you didn't like these things," he said with a grin as he caressed the gun's polished body.

"I never said that," Tanya replied, "I just think you shouldn't rely on weapons too much. I can appreciate the elegance of a fine rifle as much as anybody. Look, I've been entrusted with Winona here, but I'll admit I can't use her – or look after her – as well as you or Iain can. Would you take her?"

"I'm tempted, but I've already got a laser carbine I'm comfortable with, and I don't want to be greedy."

"Iain?"

"She's exquisite." He took the rifle and cradled it lovingly. "Thank you. I promise to take really good care of her."

"You might remember the trader in that village," Tanya told Peter. "He's sympathetic to your cause, and he might prove a useful contact." The boy nodded thoughtfully.

They continued their way through the woods around Varlov. There were quite a few people about, and they exchanged greetings with them. They seemed cheerful, but somehow a little tense.

"Everybody we meet seems to be on edge," Tanya remarked to Peter.

"It's been like this since we were annexed. You've got to be careful what you say – or even think, sometimes – or you might get reported to our new lords and masters." He spat through the window into the dust.

They located the rail to the south of Varlov, mounted it and headed in towards Tureskow. They made good time throughout the day, encountering no one until mid-afternoon, when Joseph spotted a tractor coming in the other direction.

They waited at the next passing point, and waved as the other tractor drew level. To their surprise, they stopped. Bartes raised an eyebrow at Peter. "They probably just want to swap news," he said, and this indeed proved to be the case.

The other tractor's foreman, a grizzled veteran who had identified himself as George, asked, "Where have you come from? I haven't seen you this way before, and I thought I knew everyone who worked this area of the forest."

"We're a new team," Iain said, "a bit wet behind the ears. We just wanted to try our hands at some good, honest, open air work, as far away as possible from the restraints of city life –" he lowered his voice "- and State Security."

George nodded and tapped his nose. "That I understand. How are things up Varlov way?"

"More security than you'd expect. You hear that someone's threatened to kill the President if we go to war?"

"Rumours, yeah."

"We saw it on public video. Some slip of a girl gave him a warning at his shindig in Kije. What's more, to emphasize her point she took out several vehicles and troopers, plus the Minister for War, *on her own*. Best thing I've seen on the vid since before the invasion."

George laughed, and slapped Iain on the back. "You'll do well out here, lad – you've got the right attitude."

"How about you? You got enough stashed away yet to retire?"

"Oh, I like the freedom I get out here. Maybe one day, if Silvana's liberated…"

"One day, perhaps." Iain gave him a wistful smile. "Anyway, what's happening near Tureskow?"

"Nothing much. Anyway, we must move on. Good luck to you."

They left the track a few miles before they reached Tureskow and drove through the trees, heading for the River Vistra. They had nearly reached the edge of the forest, so they came to a halt by the last copse of crystal woods and, for the first time since they left Lake Kuraken, set up camp openly.

They found some tents in the tractor's lockers, and RD and Iain pitched them with Joseph's aid while Peter helped Anoushka and Tanya to cut up the remainder of the boar meat and a selection of the fresh vegetables Anoushka had bought back in the village, in preparation for a substantial stew.

In the meantime, Bartes wandered off in search of wood to burn. He returned after a while with an armful of branches and proceeded to build a fire. He soon had a good blaze going, and they set the stew to cook.

"We've been travelling for nearly twenty-four hours," Tanya pointed out when they gathered to eat. "We need to rest."

"You're right about that," RD admitted. "We seem to be on the edge of the crystal woods. The trees ahead look more conventional. And the land seems pretty cultivated, so we shouldn't go much nearer the river in such a conspicuous vehicle. We're going to have to walk from here, and we're in no shape for a long trek at the moment. Let's get a good night's sleep, and spend tomorrow resting up too, to regain our strength. If anything flies over or comes near, we can always pretend to do some logging."

They were all grateful for the chance to relax, and – apart from exercising with Anoushka – Tanya spent the morning in repose and deep meditation. She noticed with gratitude that Anoushka spent a fair amount of time with young Peter. He was looking happier, but RD gave him a resentful glare every time he saw them together. Slimmest toured the group – apart from RD – enhancing their recuperation with her restful presence and her therapeutic purring.

Once they'd had lunch, Tanya had an idea. *This is a good opportunity for me to check out my psionic abilities,* she thought. *I know my telepathy's OK, but I ought to see what else I can do.* She walked a distance into the trees, sat down cross-legged, calmed her mind and found her true centre.

Telepresence first. She reached out with her mind and found that she could 'see' and 'hear' forest creatures for some miles around. She tried something that felt natural: she carefully inserted her psyche into one of the nearby animals, a tree-dwelling rodent. She rode in its mind for a while, enjoying the sensation of skittering up and down tree-trunks and leaping from branch to branch. She realised that she could try to take control of her host, but since she wasn't used to four legs, she might cause it to fall and injure itself. She returned to her own body with a strange urge to bury some food for the winter.

My telekinesis works, at least on the small scale. After all, I used it instinctively when Joseph attacked RD. And my self-awareness, particularly the self-diagnosis and regeneration aspects are – necessarily – working well. All that remains is to see if I can teleport.

She closed her eyes and concentrated. There was a feeling of translocation, and she suddenly felt an exposed breeze against her skin. She looked down in surprise at her naked body. Gazing to the right, she saw that her garments lay in a crumpled pile where she'd been sitting. *Dammit,* she thought with chagrin, *I've forgotten to bring my clothes. I'm glad I decide to do this in private. I hate to think how some the others might have reacted.*

She had a sudden vision – or was it a memory? She was running, naked and embarrassed, down a stone corridor lined with tapestries. The picture faded and wouldn't return. She shook her head and sighed in frustration.

Chapter 25

There were no alarums during the day, so by the time evening fell, they were completely recovered and fully prepared to leave. Having fortified themselves with the reheated remainder of the stew and more of the bread that Anoushka had purchased back in the village, they set out on foot through the forest. They travelled through the night, and dawn found them in a small clearing, where we decided to pause and have breakfast.

"Any idea how long before we reach the river?" Iain asked Peter.

"About four to five hours, I'd say," the boy said. "We'll be able to move more quickly now it's light, though it's best we keep hidden as much as possible, to avoid any farms or villages we see."

"What are we going to do when we get there?" Anoushka asked.

"The people we've met seem pretty friendly," Tanya said, "and I've got some money to buy us passage if we find a boat willing to take us."

"Or we could hijack one," RD added.

Tanya glared at him. "Is violence always your answer?"

"Pretty much – it usually works."

"Come and eat," Anoushka said, her smile defusing the tension.

It was about midday when they entered a broad clearing in the woods, surrounding a path that stretched away to their left and right.

Bartes saw the glint of water through the trees on the other side. "Over there," he said, pointing. "It must be the river."

In their eagerness to confirm his discovery, they increased their pace, and they had almost reached the far side when a young man in the uniform of a Security

Lieutenant stepped out from behind a tree and blocked their path. He held a pistol negligently in his right hand.

"Put your hands on your heads," he said, as several black-shirted troopers emerged on either side of him.

Tanya looked round to see that others of the Lieutenant's platoon had surrounded them. *:Oh, shit*: she sent to Bartes.

The lieutenant strutted forward. "Surrender," he said. "We don't really want to hurt you, but we will if we have to. My superiors want you back, but I think they'll be satisfied as long as you're still breathing."

"How did you find us?" Tanya asked, the despair showing in her voice.

"Oh, we always knew where you were. We were just waiting for *you* to come to *us*."

The fugitives stood uncertainly for some seconds. RD drew himself to his full height and said, "We're not going back with you."

"Oh, I think you are," the lieutenant said smugly. "Restrain them."

As several of the troopers moved to do his bidding, the lieutenant lurched sideways. He fell as if pole-axed. Milliseconds later, the crack of a rifle was heard, followed by the rattle of a light assault weapon. Four of the troopers to the fugitives' right fell as the others dived prone and began returning fire.

A figure about 30 yards along the right-hand path momentarily stood up and beckoned. "This way," he called as he ducked back into the bushes.

"Follow me," RD said, as he dived sideways to avoid the crossfire. Crouching low, he dashed toward the trees on the side from which they'd been hailed.

Tanya took hold of Anoushka's arm and followed him. *:Bartes – bring Joseph. And Iain, you bring Peter,*: she sent.

RD led them cautiously along the tree-line. There were shouts from the Zelynans, and an occasional warning shot flew over their heads, but most of the soldiers seemed keener on staying alive than on stopping their escape. One conscientious but foolhardy trooper tried to follow them, but just got a bullet in the neck for his trouble. He clutched his throat and fell, blood fountaining from his mouth.

As they neared the point from where they'd been hailed, they were met by the man who'd gestured to them.

"Follow me," he said, and led them off into the trees. A hundred yards or so further on they came to an outcrop of rock, which their rescuer walked directly into and disappeared. They hesitantly followed, only to find that they passed through a hologram into a large cave. "Wait here," their rescuer told them, as he left to re-join the fire-fight.

Tanya and Bartes looked at each other, dumbfounded. "Perhaps this is something Sophie arranged?" Tanya said.

"Ask that blasted cat of hers," RD said. "Where is it, anyway?"

"I don't know," Tanya replied in a puzzled tone. "I haven't seen her since we left the tractor."

"She probably doesn't like long walks," Iain suggested.

"It's not that," Tanya replied. "Remember, she followed us for a long way after we left the dacha. Anyway, she knows she can always ride on my shoulders. No, her mistress must need her at the moment."

They were left by themselves to recover from their trek. They relaxed as much as they dared, though the sporadic gunfire outside their hideout made that difficult.

After some time, there was a noise from the front of the cave as the last person they expected entered: Major Valentine. He smiled at their astonishment. "Just a few more minutes and we'll be on our way, my friends. Get some more rest while you can – we'll be moving fast when we leave here."

Tanya smiled. "I always hoped you were on our side, Major," she said.

"There's no need to use that title any longer, Dr Miller – or should I use your first name?"

"I already told you to do so once – although that time it *was* a different name."

"Okay – Tanya," he added with a grin. "If you'll call me Valentine – it *is* my real name, after all."

"I've never seen you out of uniform before."

"The time for deception has passed – I'm here to get you to Telphania, by way of Duplif, so I can show my true colours."

"But you had Karla and me tortured." Peter snarled.

Valentine shook his head sadly. "I'm sorry – that wasn't my idea. Reynard enjoys that sort of thing. When I found out, I stopped her."

"And pulled my thoughts from my head," the boy said. "You forced me to betray my friends."

"It was either that or let Reynard continue to interrogate you," the Major said. "If it's any consolation, your friends were gone when we checked the locations you knew. You held out long enough for them to escape."

"I still don't trust you."

"Then I'll have to do something to earn that trust – like reunite you with your sister."

"We'll see."

"Now that you're here and everything's out in the open," Iain said, "perhaps you can explain something: how is it that you – and everyone else in Zelyna, it seems – were able to track us? We've checked every member of our party and all of our equipment for bugs several times over and found nothing."

"The state-provided food and all the water you ate and drank at both dachas – and even back at your apartment block – was impregnated by identifiable radioactive trace elements," Valentine replied. "Whenever you relieved yourself – even when you breathed – you left a slight but perceptible trail behind you."

Tanya put her head in her hands. "I should have realised," she said with a sigh.

"What do you mean?" Bartes asked.

"Our drug dispensers," she said. "They contained a radiation palliative, and since we weren't actually at Pregeor, there had to be some other reason for it to be included."

"Are we in any danger?" Iain asked.

"I doubt it," Tanya told him. "It could only have been a trace. What's more, we've gradually been eating less and less of our original supplies, and the water from the dacha ran out a while ago. I'm betting most of it has been leached out of our system by now."

"It *has* been getting harder to follow you," Valentine agreed.

"That explains how the security forces have been able to track us," RD said, "but not how our other enemies have been able find us so easily."

"That's indirectly my fault." Valentine gave a rueful grimace. "You'll have gathered that Reynard has been after my job?"

"She didn't exactly go to too much effort to disguise the fact," Tanya pointed out.

"Exactly. Well, she wanted to demonstrate to our superiors that I was incompetent, so, to make my job of keeping you safe more difficult, she's been feeding information about your whereabouts to the resistance."

"The bitch," Anoushka exclaimed.

"That explains most of it," RD said, "but I've been thinking back to Plune, and there should have been no way that anyone would have been able to set up a mortar to attack us when we were sailing back to the dacha. How could she know our plans when she wasn't there when we decided?"

"I wondered about that at the time," Valentine said, "so I made a few enquiries and found that she'd been paying one of my closest aides to spy on me. He must have tipped her off."

"I hope you dealt with him most severely," Iain said.

"Permanently," said Valentine. His smile did not reach his eyes.

Bartes still couldn't relax. Perhaps it was only his natural paranoia, but he felt he couldn't trust their rescuers. The ex-Major sat with his back against the cave wall and seemed to be dozing, so Bartes reached out with his mind.

He'd been told that Valentine was highly psionic, and that indeed proved to be the case: his mind was so well shielded that a surface scan told Bartes nothing. He pondered digging harder, but was nervous that the ex-Major would detect his probing. Just as he was about to give up, Valentine was distracted by a burst of machine gun fire from just outside, and Bartes was able to get a rather disturbing picture from his mind.

> A thick cloth was being held over a fire.
> Eight chitinous, taloned legs took hold
> either side of the central seam and pulled.
> A stitch broke, opening a small tear. The
> light of the hungry flames that sprang
> through the rent showed that the cloth was
> a map of Ruine, a map that quickly caught
> alight and was consumed utterly.

Bartes also picked up what Valentine was thinking: *I wish I could do something about my mistress's plans, but I can't afford to defy her openly. I've spent such an effort on these poor fools, and now they must be sacrificed. I've got quite fond of some of them, too. It's a pity, but what alternative have I got?*

It grew quiet outside, and soon one of their rescuers came through the cave entrance. "We think it's OK to move on," he said.

"I'll come and check." Valentine got to his feet. "Be ready to move when I get back," he said to the fugitives as he left the hideout.

Now it was safe to talk, Bartes looked over at Tanya and said, "I'm afraid I've got bad news." He showed her telepathically what he'd picked up from the ex-Major.

She looked stricken. "But I thought... I'd hoped..." Her tone was anguished.

"What?"

Her face took on a look of grim determination. "Never mind. We're in deep trouble. What do you think we should do?"

"I don't know..."

They'd lapsed into silent circumspection when RD woke from a doze in a sweat. "What's the matter?" Anoushka asked him.

He clasped her hand, his eyes wild. "I had a dream," he said, quietly but with urgency. "A sort of premonition – we were walking through the woods with our rescuers, and we reached a barge moored by the riverbank. Valentine ushered us aboard, but when we went below, the compartment filled up with some sort of gas..."

"That fits with what Tanya and I suspect," Bartes whispered, and he described what he'd 'overheard' from Valentine.

RD looked grim. "I know what to do now. But if you don't mind, I won't tell you in advance. The fewer that know about it, the less likely it is that Valentine picks it up from any unguarded thoughts. Pretend to go along with whatever he says. Just be prepared to act when I do."

"Valentine is mine," Tanya said.

RD raised a quizzical eyebrow. "You realise that we can't afford to leave him alive?"

Tanya nodded reluctantly.

"Very well. I reckon it's time you broke out some of your home-made combat drug."

By the time Tanya had administered her concoction, the gunfire outside had stopped. Soon Valentine returned with a half-dozen of their 'rescuers'.

"We must leave immediately," he said. "It's getting late, and we'll be trapped if reinforcements arrive."

"Is that all that's left of you?" RD asked.

"All that can walk. There are a few that can't, but can still hold a gun – they've volunteered to stay behind and delay any more troops that the Zelynans send. Let's move.

Chapter 26

As they set out for the boat, RD hung back and started limping on his left leg.

"What's the matter?" Valentine asked.

"I think I must have pulled a muscle running from the fire-fight."

"We can't afford to wait for you. You two –" (he pointed at two of the soldiers) "help him along as fast as you can. The rest of us will go on ahead."

One of the soldiers put RD's left arm over his shoulder and took some of the weight off his leg, while the other led them along the path. They were soon out of sight of the rest of the convoy, and when RD judged they were also out of earshot, he gasped and put all his weight on the soldier supporting him. The man stumbled, cursing as his knee hit the ground.

"What's wrong?" their escort asked. "Do you need help?" He turned back towards the pair.

"Sorry, my leg gave way," RD said. "Here, let me help you up." He extended his hand towards the kneeling soldier.

As the man reached out, RD thrust his other hand into his boot and drew his combat knife from its sheath. In one smooth movement, he buried the blade in the soldier's neck, just under the chinstrap of his helmet, driving it through the man's vocal cords and into the base of his brain.

"What the hell?" the other soldier said, raising his rifle.

RD rolled aside of the toppling corpse, gathered his now-fully-functional legs beneath him, and launched himself almost horizontally towards the other soldier. He buried his fist in the man's crotch.

The soldier's breath whooshed out of him and he toppled over. He lay curled up in a foetal position, moaning, until RD cut his throat.

"Sleep well," he said, briskly cleaning his knife on the dead man's uniform and returning it to its sheath. "I'll take your rifle, if you don't mind. Or even if you do. I think I can find a use for it."

Meanwhile, the rest of the party had reached the barge, which was manned by three heavily-bearded men in boiler-suits.

"Those men look like Duplifis," Bartes said.

"That's exactly what they are," Valentine said. "The authorities treat them as harmless idiots, so they can get away with smuggling whatever – or in this case whoever – they want. Now I suggest you all get aboard."

"Shouldn't we wait for the others?" Tanya asked.

"We should be ready to go as soon as they get here," Valentine said. "Let's get you below deck."

They crossed the gang-plank in a single file and made for the open hold. Anoushka, Joseph and Peter descended the ladder one after the other. Bartes lingered, reluctant to follow them. *Where the hell is RD,* he thought to himself. There was the sound of a single shot and a cry from the Duplifi at the wheel as he crumpled and fell with a bullet in his brain. *Ah, there he is.*

"Sniper!" Valentine shouted. Bartes, Iain and Tanya took cover behind the boat's superstructure, while Valentine's men turned towards the trees, went prone and returned fire.

The two remaining Duplifis, who were not trained for situations like this, reacted more slowly. One stood as if stunned, then shrieked as a bullet hit him. He fell, clutching frantically at his stomach. The other looked wildly about him and ran towards the other side of the boat. For a moment, it seemed as if he'd be able to reach the relative safety of the water, but a hole appeared in his back, below his left shoulder-blade. With a pained grunt, he stumbled forwards and lay, twitching, over the far railing.

"Now's our chance," Bartes whispered. "They think they're in cover – but we've got the drop on them." He and Iain drew their pistols. "Lower your weapons and put your hands on your heads," he said aloud.

"What are you doing, Bartes – Iain? We're your friends," Valentine said.

Bartes raised a sardonic eyebrow and held his pistol ready.

Tanya had also drawn her pistol, and was pointing it at Valentine. She could sense that the ex-Major was gathering his will, but she hesitated.

:Tanya! Now!: Bartes sent.

:I can't,: she cried mentally.

:You must!:

I know, she thought, *but –* Her mind froze. He'd been their friend – she'd trusted him. She still wanted to believe in him, even though he'd deceived them all, even though he was working for someone – something –

Her finger seemed to move of its own accord. Valentine's stunned expression as her bullet hit him right between the eyes imprinted itself indelibly in her brain. His body arched, and he fell backwards over the low railings on the deck. The river swallowed him as if he'd never been...

RD emerged from the trees as Bartes and Iain began to bind and gag their prisoners. "Well done," he said. "Like a well-oiled machine – as always. But why didn't you save us some trouble and just shoot them all?"

"It wasn't necessary," Bartes said.

"And I, for one, am grateful," Tanya added. "Excuse me." She walked away, into the woods. Bartes and Iain watched her go with sympathy in their eyes.

As soon as Tanya was out of sight, she threw up. She found a quiet spot where she could curl up in the leaves and let go of her emotions. After a few minutes, she became aware that a soft body had insinuated itself into the gap between her chest and her thighs, and was vibrating gently.

:*Thank you, little sister,*: Tanya sent.

:*No problem,*: Slimmest replied gently. :*You know, it even gets to my mistress sometimes.*:

:*It's not just the death and the pain,*: Tanya told her. :*I was beginning to care for Valentine, and when he turned up I* knew *he was on our side, and the bastard betrayed us and I had to kill him. It tore me up inside to do it. I had no choice but to put a bullet in his brain.*:

:*Oh, I wouldn't be too sure he's dead. His kind are notoriously hard to kill.*:

:*His kind?*:

:*Kailyphs. Look, let's not complicate this unnecessarily for now. You'll remember about his people when you get your other memories back.*:

:*I* am *beginning to remember my past – who I really am – and some of the things I've done, and I'm not so sure I want to learn any more. Was I – am I – really a stone-cold assassin?*:

:*No – you're not. You have killed, yes, but only when really necessary. Some people – like you and my mistress – have to make uncomfortable decisions in order to keep other people safe. Now relax and let the pain drain away.*:

Back at the boat, Bartes had finished interrogating the prisoners, and RD & Iain were looking through the vessel's travel papers.

"Do they know anything?" RD asked as Bartes crossed the gang-plank.

"No – they're just mercenaries Valentine hired." Bartes looked frustrated. "I even checked psionically, to make sure they were telling the truth."

"We've found a map of the region that might help." Iain laid out the sheet and they gathered round it.

"Peter?" Bartes said, looking round at the boy. "Come and have a look at this. Does it show that pass you mentioned?"

"Here." Peter pointed to a narrow section of the southern mountain range. "You can see that the Telphanian border is just on the eastern side."

"And you believe we can get through?"

"It's our best chance. It'll be guarded, but hopefully we can slip through unnoticed."

"It's still a long journey," RD pointed out

"Look here." Bartes pointed at the map. "The river wanders a bit, but if we could reach this point, just south of Gomsk, we could save at least part of the trek – and who knows? We might find an unmarked tributary which would take us even further."

"It would definitely help – if we could fool the Zelynans patrolling the river," RD said. "We'd have to pass by Tureskow, and according to this permit, we'd have to spend the night tied up there – and we don't exactly look like Duplifis."

"But you could." Tanya had recovered her composure and re-joined them.

"What do you mean?"

"Most Duplifis have masses of facial hair, like the three men that were crewing this boat, and they all wore shapeless overalls. If I could remove their beards relatively intact – well, I've got some surgical adhesive in my medkit…"

Iain pondered for a moment. "It's worth a try. I'm sure that RD, Bartes and I could put on a show."

Shaving a dead man is not an occupation to be desired, but Tanya coped with it while RD, Bartes and Iain removed the Duplifis' overalls and put them on.

Tanya came over to them, gingerly carrying three hunks of something dark and unsavoury. "Here you are. They obviously weren't terribly keen on personal hygiene, but it made it easier for me to get their beards off in one piece. I'm willing to lay odds that you're not going to like wearing them, though."

RD's mouth puckered. "Do we have to? They smell. And they could have Things in them."

Bartes shrugged. "Come on. A man's got to wear what a man's got to wear. Give me that adhesive, Tanya. Is there a mirror around?"

"Hmm." Tanya viewed the effect critically when they had finished. "Not bad. But we'll need to do something about the blood on those overalls. Can you smear some engine grease over it? That'll do something to camouflage it."

They hid their prisoners and the bodies of the crew members in the undergrowth, stowed the weapons aboard, and set out for Tureskow. Joseph and the girls hid below, while Peter sat on the deck, trying to teach the three impostors to speak with Duplifian accents. Iain took to it easily, but neither Bartes nor RD could manage very well, so, by common consent, Iain became the boat's captain. Once Iain sounded sufficiently convincing, Peter joined the others in hiding.

It was completely dark by the time they reached Tureskow and tied up at the jetty. "What are you doing here?" a voice demanded.

"Please, sir," Iain said in a deeper register than his normal voice, every syllable dripping obsequiousness, "we have permit."

There was a grunt, and the voice continued, "You're supposed to dock before sunset."

"So sorry, sir – we have problem with engine."

"Humph. Typical Duplifi workmanship. Where are your papers?"

"Here, sir." They had retrieved the papers of the dead men. In the dark, with the false beards, Tanya's team-mates looked enough like the fuzzy pictures on them to pass muster.

There was a pregnant pause. "You there – is that blood on your overalls?"

There was a grunt from RD before Iain continued. "Very sorry, sir. Achmed is half-witted. He speak Duplifi bad enough, and could not learn your tongue. Ishmael, too, cannot. See what I have to work with? But they my cousins, so my mother, she insist I employ them." He gave a theatrical sigh. "As for blood, Achmed cut himself while repairing engine."

The guard seemed mollified. "You'll have to sleep on your boat."

"Thank you, sir. We lose much time, so we go early in morning." Steps receded into the distance, and Iain's real voice said quietly, "Well, that went well."

"Half-witted?" RD hissed indignantly.

"Merely corroborative detail, intended to give artistic verisimilitude to an otherwise bald and unconvincing narrative," Iain quoted, as he opened the hatch to the compartment.

"You've done something like this before," Tanya said.

"I believe that I have," Iain simpered. "You'd better stay in here for tonight – with the hatch open for extra air. We'll sleep on deck. If we leave before dawn, we should manage to avoid detection."

Those below found it difficult to sleep. They were tired enough, but as the boat moved in response to the river's flow, it creaked and groaned in a most disturbing fashion.

"Tanya?" Anoushka's whisper sounded troubled. "I don't like it in here."

"Nor do I," Peter added. "It seems almost alive."

"Wrong expression," Tanya said. "There's death here: death, fear and pain. I can't be sure exactly what happened, but it must have been really awful to leave such a deep psionic impression." They huddled together and soon Slimmest joined them, her purring dispelling some of the ghastly presence. Eventually, they slept.

Sunset in Silvana

Tanya opened her eyes. The hold was filled with people. She and her friends were packed in with many others – men, women and children. Some looked at her with dead eyes, others with terror. Some were moaning, others whimpering. Mothers were trying to comfort their children, and families held each other tightly.

Valentine was kneeling beside her. He didn't seem angry, or even sad, merely concerned. "Come with me," he said, helping her to her feet, taking her hand and leading her out of the hold and on to the riverbank, where he indicated that she should look back at the barge. An endless stream of struggling victims was being dragged toward a greasy black spiral on the deck of the boat, following its path inwards before disappearing with wails of despair.

Valentine turned her to face him. She looked down and away, trying to ignore the awful wound she'd inflicted between his eyes. His voice echoed, hollow, around the hold. "Escape. Escape. Escape, or their fate will be yours." And as she watched, his face became her own, but filled with agony, her eyes lifeless and her mouth agape...

...and she woke.

She was sweating, curled into a foetal position, and it was all she could do not to scream. Slimmest was rubbing against her and purring. She looked around frantically, and saw Anoushka and Peter gazing at her, eyes wide. The terror slowly ebbed away. Even so, it was some time before she could trust her voice. "I take it that you've had b-bad dreams, too?" she asked, somewhat unnecessarily. Her companions both nodded in response. None of them dared to close their eyes again, so they huddled even closer together and waited. It was a relief when dawn arrived.

Mid-afternoon found them nearing the foothills of the mountain range, and they were lucky enough to find a large tributary which led east. Trees arched out over the water, almost meeting midstream, and they now felt safe enough from observation to emerge from that chamber of horror and breathe clean air.

RD, Iain & Bartes stripped off their overalls with obvious relief. "How do we remove these beards?" Iain asked. "I don't mind a bit of hair, but this is like having an animal hanging from my jaw. And it itches." He scratched vigorously.

Anoushka's eyes sparkled. "I could pull it off."

Bartes sighed. "Tanya, you must have some alcohol that'll dissolve this adhesive."

"Spoilsport." Anoushka stuck out her tongue.

"Here you are." Tanya passed them a bottle of surgical spirit. "This should do the trick."

"Ah, that's better," Iain sighed, rubbing his naked and somewhat reddened chin. "I think I'll shave as well."

"I don't know." Bartes examined his stubble in the mirror. "A beard might prove useful as a disguise. I think I'll grow mine out."

"Could you make us a drink?" Iain asked Tanya.

"Why not," she said. "A little bit of activity might help me shake off this feeling of oppression. I'll make up a snack, too, if you'd like. Would you give me a hand, 'Noushka?"

"I'd love to."

The galley was quite well stocked, and, while Anoushka brewed some tea and coffee, Tanya sliced up a couple of loaves of rich, dark bread and made some sandwiches. The team fell on the food with gusto, and wolfed down every crumb with obvious relish. Tanya brought out some oatcakes, and they were devoured in a similar fashion.

"At least the food isn't haunted," Peter said as he picked up and finished the last fragments from his plate.

"No indeed." Iain smiled contentedly.

"There's plenty more stuff in the galley," Tanya said. "We'll soon be leaving this boat behind, so I'll make up some more sandwiches, and add them and anything else we can carry to our trail rations."

She ransacked the galley, looking for foodstuffs they could take with them. At the back of one of the cupboards was an earthenware jar. She pulled it out and examined the contents. *Flour,* she thought, *and it's nearly empty anyway.* She almost discarded it, but something stayed her hand. *Hmm...* She looked around. *Yes, there's enough molasses...* She added some of the treacly substance to the flour, and took the pot out to RD.

"Can I have a little oil, please?" she asked, "and some petrol?"

When he saw what she was carrying, his eyes glinted maliciously. "If that's intended to be what I think it is, we've plenty to spare."

She half-filled the jar with petrol and oil, and capped it with a piece of rag. Joseph had been watching what she'd been doing and said, "Can we make some more? I'd love to learn how." In the end, they managed to create three more fire-bombs, which they stashed carefully upright in their packs.

There was a whisper ahead that gradually increased in volume until, motoring around a bend, they found themselves at the base of a waterfall some fifty feet high. "End of the line," RD said. "Time to starting walking."

"I'll be glad to be shot of this boat," Tanya told Bartes as they ferried their packs ashore. "It makes me feel unclean."

"I don't think anyone will disagree," he replied. "It's spooked us all, even RD. We'd better sink it to minimise the chance of its being seen from the air." He and RD knocked holes in both sides of the barge below the waterline, and as it started to fill with water, RD started its engine and aimed it towards the waterfall.

As they were climbing up beside the cascade, Tanya looked back – and immediately wished that she hadn't: the boat's deck was awash, and there, to her horror, was the spiral of her dream. It briefly glowed a sickly green before it sank out of sight.

They walked and climbed all that night and the following morning with only short breaks. About noon, as they made their way down into a broad valley, Anoushka's foot slipped and she sat down rather heavily. "I – I can't go any further..." she said.

Tanya sat down beside her. "Yes, you can," she said gently. "We'll have a short rest, and then I'll carry your pack for a while."

Bartes was gazing forward. "I can see something glinting through the trees," he said. "Stay here and relax while I scout ahead."

Even RD didn't cavil at this, and they all sank down onto the ground. Joseph eased his shoes off and wiggled his toes with a sigh, and Tanya lay back and let Anoushka rest her head on her shoulder. The latter's eyes were beginning to close when Bartes returned.

"I think you ought to see this," he said to RD. "We've got a problem. Leave Anoushka and the boys to recuperate."

Tanya gently slipped out from under Anoushka, laying her friend's head on a bedroll, and followed the men through the trees. Running across the path was a broad swathe of clear ground stretching in a straight line to the north and south as far as the eye could see, with barbed-wire fences either side. Down the middle of the channel ran twin rails at roughly head height.

"What's this?" Tanya asked.

"It looks like some sort of guide-rail for high-speed anti-gravity trains," Bartes said.

Iain looked worried. "How're we going to get across?"

"We'll need holes on both sides," RD said, "but we'd have to cut this fence first, and whoever goes over to cut the other one is going to be pretty exposed."

"D'you think they're alarmed?" Tanya asked.

"Probably," Bartes said, "but what alternative do we have?"

"None," RD said. "And because the enemy are hunting us, they'll be alert. We'll rest up for a while and plan how to do this, and try to get over and away before they can react."

"I could teleport over to the other side, beyond the wire," said Tanya. "If I cut a hole that side at the same time as Bartes cuts a hole here, it would be quicker and lessen the enemy's chance to respond."

"You can *teleport*?" RD looked at Tanya suspiciously. "What sort of witch *are* you?"

"The useful sort. Leave her alone." Bartes' sudden belligerence cowed RD to silence.

"It'll take a lot of energy, and I can't carry much. A single layer of clothing and, if I hold them tightly, some wire-cutters is about all. And it'll take me a while to recover fully afterwards."

They found a place which was well hidden from the infrequent but insistent fly-overs and settled in to wait. Tanya sat and prepared herself while RD, Iain and Bartes took it in turns to watch the tracks. They could hardly miss the trains anyway, as their passing sent a fierce wind blowing through the trees.

"Look, I think we've established the pattern," Iain said after a couple of hours. "There should be a long enough gap after the next southbound express to get across."

"Unless they change the schedule," RD pointed out morosely.

"We've got to risk it some time," Bartes said. "It's either that or wait here till we're found and captured."

Once the train had rocketed past, Tanya took a deep breath and disappeared. She reappeared instantly on the other side, just beyond the fence. She signalled Bartes, and they started cutting holes in the wire while RD and Iain watched the tracks in both directions for any unexpected visitors. As Bartes cut one of the wires, there was a slight discharge.

"Some of the wires are alarmed," he called to Tanya.

"Not half as alarmed as we'll be if anyone appears. Let's hurry this up."

As soon as the gap was big enough, Iain squirmed through and ran for the nearest rail. The size and number of the supports made it tricky to get underneath, so he simply threw his pack over and vaulted nimbly after it.

Bartes ran to the first rail while Iain leapt over the second, and they prepared to help the less athletic members of the party across, beginning with Anoushka. Bartes lifted her up so she could straddle the rail and drop between the tracks, and passed her pack over. Iain hauled her over the next one, and she was soon crouched beside Tanya in the undergrowth.

As soon as she was clear, Bartes signalled Peter, and he, too, reached the other side successfully. Then it was Joseph's turn.

As the boy touched the ground between the rails, there was the chatter of gunfire and dust spurted around him. He, Iain and Bartes dived next to the rails for the small amount of cover they provided.

Hovering over the trees was a black helicopter gun-ship. An amplified voice issued from it: "Put your weapons down and surrender!"

:*Where the hell did that bastard come from so quickly?*: Bartes sent to Tanya.

:*It must have already been in the area,*: Tanya replied. :*Whatever we try, they're dogging our heels, every step of the way.*: She shook her head in exasperation.

Beyond the rails, RD dropped to one knee and aimed his rifle at the helicopter. A stuttering of shots pinged off the armoured shell of the intruder, and there was an immediate response: RD had to leap aside smartly as the chain gun shredded the place where he'd been kneeling. "So much for taking us alive," he called to the others.

"Take Anoushka into cover," Tanya snapped at Peter. He opened his mouth to protest, but, seeing Anoushka's terrified face, thought better of it. They disappeared into the undergrowth.

My God, what can we do? They're sitting ducks, Tanya thought. *If only I could distract the pilot...* As she lay prone, her hand brushed against a fallen leaf and she had an idea. *I wonder...*

She laid the leaf in the palm of her hand and, despite her weariness, focussed her attention on it. Once she had it fixed in her head, she stretched out mentally towards the gun-ship and located the pilot's mind. He didn't detect her presence – controlling the helicopter was taking all his concentration. She moved her focus down to his larynx and created a representation of the leaf within it. She compressed the connection between the two leaves and released her end; suddenly, her hand was empty.

The gun-ship jerked and veered suddenly sideways, before swinging round, exposing its more lightly armoured side. RD fired again as it lurched backwards and its rotors caught the trees. It spun uncontrollably and crashed headfirst into the tracks, spraying shrapnel in all directions.

They waited in stunned silence for signs of life from the wreck, but none were forthcoming. Bartes broke the spell. "Are you OK, Tanya?" he called.

"I *think* so," she replied, looking up at the sharp piece of metal embedded in a tree-trunk a few inches above her head.

"I'm fine, thank you for asking," Iain interjected sardonically. "What about you?"

"I'm not hurt," Bartes replied. "The rail sheltered me from most of the blast. Where's Joseph?"

Iain stood up and looked over the rail, where he could see a crumpled figure. "There he is," he called. "Joseph, are you all right?"

To his relief, the figure moved, and slowly raised itself to its knees. The boy's right arm hung uselessly, and blood was pouring from his scalp.

"Come over here, boy – I'll help you over," Iain called.

Whether he had been deafened by the explosion, or was simply stunned, they never knew, but instead of fleeing, Joseph started to stumble towards the smouldering wreck.

"Come back," Tanya yelled. "It's not safe."

"I'm going to get him," Iain called, and braced himself to leap over the rail.

"No!" Tanya cried. "It could explode any second."

It was too late. The fuel tank erupted, igniting the munitions in the burning carcase. Tanya dived back into the bushes, and Iain and Bartes ducked behind the rails as bullets and a second wave of shrapnel flew past them.

They hid until the storm of metal subsided. Silence fell, punctuated only by the crackle of flames and the ping of cooling metal. Iain slowly raised his head.

The rails had been buckled and broken out of recognition, and there was now a large crater full of twisted metal where the wreck had been.

And between the crater and the rails lay a shattered, bloody shape.

Iain moved cautiously over to the body, picking the best route through the wreckage. He bent over the thing which had been Joseph, before it had been torn apart by the force of the blast and flying shards of metal. He looked up and shook his head.

Carefully he made his way back to the others. "There's nothing we could have done. But he couldn't have suffered. The blast would have killed him instantly." He helped Tanya to her feet. "Are you injured?"

It was all she could do to shake her head in mute denial. She shuddered as she looked towards where the boy's remains lay. "Poor Joseph," she said.

RD was a few yards away, kneeling by something on the ground. "Pull yourself together and come look at this," he said. There, lying face down in the dirt, was Joseph's head. "What do you make of that?" He pointed to the base of the boy's skull, where the flesh had been burnt away to show something embedded in the bone. "It looks like an implant."

"I've never seen anything like it before," Tanya said. Whatever it was, it was black and slimy but vaguely metallic, yet, at the same time impossibly, it writhed as though alive. Even the sight of it made her want to throw up. As they watched, it began to vaporise. "I don't know what it is – or was – but I hope I never encounter another one," she added with an involuntary shiver.

"It appears that Joseph was more – or perhaps less – than he seemed," Bartes said.

They made their way to where the others were waiting. Anoushka looked at each of them in turn and asked "Where's Joseph?"

"I'm sorry – he didn't make it," Iain told her.

"Oh, no!" she said, her eyes filling with tears. "We heard an explosion, and I was scared..."

"The helicopter crashed," Bartes said quietly. "He was caught in the blast. There was nothing we could do."

Peter sighed. "It's a pity," he said. "We were on such bad terms after he found out who I really was. I'd have liked to have a chance to rebuild our friendship – it wasn't all pretence."

"After the explosion, we noticed something odd," Iain said. "Joseph had this strange implant in his head: it was black and metallic, and highly sophisticated."

"It didn't look like something the Zelynans would have," added RD.

"No." Tanya said slowly. "And it wasn't anything I've ever met before – as far as I remember. I didn't like it at all."

"We ought to bury him," Anoushka said. "It's the only decent thing to do..."

"We haven't the time," Iain said. "The Zelynans must know where we are now. If we stay around here much longer, we'll be captured. There'll be time to mourn later."

"You're right." RD shouldered his pack and set off through the woods. Reluctantly, one by one, they turned their backs on their dead companion and silently followed RD.

Chapter 27

They knew they had to get away from the area as quickly as possible, so despite their exhausted state, they pushed on with as much haste as they could. They walked until, just as the sun was setting, they came to a swift-flowing river that ran through a broad gully across their path. "I don't think I can take another step, let alone cross that," Anoushka said breathlessly as she slumped down on a fallen tree-trunk.

Tanya looked round at her bone-weary friends. "We don't dare go any further," she said, "In our current state, we'd be stumbling around in the dark. We'd only end up injuring ourselves, and a broken ankle would slow us down even more than a brief rest. Let's look for somewhere to hole up overnight."

"What's that?" Iain asked, pointing ahead to the left. "There's something on the top of that hillock." There was a strange overgrown shape on the mound he'd identified. In the dying sunlight they could just make out what looked like the stump of some sort of derelict structure – a watchtower, perhaps?

"Let's go have a look," Bartes said. "If nothing else, we can shelter on its leeward side."

Anoushka and Peter waited at the bottom of the hill while the rest of them trudged wearily upwards to inspect the wrecked building, which did indeed prove to have once been a circular tower. The upper levels had fallen in on themselves to form a solid pile of masonry, which had been covered by undergrowth over many years.

"This is old," Iain said, "really, really old. It must date back to the time of the elder races."

"This damage isn't just erosion, either," Bartes pointed out. "There are blast marks on some of these stones."

"And not just from hand weapons," Iain said in awe, pointing through the bushes at a huge granite slab that had been burnt and shattered by a single impact.

"I'm as impressed as you are," Tanya said, "But whoever did this is long gone. I'm concerned that we all get a good night's rest. This place would provide a little shelter from the wind. It's better than nothing, but I don't like the idea of a night in the open – especially when we're under pursuit. It's a pity there's nowhere to shelter inside this ruin."

:*Oh, but there is,*: Slimmest told her.

:*What do you mean?*: Tanya asked.

:*The underground part of the building is still usable. I've found a way in, over here, hidden behind some bushes.*: She was sitting off to the right by a patch of dense undergrowth. :*I've been inside, and it's ideal for your party, though the entrance might be a bit of a tight squeeze for* some *of you.*:

:*Is it safe?*: Tanya asked. :*I don't like the idea of being trapped underground.*:

:*Perfectly safe,*: the cat assured her.

"Slimmest has found a way inside," Tanya told the others. "Follow me."

They pushed aside the vegetation to reveal a hole in the tower's wall which was mostly blocked by a slab of fallen stone. "Hmm... Looks stable enough," RD mused. He looked at Tanya. "You're the slenderest – apart from the boy, and I trust you marginally more than I do him. You reconnoitre while we stand guard out here."

"As you wish, O Master" Tanya said with a mock bow. She dumped her gear to avoid getting it caught on protruding masonry, but before she went down into the darkness, she sent to Slimmest, :*Are you sure there's nothing dangerous down there?*:

:*Not a thing,*: came the reply.

"Can you detect anything living down there?" she asked Bartes.

"Only some bugs, and a rodent or two," he told her after a few seconds. "And a few fish," he added in a puzzled tone. "Anyway, Iain and I'll go and get the others while you're inside."

Tanya lit her torch and held it between her teeth as she squirmed through the aperture. Something seemed to brush her skin as she passed through the tower's wall and there was a faint electrical odour. The air inside smelt a bit musty and slightly damp, and she almost felt like she was being watched – not by any person, but by the tower itself. It didn't seem a hostile gaze, though, and a few feet in the tunnel opened up into a short passageway that ended in an arch. She stood up, and looking back it became clear that this had originally been an entrance to the tower.

Passing through the arch, she found herself on a small landing facing a blank wall. On her left, stairs spiralled down, and to her right more continued upwards. The walls, floor, ceiling, all were made of the same smooth grey material. It seemed a bit like stone and a bit like metal, but above all very solid and very hard. The whole structure seemed to have been carved from a single block, or perhaps extruded or moulded in some way. It seemed less dark than she expected, and when she doused her torch to check, she found that, whatever the substance was, it gave off a soft glow. She laid the palm of her hand against it and felt a slight warmth, almost as if the building were alive.

She turned right and started to climb, but after a dozen steps she was blocked by a wall of the same material, in the middle of which was a crystalline panel made up of different coloured sections, each of which also seemed to glow with a dull inner light. She couldn't make up her mind whether it was a sign, a door control or a piece of artwork, but, remembering her companions waiting outside, she realised that whatever else it was, it was definitely a mystery for another time.

Turning around, she descended to the small landing and started down the opposite staircase. As she walked, she became aware that although the width of the passage was constant, its curvature was gradually lessening. She had nearly completed one full turn of the spiral when she realised that the light in front of her was increasing.

The source of the extra light was an opening on the inner side of the staircase. She stopped and looked through, down into a large conical area. She was near the ceiling, which was roughly the diameter of the tower above, but the chamber opened out to about a hundred and fifty feet across at the bottom. In the centre of the floor, which was a fair way below, was a large circular pool. Everything seemed to be constructed of the same grey material, the inner glow of which was now enhanced by a soft, warm, white light that emanated through one of two arched openings in the base of the wall, and from under the water below.

The lower third of the walls were circled with troughs that were filled with soil. Similar troughs were dotted around the floor of the chamber, and continued down to the very edge of the pool, interspersed with couches and tables. Tanya remembered that one of the elder races, the Forerunners, delighted in the natural world, and installed gardens wherever they could. Her heart rate soared with excitement as she realised that she was looking at the remains of one of their creations.

She could hear the sound of running water, and, looking closer, she saw small streams issuing from apertures in the wall just above the highest troughs and circling downwards, irrigating the trapped soil as they did so. For such a system – and the lighting - to still be operating, even after an unguessable passage of years, was astonishing.

Her mood of awe turned into laughter as Sophie's small spotted cat came skittering from the darker archway below and hurled herself belly deep into the shining water. With a light heart she ran down the remaining stairs, and reached the bottom far more quickly than she expected. By the time she got to the water's edge, Slimmest was happily splashing through the water pouncing on small minnow-like fish that easily evaded her paws. Tanya knelt down and called her.

:*What kept you?*: she asked.

:*I'm not as lithe as you, little sister,*: Tanya told her. :*Thank you for finding this place.*: She scratched Slimmest between the shoulder blades and the cat reared up ecstatically.

The chamber was uninhabited, apart from a family of rodents that had built a nest in one of the troughs at the base of the wall. The lit archway opened onto a passageway that continued downwards. At first glance it was an exciting discovery but Tanya's hope of a major find soon turned to chagrin when her foot disturbed the water covering the floor, a liquid so still and clear that she had failed to see it until the ripples of her footstep marred the surface. She took several more paces, but as the path spiralled downward the water deepened, and she thought that, if she continued onward, it would soon fill the whole tunnel – here was another mystery that would have to wait. Everything seemed safe, so she returned to the top of the stairs, again arriving more quickly and with less effort than she'd have expected.

"You took your time," RD said as she squirmed back through the opening.

"Sorry," Tanya replied. "It's fantastic down there – like another world. You wait till you see it. Iain, you go through and we'll pass you our equipment. Bartes, see if you can find any fallen branches so we can light a fire inside."

It took some time to pass all their gear, plus the firewood, through the cramped passage, and for everyone to follow it through. As they worked, Tanya gave the others a running commentary on what she'd discovered, but she could see they thought she was exaggerating until she led them to the window she'd found earlier. They were every bit as amazed as she had been. For once, even RD had nothing negative to say. Only Anoushka seemed less than enthusiastic about their new hideaway.

"What's the matter?" Tanya asked her as they started down.

"Nothing, really," she replied. "It's just that it's so far down, and I'm so tired..."

"Don't worry," Tanya reassured her, "there's something a bit odd about this place. We'll be at the bottom before you know it." Indeed, they seemed to take only a couple of dozen paces before they entered the chamber and were able to collapse onto the couches they'd seen from above. These were surprisingly comfortable, made of a material that yielded to the touch. They did, however, seem to have been made for a humanoid race somewhat taller than the refugees.

In the end RD broke the silence of exhaustion. "We ought to keep watch," he said.

"Not outside, surely," Bartes said.

"Of course not. We don't want to give ourselves away to anyone who's passing by – or flying over. No, in the entrance passage."

"There's not much chance of anyone else finding it," Tanya pointed out. "Not unless they've got a highly intelligent cat with them."

RD grunted. "I suppose that animal has its uses," he admitted grudgingly. "Still, we ought to keep an eye on anything that might happen outside – just in case. And we ought to eliminate any traces we left out there, as soon as it's light."

"You're right," Bartes agreed, "but Anoushka and Peter are in no state to do anything without some recovery time. The rest of us will have difficulty keeping awake."

"You're right. The best we can do for now is staggered watches, two at a time, four hours on and four off, changing one person every two hours. I'll go first with Iain. Bartes will replace him in two hours, and Dr Miller will replace me in four. Could you get us some food before you rest, Doctor?"

Tanya sighed. "A woman's work..." she muttered, but smiled as she did so. She was just too glad to find such a haven to take any real offence.

There was a hearth in the wall of the tower where Tanya carefully laid out some of the wood Bartes had found. Since most of it was tinder-dry, she had no problem igniting it. The flue seemed to be blocked, but by keeping the conflagration small, she managed to avoid too much smoke. *At least none of it will escape the tower and give away our position,* she thought.

She made her way across the floor to the edge of the pool. *I wonder what the water's like? It* looks *clear and clean.* She knelt down and scooped up a little of the water in her palm and touched it with her tongue. *It seems OK, but I'll run it through the biofilter anyway.*

She soon had a kettle-full of clear water which she set to boil. She toasted some bread, covered it in butter, and distributed it, along with the hot drinks. She lay back on a couch with a slab of toast in one hand and a mug of coffee in another, and sighed contentedly.

Bartes sat down beside her, and they ate and drank together, enjoying the quiet and serenity of their haven. "Who d'you think built this place?" he asked.

"One of the elder races, probably the Forerunners. From what I've heard, they had a special affinity for gardens – and for water."

"But where does the water in the streams come from, and where does it go?"

"It's fresh, and the pool is about level with the river we saw. They must be connected somehow."

"The cat seems happy to drink it."

They watched Slimmest lap from the pool. After some minutes, the cat suddenly stiffened, waggled her bottom, and dived into the water. After a brief flurry, she pulled herself out, wet and bedraggled but with a large fish flopping about in her mouth. Exuding both triumph and pleasure she proceeded to eat her catch.

"That clinches it," Bartes said. "That fish is too big to live in such a small pool. It must be fed from outside." He sighed deeply. "I'm exhausted. The others are asleep already. Let's join them."

"You go on. I'll join you in a while. There's something I want to do first – something I've been wanting to do for days."

Once the others were all asleep, Tanya stripped off her clothes and walked down to the pool. She tested the temperature of the water with her toe. As expected, it was cold and refreshing. There were steps that led down into the sunken pool, and soon she was in it up to her neck.

She lay for a while, floating on her back and soaking up the calm that the tower exuded. The firelight reflected off the walls and the surface of the water, and that and the soft glow from all around gently illumined her sleeping companions. For the first time that she could recall, she felt truly at peace.

She almost wished she could stay there forever, but the cold eventually got into her bones and she began to shiver. She swam to the edge and hauled herself out, towelled herself dry and lay down by the fire. Soon a warm, furry body stretched out next to her – between her and the fire – and she fell into a deep, dreamless sleep.

Chapter 28

Tanya woke with the dawn, her morning hymn on her lips for the first time since her nightmare on the boat. She was about to yawn and stretch, but froze when she heard Anoushka talking.

"This place is so peaceful," her friend was saying, "but we can't stay here forever, and I don't really think we'll ever escape this planet. When Tanya says we will, I believe her – for a while – but then something happens, like that horrible fight at the boat, or – or Joseph..." Her voice trailed away.

RD and Anoushka were sitting together, and she was resting her head on his chest, while he had his arm around her, and was stroking her hair. "I'm not normally an optimist," he said with masterly understatement, "but I'd like to think that we'll get back to Regni someday soon." He paused. "If – and when we do, could you, I mean, do you think it might be possible for you and me –" Tanya could tell his mind was a turmoil of confusion, resignation and a wild hope.

Anoushka looked up at RD and gave him a wan smile. "Let's discuss it over a candle-lit dinner, just the two of us – if we ever do get home." At this point, Iain stirred, and they said no more, but from then on it was noticeable that they passed as much time as possible in each other's company.

Once any traces outside were covered, the group spent the rest of the day resting up and recuperating. Tanya insisted that they all bathed and washed their clothes. Though one or another of them kept watch by the entrance throughout, nothing significant happened outside. The adult members of the resident rodent family went in and out, providing food for their young, but they seemed unworried by the intruders. If anyone was in their way, they simply scampered over them.

Later that afternoon, Bartes was stripping down and cleaning his laser carbine when Tanya hurried over. "Come with me," she said, her eyes sparkling.

"What is it?" he asked.

"Do you remember that panel of coloured crystals I told you about at the top of the stairs? Where the passageway stops?"

"Yes. I had a look at that earlier. It appears to be some sort of door release, but none of the crystals responded to my touch."

"Well, I've got a reaction."

"You've opened up the passageway?"

"Well... no..." she hesitated. "Oh, come and see."

RD and Iain had overheard their conversation and followed them up the stairs. At the top, Tanya stood opposite the panels and concentrated. Almost instantly, one crystal then another started to glow more brightly. "It's psionically activated," she said. "It took a while, but in the end I hit on this combination. Brace yourselves." Broad circular bands of brilliant red rippled out from the panel across the end of the passageway, accompanied by a strong psionic sense of danger. When it subsided, Tanya continued. "I *think* it means access is blocked. Given the damage we saw from the outside, the tower itself may have decided that to let us go any further is hazardous."

"You could be right," Bartes said. "You know, it's amazing that this place still has power."

Iain studied the glowing red panel. "My guess is that there are geothermal generators deep below us."

"It's a pity we can't get down there," RD said, turning back toward the stairs.

"Yeah," Iain agreed. "I tried to swim as far as I could down the drowned corridor, but I couldn't find any air pockets, and the few doors I could reach wouldn't open. D'you think that passageway was always flooded?"

Sunset in Silvana

"No." Bartes shook his head. "There's a crack in the floor on one side of the pool. I think it must have been made during the battle that trashed the top of the tower. The fish in the pool show that it's connected to the river, which must supply fresh water, and also cool the generators. If you think about it, the floor of the chamber is just above the level of the river outside. That crack probably means that everything below us is completely inundated."

Later that evening, Tanya and Bartes were on guard duty together again, lying side-by-side under the collapsed entranceway. The moon was hidden by clouds, and darkness surrounded them.

"This isn't exactly a *watch*," grumbled Bartes. "I can't see a bloody thing."

"So listen," whispered Tanya. "There's something out there – did you hear that twig snap? Over to the left."

There was a tense silence, broken by a voice about fifty metres away.

"Look, it's pitch black now. We could walk within inches of them and not see them."

"But the Sergeant said to check this mound," responded another voice doggedly.

"I don't care what the Sergeant said! He just sits around on his fat behind and orders us about. Let's just rest here for a few minutes, then go back and tell him we didn't find anything."

"Well…"

"I've got a bottle…"

"Okay…"

For several minutes there were sighs and the occasional gurgle. After some time, the first voice said, "Shh… Did you hear that…?"

"Yes – some sort of slithering noise…"

There was silence for a few seconds before twin screams of terrible agony rent the air. Tanya stopped her ears but couldn't exclude the pain from her mind.

There was something else, too: something repulsive and dirty that her brain flatly refused to contemplate. The life signs of the two soldiers faded, and shortly afterwards the sense of evil diminished.

Once he felt it was safe, Bartes lit his torch. Tanya was as white as a sheet, and there was a patch of vomit off to one side of her. "Go – go and see how the others are," she told him, her breathing unsteady, "but leave me your torch."

He made his way down to where the others lay asleep, but they seemed blissfully oblivious to the carnage above. Slimmest was the only one awake and alert. :*Did you sense what happened out there?*: he asked her.

:*Yes,*: she sent, :*But it felt as if it was occurring a long way away – almost like it was a story I was being told. I think this place must have been a Forerunner stronghold. It protects those it judges to be its own – and not just physically.*:

:*Didn't the others react at all?*: he asked.

:*RD stirred slightly, like he was having a bad dream, but no-one else even twitched.*:

He returned to find Tanya peering through the entrance into the night, her body taut, as if every sense was straining to pick up any movement outside.

"What is it," he asked putting his lips close to her ears.

"Whatever those things are, they're still out there," she replied, her voice pitched normally to avoid a whisper's betraying sibilance, but a mere thread of sound. "They seem to be searching for us – it's like they know we're here somewhere, but can't find us."

Bartes reached out with his mind and sensed a wave of corruption that made him feel ill. Unthinkingly, he sent a lance of thought towards its source, trying to repel it. This proved to be a mistake: there was a malignant chuckling sound in his head, and after a few seconds they could hear a slithering coming nearer. Soon an indistinct dark shape overshadowed the entrance as it cut out the starlight beyond.

The fugitives seemed to be held paralysed in the grip of fear. A pallid tentacle reached out for Tanya, but, as it passed between the tower's still-solid walls, there was a flash of indescribably bright sapphire fire. The creature reared up and backwards. It screamed in pain and frustration before fleeing, its appendage blackened and still burning, back into the night.

Bartes held out his hand to Tanya, who took it in her own and grasped it tightly. It was some time before she stopped trembling, and even longer before he felt he could break the silence. "Are you all right?" he asked at last.

"I will be," she replied with a shudder, "but not just yet."

"What *was* that thing?"

"I-I've no idea – a-and I'm not sure I want to know..." She shivered again.

They were still holding hands when RD turned up to relieve Tanya. "Oho," he said, "is there something you want to tell me?"

"Yes," Bartes said, "but not what you suspect. Tanya, you go and try to get some sleep." She took a deep breath, nodded, and retreated quickly to the safe depths of the tower. Once she was out of earshot, he told RD about what they'd overheard and the subsequent attack.

"That's odd," he said when Bartes finished his tale. "I didn't hear anything." He paused, then shrugged. "Do you think they're gone?"

"I can still feel them out there. The tower wouldn't let them in, but they've been circling, looking for another entrance."

When Iain arrived to take Bartes' place, he was more than happy to go below. He soon settled down to rest, but despite the atmosphere of peace in the tower, it was some time before he could close his eyes. Tanya had banked up the fire so it gave extra warmth and light, but it did little to ease the cold in his soul. She, too, seemed restless, and they both slept only fitfully. He was actually grateful when he was called to take over watch again just as dawn was breaking.

"Are they still out there?" he asked Tanya as he lay down beside her.

"No, thank God," she replied, the relief in her voice almost palpable. "As soon as the sun came up, they left."

It was only a few minutes later when they heard another voice outside: "Up here, Sarge, they're here…" It trailed off. There was the sound of retching.

"What's wrong, Private. What happened to them?"

"I don't know, Sarge… and I don't think I want to know…"

"Get back to the others, Private – and clean yourself up, for God's sake. Corporal?"

"Yes, sir?"

"Get two of the squad with the strongest stomachs and put those corpses into body bags."

"What the Hell happened to them? They look half burnt and half... eaten…"

"I don't know. They'd be on a charge for drinking on duty – if they were still alive – but nobody deserves that…"

There was an interlude, presumably while the remains of the two soldiers were retrieved, and then the Sergeant said, "I can't see any sign of our targets. There's no way we'll catch them now – they'll be long gone. And I don't want to stay round here, given what happened to those two slackers. Radio for extraction."

Bartes and Tanya waited on tenterhooks until they heard a helicopter land some distance away and take off again soon afterwards. They remained where they were for some time. In the end, Tanya said, "D'you think we ought to have a look?"

"I guess so..." Bartes replied reluctantly. "I'll check it's safe." He reached out with his mind. "There's nothing dangerous out there now. Let's go."

The greenery was soaked with blood, with a few shreds of flesh and cloth hanging from the bushes – and superimposed over it all was a strange silvery deposit. This slime formed a couple of trails that came from the west and subsequently wandered about the area. One of them came up to the tower's entrance, where there was a scorch mark, and both trails circled the tower a number of times before disappearing into the undergrowth.

They scrambled back into the tunnel, and while Tanya continued her vigil, Bartes went below and reported their findings to the others.

"Is the area clear now?" RD asked.

"Yes."

"Then it's time we moved on. This place has been a real haven, but we've got a job to do. Iain, pack your stuff, then go and relieve Dr Miller. The rest of us should be ready to move by the time she is."

So it was less than half an hour later that they emerged from their sanctuary and set off towards Telphania. Rather than crossing the river, they followed its bank upstream. As expected, it soon turned in an easterly direction, towards the mountains, and they were able to climb gradually higher, heading (they hoped) for the border. Tanya and Bartes took it turns to check ahead for life-signs, but detected nothing significant.

Several times during the day they had to hide under the trees as aircraft flew over. Their pursuers seemed to know the direction they were heading – the wreck of the helicopter would have told them that – but not the precise route. Late afternoon found them on a high, grassy plateau, when Tanya noticed the approach of a jet from the north.

"Everybody lie down, as flat as you can. We might not be spotted." She breathed a sigh of relief as the plane flew past their still, prone forms and headed south, but at the last minute it banked and came round for another pass. "Oh well," she muttered. "Time for my party trick."

Bartes glanced over at Tanya, who lay in the grass, nose to nose with Slimmest. Their eyes were closed, and they both seemed to be concentrating. The cat's voice in his head asked, :*May I borrow some of your psionic energy?*:

:*Whatever you need,*: he replied, and a blue light flared under the cat's chin as he felt his power draining away. The plane flew directly over them, banked again and continued south.

"Thank you, little sister," Tanya said, breathing heavily, as it disappeared from sight, "and you too, Bartes. I thought we'd be seen for sure that time."

"What do you mean?" he asked. "I thought that we *were*."

"Oh, Slimmest and I managed to persuade the crew that what they saw on their first pass was really just a small group of deer."

They continued their weary trek through the foothills.

As the sun set behind them, RD pointed at a narrow valley just ahead of them. "That looks a good place to spend the night," he said. "The bushes will shelter us, and the creek will provide water."

"Do you think we can risk a fire?" Iain asked.

"I don't think so – in case we're spotted from the air."

The water in the stream was straight off the mountains, cold and clear. They drank all they wanted, refilled their water bottles, and settled down in the thicket to rest.

"I think we ought to keep watch," Bartes said.

"You're right." RD looked at the others. "Though I reckon it's up to you, me, Iain and Doctor Miller."

Sunset in Silvana

Indeed, Peter had already drifted into a doze, but Anoushka roused herself. "I can take my turn," she said. "All this exercise is toughening me up."

RD shook his head and smiled at her. "No, dear – you get some sleep. We'll be moving quickly tomorrow and I'd rather you were fully rested. We'll take single person two-hour watches so we can maximise our rest as well. I'll go first, then Bartes, Iain and the Doctor"

RD's watch passed without incident, but shortly after Bartes took over from him, he began to feel uneasy. *There's something out there,* he thought. He reached out with his mind and immediately began to feel foolish. *What an idiot! How could I have failed to recognise my own mother?*

A voice in his head said, :*Is that you, Bartes?*:

"Mother?" he called out as he got to his feet and started walking out to meet her. "What are you doing here?"

:*Yes, dear – it's your Gran and me. Can you help us? We're lost.*:

"Of course." He'd gone a few involuntary paces towards the two helpless old dears when a furry cannonball hit him between the shoulder-blades. He fell on his face just as twin streams of acid passed over him, through the space where his head had just been.

Chapter 29

:Run!: Slimmest's thought was urgent. *:Wake the others and run!:*

The spell shattered. Looking up, Bartes saw the two old ladies as they really were: grey and cylindrical, about eight feet long and two feet across, with a large circular mouth lined with multiple rows of sharp, hooked teeth and surrounded by tentacles. Above each mouth was the travesty of a human face. "What *are* those things?" he asked, as he sprinted back to the others.

:Nightcrawlers. Mutated slugs that pretend to be harmless and in need of help. They can make you see them as your friends, or even your family.:

"How fast can they move?"

:Not very,: she replied, *:but they're implacable. Once they have your psionic scent, they'll follow you all night, or until either you or they are dead.:*

"I've never met anything like these things before. They're not natural."

:No – they were created by the Da'ark. Our enemy is getting desperate, and bringing in help from their home dimension.:

Bartes roused the others. "Those monsters Tanya and I encountered back at the tower – the ones that killed those soldiers – are coming after us. Don't look at them or listen to them. They can bewitch you into thinking they're people you know, or that they're harmless and need help. Grab your stuff and get moving – they'll be here soon."

"But that's my mother out there – with Karla!" Peter cried, and started running toward the creatures.

Tanya grabbed him by the arm as he sprinted past her, swung him round and slapped his face. "Pull yourself together," she said harshly. "Your mother's dead, and Karla's still in the Blockhouse. Those things can make you see and hear what they want you to. Now come on."

The boy shook himself, gave her a look of terrible loss, but nodded. "What's Iain doing?" he said, looking over her shoulder.

Tanya glanced behind her. Iain was walking directly towards the oncoming beasts. She was filling her lungs to scream his name when, to her relief, he stopped, knelt, levelled his rifle and fired at the monstrosities.

The bullets hit one of the creatures dead centre, but seemed to have no discernible effect on it. In response, it spat back at him. He dodged the stream of acid, but a few drops splashed his hand. He cried in pain and retreated quickly.

"Don't run," Bartes called as they prepared to flee. "We can keep ahead of them, for now at least, but not if one of us breaks a leg, or twists an ankle. Watch where you're going."

They started moving as quickly as possible away from the oncoming horrors. Slimmest trotted ahead and acted as a scout, guiding them away from the worst terrain.

Tanya noticed that Iain was shaking his hand and wincing, so she drew over beside him. "How is it?" she asked.

"I cleaned it off but it still hurts," he said.

"Show me."

He held out his hand, striped with red weals.

"We can't stop now, much as I'd like to." She rummaged in her medkit and retrieved some salve. "Rub some of this on the wounds."

They paused for a moment, and he extended his other hand so that she could squeeze some of the cream onto it. He gently applied it to the damaged skin and sighed in relief. "That's better."

"It'll neutralise any remaining acid and ease the inflammation as well as the pain. I wish I had my

Mercy kit, though – our salves actually coat the area with synthiskin as protection."

"I'm just grateful for this. We ought to pick up the pace, though – the others are pulling ahead."

As they drew level with Bartes, Tanya called out to Slimmest. "Do you know of any way we can kill those things?"

:*They have no discernable vulnerable spots, and they're not susceptible to psionics,*: Slimmest broadcast. :*The best way is to use desiccants – such as large amounts of salt – or extreme heat. Even blowing them apart doesn't always finish them off.*:

"That's not a lot of use, you know," Bartes said, but Tanya stopped, took out one of her improvised flour and petrol cocktails and heaved it in the direction of the slugs.

"Try to hit the rag with your laser carbine," she told him.

He paused, shouldered his weapon and fired. There was a satisfying explosion and burning material was flung in all directions. The creatures paused on the other side of the conflagration before starting round to the left. Tanya threw another pot in that direction. It shattered and the flames spread. They moved the other way, and she blocked that path with the third.

She augmented her last throw psionically, and the final pot smashed just in front of one of the monsters, covering it liberally in fuel oil, petrol and molasses. The flames spread over it and it writhed and screamed in their heads as it shrivelled and died. The other was splattered, but the flames soon dwindled to nothing on its slimy skin.

Tanya cursed. "I should have tried that first," she said. "Now I'm out of bombs and there's one of those things still alive.

:*We'll have to find somewhere that it can't get at us,*: Slimmest sent. :*It's either that or we keep ahead of it till dawn – nightcrawlers don't like daylight. At least you bought us some time.*:

They stumbled on through the darkness. Every time they paused for breath, their pursuer was closer behind. Had they not already been tired, they would have stood a chance of outrunning it, but with dawn still a couple of hours away, they realised they wouldn't survive the night.

"It's no good," Anoushka cried. "We're not going to get away." She paused, her hands on her knees.

The others were too breathless to reply, but Tanya grabbed her arm and pulled her along. *I wish I had four legs, like Slimmest*, she thought. *Where's she gone now?* And as though she'd read Tanya's mind, Slimmest came racing towards them.

:*There's an old stone circle ahead. I* think *it's Forerunner, and – if so – it may protect us.*:

A ring of weathered monoliths reared up in front of them. It was about 50 feet in diameter, and made of a couple of dozen equally-spaced vertical blocks.

"I don't see this helping much," RD said.

"There's a smaller circle further in," Bartes said. "Perhaps we can build some sort of barricade."

As they made their way inwards, they found a third structure: about ten feet across and ten feet high, and roofed by a massive slab, it formed a sort of stone hut. They dived inside and waited, still panting.

There was a scream from the edge of the circle. "Keep your weapons ready," RD said, somewhat unnecessarily. "Maybe we can't kill that thing, but we can do our best to make it regret following us."

They stood motionless, hardly daring to breathe, while there were further screams and hisses, and the sound of slithering.

"What's keeping that monster?" Bartes whispered. "It seems to be moving around to the side."

"I'll go have a look," Iain said, and wriggled out of the hut on his belly. A minute later he returned. "It can't cross into the ring," he said. "I saw it try to enter – there was a brilliant blue light and it screamed."

"Did it see you," Bartes asked.

"Yes – it spat at me, but I was too quick for it." There was a patter of liquid from above them. "It must know where I went."

They huddled together and spent a restless night listening to the creature slithering around their refuge and screaming periodically as it failed to cross the invisible barrier, punctuated by occasional showers of venom.

After what seemed an eternity, the sky lightened, and the creature's attempts to get to them became more frantic. Eventually, they heard it slink away, howling in frustration.

"Can we find some wood and start a fire?" Tanya asked.

"I don't think we can afford the time," Bartes said. "We need to get as far ahead of that horror as we can before evening. Anyway, I can feel it lurking out there. I don't think it's safe to forage in the trees."

Tanya shared out some sandwiches, and they set out. Fortunately, the vegetation was becoming sparse. Bartes could sense the nightcrawler trying to follow them, travelling beneath the few trees in the deepest shade it could find, but they soon pulled ahead. By late morning, he couldn't feel its presence any longer.

They passed through a rock-strewn col and descended a couple of hundred feet onto what seemed to be the final plateau before the mountain peaks. It stretched across their path, about a mile wide.

"Can you see that?" Iain asked, shading his eyes.

"What?" Tanya asked.

"On the other side of this plain, a little way south."

Squinting, she just made out what looked like the entrance to a valley. "Peter, is that the path that leads through to the other side of the mountains?"

"I think so," the boy said.

Iain rubbed his hands together in anticipation. "Next stop, Telphania."

:*If we head that way,*: Slimmest said, :*the nightcrawler won't follow us. There's nothing to shade it from the ultraviolet rays.*:

The fugitives looked at each other in relief. "Time for a break – and some food," Tanya said, and not even RD disagreed. They sat down on a rocky outcropping, eating their first leisurely meal since they left the tower.

Bartes was about to stretch out for a postprandial siesta when his life sense flared. He reached out mentally and detected three men approaching them stealthily from above and behind them. "Incoming!" he yelled, and they threw themselves behind the rocks just as several shots pinged off the impromptu picnic bench.

"I can feel three of them," Bartes called. He seemed to concentrate for a couple of seconds, raised himself on his elbows, and fired. "Two, now. One's trying to flank us on the left."

"I see him," Iain said as he fired.

"Good shot," Bartes said. "The other one's trying to get away."

"Well, he won't manage it," RD said. He steadied himself on one knee and shot the fleeing security private between the shoulder-blades. His target gave a cry, flung out his hands and fell on his face. He twitched for a few seconds, and went still.

Tanya looked over at Bartes and frowned. "You were extremely accurate," she said. "Were you using psionics?"

"I was using my life sense to aim with," he said.

She shook her head. "Don't you know how dangerous it is, opening yourself up like that, particularly if your target turns out to be psionic himself? Do you have a death wish or something?"

He shrugged. "Maybe, but I just felt that the risk was worth it. Let's go and check out our attackers."

The dead men turned out to be a security sergeant and two privates. The former's papers identified him as Sergeant Sergei Krislenko, and gave him authority to search and detain anyone within his demesne – and to act as he saw fit in service of his country.

"That's strange," Tanya said. "They're just dressed in fatigues, and they're carrying no rations or supplies."

"Did anyone hear any helicopters?" RD asked.

They all shook their heads.

Iain looked down at the bodies. "Three men don't make a platoon, anyway."

"They can't have come far." Bartes shaded his eyes and scanned the surrounding area. "Perhaps there's some sort of encampment nearby."

"Let's go see where they're from," Iain said. "Tanya, would you look after the others while RD, Bartes & I investigate?"

"OK, but don't take too long. The hairs on the back of my neck tell me we're not far ahead of our pursuers." She shivered.

The three men spread out and searched the rocky ground in the direction from which their ambushers had come. It was Iain who first noticed the partial imprint of a boot in a patch of earth. From there, they followed a trail of boot prints that led up to the hills behind them.

They reached a doorway set into a rocky outcrop. "I can't detect anyone in there," Bartes said, "but let's not take any chances – there could be some sort of booby-trap." They stood to each side of the door, drew their pistols and cautiously pulled it open. No hail of bullets ensued, so they entered as quietly as possible, keeping an eye out for trip-wires.

The living room was deserted. Four comfortable chairs were ranged around an oil-fired heater, with side tables containing books, magazines, and some electronic games. Over the heater a vid screen was attached to a player and a game console: a multi-player first-person shooter was paused in mid-combat.

An alcove to the left contained a dining table and four chairs, with a small kitchen on the far side. On the table were the discarded remains of several meals.

Ahead of them were some stairs. Slowly and carefully, Bartes led them upwards. He cautiously peeked into the room above, which was also empty of life. They ascended into a communal bedroom with four bunks in it, plus a wash-basin. They checked everything but found nothing of interest.

On the other side of the room was a further flight of stairs, which they mounted. At the top was an observation post, similarly unoccupied, with slits covering the whole visible arc toward the border. From it, they could see the whole plateau, including a military outpost on a rocky platform on the south side of the valley they'd seen earlier.

"This place was set up for four people," RD pointed out, "but we only killed three. I wonder where the fourth is."

"Let's have a look," Iain said. He picked a pair of binoculars off a shelf and looked through the middle slit. The others followed suit, looking north and south, but it was Iain who spotted the fourth security officer. He was half way across the valley, heading for the outpost.

"Hold this," he said as he passed Bartes his ACR and unslung Winona. "This needs precision." He rested the rifle in the slit, aimed carefully through her telescopic sight, and brought his target down with a single bullet.

"Bravo!" Bartes said, and Iain gave a mock bow, but RD curtailed their celebration.

"Keep looking," he said. "Let's make sure we haven't stirred up a hornet's nest."

They trained their binoculars on the garrison and watched for some time, but surprisingly there seemed to be no reaction to the gunshot. "You'd think they'd at least come out and investigate," Bartes said, bemusedly.

"I'll bet they're ignoring it because it involves the security forces," Iain said. "If they're anything like most regulars, they hate blackshirts."

"And think what this observation post is for," RD added. "There's no way it's guarding the border. It's here so they can spy on their own soldiers."

Iain glanced through the northward-facing slit and swore. "Look," he said, indicating a transport helicopter which was taking off from a clearing several miles away.

"It'll have landed some security troops," RD said. "We need to move – and fast."

As they made their way back to the others, Bartes sent to Tanya, :*We've got company coming.*:

:*What d'you mean?*: she asked.

:*We've just seen a transport helicopter,*: he replied. :*Some miles to the north.*:

The others were on their feet and ready when Bartes, Iain and RD reached them. "Do you think we should we stay and fight?" Tanya asked. "We could set up quite an effective ambush."

"There'll be too many of them," RD said. "And there's a garrison on the south side of the mountain pass we're heading for. They've ignored what's happened so far, but they couldn't disregard a fully-fledged firefight. No, our best option is to keep going, but we'll have to hurry. The search party don't know exactly where we are yet, but they'll come in this direction, and then fan out and look for us. We've got thirty minutes at best."

"But what about the outpost?" Iain asked.

"Hopefully, we can slip below it. It's there to stop an invasion from Telphania, and with any luck, they won't be prepared for anyone coming from this direction. I can't see much of an alternative."

Sunset in Silvana

As they approached the canyon, they came across a clearing where several posts had been set up. Tied to three of them were freshly-dead corpses in regular army uniform: a lance corporal and two privates. They had been shot. There was a sign around the neck of each body that read DESERTER. Execution warrants signed by Security Sergeant Krislenko were pinned to their fatigues.

Tanya turned aside, looking rather sick. "No wonder the soldiers at the garrison ignored what happened," she said.

"And this place has been deliberately chosen to be visible from the military outpost," Bartes said. "I'd guess – if they did see our little fire-fight – they cheered us on."

"Let's hope their antipathy stretches to letting us escape," RD added.

Iain stopped to check the bodies and, as he reached into the breast pocket of the first, something slid up onto his arm and bit him. His body jerked as pain lanced through it, and he screamed.

Chapter 30

Tanya was startled for a second or two when Iain screamed, but then her training took over and she ran to his side. She was about to ask him what was wrong, but one glance answered that question – there was a pallid, caterpillar-like creature latched onto his right forearm.

Iain was thrashing around in pain, desperately trying to wrench the creature free with his other hand. Gradually, his movements grew feebler as the hook-like claws clung on, allowing two pairs of wicked looking curved fangs to dig deeper into his arm, until, with one last faint moan, he collapsed and was still.

RD dropped to his knees, took out his knife, and sawed at the creature's neck. Its skin was scaly, and tough as old leather, and despite his frantic efforts, it took him several seconds to penetrate. A green slime began to ooze through the small slit as he stabbed downwards to widen the hole, and a spray of gunk striped the back of his hand. He yelped, then gritted his teeth and redoubled his efforts. It took a couple more minutes but he finally managed to slice through the rest of the skin and the underlying tendons. The body fell to the ground, leaving four lines of red weals behind. He reached for the head, which remained locked to Iain's arm, intending to wrench it away.

"Don't!" Tanya snapped. "You'll do more damage." She took a pair of forceps out of her medical kit and pushed them to between the creature's fangs. She tried to prise them apart, but even in death, the thing would not relinquish its grasp. She took a deep breath and pulled her hardest. For some seconds, the jaws would not budge. Tanya felt herself sweating, and the metal of the forceps bending. She gave a loud cry and a final heave, and the head dropped to the ground.

Iain's forearm was already beginning to swell and take on an unhealthy green tinge, so she ignored her own fatigue and carefully opened his wounds with a scalpel and slapped a venom extraction pad over them. She looked at Slimmest, who was lying on Iain's chest and purring, with the same glow beneath her chin she'd seen when she was gored. *:Do you know what that thing is?:* she asked.

:It's another creature from outside this plane,: the cat replied. *:Be careful. Its ichor is corrosive.:*

Tanya looked at RD's expression. His eyes were screwed up and his lips were set hard. *:Ya think?:* she sent back to the cat. She took out a couple of absorbent cloths and handed one to him. "Clean that gunk off your hands – they're beginning to blister," she told him as she wiped her own hands with the other. "Hold out your arms." She squeezed some Dermoflex gel onto her palm, wrung her hands together, and gently rubbed the unguent over RD's lesions.

The tension on RD's face subsided, and he said, "Thank you, Doctor."

Tanya smiled. "Thank *you*. Your quick reactions may have just saved Iain's life."

"How's he doing?" Bartes asked. "We can't stay here much longer."

She reached out with all her senses as she removed the pad from Iain's wound. *Heartbeat strong and regular,* she thought. *Heart rate normal. Respiration good. No sign of neural damage. What the devil is going on? That venom must have* some *effect.* Her brow wrinkled in puzzlement. "Apart from the obvious, he seems fine." She shook her head. "If you deal with the detritus, I'll see what I can do to get him moving."

Bartes picked up the forceps and used them to gather together the creature's head and body and the soiled cloths, before using the wide-beam setting on his laser carbine to incinerate them.

Meanwhile, Tanya injected Iain's arm with both a local anaesthetic and a generalised antibiotic, and gave him a shot of her patent combat drug as a stimulant.

"We'll have to move on," RD said. "That search party must have heard Iain's scream."

"Perhaps the echoes from the canyon obscured our exact location," Anoushka said, more in hope than conviction.

As Bartes and Tanya helped the groggy Iain to his feet, Slimmest's voice in their heads said, :*I've got an idea that might buy us some time. You go on. I'll catch up with you later*:

They reached the mouth of the valley without further incident and, clinging to the walls so as to keep out of sight of the soldiers above them, began to make their way down it. Their hope that those in the outpost would remain disinterested bystanders seemed to be fulfilled. Indeed, though they had obviously seen the fugitives, the soldiers only fired a few desultory shots in their general direction. *They're only shooting so that they can honestly say that they tried to stop us escaping,* Bartes thought.

Tanya and the others were just beginning to feel a bit more optimistic when Bartes drew their attention to two emplacements half-way up the valley wall. A couple of heavy flamers were installed on one to their left, and the one to their right mounted four large auto-cannons. "No wonder those soldiers couldn't be bothered," he said. "We're trapped."

"I'm not so sure," RD said. "They're here to help stop an invasion from the other direction, and they look to be automatic. If we can avoid activating them, we might get through. Anyway, we've no option but to try."

They moved forward as quickly as they could whilst checking for tripwires or anything else that might bring Armageddon down on them. The hairs on the back of Tanya's neck were standing rigidly to attention at the thought of being in the cross-hairs of such massive weapons – or of the search party that would undoubtedly be on their trail by now.

They were just past the artillery when Slimmest caught up to them and jumped up onto Tanya's shoulders. :*Call a halt,*: she sent in a peremptory tone, :*I can feel something strange just ahead of us.*:

"Slimmest thinks we're approaching something that smells fishy," she announced.

"Well, she's the expert on fish," Bartes said. He examined the valley immediately in front of them with his purloined binoculars, and then with night glasses. "She's right," he said, "There's a laser detection web across the valley. I can see it in the infra-red. It probably triggers the heavy artillery."

"Could we thread our way through using the night glasses to help us avoid the lasers?" Tanya asked.

"We could try, but the holes in the web are pretty small, and if we made any mistakes, it could prove disastrous."

"I think that our best chance is to climb up the left hand wall of the canyon – that looks the easier side – and over the top of the web," RD said.

:*Do we have the time?*: Tanya asked Slimmest.

:*Oh, yes,*: came the reply. :*I've spent the last couple of hours leading the search party on a merry chase, and I've left them a little present by the dead soldiers – courtesy of my mistress.*:

"I'll go first," RD said, "then Anoushka. The boy can go next, then the Doctor and Bartes. We'll have to leave Iain behind."

"Not a chance." Tanya was vehement.

"I agree," Bartes said. "Tanya and I can help him over."

"I don't – need any help," Iain mumbled. "I can manage – by myself"

Bartes laughed. "It's not the time to revert to being Ivan, you idiot. I've got some rope – let's tie ourselves together."

That's a good idea," said Anoushka. "Let's all tie ourselves together."

RD shrugged, took the rope and cut it into two pieces. "OK, but in two batches – Anoushka and me, and the rest of you together."

That's symbolic, thought Tanya as she wound the rope around her waist and tied it firmly.

"I'll see you the other side – if you make it," RD said as he started clambering up the cliff-face. He moved slowly, testing each foothold and ensuring that Anoushka put her feet in the same places. A couple of times those watching held their breath as tentative footholds gave way and cascades of small pebbles fell, but soon the pioneers had reached the far side of the laser net. RD hurried Anoushka away.

"Where are you going?" Bartes called. "We could do with your help."

RD shrugged again and continued walking. "I don't want to be hit by the firestorm if you trigger it," he said over his shoulder.

Tanya led the second party, using the footholds RD had found, with Slimmest in front of her acting as guide. Peter came second – his light weight and easy athleticism made climbing easy. Bartes, who took up the rear, was less nimble, but had a reassuring solidity. It was Iain who was the problem. He was still rather dazed, and he couldn't use his right arm to hold on, or to balance.

This made climbing a ticklish business. It didn't help that the scree was unstable, and often moved beneath their feet. Their pace was incredibly slow, and they had to pause frequently to steady themselves.

They were slowly inching along a narrow ledge just over the top of the web when there was a terrible screaming noise behind them and their silhouettes were thrown onto the rocks ahead by a flash of searing blue light.

:It appears your pursuers have found my little booby-trap,: Slimmest told her smugly. *:I don't think they'll be in any shape to follow us – any that survived.:*

:Thank you,: Tanya replied, *:but a little warning would have been nice.:*

They had dislodged several stones that rained down through and between the laser beams. They waited tensely to see if anything would be triggered, but there was no reaction from the artillery behind them.

Bartes gave a long exhalation. "I reckon they don't want their toys triggered by animals – or minor rock falls," he said. "Luckily for us."

They reached the point at which it was safe to descend. Step by step they inched downwards, each guiding their neighbour's feet into cracks and crevices that could take their weight. Several times hand- or footholds crumbled but the closest they came to disaster was when Peter's boot caught Tanya's forehead.

"Careful," she called.

"Sorry."

Eventually Tanya reached the valley floor. She breathed a sigh of relief, looked up, and said, "We've made..." when Iain's left foot slipped. His left hand grasped at the air as he lurched sideways. As he fell, he managed to grab hold of Bartes' ankle. Bartes held on grimly for several seconds, then his hands were inexorably pulled from the cliff face, and both men plummeted past Peter.

Tanya muttered a most unladylike expletive, and knelt down beside Bartes, who was groaning in pain. He'd landed on his right ankle, which was now bent at a very unnatural angle. *:How's Iain?:* she asked Slimmest, who was checking the other man's injuries.

:He's fractured his left wrist,: the cat told her, *:but that's all.:*

Sunset in Silvana

That's both arms out of action, Tanya thought, *but at least he'll be able to walk – and carry a pack. No such luck for Bartes...* She gave Bartes a strong shot of local anaesthetic just above his injury and waited for it to take effect. Once his moans had stopped and his face relaxed, she telekinetically straightened his shattered bones, which luckily hadn't pierced the skin. She held the pieces in place while she immobilised the joint with an insta-splint.

While Tanya was dealing with Bartes, Anoushka arrived, dragging a reluctant RD with her. "I can help," she said. "Give me the anaesthetic spray and a bandage." She numbed Iain's arm and wrapped it carefully, then helped Tanya mould the quick-drying plaster around his wrist.

"Can we move on?" RD asked once they'd finished.

"We're going to have to," Tanya said with a sigh, "but these injuries need proper treatment, and rest, and I'm running out of medication. We've got to reach Telphania soon, or I can't answer for the consequences. Slimmest & I can help psionically when we have time – and I'm not exhausted – but for now we've got to keep moving."

"Let's lighten our loads as much as we can," suggested Bartes.

They emptied their packs of everything non-essential: extra clothes, most of their equipment – even some of their extra weapons. The little they retained was shared between Iain, Anoushka, Peter and Tanya, so that RD could help Bartes.

Their progress was achingly slow, but having RD occupied meant that Tanya could talk to Anoushka privately for the first time since they left the ruined tower. She came straight to the point and asked, "What's going on between you and RD, Anoushka?"

"Oh, nothing much," Anoushka replied, but there was a little colour in her cheeks and she seemed to be deliberately looking the other way.

"I thought you had a thing for John D'Arcy."

"Can't a girl like more than one man?" She sounded rather resentful of Tanya's interest.

"I'm sorry, 'Noushka – I didn't mean to offend you."

They walked in silence for a while. Finally, Anoushka said, "No, *I'm* sorry, Tanya – I shouldn't have reacted like that. It's just that I'm not really sure of my own mind. John's never shown any real interest in me, but on the other hand, RD really cares."

"But do you care for him?"

"That's just it: I don't know. The one thing I *do* know is that he's comforting to be around at the moment. I feel safer when he's near me. And he is rather appealingly vulnerable."

This took Tanya aback. Officious, yes; obnoxious, often; competent, yes, very; but vulnerable? She looked over to where RD was supporting Bartes' weight on his shoulder. Perhaps she should re-evaluate him.

The valley began to open out, and they could see the tops of trees ahead. Anoushka ran to a ridge a little ahead of them. "We've made it," she cried.

As Tanya caught up with her, the vista below unfolded: the sun was setting behind them, but ahead of them, in the shadow of the mountains, was a long wooded slope that led to a range of foothills. Several rivulets trickled down the sides of the valley to form a mountain stream that flowed down the hillside and onto a cultivated plateau.

RD helped Bartes to a flat rock and, having settled his burden, strolled forward to survey the land ahead through his binoculars. "I think you're right," he announced after a few minutes. "I can see a barbed-wire fence beyond the foothills that must mark the border, and I can make out a small town some miles beyond it. Perhaps the night after next we'll sleep in a Telphanian hotel, and – you never know – there might even be a restaurant... with candles..." He smiled, and raised an eyebrow in Anoushka's direction.

She giggled, then frowned. "But could we afford it?" she asked.

"That shouldn't be a problem." There was an uncharacteristic playfulness in his voice. "I'm certain our good doctor has enough left from her illicit trading for a few drinks. And after we've spent her profits, we can contact Mercy, and find out how senior a field agent we've been nurturing in our collective bosom. I'm sure she has access to enough credit to put us all in the lap of luxury, eh, Tanya?"

He rarely used Tanya's first name before, and she was trying to work out how to respond to his olive branch when the rocks behind him started to shift, as if the stone was turning to mud, and something emerged from the cliff face. It was as large as a man, but black and chitinous, and it moved with inhuman speed.

"Oh God," breathed Tanya, pulled back into the past...

..."Tell me another story, Mama – *please*."

"Just one more, darling. (Stop wiggling if you want to stay sitting on my knee.) You remember that I told you about Lyra?"

"Yes – Lyra the Brave. She was my great-great-great-great..."

"Well, let's just say she was your ancestor. And you remember that the Ancients made our people slaves for a long, long time? And how we fought for our freedom?"

"And there was a bear, wasn't there?"

"Well, Lyra's husband was called Beran, but I don't think he was a bear! But he *was* a great fighter, and led the resistance in our province. Well, one day, while he was away fighting, the Ancients sent a Ripper to attack his family."

"What's a Ripper, Mama?"

"The Rippers were made by the Ancients to kill our people. They were partly like us, and partly like giant insects. They were covered in sharp bits, and had big knives for hands. They had one purpose: to chop people into little pieces. And once they came after you, they didn't stop until you – or they – were dead."

"But - but Lyra killed this one, didn't she?"

"She did. She defended her children with the great sword Dragonfang, and the Ripper couldn't get to them. But the Ripper sliced her apart as they fought, and when Beran got home, she and the Ripper were lying in a pool of blood in front of the nursery door."

"Oh!" Tanya recalled how she buried her face in her mother's hair and sobbed. "But it's just a story, isn't it?" she wept. "It didn't really happen, did it?"

"Sweetheart, it's a story – but not 'just' a story. It really happened. Our freedom was hard-won, and cost many lives. Why do you think we've sung of it every dawn since?"

That night, she dreamed of running down endless corridors, followed by the click of claws on stone and the grating sound of scales rubbing together. It had triggered her first – involuntary – use of teleportation. She had woken with a scream, naked and shivering, in her parents' bed.

Her mother's description of the Ripper was etched in her brain, but it was just a pale reflection of the horror that stood before her now. It had a face, but more like an insect than a man, with mandibles like a cockroach but the size of a scimitar, and compound eyes like an enormous fly. Its body was almost human in shape, though no human would have an extra pair of limbs extending from the lower torso. It was covered in black armour-like scales with spikes protruding from every joint. What caught her eyes, though, were the curved blades that took the place of forearms and hands. They were well over a foot long and razor-sharp, and the way they swept back and forth was mesmerising.

Anoushka screamed and hurled herself towards RD in a desperate attempt to save him. Suddenly, it seemed to Tanya as if everything had slowed down and her companions were dancers in some weird low gravity ballet. Everything? No, the monster was still moving quickly, though not in the blur of movement she had just seen. It occurred to her that she was cursed to witness RD's death in terrible slow motion.

She stood there, paralysed like a rabbit in front of a snake, until Slimmest raced past her. Almost without volition, her hand clawed at her pistol. She levelled her gun and started firing as soon as its barrel cleared the holster. It was a lightning draw, but still far, far too slow.

Anoushka thrust her hands against RD's shoulders, knocking him to one side. She was still airborne when the creature reached her, and one of its scythes caught her just about the level of her left breast. The impact spun her round, and they saw her face contort with a scream that she suddenly had no breath to make as the razor-sharp talon sliced right through her torso, leaving the two pieces of her body to fall to the ground.

Through desperate tears, and screaming imprecations, Tanya emptied her gun into the hideous thing's face, firing as fast as her pistol would cycle, watching the bullets emerge from the barrel like a train's carriages emerging from a tunnel. She threw the now-empty gun at the demon and, wanting to reach her dying friend, found herself on her knees by Anoushka with no memory of having crossed the intervening ground.

There was nothing she could do to save her friend – all she could do was to take her hand and squeeze it. Slimmest was standing with her forehead pressed to

Sunset in Silvana

Anoushka's. She was purring, and the terrible surprise and agony cleared from the dying girl's face. She looked up into Tanya's tear-filled eyes and gave a slight smile. Suddenly, for a mere moment, an expression of hope and joy filled her eyes before the life in them vanished.

Tanya closed those still, blue eyes and whispered a prayer. Slimmest reared up on her hind legs and gently patted Tanya's face before leaving her to her grief. Without warning, there was a brief pain in Tanya's thigh, and she found herself standing up.

Chapter 31

When the attack came, Bartes had been relaxing, grateful for the opportunity to rest. Anoushka's scream had roused him from his reverie, and his training had taken over: he'd swung his ACR up and been firing almost before the stock was resting in his left hand. His ankle might have been injured, but there was nothing wrong with his aim, and he'd pumped continuous fire into the monstrosity, with Iain and Tanya matching him on either side.

He'd watched as many of the bullets had glanced off the fiend's armour, but had noticed that enough got through to slow its inhuman speed. It had begun to leak a greenish ichor in multiple places, had faltered then sunk to – no, into – the ground. When he inspected the area later, even the demon's vital fluids – if that's what they were – had disappeared.

He'd looked on helplessly as Tanya fell to her knees by her closest friend's riven corpse. Now he saw a shiver go through her body.

Tanya rose to her feet. "We must move on," she said tonelessly.

"What do you mean, you bitch?" RD cried. "Anoushka's dead. Don't you even care?" Tanya ignored him, and started to remove Anoushka's blood-soaked pack from her remains. "Stop right there or I'll shoot you down."

She turned. Her face showed no emotion, nor did her voice. "Oh, I care – but we have to escape. The mission comes first."

"Tanya?" Bartes said.

"Of a sort. As a senior Mercy operative, I have a pharmacopoeia implanted in my femur. It has a very special drug in it, designed to help save my life – and those of my team – in extreme situations. It triggers if and when I can't cope with my feelings, and temporarily cauterises my centres of emotion. It brings a more – efficient – personality to the surface so that I can function."

RD did not seem to be listening. "You snake! You should have died instead of her."

"If you want a shouting match, I can't help you there," the woman said. "Believe me, you can't blame me any more than I blame myself. Part of me desperately wants you to stop waving that gun around and put me out of my misery, but I'd have to advise you that such an act would be detrimental to the mission. You're only trying to assuage your grief – and your own feelings of guilt – by taking them out on me, anyway."

RD stopped dead, and sank to his knees by Anoushka's body, angrily brushing away the moisture which filled his eyes. "You're right, damn you," he said. "If she hadn't pushed me aside…"

Iain shook his head. "She clearly cared enough for you to sacrifice her life in your place. There was nothing you – or any of us – could have done."

"I know," RD said miserably. "But what shall we do about her body? We can't just leave her like this."

"There's nowhere here to bury her," the woman that was Tanya said. "We should cremate her remains. I'll appreciate that – when I'm myself again."

She helped RD and Peter gather some fallen pine branches and lay out Anoushka's body on them: she coldly efficient, the others both weeping openly. Iain and Bartes could only watch in solemn silence. They gathered around the pyre.

"Does anyone want to say anything?" Tanya looked around the others, but one by one they shook their heads. "Very well. I know how you're all feeling and – if I were myself – I couldn't find any words, either. As it is, though…" She closed her eyes. "Dear Lord, we ask you to receive the soul of our dear friend and companion, Anoushka. There is no greater testimony to her love than she gave her life for another.

Please welcome her into your arms. We will miss her, and pray that we will all one day meet again in your presence."

They ignited the pyre, stood for a moment watching the flames take hold, and set off eastwards again. They trudged downhill through the pinewoods, along the side of the burgeoning stream, until night fell, and sought shelter in a thicket.

In the early hours of the morning, Bartes was disturbed by someone laying down beside him. He blinked himself awake and in the moonlight he could see the tears running down Tanya's cheeks. She didn't have to say anything. He put his arm around her and held her as her shoulders heaved.

As if in sympathy, a steady, unrelenting rain began. The trees were scant cover, and it seemed an age before the Eastern sky was tinged with a paler shade of grey. "We'd better move on," Bartes said.

"What's the point?" Tanya's voice was nearly inaudible.

"We have to get back to Regni – people are depending on us."

"Like Anoushka did?" Sorrow and anger fought for control of her face.

"Yes." He sighed. "But she was only one person."

"You bastard!" She pushed him away.

"That's it – let it out." He caught her wrists and held them firmly. "Look, I know you blame yourself, but you did all you could."

"There must have been *something* more." Her body went limp. "It's happened again. I've b-been given these abilities, but when I need them most – they fail me."

"There'll be time to talk about all this later, but for now we must get moving."

"You're right." Tanya shook herself and sighed. "Can you walk? How's your ankle?"

"Improving. The cat's been doing all she could, and she's been showing me how to use my own talents to regenerate the damaged tissue."

"I'm sorry. I've been so turned in on my own misery, when I should have been helping you and Iain."

"Well, I can put a little weight on the injured leg, and with a stick, I should be able to make reasonable time. This'll do." He picked up a nearby fallen branch, shaped it with a few deft strokes of his combat knife, and lifted himself to his feet.

Nobody wanted breakfast, so they were soon stumbling on through the trees under overcast skies in their individual cocoons of misery, putting one foot in front of the other, hardly noticing their surroundings. They paused several times by what was now becoming a small river for a brief rest and some food, but nobody ate a great deal. They spent another miserable night, huddled together in what shelter they could find.

By late afternoon of the next day, the rain had stopped, though the canopy still dripped water down their necks. Suddenly, Bartes, who was leading, raised his hand. "I can see something through the trees," he said. "Wait here."

They slumped wearily to the turf, too tired and wet to care where they sat.

Bartes was back after a few minutes. "That fence we saw from the mountains is just ahead," he said. "There are a couple of wooden towers just this side of it – the one on the left is quite close, but the one on the right is several miles away. They look like they've been built recently, and in a hurry."

"To watch for us?" Iain asked.

"Possibly – or maybe just because of cross-border tensions," Bartes said.

"What's on the other side of the wire?"

"A broad strip of ground that looks barren and scorched. I'd reckon it's so the Telphanians could watch for anyone coming from this side, but I didn't see any buildings over there. We'd better move round to the right till we're about equidistant from the towers, and make a run for it after dark."

They moved as quietly as they could for a mile or so through the woods, and Bartes was about to call a halt, when a voice said, "I thought there were more of you."

They grasped for their weapons and looked around frantically. On their left, leaning against a tree with his arms folded, was a tall, lean man. "You won't need those," he said. "I'm Sub-Major Gilbert of Telphanian security, and I've been sent here to retrieve you."

RD pointed his rifle at the newcomer, but Bartes pushed it aside. "I'd like to believe you," he said, "but we've been let down and betrayed so much that it's not easy. Have you any proof?"

The Sub-Major shrugged. "I could hardly come across the border in uniform – and to carry Telphanian papers would be suicide."

"I wouldn't have trusted any of that, anyway," RD replied. "We've been fooled once too often."

"I do have this." He reached into his pocket. "It's for one of your group – Tanya?"

Tanya snatched the paper and scanned it. Her eyes filled with tears and she crumpled the note and thrust it into Bartes' hands before turning away.

Bartes straightened out the note. With a catch in his voice he read it aloud. *"I'm looking forward to our girls' night out – the three of us will paint Brogovel red! S.".* He sighed. "Well, that's good enough for me." He turned to the Sub-Major. "We left one of our team behind, to escape by another route – so as not to put all our eggs in one basket – and two didn't make it. A few days back, one of them had a fatal accident – and the other was killed by some sort of hideous creature, just when we started believing we were going to escape..."

The Telphanian sensed their sombre mood. "I'm sorry," he said.

"Well, if you can get us into Telphania, you have my vote of confidence," Iain said. "How do we get across the border?"

"That barren strip of land just ahead *is* the border," the Sub-Major said, "but you can't just walk across it – there are satellites in orbit whose task is to detect and destroy anything much bigger than a squirrel that tries to cross it. The satellites are ours – Mercy provided them to help protect Telphania from being invaded. I have a transponder which gives off a signal that prevents me, and those with me, from being targeted."

"How did you get across without being spotted?" Bartes asked. "And how did you know where we would be anyway."

"As for that, your friend Sophie – the one who gave me the note – told us. And I crossed last night, by way of the culvert this river runs through. I was lucky – with the sky overcast, it was very dark, and the cold water prevented them from seeing me on infra-red."

"Could we get out the same way?" Iain asked.

"No – I could only manage to bring the camouflaged wet suit I wore and a single re-breather. And anyway, the sky's clear again, and we couldn't hide from the ringlight while we crossed the ground to the culvert. We're bound to be seen, but hopefully, if we move quickly, we can be across and into the trees before the enemy can react."

They waited till the sun had fully set and, in the blue-grey light of the rings, the Sub-Major led them along the fence to a hole in the wire. They scrambled through one by one and waded through the intervening bushes as quickly as they could, then the Sub-Major switched on the transponder and they stepped out onto the strip.

Before they'd gone more than a dozen paces, their silhouettes were projected in front of them by a bright light, several spurts of dust flew up, and an amplified voice said, "That's far enough."

They turned, and through the glare of the spotlight, Tanya could just make out the shape of a helicopter. She muttered a very unladylike expletive. "Another bloody helicopter!"

"Dammit!" Bartes said. "They must have been in the air already, patrolling the border."

"Stay right where you are until we can retrieve you," the voice said.

"I can see movement from the tower on the left," Iain said.

"And from the one on the right," RD added.

Tanya turned to Bartes. :*I'm not going back,*: she sent.

The look in her eyes sent shivers down his spine. :*What are you going to do?*:

:*What I do best. I failed Anoushka, but I won't fail you. Warn the others to be ready to run while I distract the enemy. Do it psionically – RD can bitch about it later. I've got to prepare myself.*:

He did as she bade him, and then sent to her, :*What exactly do you mean?*:

Her answering grin was barely sane. :*You remember that drug dispenser I've got embedded in my thigh?*:

:*After the other day, how could I forget?*:

:*There's a special mixture of drugs in there which will give me the ability to do things the enemy won't be prepared for.*:

:*There's something you aren't telling me, isn't there?*:

Tanya shrugged. :*It puts a massive strain on the body. There's a chance I won't survive.*:

:*What sort of chance?*:

Sunset in Silvana

:Oh, upwards of 90%. Now run as soon as the spotlight swings away.: She disappeared, and there came twin screams from the direction of the helicopter. True to Tanya's prediction, the spotlight swung back towards the fence. The 'copter's mini-gun started firing, but not at the fugitives – at the troops from the tower.

As soon as Tanya was ready, she mentally triggered her pharmacopoeia. *:Black, black, zero, zero, black,*: she sent deliberately. *:Authorisation: extreme prejudice.*: She shivered as the drug cocktail coursed through her bloodstream. *That should do it: level 4 blur – 16 times normal speed, and freedom from natural self-preservation restraints.* She instantaneously teleported into the helicopter's cockpit. *So this is what it feels like to be invincible. It doesn't seem that different – though everything else seems to hardly be moving – and I can't remember my senses ever being so intense.*

She pushed at the gunner on her left and felt his ribs cave in under the force of her blow as he began to slowly topple out of the door. Pain lanced up her arm and she glanced down at her mangled hand.

Careful, Tanya, at the speed you're moving, your hand could have disintegrated. It's lucky you've got energy to spare. She moved the bones back into position, concentrated for a subjective second and her hand was whole again.

The push she gave to the pilot was more circumspect, but enough to lift him out of his seat and start him on his ponderous way toward the ground, still clutching his microphone.

Tanya swung the joystick to the left, and slowly but inexorably the aircraft slewed sideways. *I should have brought a book,* she thought as she waited for the fuselage to swing round. After an apparent age, her friends were no longer illuminated.

Sunset in Silvana

:Fly, you fools!: she sent them. She giggled, and shook herself. *Don't get carried away, you idiot – you've still got a job to do.* She steadied the joystick, aimed the mini-gun at the oncoming troops, pulled the trigger and locked it.

Before the first bullet had left the gun, she had teleported to the ground. *That's funny, my clothes have stretched.* Looking down, she saw that her skin, as well as her costume, hung loosely on her. *I should have remembered – my fat reserves are almost exhausted. This is an effective way to lose weight – though it's a bit of a drastic solution. I'd better get moving while I still can. If I can just disable the other troops while my heart's still beating...*

The soldiers under fire from the helicopter were beginning to dive for cover, so she zigzagged among the troops coming from the other direction, delivering incapacitating blows wherever she could. *This feels more like swimming than running. It must be the increased wind resistance – after all I* am *moving at a couple of hundred miles an hour.*

Her dance of mayhem was complete before her first victim hit the ground. She looked down at her body, her vision blurring and her heartbeat faltering. She was drenched in sweat and realised that, since she couldn't disperse the heat she was generating fast enough, her core temperature was far too high and her organs were failing.

She could see that her friends were most of the way across the strip, and could tell that, as the drugs were beginning to fail, her speed advantage was dwindling. *I'm probably too far from the Sub-Major's transponder for it to protect me,* she thought. *Let's see if I can outrun those satellites...*

She launched herself across the strip. She was barely half-way across when there was a concussion and a blast of heat behind her and she felt the skin on her left heel blister.   Her last conscious act was to hurl herself through the air towards the trees.

Sunset in Silvana

About the Authors

Paul Sims

The Author works as a Software Engineer for a major company. Although he is talented at what he does, he is, at heart, a storyteller.

He is married with three sons. Three cats condescend to share his house and he is looking forward to retirement, as he will have more time for writing, and to raise the spaniel(s) he wants to add to his menagerie.

This is his first published work of fiction.

Robert Warr

The Author was born in the South of Africa on New Year's Day, a fact that was reported in the local paper. This was his last brush with any type of fame.

A good education was followed, eventually, by an engineering degree, and having tried the army and the police force (as a reservist in both cases), he went into the world of industry. This industrial career was mercifully cut short following an accident while playing cricket in India. As a part of his physiotherapy, he started writing again and found a satisfaction in fiction that no management meeting could ever match.

Having had animals all his life the Author lives in Bournemouth and is currently owned by a Bengal who graciously shares his time with a Labrador and a ginger tom.

More information on his work and forthcoming novels can be found on his Amazon Author page.

Sunset in Silvana

For more information about the setting of this book, see:
www.eranian-empire.co.uk

Twilight in Telphania (extracts)

1

Commander John D'Arcy, of Section 6 (Counter-Espionage) of the Terran Union's Naval Intelligence Service, stood outside his superior's office door. His heart, normally so well controlled, was beating faster than was comfortable. After all, a summons from the Admiral was rarely for a chat – and this was the first time he'd been called to see the Old Man since... He took a deep breath and knocked.

"Come in."

He squared his shoulders and entered.

Admiral Neville looked up from the file he was reading. "Ah, Commander D'Arcy, thank you for coming so promptly. Take a seat. How are you feeling?"

"Fine, sir."

"Have you got used to your new hearing yet?"

"It's still a bit odd – slightly echoey – and hearing sounds outside the normal spectrum can be rather disconcerting. The adjustable volume is useful, though, and should prove invaluable in the field. And it's better than being deaf – or worse."

"To be honest, when I saw what that bomb did to you, I thought I'd never see you in my office again."

"When I came to, I must admit I thought the same – but now, thanks to the marvels of modern medicine, here I am: John D'Arcy 2.0."

"Are any of the replacement parts metallic? That could cause problems on high-tech worlds."

"No – they're all organic, grown in a vat from my own stem-cells; even the drug filter and the dispenser built into my new right kidney were constructed using my own DNA. After some intensive physiotherapy – with a very attractive physiotherapist, I might add –" (he grinned boyishly) "– I'm raring to go."

"Ever the man of action, eh?" The Admiral laughed. "Well, I've got a new assignment for you, if you're sure you're ready to get back into harness."

John couldn't suppress his smile. "All too ready, sir. To be honest, I've been getting a bit impatient. After all, the medics cleared me a month ago. I was beginning to be afraid you were going to chain me to a desk forever."

"Not a chance of that – you're one of our best operatives. This is a long-term job: you're going to join the personal bodyguard of the Regnian Sector Governor – without anyone knowing who you really are, of course."

"What's the problem?"

The Admiral frowned. "The medic on the team recently retired early, and another took his place."

"There's nothing suspicious about that; it's a high-pressure job, with a lot of burn-out."

"Normally, I'd agree, but when the new doctor is a volunteer from Mercy, I find it suspicious, especially since the retiree has been offered a sinecure of a job with the same organisation."

"Hmm… you think the Eranians are up to something?" It was an open secret in the intelligence community that Mercy Incorporated, an interstellar aid agency, was covertly operated by the Eranian Empire. "What do we know about the replacement?"

"Her name's Tanya Miller, and she was born and brought up on Ataraxia. That makes her a Union citizen, but the fact that she was recruited by Mercy is of concern."

"How long has she worked for them?"

"Several years."

"What benefit would the Eranians gain from having an agent in the Governor's bodyguard?"

The Admiral shrugged. "That's what I'd like to know – and why I'd like someone I trust keeping an eye on her. Either she's there for some skulduggery, or the

Eranians know something we don't. Both possibilities make me nervous."

"Is she psionic?"

"Not that we know of. That's one of the things I want you to look out for."

"Hmm... Relations with Eran have been good for a decade or more. Why would they rock the boat now?"

The Admiral raised one eyebrow. "You never know with those psionic bastards. I served in the last border war. It may have been over in less than a month, but it was pretty bloody, and I lost a number of good friends to their dirty tricks."

"Actually, I was involved too. I was just out of Staff College. I graduated early because of the crisis. I was on the *TUS Intrepid* when we beat the *Pride of Hurrn*."

"Sorry. I didn't realise. You must be proud."

"Of being on the only ship to take out one of the enemy's? Of having the dumb luck to take advantage of their mistake? Not really. I rescued some of their survivors, and – believe me – most Eranians are just like you and me. I can understand you being suspicious about people with psionic abilities, sir. After all, nobody wants their innermost thoughts exposed to strangers – but it's a fact of life that such talents exist, and are by no means restricted to the Eranians and the Aelumi. And they can be useful, particularly in our profession. I sometimes wish I was psionic – it would certainly make my job so much easier."

"That's what worries me: people with talents like yours *and psionic abilities as well*, working for our enemies. It's bad enough having registered psionics – there's one on the team you're joining already – but it's the *unregistered* ones that worry me."

John cleared his throat. "Well, I'll make sure this doctor's kept under strict surveillance. How am I to infiltrate?"

"We've been a bit lucky there. The current pilot on the team has recently become pregnant, and has resigned from her post. You're to be her replacement."

John frowned. "Surely they'd normally draft in a local. Won't they smell a rat if I'm being imposed on them?"

"You're right." The Admiral's brow wrinkled, and then cleared. "I know. You're officially one of my aides, right?"

"Yes…"

"Well, what if you were having an affair with my wife?"

"What?"

"Yes, yes – I can see it now. I come home unexpectedly and find you and her in flagrante. I'm outraged, and have you transferred somewhere far away – Regni."

"But wouldn't Lady Neville object?"

The Admiral laughed. "Not Elizabeth. Before we married, she was one of Section 5's best agents. She agreed to retire, bless her, because I didn't like the idea of her seducing any more naïve ambassadors or envoys, but she's always chafed a bit at that. I'm sure she'd enjoy having a swan-song."

"We could just pretend it happened."

"Not if I know Beth. She'll insist on playing out the full scene to make it believable. I'll try to hush it up, of course, but sufficient hints should surface to back up your story when you tell it to your new team-mates."

So it was that a few days later John was sent on a shopping expedition, and when he arrived back at the Admiral's quarters, the front door was open.

"Hello?" he called.

"Come along in, John," came a sultry voice. "Put the bags in the kitchen, and come and join me in the living room."

"Shall I put the ice-cream away? It's half melted already."

"Most of it – but bring me the strawberry sundae." There was a low-pitched laugh.

He did as he was told, but the sight that met him as he entered the lounge almost made him drop what he was carrying.

Elizabeth Neville was draped across the sofa in a black negligée that was obviously designed to show off her voluptuous figure. The cups that covered her breasts and the thong were of lustrous silk, and the rest of the assemblage was also silk, but diaphanous. It was obviously designed less to be worn than to be removed.

"Oh, do close your mouth, John – you look like a fish." She gave another laugh. "Now bring me the ice-cream."

Wordlessly, he crossed the room and held out the tub and the spoon he was carrying.

She took his wrist firmly, and with surprising strength, swung him off his feet. He sat down with a bump on the sheepskin rug, the back of his head resting on her thighs.

"Oh, that's better." She took the ice cream, levered of the lid of the tub and carefully spooned out some of the contents. Slowly, and with obvious pleasure, she sucked the semi-liquid dessert off the spoon before licking it clean. She took another spoonful and deliberately let some of its contents dribble onto her breast. "Oops." Another throaty laugh. "Be a dear and clean that off, please." John reached for his handkerchief, but she shook her head. "Silly boy – use your tongue."

This is too real, John thought, aware that his trousers were definitely feeling tight. "But, Lady Neville," he began *sotto voce*.

"Don't you find me attractive any more?" There was a catch in her voice, and her lower lip trembled slightly.

God, she's good. She can even produce tears when she wants to. "It's not that," he whispered. "It's just that I respect your husband, and I'd hate to…"

"Hah! He doesn't love me like you can. Now use your tongue for what it was designed for."

Tentatively, he leaned over and gently licked her breast clean.

She shuddered in delight as he did so, then slithered down so her face was level with his and gave him a long lingering kiss.

The pressure below was eased as she loosened first his belt, then his trousers. He was wondering just how far this would go when there was the sound of the front door slamming, and the Admiral's voice said, "Beth? Where are you?"

Lady Neville gave a theatrical cry and pushed John away, just as the Admiral appeared in the doorway.

"Th-this isn't what it seems," John stammered as the Admiral strode towards him.

"Yes it is." Lady Neville was suddenly between them, facing the Admiral defiantly. She tossed her head. "You leave me here all day to rot, Roger. John, at least, cares for me."

"Go to my office and wait for me there, Commander D'Arcy," the Admiral said through gritted teeth, his eyes flashing.

He's good, too, thought John. "But, sir.."

"Now!"

"Yes, sir!" John quickly adjusted his trousers and fled, the voices behind him becoming more and more impassioned as he did so.

About an hour later, John was sat in the Admiral's office when the Admiral himself returned, his face like a thunder-cloud. He strode in, slammed the door, and broke into a smile. "Well done, my boy," he said, rubbing his hands with glee. "You sold that brilliantly."

"It's all down to your wife, sir – she's amazing."

"Isn't she just!"

"She made *me* believe we were having an affair."

"Section 5 hated losing her. I'm not sure they've forgiven me yet."

"How did it go when I'd left?"

"Oh, we had a shouting match that no-one within miles could ignore. It ended when I slapped her face."

"You didn't!"

"Oh, yes, I did – but I can do it with a lot of noise and little pain. And she can use make-up to simulate a bruise."

"What happened then?"

"She collapsed into a storm of tears. I was immediately contrite, and took her in my arms. She batted those big brown eyes of hers and promised never to cheat on me again. I accepted her promise. She blamed the whole affair on you. I left, promising to return as soon as I'd dealt with you."

"What a performance! A pity there wasn't an audience."

"Oh, I'm sure there was. The walls of our quarters aren't very thick. I'm sure Beth is looking forward to the rumours spreading. She'll love playing the *Femme Fatale*. By the way, she sent her thanks for the negligée, and you have my thanks as well." He smirked. "It'll come in handy tonight, when we 'make up'."

John was puzzled. "I don't remember buying that."

"Oh, but you did – via the Quartermaster of course. That woman obviously knows as much about lingerie as she does about munitions. There's a virtual paper trail in your name from an online store. She did the same for a rather nice agate bracelet and a jade locket. There's also subtle traces of several assignations you had with Beth over the last few months. They're hidden just well enough that a determined investigator will find them. You can claim for everything we've paid for on your behalf on expenses once the furore has died down."

"I wouldn't dream of it. I'm a gentleman. Please tell your wife…"

"Call her Beth, please – let's sell this properly."

"Please tell Beth that I don't regret a second of our time together, real or imagined."

"Good man. Now, you'd better act contrite. Avoid people as much as possible, and concentrate on doing paperwork until you leave."

2

The fugitives set off for the woods as quickly as they could. The sudden darkness after the bright spotlight made even walking hazardous, but, with the agility of youth, Peter ran on ahead and found a suitable gap in the trees. Iain stumbled after him, while RD helped Bartes limp across the broken ground, and the Sub-Major made sure they all stayed within range of his transponder.

Bartes had been listening to the shouts and screams from behind them, and risked a look back. The troops to the south were diving for cover, trying to avoid bullets from the helicopter's mini-gun, and those to the north were toppling like dominoes as a blurred figure sped among them.

He and RD were approaching the path Peter had located when a laser blast came out of the sky and hit the earth a hundred yards to the north. Bartes glanced in that direction. He was just in time to see an indistinct human shape hurtle into the trees.

The others were waiting just out of sight, and escorted them to a small clearing some thirty yards beyond the edge of the forest. They sank to the ground as one.

"Do you think we're safe here?" Peter asked.

"I believe so," The Sub-Major said. "The enemy can't cross the border, and the trees will stop any bullets. And by the time they get any heavy weapons here, we'll be long gone."

"What about the mini-gun on the helicopter?"

"The last I saw of that 'copter, it was unmanned, and heading towards the tower to the south." Almost as if on cue, there was a loud explosion to the south-west with an accompanying flare of light which lit the clouds above. "I think we're in the clear."

As soon as he had caught some of his breath, Bartes said, "I'm going to look for Tanya. I think I saw her dive into the trees north of here."

"I wouldn't bother," RD said. "I saw the laser blast, too. She couldn't have survived."

"Then I'll find her body." Bartes glowered at him. "I'm not abandoning her."

"I'll help you look," Iain said.

"Me, too," Peter glared at RD. "I've few enough friends – I don't want to lose another."

"I'll come along as well," the Sub-Major added. "It's the least I can do – after all, she saved my life too. But we can't risk using lights at the edge of the trees – they might give us away to any surviving enemy snipers. I've got a pair of night glasses, so I'd better lead the way."

"Well, I've got some as well," Iain said. "We 'liberated' them from a Zelynan observation post."

"Good – then it's not as hopeless a task as I thought, but we must keep the noise to the minimum." The Sub-Major helped Bartes to his feet, and supported him as they, Peter and Iain made their way carefully towards the north-east, with RD reluctantly following.

They'd reached the treeline and had been walking along it for a fair distance when Iain raised his bandaged arm. "I can see her," he whispered over his shoulder. "I'm sorry, Bartes – I'm afraid it looks like RD was right." He inclined his head towards where Tanya's body was draped limply over a branch.

14872283R00178

Printed in Great Britain
by Amazon.co.uk, Ltd.,
Marston Gate.